SECRET LIES

Visit us at www.boldstrokesbooks.com

SECRET LIES

by

Amy Dunne

2013

SECRET LIES

ISBN 13: 978-1-60282-970-1

This Trade Paperback Original Is Published By
Bold Strokes Books, Inc.
P.O. Box 249
Valley Falls, NY 12185

First Edition: December 2013

Credits
Editors: Lynda Sandoval and Ruth Sternglantz
Production Design: Susan Ramundo
Cover Design By Sheri (graphicartist2020@hotmail.com)

Acknowledgments

The first person I wish to thank is Radclyffe—for being an inspiration, making my dream come true, and also for coming up with such a great title. I can't express how grateful and privileged I feel for being welcomed into the BSB family. I've been fortunate to work with two amazing editors on *Secret Lies*, and they have made this book so much better than I ever imagined it could be. Lynda Sandoval gave me a whole different perspective on writing, and as a result, my tenses, characters, and the story have improved. Ruth Sternglantz has made me laugh, been patient, supportive, and has vastly improved my knowledge. Sheri, I absolutely love the cover. Thank you to Connie Ward, Sandy Lowe, Cindy Cresap, and all of the other wonderful people who work behind the scenes at BSB. I'm astounded by the hard work and dedication that goes into producing such high quality LGBTQ fiction.

I also wish to thank Katherine V. Forrest, whose books inspired me to start writing in the first place. I'm grateful for the time, advice, and guidance that she gave to me at the beginning of this process, as without it, *Secret Lies* would have remained an unruly mess, stowed away in a dusty file.

I'd like to thank my two trusty beta-readers, Kat Doyland and Sue Chittock, for your time and constructive feedback. I hope you're both as proud of the finished result as I am.

I'm lucky to have amusing and gifted writer friends—Vic Oldham, Andrea Bramhall, and Gill McKnight. Thank you for answering my many questions, inspiring me, encouraging me, and making me laugh so hard I cry.

I'm blessed to have such a loving and supportive family. Mum, Dad, my amazing sister Anna Rigley, Luke Rigley, Sue Smith, Maria Cocking, Grandma, and Granddad—thank you all from the bottom of my heart. (Grandma and Granddad—please don't read this book. Ever.)

I owe so much to my Keele friends—Dobby, Beth, Catherine, Mabel, and Roch. Thank you for seeing me through my darkest time and helping me pick up the pieces afterwards. In the last few years, we've all celebrated many happy occasions, and I know there are many more to look forward to. I'm confident we'll always be friends...you know too much.

And to the readers, I hope you enjoy this book as much as I enjoyed writing it. I'd love to hear what you think. On a serious note, I want you to know that if you or a loved one is being affected by abuse or self-harm, you're not alone. There's a vast wealth of support and guidance out there, and it can really change lives for the better.

Last, but certainly not least, I want to thank my beautiful wife, Lou. Without her constant love and support, I would never have been able to write this book. She took on the role of a domestic goddess so I could spend the evenings writing. Whenever I felt frustrated or like I wanted to give in, she was there to sit my ass back in the chair and get me writing again. I never in my wildest dreams believed it was possible to love someone so very much, or to feel so happy and content—until now. You're my world.

Dedication

Lou, I love you with my heart, body, mind, and soul.
You complete me.

❖

In loving memory of:
Emma, Rebecca, Bridie, and Joe Dunne.

CHAPTER ONE

The unexpected heatwave across the UK had caused mixed reactions. Some claimed it was yet another sign of global warming, while others argued it was just the good old British weather being unpredictable.

In Brassley, a large town in the East Midlands of England, the sun had reached its highest point and burned brightly against the endless backdrop of the blue, unblemished midday sky. The air was thick and oppressive, with not so much as a gentle breeze to offer relief.

Jenny O'Connor idly shifted position on the dry, itchy grass. Her sleeveless, tight-fitted school shirt clung to her damp torso as she lazily sunned herself.

The beast of a hangover that was plaguing her was growing worse with each passing second. She moistened her parched lips with her tongue and then lit up a smoke, savouring the simultaneous sensations of her quickening heart rate and the light-headedness from the nicotine rush.

"So, are you going to tell us about last night or what?" Corrina asked as she also lit up a smoke. Sarah and Laura shifted their positions to look up at Jenny.

Normally she loved being the centre of attention, but not today and not in her current state. "There's not much to tell," she answered evasively, hoping that by some miracle her three friends would actually drop the subject.

Laura's brow creased. "You did go to Matt's, didn't you?"

Jenny shot her a warning look. The last thing she wanted to do was talk about last night; just the mention of it made her queasy.

"Come on, Jenny. What did you do?" Laura encouraged with blushing cheeks.

"What do you think we did? Is your life really that fucking boring that you have to hear every little detail of mine?" She immediately felt guilty. Laura was harmless, and she shouldn't take her vile mood out on her and be a bitch for no reason. "I'm sorry, Laura, that was shitty of me."

Laura smiled weakly. "It's okay."

"No, it's not okay. You shouldn't take shit off people."

"We've established that she's pathetic, tell us something we don't already know. Christ, just ignore her and tell us about last night," Corrina said.

Jenny took a deep drag from her smoke and tried to ignore the anxiety building inside of her. She glanced at her left wrist and tried to take solace from the tight pink elastic hairband she saw there, hidden amongst her collection of bracelets. With a slow, deliberate flexing of her wrist, she felt the freshly hidden bruise flare painfully and then allowed herself to exhale. "His parents were out, so we had the place to ourselves. We drank, smoked a little weed, talked, and listened to some music. One thing led to another."

All three listened in silence, and Jenny felt the urge to laugh bitterly at their naivety but swallowed it down.

On the surface, she knew she was the epitome of everything they wanted to be, even though they'd never actually said it out loud. She was the girl every guy in school fantasized about being with and the girl every other girl desperately longed to be. But she'd sacrificed a lot for her popularity, more than she dared to admit, and the idea of her friends and others discovering it was all an act terrified her. So far, she'd managed to keep her fucked-up issues hidden from everyone, but every day they seemed to bristle ever closer to the surface, threatening to crack her fragile façade and reveal all. She couldn't let that happen.

"Like what?" Laura asked, bursting Jenny's trail of thought.

Jenny decided she'd tell her friends the romantic story they wanted to hear just to shut them up, and then she'd seek sanctuary in the solitude of the cool art room.

She described a fictitious night of romance and pleasure. Her friends believed every word, just like they always did, and her anger seethed. Had she ever been so gullible?

"Did it...hurt?" Corrina asked quietly, as if trying to mask her bashfulness.

All three waited in anticipation for her answer.

Jenny stubbed out the remains of her cigarette, tossed the butt away, and immediately lit another one. "It hurt a bit at first, but then after a while it felt great." An involuntarily shudder tore through her body as she recalled the actual events of the previous night.

Matt had barely spoken to her, but to be fair she hadn't exactly tried to initiate an in-depth conversation either. In the end, they both drank way too much vodka and smoked way too much weed just to fill the awkward silence.

They'd undressed quickly at separate sides of his bed, purposely facing away from each other. She'd stared at the floor while he sorted out putting on the condom, and then they both climbed beneath the musty-smelling sheets. They didn't kiss, not even once.

He'd grabbed painfully at her breasts, which she could only assume was his Neanderthal attempt at foreplay. Eventually, he'd clumsily clambered between her legs and rested his weight on top of her. The pungent smell of body odor and weed radiated off his body. After three failed attempts, he finally managed to enter her, and it hurt like hell. She'd been so tense trying not to gag, that pain pierced her with every thrust. The only blessing was that he finished quickly.

Unable to endure his overwhelming stench or sweaty body for even a single moment longer, she'd climbed out of bed and begun to dress. As she'd fastened her bra, she'd noted her breasts were already bruising.

A sudden blare of sound from the TV had startled her, and she'd turned to find him dressed in boxers, casually sitting on the bed with a game controller in hand.

"I'm ready to go," she'd said, stepping over a moldy plate and waiting by the door.

With his back to her and his concentration focused solely on the TV, he'd said, "See you tomorrow."

She'd headed home, and with every step, self-loathing clawed at her from inside. She felt like a used, pathetic whore, and as much as she wanted to, she refused to cry. The situation was all her own doing, the price she had to pay for being the most mature and popular girl in school. She still hated herself, all the same.

When she'd gotten home, she'd avoided her parents and gone straight to the bathroom. She adjusted the temperature of the shower, stripped, and stood beneath icy cold spray, feeling it wash the touch and stench of him down the drain. At first, her body had flinched and tensed in protest at the unbearable cold, her breathing changed to short gasps, and her heart pounded in her chest. She'd resisted the urge to move away, even when her body and mind both seemed to be screaming for it. She remained beneath the water, punishing herself with unwavering resilience. Soon she had begun to shudder violently, and the pain from the cold eventually faded, leaving her body uncomfortably numb. Her flesh had turned greyish in colour; her nails and the collection of previous scars all had a blue tint to them.

With her teeth chattering loudly, she'd fumbled to switch the shower off, feeling as if her body was slow to respond to her brain's requests. Her hands had struggled at first to grip and pick up her towel, but eventually she managed to wrap it around her body, noting that she couldn't feel the dense material at all.

Carrying her clothes, she'd headed into her own room and discarded them in a heap on the floor. She'd then collapsed on her bed, lying alone in the darkness, finding sleep impossible. Her body gradually thawed out, leaving her with uncomfortably sensitive skin. Worse still was her overly active mind, which allowed the constant stream of sinister thoughts to return. They'd started by tormenting her with her worthlessness and replaying what had happened at Matt's.

As the negative emotions intensified, the darker her thoughts had become, tempting with promises of release—just a burn from her lighter or a few well-placed cuts to her skin and the simultaneous hit of relief that she'd been desperately craving for the last four months.

She'd almost given in, almost resigned herself to admitting she was too weak-willed to fight it any longer. In one last desperate attempt, she resorted to using the elastic band. Grinding her teeth and holding her breath, she gripped the band and pulled it taut, feeling it strain against her fingertips. In a single fluid motion, she exhaled and let go, and the band snapped back with an audible slap, painfully hitting the soft, sensitive inside of her wrist. The shock and pain momentarily caught her breath in her throat. Curious, she moved the band aside and studied the fresh red line on her skin. She traced it with a fingertip and felt nothing. The initial sharp sting of pain was now forgotten and her adrenaline numbed any pain she should feel.

The whispered thoughts had returned, and so she'd repeated the act several more times. And although the marks faded a little with time, some red bruising remained. The natural anaesthetic from her adrenaline gradually wore off, and the residual dull pain of her inside wrist became a comfort. The dark thoughts receded from the forefront of her mind, but she knew they'd come back. They always did.

The night had crawled by, and when dawn finally arrived this morning, she felt exhausted. Her wrist was bruised and sore, but in comparison to what she could have done to herself, it was nothing of significance.

Her thoughts were interrupted when the year-ten girl on lookout spun around. "Someone's coming!"

Jenny was on her last official warning for smoking, and if she got caught once more, her parents would be informed and her life would become shittier. As punishment, she'd be subjected to hours of parental disappointment, be grounded for the rest of her life, and—worse still—be compared to Elizabeth, her perfect older sister. Smoking was enjoyable, but it definitely wasn't worth the repercussions of getting caught again.

All four of them scrambled to stub out their cigarettes and throw the butts away, then tried to act casual while watching the corner.

When someone did appear, it wasn't a teacher or a prefect, it was just a girl by herself. Her long dark hair was tied up in a simple ponytail. She wore no make-up, and her pale skin was freckled. It was her startlingly big blue eyes that captured Jenny's attention. Stunning.

Feeling incredibly self-conscious but unable to look away, Jenny watched as the strange girl walked out towards the deserted playing fields.

"Are you actually shitting me? I wasted a decent smoke for that freak? That's coming out of yours," Corrina said to the year-ten girl, who turned scarlet while mumbling an apology.

"Did you see what she's wearing?" Sarah asked.

Jenny had only noticed the blue eyes, but now she saw that the girl was dressed in a long-sleeved shirt and black woolen trousers.

"Someone needs to tell her we're in the middle of a heatwave," Corrina said, lighting up another cigarette.

"Her name's Nicola," Laura said softly. "She's quiet but seems nice. I don't think she has many friends. She always seems to be alone—"

"If it bothers you so much, why don't you go and join her?" Corrina asked.

"Yeah, you'll probably get on well, considering you're both freaks," Sarah added, and both she and Corrina laughed.

Laura blushed and looked beseechingly at Jenny to intervene.

Choosing to ignore the look, Jenny got to her feet. She'd had enough of the heat and the bitching for one day. She brushed a few stray blades of dry grass from her skirt and picked up her bag.

"You're not going already? There's ten minutes left..." Laura's expression looked every bit as desperate as her voice sounded.

Jenny shrugged dismissively. "I need to set up. I'll see you tomorrow."

"We'll see you tonight at Jake's party, won't we?" Laura asked.

Jenny shook her head. "I'm not going. I've got a hot date. I'll fill you in on all the juicy details tomorrow." In reality, she had her weekly counselling session, and then she planned to go home, take a tepid shower, change into fresh pyjamas, and have an early night.

She pushed open the heavy door and sighed with relief. The deserted art room was the perfect hideaway from her friends and the heat.

She placed her bag down at her desk and walked over to the sinks. She dabbed cold water onto the scorched skin of her neck and throat, avoiding splashing her face as she didn't have the time to reapply her make-up.

While drying her hands with a paper towel, she looked out of the window onto the playing fields. Beneath the shade of a large tree, the weird girl sat alone. Jenny had already forgotten her name but found herself content to watch her for a while.

As soon as the bell sounded, other students entered the room and started setting up their work. Reluctantly, Jenny took one last glance at the strange girl and then returned to her desk.

Fifteen minutes later, she was totally immersed in her artwork and all thoughts of the strange girl with blues eyes were gone.

❖

The room was cool, thanks to the large electric fan that stood in the farthest corner. Jenny watched the white blades rotating so fast they appeared to almost not move at all. The encased head slowly turned direction, spreading the cool air throughout the room. When the air reached the small table that stood by the wall, the stack of magazines on top of it had their pages flutter for a few seconds. She found the humming sound almost therapeutic as it filled the silence.

"So, the mental-health questionnaire you've filled out shows that your anxiety and depression scores have increased since the last time we met. Would you agree they reflect how you've been feeling?"

Jenny reluctantly removed her gaze from the blades and focused it on Kathy. She sat in the only other chair in the room, legs crossed, her fingers interlocked with her palms resting in her lap, facing upward. She looked comfortable and relaxed. Her short blond hair was casually swept behind her ears, her tanned skin remained free from perspiration, and Jenny felt envious of the plain white cotton top and trousers she wore, as they looked comfortably cool. Her head tilted slightly to the right as her brown eyes watched Jenny carefully.

Jenny fidgeted in her seat, feeling hot and uncomfortable. She could feel Kathy's gaze taking in everything about her. That was the problem with counselling—it was entirely about the *real* her and there was nowhere to hide. It was six months since she'd attended her first appointment, and it was still hard to attend. But this was the price of freedom from hurting herself, and her desire to stop was the only thing that kept her coming back.

"Yeah. I used the band last night." Even to her own ears, Jenny's voice sounded flat and emotionless. "I ended up using it five or six times."

"Okay," Kathy said calmly. "Do you want to talk about it?"

"It was too late to go for a run, so I tried having a cold shower. It worked for a bit, but afterwards I kept thinking about things and it was using the band or...you know."

"Did something happen yesterday—or recently—that's upset you?"

Jenny chewed on her bottom lip while her left leg danced up and down on the spot. She didn't want to talk about Matt. She wanted to just forget the whole stupid thing and move on.

"You don't have to talk about it." Kathy's voice was reassuring. "We can talk about something else if you'd prefer."

"It's nothing. I just went to a guy from school's house. We drank and smoked some spliffs, then we…I slept with him." Jenny refused to look up at Kathy, she waited for her to speak, but after a few seconds it became clear she wasn't going to. This was the other annoying part of counselling—there were always long silences, which she then felt obligated to fill. "I felt like shit afterwards and all I wanted to do, all I could think about, was cutting myself."

"But you didn't."

"I came so fucking close. I honestly thought I was going to do it."

"What stopped you?" Kathy asked, leaning forward.

Jenny slumped her shoulders and sighed. "I kept thinking about what we'd talked about. I knew if I did it, I'd feel even worse afterwards. I don't want to feel the guilt and all the crap that comes after doing it anymore. I'm sick of looking at what I've done to myself and wondering if this is the one time I've gone too deep. Or if this time, it's going to get infected and I'm going to have to go to the hospital." She folded her arms and slunk further down into the chair. "It's exhausting, being constantly terrified that someone's going to see what I've done. I don't have the energy for it."

"Jenny, you're doing really well. That's a massive improvement, in such a small space of time."

"I used the band, though."

Kathy nodded. "Yes, but you used it as a last resort to stop yourself from cutting. That's why you have it." Jenny shrugged unenthusiastically in response. "Keep trying the other things, like the cold showers and the running. You said last time that they've been helping you fight the urges."

"The running has been helping. The problem is I can't run at night. The cold showers work for a bit, but after them I feel wide awake, and then I start thinking about stuff and can't stop. That's what happened last night. I just couldn't stop thinking or feeling. I didn't know what to do."

"If things get to the point where you think you're actually going to hurt yourself, like last night, the band is there for you to use. While we go through this process, it's only natural that you're going to be thinking and feeling more. Would you say evenings are when you feel the urges most?"

Jenny considered it and then nodded. "Yeah. I suppose so."

"Why do you think that is?"

"Probably because I hate being by myself. When I'm around my parents or friends, I'm okay because I'm acting exactly how they expect me to."

"You described yourself as *acting*. Do you feel like you're playing a part?"

"I play lots of different parts."

"Such as?"

"The popular girl at school. The innocent Catholic daughter. The girl who's experienced in all things sex related." Jenny couldn't believe she was actually admitting this stuff. She knew that Kathy wasn't allowed to tell anyone what she said, but the fact she was being honest felt like a massive weight was lifting from her shoulders. "Does that make me a psychopath?"

Kathy smiled. "No, it doesn't make you a psychopath. Everyone acts differently, depending on the situation they're in and who they're with. It's normal. The problems occur if the acting leads to potentially dangerous situations or harmful behaviours. For instance, if someone feels they have to drink alcohol, take drugs, or have sex, when deep down they know they don't want to go along with it. Afterwards, the negative thoughts and feelings set in and affect the real person. Does that make sense?"

More than you know! Jenny swallowed hard and nodded. "Some of the stuff I do makes me feel a million times worse afterwards. When I'm by myself, I can't stop thinking about it all and eventually it gets too much and that's when I hurt myself."

Kathy picked up her pen and pad of paper and began writing. "I think we should start working on identifying the triggers that lead to those harmful thoughts and emotions. Is there a type of situation that makes it worse? Do drinking alcohol and smoking cannabis have negative effects on your behaviour and thoughts? I want you to try and reflect on the occasions when the urge to hurt yourself is at its most extreme. Okay?"

"Yeah."

"Once you identify them, we can work on how to overcome them. Have you considered what we spoke about last time?"

Jenny sighed. "I can't keep a diary, my mum's too nosy. If she found out about this, it would really upset both her and my dad. I can't hurt them. As far as they're concerned, I'm a normal, happy seventeen-year-old. If they even suspected anything, they'd blame themselves."

Kathy lowered her pen. "What about talking to someone else?"

"I don't have anyone."

"What about friends?"

"I don't trust or really even like my friends."

"Your sister?"

"She's at university. She really wouldn't understand, and she'd probably try and perform some kind of exorcism on me. I've got to do this by myself."

"All right. What about the antidepressants? They can genuinely help, especially when used in conjunction with the counselling. Like I said before, thoughts and emotions are going to become more frequent, they can help you to cope with the influx."

Jenny shook her head. "It's hard enough taking the pill in secret, if mum found antidepressants she'd automatically think I was suicidal or something. No one knows just how fucked up I am—apart from you."

"Don't be so harsh on yourself. The fact that you've identified the negative consequences of hurting yourself and are now using them as motivation to fight the urges is excellent. Maybe try reading or watching a film before bed. Something to distract yourself."

"Okay."

"Our session has come to an end today." Kathy gave a small smile. "You really are doing great, Jenny. Does the same day and time next week suit you?"

"Yeah." Jenny stood up and stretched out her arms before picking up her bag and searching for her cigarettes. *Same shit, just a different week*. "See you then."

CHAPTER TWO

Nicola Jackson lay on the stain-encrusted carpet, curled up in a tight protective ball. Her back, arms, and legs were stinging from where his fists and shoes had struck. Adrenaline pumped temporary pain relief through her veins, but she knew in a little while she'd suffer the full extent of the agony caused by this beating. It was always the same.

Straining hard, she listened but could only hear the rapid pounding of her heart and the rushing of blood in her ears. Had it been seconds or minutes since he'd last hurt her? She couldn't be sure, which tore her already frayed nerves into finer shreds.

He could've gone to get a beer, like usual. Beating her always seemed to work up a thirst for him. If that was the case, she was wasting her only opportunity to escape. Or he could be waiting for her to make herself vulnerable, so he could really cause some damage.

Desperate to escape, she decided to risk it. She cautiously raised her head, ready to duck back down in an instant.

Alone.

Her gaze was drawn to the doorway, which led to the kitchen. His shadow flickered in the light.

It's now or never.

Having been bound so tightly in her protective ball, her body refused to loosen up. Crawling on her hands and knees, the painful tension in her shoulders and neck cried out in protest. Persevering, she finally managed to stand.

Her stomach dropped at the sound of the fridge door opening and the clinking of a beer bottle. He'd return any moment, and if he saw her standing there, he'd most likely start all over again.

Time's running out!

Begging her legs to work, she took a tentative step forward, as the shadow in the doorway transformed into a man. Frozen with terror, she helplessly watched him.

Dark eyes filled with hatred pierced her. Grey speckled his once-dark hair. Scalp shone through the thinning spots. He stood only a few inches taller than her, but his stocky build made him formidable. Thick stubble grew on his jaw, but the ugly jagged scar on the left side of his face stood out like a whispered challenge. Her mum had told her years ago never to ask him about the scar. Nicola had asked why not, but her mum had evasively explained he'd had a difficult childhood and the scar was a bad reminder. She'd never asked him about it and never would.

From the doorway, he watched her while taking a mouthful of beer. He acted casual, as if nothing had happened only minutes before, but his reddened knuckles told a different story.

"Did I say you could get up?" he asked.

She could barely breathe, let alone form a reply. No escape now. Too late.

"Answer me," he said, walking towards her while lighting a cigarette. "You're pissing me off."

She automatically stepped back and gasped as the wall jabbed painfully into her back. Cornered. Again.

In a sudden flash of movement, he raised the bottle to his mouth. She was used to things being thrown at her, so she flinched. She regretted her reaction immediately. His grin widened and his eyes shone with excitement.

He gulped down a few mouthfuls before placing the bottle onto the coffee table with an ominous clank. "I'm not gonna ask again." The dangerous edge to his tone washed over her like icy water.

"No," she whispered, unsure if she was answering his question or pleading for him not to hurt her again.

"No." He closed the remaining distance between them. "I didn't say you could get up, and you know what happens when you go against me, don't you?"

Tears born of anger and humiliation brimmed in her eyes, but she refused to cry in front of him.

He suddenly charged forward. "I have to teach you another lesson!"

As his fist punched her stomach, the breath was forced violently from her lungs. Winded, she fell into a heap on the carpet. Hot tears streamed down her face as she gasped, desperately trying to catch the breath her burning lungs needed.

He stood over her. "You're pathetic and you make me wanna puke. Look at you, crawling on the floor, like the scum you are." He spat on her. "You're her biggest mistake—she wishes she never had you."

The fire in her lungs was almost too much, and her head began to swim dizzily. *This is it. You've actually killed me, you bastard, and I'm going to die right here and I welcome it!*

As darkness began to claim her, the vital breath she needed filled her lungs, and it was tainted with tobacco smoke.

He grabbed a fistful of her hair and used it to drag her up to her feet. He rammed her body against the wall, which caused her head to ricochet painfully. He pinned her with the weight of his body and raised the cigarette towards her face. She turned her head away, clenching her eyes shut.

"Look at me!" He gripped her jaw with his free hand and forced her to face him. "You don't deserve to live. Your mum can't stand you. Do us both a big favour and fuck off—or even better, just end it. No one would give a shit if you killed yourself, so do it."

He shoved his contorted face forward, forcing their noses to touch. The rancid stench of stale cigarettes and beer from his breath filled her nostrils, and she fought not to heave. His eyes bulged and his chin glistened with spittle.

"Say it, or I'll stick this in your eye."

He thrust the cigarette close to her right eye. She was blinking uncontrollably against the searing heat and burning smoke, the tips of her lashes singeing, while boiling tears tried to escape.

"I should be dead…I should kill myself and no one would care. Please, Chris, don't…please," she said hoarsely.

He moved his body away and released her. After a few seconds of lingering torment, he also finally withdrew the cigarette.

"Take it off now and don't mess around. I'm not in the mood." He took a deep drag from the cigarette, the tip glowing red once more.

Refusing to look at him, she fumbled open the buttons of her school shirt and instinctively felt his eyes undressing her. It wasn't her naked body he wanted to see. It was the scars he'd inflicted on her that gave him his perverse sense of pleasure.

Her flesh chilled under his gaze, making her feel vulnerably naked, even though she remained dressed in her bra and school trousers.

He continued to look her up and down while he absent-mindedly used the back of his hand to wipe his chin. "Face the wall."

She didn't want to turn her back to him, but she had no other choice. Before she could fully register what was happening, she heard the hiss. A split second later, a searing pain stung her back, followed by the smell of her own burnt skin.

Clenching the shirt tightly with both hands, she watched as her knuckles turned white, as he repeated the process several more times. She bit down hard on her tongue to silence her cries, and a trickle of warm, coppery blood filled her mouth.

He moved closer and she flinched, expecting the hiss and pain to be repeated again, but he pressed himself against her instead.

"She loves me. She needs me. You mean nothing to her. She knows about this, she's known from the beginning. How could she not know? And the truth is, she doesn't give a shit, 'cause you're nothing but an annoying mistake from the past that won't go away. Leave soon, or I'm gonna make you go."

Moving away from her, his savage words continued to inflict pain in a way his fists never could. The possibility that his words harboured some truth tortured her every day. How could her mum not know the truth? It'd been going on for years and it was obvious something was wrong. If her mum did know, would she care or even stop him?

"What will it take for the message to get through your thick skull? I've tried beating it into you, but I'm actually starting to think you're enjoying this. My options and your time are both running out. Leave."

Turning her head ever so slightly, she watched from the corner of her eye as he walked back to the coffee table. He stubbed out his cigarette and reclaimed his beer. He slumped down onto the sofa, and a moment later the TV came to life with the sounds of a cheesy game show.

Although his attention was focused entirely on the TV, she dared not move, as doing so would only give him another excuse to punish her. She remained silently still, listening to voices of contestants answering questions, while her injured body trembled and her humiliation grew.

After nearly fifteen minutes, he finally acknowledged she was still in the room.

"Get out of my sight, bitch."

Trying to keep her composure, she rushed towards the sanctuary of the door.

"Things are only going to get worse for you. That's a promise," he threatened, without bothering to look away from the TV screen. "It's about time someone gave it to you, and if it wasn't for the fact you make me wanna puke so much, I might even be tempted."

She didn't understand what he meant, didn't *want* to understand, but fled from the room and ran upstairs. Once inside her bedroom, she barricaded the door by wedging the rickety desk chair beneath the handle.

Pain and exhaustion set in. She undressed, placed her uniform on a hanger, and changed into her pyjama pants. The fresh burns were sore and needed to breathe, so she decided to try sleeping without wearing a top.

She fell onto her bed. Lying on her front, she buried her face into one of the pillows and finally allowed herself to cry.

Today was almost over and she'd live to face tomorrow. "When it'll start all over again," she whispered bitterly.

She wiped her wet cheeks and tried to ignore the different types of pain resounding from her body. Eventually, she fell asleep, and monsters and flames occupied her dreams.

Chapter Three

Nicola turned her bare back to the mirror and glanced over her shoulder to assess the damage. She noted new bruises, which felt as tender as they looked. Seven cigarette burns were also scattered randomly across her back. Although they looked angry and felt painful, they were starting to scab over, which was a good sign.

Her reflection repulsed her, but she was glad she'd chosen to have a strip wash instead of a shower. She turned away from the mirror and began to dress for school.

He'd ensured no one would ever find her physically attractive and had therefore sentenced her to a life of solitude. Although depressing, it wasn't an entirely new prospect. She'd spent the last five years alone. Being attractive and romantically involved with someone were hopes she no longer secretly harboured. Trying to survive from one day to the next was more than enough to keep her occupied.

Dressed, she glanced at her reflection and let out an exasperated sigh. The long-sleeved shirt and thick black trousers made up her winter uniform and were incredibly uncomfortable, but they were the only items of clothing which managed to hide all the bruises and scars. She had no choice other than to wear them, even during this hellish heatwave. She had grown accustomed to the odd looks and cruel comments, but wearing these clothes during such hot weather drew more unwanted attention than usual.

Wary of the time, she grabbed her school bag and silently crept downstairs. She left her bag by the front door, then walked through the living room and into the small grubby kitchen.

The once-pristine white walls were now stained yellow from years of being subjected to constant cigarette smoke. A few dirty dishes littered the chipped work surface, and the sink was filled with empty beer bottles. An overflowing ashtray rested on the dusty draining board.

She'd given up trying to keep the house clean years ago, but she was still the only one who actually washed dishes, dusted, and vacuumed.

The cupboards were bare and the fridge cooled only beer. It fell to her to buy food three times a week, out of her own wages. The food was to ensure her mum actually ate something, although in truth, he usually ate most of it.

Nicola never ate in the house but chose instead to eat on the way home from school or on one of her work breaks. She worked part-time, three evenings a week, at the local convenience store and received a small discount on her grocery shopping.

With the exception of buying the food and other essentials, she was saving the majority of the money she earned in her bank account, for university. Her ambitions of escaping Brassley and going far away to study teacher training were the only things keeping her sane.

In two years she'd be gone, leaving this hellhole of a town and her abuser behind. She secretly knew once she escaped, she'd never come back. It was only the thought of abandoning her mum—to *him*—which made her doubt that pledge of *never*.

Rummaging in a cupboard, she found a relatively clean glass. She filled it with tap water and drank quickly.

The shirt was aggravating her burns already. Frustrated, she found a packet of painkillers and popped two tablets from the plastic.

Food was scarce in this house, but beer for every night and painkillers for every morning were always in ready supply.

Pouring herself another glass of tap water, she swallowed the tablets down.

A sudden sense of foreboding gripped her body. An icy shiver crawled down her spine, and her skin broke out in goosebumps. Sensing danger, she spun and found him standing in the doorway, blocking her path to the living room.

Panic and fear surged, and she silently chastised herself. She'd made a promise to herself years ago, she'd never allow him to intimidate her when her mum was at home.

Bracing herself, she walked towards him. "Chris, please, can you move? I need to leave, otherwise I'm going to be late." Her voice was quiet, but she was sure he'd heard her. Raising her gaze from the filthy floor, she looked up at him.

His jaws were clenched and his nostrils were flaring. He looked furious.

Furious about what? She had no idea, but something had clearly gotten him riled up and now he was looking to take it out on his usual punching bag.

Well, it wasn't going to happen this morning. Safe in the knowledge her mum was only upstairs, she tried to instill more confidence into her voice. "Excuse me," she said, "I need to leave for school."

He didn't respond or even acknowledge her request. She was about to ask again when he silently stepped aside, allowing her passage into the living room. As she took a tentative step forward, he spoke.

"It's time, bitch."

Something clearly wasn't right with him or the situation and, worried she might unwittingly antagonise him further, she chose not to reply. As she took another step, everything changed in a split second.

He was so fast, she couldn't have avoided him even if she'd seen what was coming. In a flash he'd rammed her against the doorway and used his body to pin her there. His left hand gripped her throat and squeezed. "It's time you learned your lesson, once and for all."

Shock and disbelief at what was happening incapacitated her more than the strength of his body. Her brain could hardly comprehend what he was doing because her mum was only upstairs, asleep.

"I know you want it." He pressed his body more firmly against hers. "And I'm going to be the one to give it to you."

She could actually feel him against her. Not only his body, but the other part of him, his penis. She tried to cry out, but he squeezed tighter, silencing her. His free hand began tearing at the button on her trousers.

This can't be happening! Mum's upstairs!

He unfastened the button and tugged harshly at the zip. Excitement laboured his breathing.

Even when his hand moved inside her trousers, tearing at her knickers, her body remained paralysed. He was whispering awful things in her ear, but she barely heard them.

It was all too much.

"No!" Her voice sounded alien to her own ears. "Get away from me. Now!"

Surprised, and with an expression of disbelief, he removed his hand from her trousers and stepped backwards into the kitchen.

With trembling hands, she pulled up the zip and fastened the button, never allowing her gaze to leave him. His face was scarlet, and he looked strange, almost comical, with that part of him sticking up at the front of his trousers.

He followed her gaze down. Then his head snapped back up, and his expression turned her blood to ice. He started towards her again.

"Take one more step and I'll scream. I'll scream louder than I've ever screamed in my entire life." She heard the panic in her voice, but with the potent mix of anger and adrenaline surging through her veins, she continued. "And when Mum wakes up, I'll tell her what you've just tried to do. If she doesn't believe me, I'll show her my back and the scars. She'll believe everything I say."

Although he was furious, he apparently wasn't stupid enough to test her. Begrudgingly, he took another step backwards.

Wary, she backed out of the living room and into the hallway, grabbing her bag as she reached the bottom of the stairs. As she fumbled with the handle to escape, he appeared in the living-room doorway. His fists were clenched at his sides and his eyes bored into her. She'd never seen him look this crazy before, his rage palpable.

"Come back here and you're dead. She won't always be here for you to wake up, and eventually we'll be alone. When that happens, I'm gonna hurt you so bad, you'll beg me to kill you. But I'm gonna take my time."

His tone sounded eerily calm, which made her believe he meant every word. Not daring to waste another second, she fled into the dense morning heat, slamming the door behind her.

She knew he wasn't going to let her escape. At any second he was going to appear and make good on his threats.

Turning away from the direction of school, she bolted. She ran as fast as she physically could, tears blurring her vision, sobs forcing themselves out with each ragged breath.

She sensed his hands reaching for the back of her neck as a large blur appeared directly in front of her. Unable to react in time, she collided hard and fast with it, throwing them both to the ground.

"Shit! What the hell?"

Nicola heard the angry voice from beside her and found herself face-to-face with Jenny O'Connor. Her panic continued to intensify. She scrambled to her feet.

"Are you okay?" Jenny asked, getting to her feet and brushing herself down.

Nicola was surprised by both the question and the genuine concern in Jenny's voice. She wanted to apologize, but her sobbing made it impossible. She picked up Jenny's bag and held it out, finally managing to form a coherent sentence. "I'm…sorry, Jenny."

Scared he could round the corner at any moment, she turned and stumbled aimlessly down the street, glad to be leaving the main road. She was already sweating profusely, and the burns stung. She needed to find somewhere shady, deserted. She needed to think clearly, to decide what to do next.

Fast-paced footsteps hitting the pavement behind her induced new fear.

Run!

Bolt!

"Wait!" cried a female voice.

Relief doused her terror. It was Jenny O'Connor, not him.

Turning, she braced herself to receive the brunt of the redhead's fiery temper.

Jenny approached with caution, gave a tentative but encouraging smile. "We go to the same sixth form, don't we?"

Nicola blinked. Small talk? "I…I—"

"What's your name?"

Nicola studied Jenny warily. She was every bit as attractive as her reputation proclaimed. Her flawless, straight auburn hair fell stylishly to her shoulders. Her vibrant green eyes sparkled. She was undeniably pretty, but up close Nicola saw she wore way too much make-up.

Unlike Nicola's own slim and lanky figure, Jenny's body was curvaceous in all the right places. She wore an outfit that barely resembled the strict summer uniform. The short-sleeved shirt was incredibly tight fitting, and Nicola felt a stab of envy at the ample chest displayed before her. A flick of her gaze lower fell on the short black skirt sitting snugly at the top of a pair of shapely legs.

It's no wonder the guys are obsessed with her.

Feeling herself blushing at the inappropriate thought, Nicola's discomfort grew as Jenny continued to watch her, to…wait. At a loss, she looked away and then realized she'd not answered Jenny's question.

"I'm Nicola Jackson," she said in a tumble of words. She squirmed beneath Jenny's quiet scrutiny and added, "We're in the same psych class. We have been for the last two years."

Jenny beamed a megawatt smile. "Nicola. Yeah, now I remember."

Nicola frowned. She didn't believe for a second Jenny O'Connor had ever noticed she existed, let alone knew her name. The dazzling smile also looked incredibly fake, but she pretended not to notice. No sense inviting confrontation.

"Um—I've got to go. I'm sorry for knocking you over though." Turning, she managed only three steps, before Jenny called after her again.

"Nicola?"

Grimacing, Nicola turned and faced Jenny once more.

Jenny pointed to her hand. "Are you bleeding?"

Nicola looked down and saw her palm was in fact grazed and bleeding, but in comparison to all of her other injuries, it was barely worth mentioning. "It's fine—"

"I live literally five minutes away," Jenny said cheerily. "My parents are at work, so if we go back to mine, you can clean it up."

Nicola's initial surprise was quickly replaced by suspicion and then anger. She wasn't stupid or naïve. The only reason Jenny O'Connor would offer her something would be as part of a cruel joke, at her expense. She intended to politely decline, but frustratingly, Jenny spoke first.

"Come on, Nic. You don't mind if I call you Nic, do you?"

Astounded, Nicola shook her head.

"Cool. My house is back this way. Come on." She reached into her bag and pulled out a packet of cigarettes, then hesitated. "Do you smoke?"

Nicola shook her head again.

Jenny nodded. "You're actually the first person I've met from our year who doesn't." Beaming the fake smile again, she said, "You don't mind if I smoke on the way, do you?"

Still unable to speak, Nicola shook her head again. *Jeez, at least try to speak!*

"Come on then." Jenny walked back in the direction they'd come.

Confused by the peculiar turn of events, Nicola didn't move. *What the hell is going on?*

After a few more steps, Jenny stopped and looked back. She flicked her hair impatiently. "Come on, Nic. It's frigging boiling out here."

Unable to come up with a decent excuse to get out of it, Nicola found herself falling in beside Jenny, who talked constantly, except when she took a drag from her cigarette. As they walked, Nicola watched Jenny out of the corner of her eye and tried to work out her agenda. After a few minutes she gave up and admitted defeat. Jenny O'Connor and she were polar opposites, so she couldn't hazard a guess as to what was going on in Jenny's head.

Pretending to listen to Jenny's ramblings, she took time to consider her options.

What to do next?

Where to go?

Her bag and the uniform were all she had. She could never, ever return to the house for the rest of her clothes and possessions. But there was one factor that took precedence above all the others. It forced a lump of emotion into her throat. *What about Mum? Will we see or speak to one another again? What's he going to tell her about what happened? Would she believe him? Would she even care?*

She needed to find a quiet place to carefully think things through, which meant getting away from Jenny O'Connor as quickly as possible.

From what she'd seen and the rumours she'd heard about Jenny, she had good reason to be wary. Although this was the first time they'd ever actually spoken, she had always secretly disliked Jenny. In her opinion, Jenny was a superficial, promiscuous bitch, who bullied for personal amusement.

Her mind made up, she decided once her grazed hand was sorted and an opportunity to escape arose, she'd take it without hesitation. Nothing good could come from spending time with Jenny O'Connor, of that she was certain.

CHAPTER FOUR

Feel free to have a look around, Nic. I'll go and get the first-aid kit."

Nicola opened her mouth to speak, but Jenny had already disappeared, leaving her alone.

She looked around the hallway and felt more at ease. Everything from the cleanliness, to the faint lingering smell of coffee, suggested this was a loving family home.

The hallway was neat and tidy. A small dust-free table held a phone, address book, and pen. Coat hooks sprang from the wall above the table, and unable to resist, she hung her bag over one of them. After a few seconds of hesitation, she allowed her curiosity to get the better of her. She walked timidly through the nearest doorway.

She entered what appeared to be the living room. It was large in size, but furnished in such a way it felt cosy and snug. Two brown sofas sandwiched a large wooden coffee table and were positioned towards an elegant fireplace. The hearth was made of white marble and the wooden frame was decorated with pretty floral carvings. A mirror hung centrally on the wall, and two large unused candles were placed on either side of the fireplace shelf. An average-sized TV stood on a wooden stand and veered off to the right. An authentic-looking sheepskin rug lay at the foot of the fireplace.

Nicola turned to take in the rest of the room and was immediately drawn to the back wall, where a variety of framed photographs were displayed.

She took her time to study each one. The largest two were landscape views of countryside, filled with stone walls, thatched cottages, and vast fields of green. The rest of the photographs were of people, and she soon found herself scanning each one for Jenny.

One photo in particular captured her attention. A very young version of Jenny walked on a sandy beach, dressed in a fluorescent pink Minnie Mouse swimming costume. Her light auburn hair was blowing in all directions, and her green eyes sparkled brightly with mischief. One little hand gripped the handle of a plastic bucket and the other dragged a plastic spade behind her. Mini-Jenny's face beamed with happiness, and her grin comically revealed the large gap of two missing front teeth. Mini-Jenny seemed totally oblivious to the camera, and it made the photo all the more charming.

Nicola wondered how this innocent version of Jenny had grown into the promiscuous, bitchy bully. She quickly accepted she'd probably never know the reason why, and unable to help herself, she smiled back at the cute, smaller, and toothless version of Jenny.

CHAPTER FIVE

I've got the first-aid kit," Jenny said softly from the doorway. As Nicola turned to face her, Jenny's breath momentarily caught in her throat. The upset, plain girl she'd left in the hallway seemed to have transformed. Her blue eyes now sparkled with vitality, her cheeks glowed, and her smile was beaming.

"If you point me in the right direction, I can sort myself out," Nicola said politely, as she walked towards her. "You've already been kind enough."

Jenny swallowed and tried to recover herself. "The kitchen's this way."

As they entered the kitchen, she watched Nicola as she surveyed the room. A wistful expression flickered across her face and a half smile touched her lips. Jenny looked around too but saw only the familiar orange walls, large oak table, and four matching chairs.

"That's the biggest cooker I've ever seen," Nicola said. Her gaze focused on the eight burners on the stove, before moving to the inbuilt double ovens.

Amused by the quirky randomness, Jenny said, "My mum likes to cook a lot."

Nicola blushed and nodded. "I can tell. This is the nicest kitchen I've ever been in."

"Seriously?" Jenny asked. "You've obviously led a sheltered life." Sensing Nicola's embarrassment, she added, "This is strictly my mum's domain, but it'd make her day to know you like it so much."

Nicola continued to look around curiously, and Jenny found she was happy to watch her. There was something pleasantly innocent and calming about Nicola's presence. It was only when Nicola winced slightly that Jenny remembered her grazed palm.

She walked over to the sink and began washing her hands. Over her shoulder she said, "Have a seat and roll up your sleeve."

"I can clean it myself."

Taken aback by the snap, Jenny turned and saw Nicola looked panic-stricken. With a sympathetic smile, she said, "It'll be easier and quicker for me to do it." She raised both of her wet hands. "Two hands beat your one good hand. I promise I'll be gentle."

Nicola shifted uncomfortably from one foot to the other and nibbled agitatedly on her lower lip. Her brow was creased, and Jenny suspected she was forming an excuse, so she spoke first. "Please have a seat, Nic."

Reluctantly, Nicola pulled out a chair and took a seat. She sat upright, and her body remained rigidly tense as she fumbled with the sleeve of her shirt.

Drying her hands, Jenny tried to put her at ease. "This is a bit weird for both of us, isn't it?"

Nicola's shoulders slumped. "Weird is an understatement. But I do appreciate your help."

Unable to continue watching Nicola struggle to roll up her sleeve, Jenny knelt on the tiled floor before her. "Let me help."

As she rolled up the sleeve, her heartbeat quickened and phantom butterflies fluttered frenziedly in her stomach. She'd never done anything like this for someone before, and it felt strangely intimate.

"Uh—I'll be as quick as I can. If it hurts, tell me."

"Okay."

Trying her best to be gentle, she wiped the grazed palm with an antiseptic wipe. Nicola's skin felt both smooth and soft as it rested against her own. Nicola's fingers were slender, and the tips of all her nails were bitten.

Jenny shook her head and tried to clear her thoughts and concentrate on the task. Although Nicola gave no indication she was in discomfort, Jenny worried she was causing her pain. "Am I hurting you?"

Nicola shook her head. "I've had worse." Her expression looked melancholic.

Jenny nodded and applied a little antiseptic cream before standing up. "That should do you."

"Thank you, Jenny," Nicola said quietly. "I'd have struggled to sort it by myself."

Genuine gratitude lay behind the simple words, and it embarrassed Jenny. She couldn't quite explain it, but there was a vulnerability to Nicola that inspired protectiveness. The feeling was so out of character for Jenny, it unsettled her.

"I need a drink. Would you like one?" Jenny asked, surprised to realize she hoped Nicola would accept. She noted the familiar creasing of Nicola's brow.

Nicola looked at the floor and said, "I should probably—"

"Just one drink?" Jenny asked. "What harm will it do?"

Nicola's expression darkened, but with a defeated sigh, she said, "I suppose one drink will be okay. Thank you."

Jenny tried to suppress her grin as she poured them each a tall glass of cold orange juice. Nicola accepted the glass politely and took a long drink while Jenny sat down. For the next few minutes they sat in an awkward silence.

Nicola sipped her drink slowly, as if wanting to take her time, but also kept glancing at the kitchen clock.

"Have you got to go somewhere?" Jenny asked, breaking the silence.

Nicola shook her head sombrely. "No."

"Well, why don't you stay here for a bit? It's too late for either of us to go to school, and I hate my own company." Jenny was genuinely surprised by her own proposal. She didn't know Nicola. They were strangers with nothing in common, yet weirdly, she didn't want Nicola to leave. Curiosity was a part of it, but she also felt drawn to Nicola in a way she didn't understand. Plus she was aware this opportunity wouldn't happen again, so she wanted to make the most of it.

Nicola's eyebrows narrowed and her lips formed a thin line. "Why would you want me to stay?" she asked with testy suspicion. "We're not friends, Jenny. Before this morning, we'd never spoken. You weren't even aware I existed."

Surprised and a little hurt by the brutal honesty of Nicola's words, Jenny also found them refreshing. People usually didn't dare confront her.

"You're right. I didn't know your name before today. But I knew you existed. I've watched you sit under the shade of a tree at school…" As soon as the words left her mouth, Jenny regretted them. Her face burned with embarrassment.

If Nicola was surprised by the stalker-ish admission, she didn't show it. She crossed her arms and said coolly, "I've watched you and your friends too. I've also heard the cruel comments you've all shouted at me. And I've been shoved, pushed around, and humiliated for your personal amusement—"

"I never did that!" Jenny said, mortified. "I never shouted things at you. Christ, I've never laid a finger on you, never. That's not me, Nic."

Nicola's expression softened. "Perhaps it wasn't you directly, but it was still your friends. You didn't stop them. Isn't that as bad?"

Perplexed, Jenny tried to explain. "I'm just…I don't get involved in—"

"Well, maybe you should get involved, Jenny. You're probably the only one they'd listen to." Nicola took a slow sip from her glass, allowing her statement to linger between them. "Why have you been so nice to me today? Why ask me to stay?" She hesitated and then asked, "Is it part of a cruel joke?"

"What?" Jenny jumped to her feet, sending her chair scraping backwards. She glared down at Nicola. "You think I asked you to stay for some sick joke? What do you think I am? Shit!" She banged a fist down hard on the wooden table, needing to feel the pain to calm her. It didn't work. The urge to punch something or hurt herself in some way in order to cope with her anger was overwhelming. She glanced at the band around her wrist.

"Then why?" Nicola asked quietly.

Jenny looked down at Nicola and noted she'd shrunk back in the chair. Shaking her head, she replied, "I honestly don't know. That's the truth."

She stalked away from Nicola, trying to calm both the festering self-loathing and her temper. After a few deep breaths, she turned and faced her once more. The realization Nicola might actually be afraid of her extinguished her anger. Her temper quickly abated and was replaced solely by guilt.

"I don't know why I asked you back here. I don't know why I cleaned your hand, or why I've asked you to stay. It's not like me. This whole situation is really weird…" Jenny slumped down into her chair but avoided looking directly at Nicola. "But I didn't do those things because I'm the cold calculating bitch you think I am. You were upset, and I thought maybe I could help."

For what felt like a lifetime, they remained in silence. Jenny tried to think of something to say, but it all sounded wrong in her head. In the end it was Nicola who spoke.

"If the offer to stay for a little while is still open, I'd like to accept."

"It's still open," Jenny said, feeling relief and another stir of butterflies. "You're not as timid as you let people believe, are you?"

Nicola shrugged. "What people think is up to them. But what about you? I don't think you're half as bad as you make out, although your reputation of having a fiery temper is definitely true."

"You haven't seen anything yet." Jenny smiled and got to her feet. "I'm officially uncomfortable and too hot. Let's go to my room and find something to change into." She shot Nicola a sidelong glance. "If I'm hot, you've got to be boiling."

Nicola tensed, and Jenny decided now wasn't the time to ask about the winter uniform. To her amusement, she watched as Nicola's brow burrowed with the familiar *I'm thinking of an excuse* expression. She decided to save them both time. "We'll have a look. If you don't see anything you like, you can stay in your uniform. Okay?"

Nicola pouted. "That's getting annoying now."

"What is?" Jenny asked, feigning ignorance as they left the kitchen and started up the stairs.

"That you know what I'm thinking, so you speak before I get the chance to. Or you interrupt me and then end up changing my mind."

Jenny grinned. "That's the nicest way I've ever heard someone call me manipulative. And you're right, I am, but I get the distinct impression I wouldn't be able to change your mind if you were set against something. You'll only let me be so much of a bad influence on you." Jenny instinctively knew Nicola was timid and innocent. *I can have some fun with that.*

Nicola's cheeks flushed. "At least you're honest about yourself."

Jenny found she wanted to be totally honest with Nicola and warn her not to get too close. "I can also be a nasty piece of work."

Nicola stopped climbing. "So can everyone, Jenny. But today you've only been kind, considerate, and selfless. You're not a bad person, even if you're determined to convince me you are."

Jenny struggled to swallow. "Like I said earlier, so far I've not acted like my usual self today. Downstairs, you said what I'm like."

Nicola shook her head. "What I said downstairs was wrong."

"I think you should know what I'm like—"

"Okay." Nicola held up a hand silencing Jenny, while she studied her. "As you're so keen on confessing, do you have any other horrible qualities I should know about?"

Jenny was momentarily speechless. Her self-loathing had bubbled up to the surface, but now confronted by Nicola, she struggled to think. "I'm an excellent liar."

Nicola raised a quizzical eyebrow, and a smile twitched across her lips. "Most excellent liars wouldn't admit to it."

Jenny felt herself blush. "You're probably right about that."

"I consider myself warned."

They began climbing the stairs again, and Jenny couldn't help but smile, her morose mood lifting. "So, I've been upfront about my dark secrets. What about you? What dark secrets are you hiding?"

Nicola stiffened and looked away.

Curiosity stirred inside Jenny. She'd suspected Nicola had secrets, but now she was certain Nicola was hiding something big. She knew she'd have to gain Nicola's trust a little bit first, as she doubted Nicola would just reveal the secret to her. Her confidence was unwavering—in the next few hours she'd uncover it. *Gently does it.*

Trying to lighten the mood, she teased, "So, are you a good liar too?"

Nicola shook head. "I never lie."

"Ha! That's a lie."

"No, it isn't. I don't lie."

"Everyone lies sometimes, Nic," Jenny said. "It's human nature."

Nicola shrugged nonchalantly. "Well, I don't. I'm so bad at it, it's easier for me to be honest. I'm good at telling when people are lying to me, though." She raised her gaze and met Jenny's. "Even if they do believe they're excellent at it."

"That almost sounds like a challenge," Jenny said. "I guess only time will tell which one of us is right." She walked over to the first door on the left of the landing and held it open. "This is my room. Go ahead."

Nicola walked inside, and Jenny hesitated for a moment behind her.

The more time she spent with Nicola, the more she liked her. Which was strange, considering she generally didn't like many people. But liking Nicola wasn't enough to deter her. She remained adamant she would discover Nicola's dark secret. Another of her own darker qualities, which she'd failed to mention earlier, was she always got what she wanted in the end, even if it was at someone else's expense.

CHAPTER SIX

Nicola found Jenny's bedroom a contrast of styles. A stereotypical pink-and-purple colour scheme ran throughout the room, including a purple duvet which covered the king-size bed. A full-length mirror hung on the wall next to the largest dressing table Nicola had ever seen. Bottles and tubs of various cosmetics and other beauty paraphernalia filled the entire surface of the table.

The stark contrast began with the wooden easel and the desk which occupied the space by the window. The desk was exceptionally neat, and all of the art materials were well ordered, unlike the dressing table.

A collection of paintings hung on the walls, and Nicola surmised Jenny had painted them all. They were good, but all the themes seemed to be a little dark. She moved towards the nearest one with the intention of studying them all, but Jenny apparently had other ideas.

"Right, I'm taking these two." Jenny held up a pair of denim shorts and a black strap top. "Have a rummage through and see if you can find something you like."

Nicola scoffed at the solidly packed wardrobe. The rail seemed to be straining from the sheer volume hanging from it.

"I'm a bit bigger than you," Jenny said, as she walked over to her bed and began to undress, "so my clothes may be big on you, but they've got to be more comfortable than your uniform."

Quickly averting her eyes, Nicola reluctantly walked over to the wardrobe, feeling embarrassed. Jenny had an incredible body, so it wasn't surprising she was happy to strip in front of others. But under no circumstances would she do the same.

She went through the motions of skimming through the masses of clothes but didn't actually bother to look at anything. Her uniform was hot and uncomfortable, but there was no way she was changing out of it.

"Found anything?" Jenny asked from behind her.

Turning, Nicola found herself facing Jenny's practically naked body. Luckily, she had her back to Nicola. Only a white matching bra-and-panty set covered Jenny's modesty. Her legs and arms were delicately defined and tanned, her backside pert and round. Horrified, Nicola found her eyes seemed glued to it.

Stop looking! If she turns around, she'll think you're a total pervert!

Suddenly sensing she was being watched, Nicola raised her gaze and found Jenny's green eyes watching her with interest from the mirror's reflection. Mortified, Nicola snapped her gaze to the floor and begged the ground to open up and swallow her whole.

Pulling up her shorts, Jenny turned to Nicola and asked, "Seen anything you like the look of?"

Nicola gulped and reluctantly looked up. Her gaze leapt from Jenny's sparkling eyes down to the amazing pair of breasts that were encased in white lace. Horrified by the betrayal of her eyes yet again, she felt her face turn scarlet.

"I'll be fine in my uniform." She cringed at the unnaturally high pitch of her voice.

Jenny pulled her top on and walked over to the wardrobe with a smile. She rummaged through the tightly packed row of clothes and a few seconds later produced a pair of thin black combat trousers and a plain blue three-quarter-length sleeved top.

"How about these? The trousers may be a bit big in the waist and shorter in length, but no one's going to see you other than me."

Nicola was genuinely surprised. "They're actually nice."

Jenny nodded, with a victorious smile. "Nic, all of my clothes are nice, but I agree these are more your type of thing than mine. Do you want to get changed in the bathroom?"

Nicola hated her prudishness but nodded. "If that's okay?"

Jenny handed the clothes over. "It's fine. I'll meet you in the kitchen."

❖

"Hi," Nicola said nervously as she entered the kitchen.

Jenny actually did a double take. "Wow. Nic, you look great. You look like a totally different person."

"Thanks," Nicola said with a shy smile. "I feel loads more comfortable than in my uniform." She secretly felt pleased at Jenny's reaction. She'd admired her reflection in the bathroom mirror.

"Keep them," Jenny said, and although Nicola began to protest, Jenny continued unfazed. "They suit you. Plus, you saw my wardrobe, it's not like I haven't got enough clothes to choose from."

Relieved she'd have something other than her uniform to wear, Nicola happily agreed. "You do have an awful lot of clothes. Thanks, though."

"You're welcome. Here." Jenny presented her with a plate that held two hefty slabs of white bread. "I didn't know what food you like, or if you're allergic to anything. So I thought it's probably best you make your own sandwich."

They searched through the well-stocked fridge, and Nicola felt a stab of jealousy. She knew it was misplaced and so tried to ignore it. They sat down at the kitchen table, and they both ate with gusto.

With perfect timing, Jenny asked, "Is your sandwich okay?"

Mouth bulging with food, Nicola nodded enthusiastically.

"So, do you have any sisters or brothers?"

Nicola swallowed and studied Jenny carefully. She sensed no malice in the question and knew it was only natural Jenny would want to know more about her, but she didn't feel comfortable talking about herself.

"No."

Jenny seemed undeterred by her abruptness. "Lucky you. You probably saw from the photos in the living room that I've an older sister. Her name's Elizabeth and thankfully she's away at university. After graduating top of her class, she'll no doubt go on to have some career which will allow her to save the world, so she can secretly revel in all the glory while acting sickeningly modest."

Nicola recalled seeing a slightly older blond girl in some of the photos. "You don't get on well with her, then?"

Jenny's expression darkened. "It's no big secret we don't like one another. She's the ridiculously brainy celestial prodigy of the family."

The bitterness was clear, but Nicola sensed something darker lurking than normal sibling jealousy. Although curious, she knew it wasn't her place to ask and so remained quiet.

"So, did your mum and dad not want any more kids?" Jenny asked, expertly turning the limelight back onto her.

"They probably did, but my dad died when I was eleven."

Jenny gaped, dropped her sandwich onto her plate, and said, "Shit, I'm so sorry, Nic. That was shitty of me."

Nicola forced a weak smile. "It's okay, you didn't know." She pushed her plate away, her appetite gone.

"So, it's you and your mum, then?"

"No," Nicola said, as a shudder passed through her body. "My mum met a guy called Chris when I was twelve. He lives with us."

Jenny nibbled on her bottom lip, seeming to hesitate before asking, "You don't get on with the guy?"

"No."

Leaning forward, Jenny rested her hands on the table. "Did you have an argument with him this morning? Was that why you were running away?"

"I hate him," Nicola whispered. She regretted eating the few mouthfuls of the sandwich as they lay heavily on her stomach, causing a wave of nausea. For a short while she'd allowed herself to ignore the situation; now it all came crashing back. "I can't...go back."

Jenny blinked. "Sorry?"

Nicola brushed aside her question. "Can I use your Internet please? I need to look for a local hostel or cheap hotel to stay in tonight."

Jenny shook her head. "You're not staying at some crappy hostel! Stay here."

"I couldn't—"

"No arguments. Elizabeth's room's spare, and my mum and dad would rather I've a friend stay than go out."

Nicola opened her mouth but couldn't speak. A lump of emotion stuck painfully in her throat, causing her eyes to water.

Jenny rushed around the table and gently took hold of her hands. "Come on. I won't ask you what's going on, but please say you'll stay tonight. You'll give me the perfect excuse to stay in—surely that's better than staying somewhere you don't know and being alone? We'll chill, Nic."

Nicola couldn't stop the stream of tears flowing. For five years she'd been mostly invisible. No one had noticed her or showed any kindness towards her, except for her boss and his son Jack. Jenny's unexpected kindness overwhelmed her.

Giving a supportive squeeze of her uninjured hand, Jenny asked, "Nic, please say yes."

Wiping away tears, which were immediately replaced by new ones, Nicola managed to nod.

"Good. Why don't you go use the bathroom and I'll clear the dishes away. Okay?"

Nicola managed another nod before running from the room.

CHAPTER SEVEN

Once the tears had stopped and the snot was finally under control, Nicola sheepishly made her way downstairs. She found Jenny waiting for her in the living room. She was lying on the sofa and the TV had the opening credits of *Sister Act* paused.

"Feeling better?"

"Yes," Nicola said quietly, sitting down on the opposite sofa.

Jenny stretched out in an almost feline manner. "I hope you don't mind I chose this? Whenever I feel a bit sad or down, I watch it, and it always makes me feel better."

Nicola was surprised again by Jenny's thoughtfulness. "I've never seen it, so it's fine with me."

Jenny sat up. "Tell me you're joking?"

Surprised by Jenny's disapproval, Nicola said, "Nope. I've never seen it."

"It's amazing. You'll love it. I watched it constantly as a child." Jenny pressed play and they both made themselves comfortable as the opening credits rolled. "By the way, as predicted, my mum's ridiculously pleased you're staying over. They're going to the Irish club tonight for a seventieth birthday party, so we'll have this place to ourselves."

"Are you sure—?"

"I insist. Now enjoy the film."

"Okay, thanks."

A few minutes later, Nicola secretly glanced at Jenny, already engrossed in the film. Allowing her gaze to wander, she travelled up

Jenny's bare legs marvelling at how tanned and toned they were. *What the hell am I doing?*

The thought jolted her. She quickly turned her attention back to the TV.

During the film she found herself occasionally glancing in Jenny's direction. More often than not, Jenny would already be watching her and their eyes would lock for an instant. Each time it happened, Nicola's pulse would race. Then they'd both turn their attention back to the TV, watching it with fake concentration. A short while later, it'd happen again.

The sound of a car pulling into the driveway made Jenny pause the film and urgently whisper, "You should probably know my parents don't know I smoke, drink, hook up with guys, or that I'm on the pill. I need it to stay that way."

Panicking, Nicola whispered back, "Is there anything else? What if I say something I shouldn't?"

Jenny smiled. "Relax, Nic. As far as my parents are concerned, I'm a good Catholic girl. Stick with that and we'll be fine."

Nicola tried to calm herself and Jenny pressed play. The sound of keys in the front door made her bolt upright. Jenny mouthed, *"Relax,"* as Mrs. O'Connor entered the room.

"Well, hello, ladies. How are we keeping? Oh, I love this film. Nice nuns, nothing like what your father and I had to put up with back when we were young. They could be nasty back then."

Jenny's mum spoke with a soft Irish accent, but Nicola didn't struggle to understand her. She was shorter than both of the girls. Her blond hair fell in a cropped bob, her cheeks glowed, and her blue eyes shone brightly. She was pleasantly plump, unlike Nicola's own mum, who resembled a walking skeleton. Nicola immediately liked her.

"Or like the nuns in those depressing Irish films you and Dad made me watch," Jenny said, with a playful wink directed at Nicola. "Mum, this is Nicola. She's in my psychology class."

Mrs. O'Connor turned and beamed a warm smile at Nicola, who couldn't resist smiling back.

"It's lovely to meet you, Nicola. I'm Anne. You make yourself at home here. I hope Jennifer's been hospitable." Anne held her hand out for Nicola to shake. Her grip was firm but her hand was warm and soft.

"Thank you so much for letting me stay tonight. And Jenny's been a fantastic hostess."

Anne's smile became brighter as she dropped her ample frame down next to Nicola on the sofa.

"I'll tell you the truth, Nicola. It's not often Jennifer brings friends from school home. Her father and I think she must be embarrassed by us." Anne gave a hearty laugh, and Jenny rolled her eyes but also smiled.

"Anyway," Anne continued, "you're more than welcome here. Now, as much as I'd like to rest my old weary bones and watch singing nuns, I better go and get dinner started before the old man gets back."

She lightly patted Nicola's knee before pushing herself up onto her feet. On her way out of the room, she planted a kiss on top of Jenny's head.

Nicola's heart swelled and ached with emotion. Ever since her dad had died, her mum hadn't been affectionate towards her at all. She couldn't remember the last time they'd hugged.

Anne was almost out of the room when Nicola asked, "Mrs. O'Connor—sorry, Anne. Do you need any help with dinner?"

Anne looked slightly taken aback. Jenny also looked surprised.

"Well, that's a kind offer! You should take a few notes from Nicola, Jennifer." Anne winked playfully at Nicola. "It's very kind of you, dear, but you watch the rest of your film, my lovely. It won't take me long." She disappeared.

"Creep," Jenny whispered.

Nicola's face grew warm, and she concentrated on the film.

Twenty minutes later, another car pulled into the driveway. Nicola's nerves and discomfort surged back into action, and it must have been obvious, because Jenny leaned towards her again. "Nic, would you chill out? Jeez. You're making me nervous and they're my frigging parents."

Nicola tried to act casual. "Sorry."

Anne called cheerily from the kitchen, and a booming male voice answered back with a strong Irish accent. A moment later a man entered the room. His gaze immediately fell on Nicola.

"Well, who do we have here?"

Nicola looked up at Mr. O'Connor. He stood perhaps six foot five. Grey tinged his black hair at the sides. He studied Nicola with serious eyes the same colour green as Jenny's. He wore a smart grey suit, and Nicola felt uncomfortable under his stern gaze.

"Dad, this is Nicola, a friend from school." Jenny said.

Mr. O'Connor kept his gaze fixed on Nicola. Just as she became certain he didn't like her, his face transformed. He grinned mischievously and his eyes sparkled. Nicola relaxed. "Howdy there, Nicola. I had you going for a moment, didn't I?" He let out a hearty laugh.

Nicola nodded.

"Well, any friend of my Jennifer's is a friend of mine. I'm Michael." He glanced at the TV and then turned to Jenny. "You're not watching this old film, again? Do you know, Nicola, when she was small, she used to put a towel over her head and make herself into a nun. She'd watch this film over and over, singing along with every single word. For years, whenever anyone asked her what she wanted to be once she grew up, she'd reply—a nun! Who knows, she still might." He let out another hearty laugh, and Nicola couldn't help but join in.

Jenny had not only turned bright red, she also looked mortified and was unsuccessfully trying to hide behind her long hair. Although embarrassed, Nicola saw she was still smiling. Nicola realized Jenny was probably used to her dad embarrassing her with childhood memories, and another pang of jealousy stabbed through her heart.

Anne materialized next to her husband in a flash, wearing a bright green apron over her floral dress. She'd obviously been drawn to the room by the sound of laughter and the intention of not wanting to miss out on anything.

"Michael. You better not be bothering these poor girls," Anne scolded him playfully. Her smile grew when she glanced at Jenny and saw how flushed she looked.

Michael continued to chuckle. "I was telling Nicola here about our little singing nun. Can you remember? With a towel over her head, singing and dancing along." His large shoulders shook with laughter.

Jenny's face bordered on purple, and her expression made all of them laugh harder.

"Michael, shame on you. You're embarrassing her. Leave them alone to watch the film. Go and get changed, dinner's nearly ready." Anne left the room and Michael winked at Nicola before leaving.

"God, I'm so sorry about them," Jenny said, cringing.

"They're wonderful," Nicola said, unable to repress her grin.

As they watched the last few minutes of the film, the smell of fish and chips grew more tantalizing. Just as the film finished, Anne gave them a five-minute warning for dinner.

"Let's go wash our hands. Mum's a stickler for hygiene," Jenny said. "Oh yeah, and before you creep some more and beg her to let you wash up, you should probably know we've a dishwasher."

"There's a difference between being polite and creeping. Anyway, after tea I was hoping you might show me your nun impression. Towel and everything…"

Jenny's mouth gaped, which gave Nicola tremendous satisfaction. "I was young. You better not tell anyone. Please?"

Nicola shrugged her shoulders. "I'll think about it."

"Bitch," Jenny whispered quietly, throwing a cushion at Nicola's head, which narrowly missed her.

Nicola playfully bumped against Jenny's shoulder. "That's rude, *Jennifer*. You'll never make a good nun if you say and do things like that—"

Jenny interrupted with a few hissed words—explicit enough to make a nun drop dead from shock—before leading Nicola upstairs.

❖

The O'Connor's family meal was the nicest Nicola had experienced since her dad's death. She hadn't expected the holding of hands or the saying of grace, but it made her feel included. The whole thing had clearly embarrassed Jenny—especially when Michael asked her to offer the prayer for grace. She'd spoken beautifully, which surprised Nicola once again.

The homemade fish and chips were delicious and were followed by generous helpings of homemade apple pie and custard. At the end of the meal, when she and Jenny left the table and headed upstairs, Nicola felt uncomfortably full, but also content.

She dreaded the thought of leaving the O'Connor family tomorrow…

CHAPTER EIGHT

Jenny watched out of her bedroom window as her dad's car pulled out of the driveway and disappeared from view. She turned her attention to Nicola, who was sitting on the edge of her bed reading. "So, what do you wanna do tonight?"

Nicola looked up from the book and gave a sheepish smile, "You're not going to like it."

"Try me," Jenny said, stretching back in her desk chair.

"Well, exams start on Monday and I haven't finished reading this." Nicola's cheeks blushed, but she met Jenny's disapproving gaze head on. "So tonight I'd like to finish it."

Jenny crossed her arms and tilted her head to the side. "You're not seriously suggesting we stay in and revise? It's a Friday night, Nic. It's officially the start of the weekend."

"Wow. Thanks for pointing that out, but I'm still staying in and reading this." Nicola dropped her gaze back down to the page.

Jenny wasn't happy. She was used to getting her own way—didn't Nicola realize that? "I honestly can't even remember the last time I stayed at home on a Friday night." She watched as Nicola ignored her and sensed this approach wasn't working, so she decided to change tack. "We could go out somewhere. There's a house party—"

"Okay," Nicola said calmly, as she continued to read.

"Okay, what?" Jenny asked. She suspected Nicola wasn't going to back down that easily.

"Okay. You can go out tonight and do whatever you want. But I'm staying right here and finishing this." Nicola still didn't bother looking up as she added, "I don't want to ruin your Friday night, Jenny. Go out to the party. I'll be fine here."

"I can't leave you here alone," Jenny said and then stubbornly waited for a response that never came. They remained in silence, which only added to Jenny's growing irritation. "You're seventeen, Nic, not seventy."

Nicola infuriatingly continued to silently read.

"You'd enjoy the party, I know you think you wouldn't, but you would."

A few more seconds of silence passed.

"Don't blatantly ignore me!"

With a soft sigh, Nicola finally looked up from her book. "Why not? You're *blatantly* ignoring what I'm saying." She paused to let her point sink in. "I really don't want to go out, Jenny. I want to stay in and read. I get the idea doesn't appeal to you, but at least I'm not trying to force it on you."

Their eyes locked in a battle of wills. Nicola stared back with a stubborn calmness that showed no signs of abating. Jenny tried to make her glare intimidating, but after a few seconds, she knew she'd failed miserably.

"Fine!" she said, resigning herself to the fact she was spending the first Friday night in years at home. "You win, we're staying in."

Nicola's lips twitched. "Jenny, go out and have fun. I'm happy to stay in and do work by—"

"I'm staying too." Jenny huffed dramatically. "It's only one night and I'm not bothered about not going out." She picked up a pencil from her desk unenthusiastically.

"You're obviously bothered because you're sulking," Nicola said with a grin, as she spread out on top of the duvet, making herself comfortable.

"I'm not sulking."

"Yes, you are. But I'm sure you'll get over it." Nicola began reading again and said under her breath, "Eventually."

Holding back a smile, Jenny said, "I heard that."

"You were meant to."

Jenny looked at her empty desk and sighed. In reality, she had a ridiculous amount of work to do before Monday morning, when her art exam began. She needed to sketch a basic outline onto a canvas, so it could be painted during the exam. Her only problem was she had no idea what to draw. Her scrapbook was filled with rough sketches and ideas, but none of them appealed to her.

She'd recently found inspiration lacking and rather than admit it, she'd chosen to ignore it and procrastinate. All of her recent partying had taken her mind off the problem for a while, but it had done nothing to inspire her, and now her time was almost up.

She opened up her scrapbook, held her pencil poised above the blank page, and waited for an idea to strike. Nothing came. She turned her head slightly so she could discreetly watch Nicola.

Nicola looked both comfortable and engrossed in the book. Her eyes scanned the lines of text eagerly. Her eyebrows arched slightly in concentration, and she chewed absentmindedly on her bottom lip.

Jenny scrutinized Nicola's face, lingering briefly on her dark eyelashes and eyebrows. Nicola wore no make-up, as far as she could tell. Her lips were aesthetically pleasing in their shape, fullness, and colour. *Well, who'd have thought it?* It turned out, Nicola was a natural beauty, who didn't seem to have a clue.

Jenny was surprised. How had she never noticed Nicola before? How had other people not?

Nicola must have sensed she was being watched because she looked up at Jenny questioningly.

"Uh—what are you reading?" Jenny asked, trying to hide her embarrassment.

"'The Yellow Wallpaper,' by Charlotte Perkins Gilman. It's only a short story, but I need to memorize some quotes."

"I'm not a big reader," Jenny said honestly.

"Really? I love reading," Nicola said, her enthusiasm clear from the change of pitch and the sparkle in her eyes. "I can easily get through five books a week."

"Seriously?" Jenny asked and watched as Nicola nodded enthusiastically. "Well, I can tell you're enjoying it. I was curious." She swallowed and added weakly, "Sorry for interrupting you." She forced her attention back to the blank page in front of her. She could feel Nicola watching her for a few seconds longer before she returned to reading.

Jenny forced herself to start drawing, deciding any scribble was better than nothing. At first there was a random array of lines, but it was something. Intrigued, she continued to watch each stroke of the pencil until an image began to form. It took a few minutes longer before she realized what she was sketching.

Nicola's face gazed up at her from the page. Stunned, Jenny slammed her pencil down.

"Is everything okay?" Nicola asked with a frown.

"Yeah, I made a mistake." Jenny swallowed nervously and covered the page with her arms. "I get a bit annoyed at myself when I do things wrong."

Nicola's expression looked sympathetic. "You shouldn't be so hard on yourself. Your paintings are excellent."

"Thanks," Jenny said, "but sometimes I need to be harsh on myself."

Nicola shrugged and went back to reading.

Jenny moved her arms away and looked down at the sketch. It resembled Nicola and was actually quite good. With a frustrated sigh, she went to put the book away but then changed her mind. She wanted to finish it. And if she didn't carry on, it'd only eat away at her all night. With one last apprehensive glance in Nicola's direction, she started to add to the sketch.

The next two hours passed quickly, with neither girl speaking. Jenny found herself occasionally studying Nicola a little bit too intensely, or for too long, and then she'd quickly look away, embarrassed. Sometimes, she sensed or caught Nicola watching her, and then the phantom butterflies would flutter inside her stomach, all over again.

She placed down her pencil, turned over the cover of the pad, and locked it safely in her drawer. She swivelled the chair around and knew, from Nicola's weary eyes, she was also tired.

"I'm exhausted. I'm gonna go have a shower and then probably head to bed."

Nicola gave a tired smile, which turned into a yawn. "Sounds good to me."

Jenny got up and headed over to her set of drawers. She opened the middle drawer and took out an old pair of long-sleeved and -legged pyjamas. She threw them to Nicola, who was midway through yet another a yawn and only just managed to catch them.

"They'll be a little big, but they should be comfy. I'm going to use the bathroom. Do you want a shower tonight or in the morning?"

Nicola glanced down at the pyjamas. "I'll have one tomorrow, otherwise it'll wake me up. Is it okay for me to get changed in here while you're using the bathroom?"

"That's fine. Excuse me for a second," Jenny said, as she reached under the pillows next to Nicola's head for her own makeshift pyjamas, which consisted of a different strap top and a pair of cotton shorts.

The night was already stifling, and Jenny was looking forward to a cool shower. "Feel free to put the TV on for a bit if you want."

Once inside the bathroom, Jenny dropped her pyjamas into a pile on the floor while she turned the shower on. Steam clouds filled the room and she was starting to strip, when she realized she'd left her towel in the bedroom. With a frustrated sigh, she turned the shower off and trudged back out onto the landing.

When tomorrow came and Nicola left, she knew she'd feel sad. Although she liked Nicola, she was too strange to fit in with her other friends.

Friends. She contemplated the word bitterly.

Truth be told, she disliked Corrina and Sarah, but at least they were popular. Nicola was a nobody.

Questions niggled at her. Would she have the guts to acknowledge Nicola if they passed each other in the hallway? Would a brief knowing glance be the only reminder that today had happened?

Jenny hated herself for being so shallow, but she wasn't brave enough to go against the grain. Her head was starting to hurt with all the questions, so she decided to ignore them. A cool shower, and then bed was all she wanted. Whatever happened tomorrow and in the future could wait until then.

Absorbed in her thoughts, she turned her bedroom door handle and opened the door, remembering at the last instant she'd forgotten to knock. The door was only partly open, but it was enough to change everything.

Jenny stood frozen to the spot. Nicola's bare back was facing her, and Jenny was unable to make sense of what she was seeing.

Nicola spun around trying to cover her chest with her arms. Her eyes bulged and her expression was of complete horror. For what seemed like a lifetime, but was in fact only seconds, they stared at each other.

Nicola broke the silence, rasping, "Get out!"

Jenny tried to mumble *sorry*, but the word wouldn't come out. She tore her eyes away from Nicola and retreated to the landing, closing the door behind her.

What the fuck have I seen? Her back! Nicola's back was covered in...

Rooted to the spot on the landing, she trembled, the image of Nicola's back seared in her memory.

CHAPTER NINE

Jenny tried to make sense of what she'd seen. So many marks covered Nicola's back, she wondered if she'd imagined them. But Nicola's expression had been of genuine shock, and her reaction was enough to convince Jenny: they were real.

She pressed an ear to the door and listened carefully, wondering what Nicola was doing. She couldn't hear anything, but her gut feeling was telling her something wasn't right. She hesitated and then knocked on the door, preparing for another outburst from Nicola. There was nothing.

A few seconds later she knocked a little louder, waited, but still heard no response. Unable to ignore the overwhelming feeling something was very wrong, she managed to pluck up enough courage to slowly open the door.

Nicola had put on the pyjama top but was lying in a heap on the floor.

Jenny rushed over to her and saw her tear-stained face had turned burgundy. A high-pitched wheezing sound was coming from her.

"Nic! Can you hear me, Nic?" Jenny asked, as she ransacked her pockets. Her phone was downstairs. *Shit!* "Nic? Can you hear me?"

Nicola's eyes fluttered in response, but the raspy wheezing continued with each gasping breath. Jenny dismissed her initial thought that Nicola had choked on something. Her mind raced until she came up with an answer. *A panic attack.* It made sense. She'd watched Sarah having a similar attack in the past.

"You're going to be okay, Nic." She sat down behind Nicola and gently pulled her up into a sitting position and supported her trembling body by letting it rest against her own. She wrapped her arms around Nicola's waist and began to whisper soothing things.

Gently, she began to rock them both back and forth. "You're having a panic attack and I know it's scary, but if you listen to me and focus on breathing in and out, you'll be back to normal in no time. I promise."

Nicola's wheezing gradually calmed down, until her breathing was almost back to normal.

"You're safe, Nic. You're safe with me. I won't let anything hurt you."

Nicola's body slumped and she began to cry.

Jenny could do nothing but listen to Nicola's sobs. They were the most pathetic, exhausted, and sorrowful sounds she'd ever heard. They made her heart ache, and she wanted to relieve Nicola's sorrow but didn't know how. She hugged Nicola tighter, hoping the physical comfort would reassure her.

After a while, Nicola stopped crying, but they remained huddled together in silence on the floor.

Jenny was surprised she didn't feel uncomfortable holding someone she barely knew. The weight and warmth of Nicola's body's leaning back into her felt nice.

"What happens now?" Nicola asked in a husky emotionless tone.

Jenny winced. "I guess we need to talk. I know it's probably the last thing you want, but we have to. I'm sorry."

"Okay."

Jenny begrudgingly released her arms from around Nicola's waist, immediately missing the contact and warmth. She watched as Nicola stood and looked down at her. Nicola's eyes were red and puffy, and they no longer sparkled as they had earlier in the day. She looked exhausted.

Jenny got to her feet. "I need a drink and you need one too. Have a seat." She indicated the bed and watched as Nicola compliantly trudged over and sat.

Jenny shuffled the bottles of paints and glue in her art cupboard until she reached the back. She took out the plastic bottle of white spirit, carried it over to the chest of drawers, and picked up an unopened can of soda.

"Here," Jenny said, offering the can to Nicola. "You need to drink some, so I can pour some of this in. You wouldn't like it neat."

Nicola pulled the ring and took a drink while Jenny unscrewed the lid and lifted the plastic bottle to her lips. Nicola suddenly grasped the bottle firmly, preventing her from taking a sip.

"You aren't going to drink that?" Nicola asked, her tone a mixture of disbelief and horror.

"I sure am. It's vodka."

Nicola's eyebrows arched. "Vodka?"

"This is where I keep my secret stash of vodka, and so far, my mum hasn't found it. Don't look so freaked out, it's vodka."

Nicola still didn't look convinced, but she let go of the bottle and watched with apprehension as Jenny took a mouthful of the clear liquid. Jenny swallowed and grimaced at the strong taste, feeling the familiar warmth seep through her body.

"Hold the can still," Jenny said. She poured some of the vodka carefully into the can and ended up pouring more than she'd intended, but figured Nicola probably needed it.

She tapped the plastic bottle gently against Nicola's can and said, "Cheers."

Nicola raised the can to her lips and took her first sip. "Ugh!" She heaved dramatically.

Stifling a laugh, Jenny crossed to her desk and brought back a plastic pen. "You probably drank a mouthful of vodka. Give it a stir. It'll taste better."

Nicola reluctantly took the pen and tried to stir the contents of the can through the small hole, as best as she could.

"Just go for it, drink it down as fast as you can," Jenny said. "You'll be fine. Trust me."

Nicola still didn't look convinced. "I've never drunk vodka before." Her tone and expression were both pleading.

But Jenny hadn't missed the trembling of Nicola's hands. She knew that neither of them would want to be sober for the question-and-answer session. Her determination must have shown through because Nicola raised the can to her lips. She gave one last beseeching look, which Jenny chose to ignore, and then she drank.

Nicola's expression changed from the grimace and into a less dramatic pursing of the lips. She gulped the drink down until the can was drained, and then she belched loudly. Blushing with embarrassment, she said, "Excuse me."

"Better out than in. Well, that's what Gran always used to say, and take it from me, she was a true believer. The burping was okay, but it was the other end that was the problem. Elizabeth and I used to argue about who'd have to sit with her in Mass."

Nicola gave a weak smile.

Jenny crawled across the bed and patted the duvet, motioning for Nicola to lie down next to her. Nicola looked uneasy at the prospect but crawled onto the bed and lay down anyway.

Side by side they lay, and Jenny felt pressure to break the awkward silence. It was up to her to initiate the conversation, but she didn't know how.

The temptation to avoid questioning Nicola and talk about something else, something safe, pulled at her. In the morning they'd go their separate ways, and Jenny could ignore what she'd seen. She instinctively knew if she chose not to ask, Nicola wouldn't mention it. Jenny could choose not to ask and in doing so, she wouldn't bear any responsibility. That simple.

Jenny rolled her head to the right to look at Nicola, staring at the ceiling and seemingly lost in her own thoughts.

Is she thinking the same thing?

Jenny swallowed hard. *Can I really do it?*

Can I ignore what I've seen?

Can I live with myself if I let Nicola go without ever knowing the truth? The possibility she might be able to do exactly that scared her deeply.

"You know I've got to ask you about it, don't you?"

Nicola winced but kept her gaze focused on the ceiling. Jenny watched as the tears began to well and so offered the bottle of vodka. Nicola took the bottle and swallowed a big gulp. Her face grimaced and her jaw muscles clenched as she fought not to gag. A tear escaped and rolled slowly down her cheek. Nicola took another big swig of the vodka, gagged, and passed the bottle back to Jenny before wiping away the renegade tear.

"Your back. I saw all the...scars?"

Nicola closed her eyes and gave a curt nod.

"Some are old and some are more recent?"

Nicola nodded again. Her gaze remained fixed on the one patch of ceiling while tears continued to brim in her eyes.

Jenny knew it was hard, but Nicola needed to talk about it. "You said earlier you live with your mum and her boyfriend. You said you hate him. Is he the one...has he hurt you?"

"Yes," Nicola whispered.

"How long has he—?"

"Five years."

Five years! Nausea slammed into Jenny. Nicola must've only been twelve when he'd started. A defenceless child. While Jenny had been playing with dolls and worrying whether or not Santa would come, Nicola had been losing her childhood innocence while living in hell.

"Shit, Nic!" Jenny shook her head. "Why didn't you tell someone? Five years. How could no one notice what was going on?"

Nicola flinched and Jenny regretted raising her voice. But anger burned in a fiery rage inside her and she struggled to keep control of it. She clenched her jaws painfully to stop herself from venting further.

"I couldn't tell anyone. There's so much, I...I couldn't. My mum..." Nicola tore her eyes from the ceiling and peered at Jenny for the first time since they'd started talking. A multitude of emotions haunted her eyes.

"Couldn't you have told someone?" Jenny asked, looking away. "Surely someone could have stopped it years ago."

"You wouldn't understand, Jenny," Nicola answered angrily, but her voice also had an edge of desperation to it.

"Try me. Make me understand. God, Nic, I need you to make me understand." She knew she was being harsh, but she needed...to make sense of it. She hated her anger towards Nicola for *allowing* herself to be a victim for so many years.

Nicola closed her eyes, swallowed hard, and winced. "My mum... when my dad died, she completely lost it. She was so depressed. The doctors tried everything from counselling to drugs, but Dad's death had been so sudden, it totally destroyed her. Nothing worked. She would cry, sleep, and drink." Nicola shook her head softly. "I tried to look after her, but she'd given up on everything. I wasn't enough of a reason to go on living. She tried four times to kill herself and nearly managed twice."

"Oh, Nic."

"She took an overdose of antidepressants and alcohol. I found her slumped on the sofa…I was taken into care—"

"No!"

"Yes. And I hated it. I'd just lost my dad, and I knew if I wasn't at home to watch her, I was going to lose my mum too. When she came out of hospital, she attempted again. And no matter how hard I tried, I couldn't always be with her, watching her every second of the day. I stopped going to school, and I only left the house to run and get food from the corner store when I knew she'd passed out."

Jenny continued to listen, guilty and horrified in equal measures.

"I barely slept because I was terrified when I woke up, I'd find her dead. I honestly thought it couldn't get any worse. Then, a few weeks later…she met *him*. I don't know how they met. But she suddenly got better. It was that simple. Within a month, he'd moved in and I had my mum back, kinda. I knew she was never going to be the same as when my dad was alive, but it was the closest I was going to get. Then, three months later, it started. *He* started. And my choices were simple: I either took it and carried on, or I'd lose my mum again and end up alone. So I've taken it ever since. And in the whole five years, no one has seen and no one has cared. So you may judge me for my choices, my *weakness,* but I stand by what I've done."

Stunned, Jenny was struck dumb. She couldn't find the right words and in the end only managed to pathetically say, "I'm so sorry."

Nicola shrugged, returned her gaze to the ceiling, and remained silent.

"Why does he hurt you?"

Nicola closed her eyes again and tears flowed freely.

Jenny gently wiped away a few of the tears, feeling the hot wetness against her fingertips. Nicola had flinched at her initial touch, but now she turned her cheek towards Jenny's open palm.

"I don't know why. He says I disgust him. That I'm ugly and no one will ever love me. He's made sure of it. Who could ever love me when I'm covered in…who would ever want to…" She began to sob.

Jenny still didn't know what to say, but she knew exactly what she wanted to do. She wanted to hunt him down and kill him. She'd hurt him first, like he'd hurt Nicola, and then she'd kill him. The desire was intense and strong, but suddenly Nicola's voice snapped her out of her murderous thoughts.

"He never had to have a reason. I think he enjoys it." Nicola wiped away her tears with both hands.

"You've got to go to the police."

"No," Nicola said, shaking her head. "I can't, Jenny. I don't have any proof—"

"Proof? Nic, the state of your back is proof enough. You can't let him get away with this. You've got to go to the police. You can't just never go home again."

"Wrong." Nicola shuddered. "'I'm never going back there. Never."

"What about your mum?"

"My mum needs him more than she needs me."

"But that's ridiculous."

"I know you don't understand, Jenny. I told you, you wouldn't. But I'm not going to the police. I can't bear to have them look at me, prod me, ask questions. Telling you the ugly truth has about killed me. Please don't make me go. Please?"

Jenny watched in dismay as heart wrenching sobs racked Nicola. She decided she wouldn't upset Nicola any more tonight. In the end, it wasn't her decision. Perhaps tomorrow, she might be able to talk some sense into her, but for tonight she'd suffered enough.

"Okay. No more talking about the police tonight." A sudden sickening realization struck Jenny hard and the thought refused to leave her mind. The last thing she wanted to do was upset Nicola more, yet if she didn't dare ask tonight, she'd never have the courage to broach the subject again.

"Nic, did he…" Jenny clenched her fists, feeling as her nails dug painfully into her flesh. "Did he ever do more than…*hurt* you?" She braced herself, dreading the answer.

Nicola moved to the edge of the bed, turning her back to Jenny. "Did he do more than hurt me?" A bitter laughed escaped. "Was hurting me not enough?"

Jenny opened her mouth to apologize but then realized Nicola wasn't talking to her.

"I disgust him. He says everything about me is repulsive and nobody will ever want me. You'd think he wouldn't want to and he didn't. Hurting me was always enough, but today...I don't understand..."

Jenny waited for Nicola to continue, but after a few long moments of silence it was clear she wasn't going to. "What did he do today?"

"He pushed me against the wall." Nicola buried her face inside her hands. "Mum was upstairs in bed and he never does anything when she's home. But today, he was crazy. He was so angry. He said I had it coming, that I wanted it. He...he tried..." She hugged herself, rubbing her arms as if to rub the memory away.

Jenny felt helpless and all she could do was watch and listen, but it was bordering on torture.

"He was going to rape me," Nicola whispered. "My mum was upstairs and he was still going to rape me. I threatened to scream and he backed off. But if I ever go back, he's going to kill me. He said it and I know he means it." She broke down again.

Jenny needed to drink. To drink until she couldn't think or feel anything. That was what she normally did to try and cope with bad feelings. She'd drink and push the bad thoughts and feelings away, in the hope the drunken numbness would be enough to stop her having to hurt herself.

She screwed the lid on the bottle of vodka, placed it down, and then moved behind Nicola, gently stroking the sides of her arms. Although the night was hot, she could feel Nicola trembling.

"Come on, you're shaking. Climb under the covers."

They got up, Jenny pulled back the duvet, and they both climbed inside, resting their heads on the pillows as the duvet fell over them.

Nicola continued to cry, and after a moment of hesitation, Jenny moved closer, wrapping her arms protectively around her. Nicola moved back against her and they lay together in silence, sharing the warmth and comfort of being close again.

Jenny felt peculiar, and the phantom butterflies fluttered frenziedly in her stomach. She became hypersensitive to everything—the heat and weight of Nicola's body pressed against her own, the faint scent of shampoo in Nicola's hair, and the movement with each breath she took.

"Thank you," Nicola whispered, her voice thick with sleepiness.

"It's okay," Jenny whispered back. "I promise, he'll never hurt you again. No one will."

Jenny was beginning to feel tiredness creeping into her own eyes and body. She needed to get up and get changed into her pyjamas but was reluctant to move because she was so comfortable and didn't want to disturb Nicola.

A little while later, she began to feel overly hot and knew she'd soon start to fidget. Reluctantly she moved away from Nicola and got out of bed. Nicola remained asleep, so trying to be as quiet as possible, Jenny headed back to the bathroom and recovered her pyjamas. It felt like a lifetime ago since she'd come in there. She was too tired for a shower now, so she got changed, brushed her teeth, and removed her make-up.

On the landing, she froze, hearing noises downstairs. Loud whispered voices and clattering confirmed her parents were home. The urge to run down, hug them, and tell them how much she loved them was overwhelming. But in doing so, she'd only stress them out and make them think something was wrong. She silently went back into her room instead.

"Hey."

Jenny jumped with surprise and turned to see a sleepy-looking Nicola peering up at her.

"I thought you were asleep. Did I wake you?"

Nicola stifled a yawn. "No. I keep waking up and falling back to sleep. Should I go into the spare room?"

Jenny felt a stab of disappointment. She knew Nicola ought to go into the spare room, but she didn't want her to. She liked having her in the same bed and holding her. "If you want, or you can stay in here." *Please stay.*

"I'll go into the spare room. We'll both be boiling if we share a bed."

Jenny nodded. It made sense, but she still felt gutted. "It's the door directly across the hall, next to the bathroom. If you need anything, come and get me. I mean it, Nic." She moved aside to let Nicola pass. "I'll wake you up in the morning for breakfast."

Nicola gave a sleepy smile, which made her look adorable. A wisp of dark hair had come loose from her ponytail, and Jenny had to physically restrain herself from reaching out and sweeping it behind her ear.

"Thank you for everything. You didn't have to care, or get involved, but I appreciate you did. Sleep well, Jenny."

"You too, Nic."

She watched as Nicola made her way across the hallway and into Elizabeth's room. When the door closed, Jenny finally released the breath she hadn't realized she'd been holding.

She quietly closed her door, switched off her light, and found the darkness welcoming. She opened the windows as wide as they could go, even though the night was stifling and the windows wouldn't offer much in the way of relief. She was grateful for any breeze she could get.

Climbing on top of the duvet, she tried to make sense of the last twenty-four hours. Images and thoughts flooded her mind. Things finally began to fit into place like a puzzle. The image of Nicola's back continued to flash into her mind's eye, over and over again.

Jenny wasn't a stranger to pain, but the state of Nicola's back filled her with anger and guilt. She'd only known Nicola a day but instinctively knew she'd never hurt anyone intentionally. She was nice, quiet, and selfless and had already been through so much shit.

"I never asked if she needed to go to hospital to get checked out," Jenny whispered to herself. After a few moments, she decided Nicola would never have agreed anyway.

The things Nicola had said played repeatedly in her mind. He'd told her over and over again that no one would ever love her or find her attractive. The anger in the pit of Jenny's stomach burned hotly. Nicola was beautiful! Gorgeous big blue eyes that lit up when she laughed, beautiful pale skin, complemented perfectly by her rosy cheeks and freckles.

Jenny swore to herself she'd never let anyone hurt Nicola again.

And if this guy had made his mind up about going after her, then hostels and hotels would surely be the first places he'd look. The safest place for Nicola was to stay here, with her.

She knew she couldn't ask her mum outright to let Nicola stay for the next few weeks because she'd never agree. Although Nicola had made a great impression, her mum would ask too many questions and want too many answers. From personal experience, she knew her mum could be relentless when she thought she was on to something.

The only way she could get Nicola to stay was by doing what came naturally to her. She'd have to lie and manipulate to get her parents to give her what she wanted.

Her mum would only agree if she believed everything was on her own terms or as part of a compromise she'd suggested. Making her think that would be easier said than done.

As time passed, Jenny lay in bed thinking up different strategies and then systematically rejected them all. In the early hours, she finally came up with a plan that could work. It had to work, for Nicola's sake.

They were in this together now.

CHAPTER TEN

Jenny felt incredibly nervous as she entered the kitchen. "Morning, Mum."

Her mum turned and beamed a big smile. "Morning, Jennifer. I'm making breakfast, so you've time for a shower, if you want one. Is Nicola up yet?"

"I'll have a shower after breakfast," Jenny said, sitting down at the table. "I'll go wake her up in a minute. Did you have a good night?"

During the next five minutes, Jenny listened as her mum gossiped about the escapades of the previous night. Jenny was a little surprised at how wild the seventieth birthday party sounded.

"So, how was your night?" her mum finally asked.

Jenny took a breath and prepared to put her plan into action. "It was okay to start with. We both got loads of work done and then had an early night. The only thing that spoilt it was when Nicola got some bad news." Jenny watched as her mum's ears pricked up to the words *bad news.*

Perhaps it was the Irish in her, or just that she was incredibly nosy, either way in one swift motion, she'd turned away from the stove and scooped up her cup of tea. Within a blink of an eye, she was sat opposite Jenny at the table.

"Oh, she didn't," Mum said, her voice full of sympathy. "What happened?"

Jenny avoided looking directly into her mum's eyes but could feel them boring into her. "Her uncle in Australia has died. It's upset her." Her lie was met with condolences and more prying questions. Her mum was attracted to the sad story, like a moth to a flame.

"Her mum's flying out to Australia today. Nicola wanted to go with her, but with exams starting next week and lack of money, she's got to stay." Jenny felt a little guilty about the ease with which she could lie to her mum. As planned, her mum continued to lap up the sad story and ask questions, which she took as an indication her mum believed her.

"I didn't want to ask, but I think she mentioned something about a heart attack. Nicola lives with her mum because her dad died when she was twelve, in a car accident."

Jenny felt guilty for telling lies to her mum, but telling actual tragic truths that belonged to Nicola made her feel even shittier. But if she didn't get everything exactly right, her mum wouldn't go for it.

"Her mum thinks she'll be over there for at least a month. She's got to sort out the funeral arrangements, wait for the reading of the will, and all that stuff. So Nicola's going to be home alone and she's dreading it."

Her mum took a drink from her cup. *It was now or never.* Jenny hoped she'd done enough.

"I said I'd go and stay with her and keep her company. I think she's nervous about staying in the house alone. For a whole month as well, that's practically ages. I mean, that'll take us right up until the end of our exams and into the summer holidays."

She took the frown on her mum's face and the pursing of her lips as a good sign. Without letting her mum have a chance to interrupt, Jenny continued talking.

"Although, after the exams are over, there will probably be a few more of us staying over to celebrate…" Jenny glanced at her mum and had to suppress a smile. "I wanted to let you know."

Her mum's cheeks were pink. She clearly wasn't happy, which was exactly what Jenny wanted.

"That's truly terrible, bless her cotton socks. And although I think it's admirable you want to support her, Jennifer, I don't think this close to your exams you should be…uprooting or distracting yourself."

"Mum, I can't leave her in a house by herself. She's upset and it'll probably bring everything flooding back about her dad's death. Would you feel right letting her stay in a house by herself? She's only seventeen, the same age as me. If something happened to her, I'd never be able to forgive myself. At least we're more likely to be okay if there's the two of us."

Her mum took another small sip from her cup and then placed it carefully down. Jenny held her breath in anticipation.

"No, Jennifer. I wouldn't feel right about letting her stay by herself. But I certainly wouldn't feel right about letting you stay there unsupervised, either—"

"Mum, we'll be fine." Jenny expertly took up her cue. "You can trust us. We're practically adults anyway. And we'll only have a few friends come and stay over to keep us company."

Mum's eyebrows narrowed and her complexion paled, as she no doubt imagined all the unprotected sexual orgies, wild parties, and drug use that would happen. Jenny knew her mum was not only incredibly nosy, but that she also always used her overactive imagination to foresee the worst-case scenarios.

"Jennifer, you're not going to stay at Nicola's house for a month without adult supervision. Especially not during your exams. I'm sorry, but you're not."

"I'm not going to let her stay there by herself, Mum! She's my friend and I'm not going to leave her when she needs me the most. This is because you don't trust me, isn't it? Why don't you ever trust me?"

"Jennifer, stop raising your voice and listen to me." Her mum folded her arms over her chest. "I do trust you…"

Jenny knew this was an obvious lie, but she couldn't blame her parents for not trusting her. Up to yesterday, she couldn't have been trusted, and today, well today she was still lying and trying to manipulate them.

"You've both got your exams, important exams, and the last thing you both need on top of that stress is having to cook, clean, and fend for yourselves. Please listen to me, Jennifer. I know you're not going to like what I propose, but I think it's for the best. Why doesn't Nicola move in here until her mum comes back? We've got Elizabeth's spare room, and I always cook enough for four people. You can both revise here and help each other. That's a good compromise. What do you think?"

Jenny feigned her best sulky expression and glared. "I think you don't trust me."

"It's not about trust, Jennifer. It's about what's for the best. I'm not having it any other way."

They remained in a silent standoff for a few seconds more before Jenny spoke.

"It's not like I actually get a choice, is it?"

Mum smiled sweetly. "I only want what's best for you. One day you'll see it, perhaps when you've got children of your own."

Jenny still felt shitty. Mum was relieved she'd come up with a plan to prevent the inevitable loss of her daughter's innocence. *Too late,* Jenny thought grimly.

Mum got to her feet and returned to the stove. "Go wake Nicola up and see how she feels about it. I'll finish making breakfast. You've got fifteen minutes."

Jenny took a glass off the draining board, filled it with water, and made her way upstairs to wake Nicola. She couldn't hide her grin.

CHAPTER ELEVEN

Nicola was dying. A slow and painful death—of that, she was certain.

Her head pounded as if someone was using it as a drum. A dull ache resided behind her eyes, and her mouth tasted dry and stale. Whenever she moved, her headache worsened tenfold.

I'm never, ever, going to drink vodka again! Or any other form of alcohol. Or soda. Her body shuddered at the mention of the evil substances that had poisoned her. *How can people inflict this upon themselves, over and over again?*

"Never…again," she whispered to herself. "She better be suffering as much as I am."

As if speaking of the devil had somehow summoned her, there was a quick knock on the door before Jenny burst straight in without waiting for a reply. Nicola watched through squinted eyes as Jenny made her way over to the bed. Her annoyance grew. From all appearances, Jenny didn't seem to be dying, or suffering at all.

"Morning, Nic," Jenny said, grinning, as she dropped down on the bed. "No offence, but you look like shit."

Nicola's mood darkened significantly. Yes, she probably did look like shit, but in all fairness, they should both look like shit! She chose to remain silent and glare, hoping Jenny would recognize both the dirty look and the silent treatment.

"Jeez. You weren't joking when you said you hadn't drunk before, were you?" Jenny said, with a chuckle.

Nicola could feel the restraints on her temper fraying, as Jenny's irritating laugh stabbed through her head like a knife.

"So is this your first hangover?" Jenny asked.

"My last," she said gruffly.

All the good qualities she'd seen in Jenny yesterday had now disappeared. She realized she didn't like her after all. And she especially didn't like the grin or the stupid laugh.

Jenny held out a glass of water. "Well, if you don't want this, I'll—"

Nicola snatched the drink from Jenny's hand and gulped down a few mouthfuls. She watched as Jenny held out her other hand and said, "Here."

Nicola watched as two white tablets fell into her palm.

"Painkillers," Jenny said. "They'll make you feel more alive. I've got to tell you some important stuff, and I need you to concentrate."

Nicola stopped her glaring and swallowed both tablets. The water felt wonderful as it cooled her parched throat. "Thank you," she said finally. "I'm sorry for being horrible, I feel awful."

Jenny shrugged. "It's fine. It's nothing a few tablets and an O'Connor fried breakfast won't sort out. Anyway, I've got some news for you."

All of Jenny's fidgeting and grinning like the Cheshire Cat was making Nicola suspicious, but she decided to give her the benefit of the doubt.

"I know this is going to sound a little bit stressful in your current state, but I've managed to convince my mum to let you stay here, with me, for at least a month. We'll have to go buy you some clothes and things, but you get to stay here and not at some shitty hostel."

Nicola was stunned and her hangover was forgotten for the moment. She struggled to take in Jenny's words. "What? How?"

"I came up with it last night. To get my mum to agree, I had to tell some tiny white lies, some of which you're going to have to keep up."

"Oh, what've you done?"

"Don't look so stressed, Nic, it's all going to be fine."

Lies? Had Jenny not listened to a word she said yesterday? Or was this some kind of stupid game to prove she was right? Nicola could only watch as Jenny continued speaking, totally oblivious to her anger.

"Your uncle in Australia has died of a heart attack. Your mum phoned you last night."

Nicola shook her head, which only succeeded in making her headache worsen and a fresh wave of vertigo assault her senses. "I don't have an uncle in Australia. What are you going on about?"

Jenny's grin faltered slightly. "I know you don't, but you have to pretend you do. He died of a heart attack. Your mum's already got a flight out there early this morning. She phoned you last night. She's going to be gone for at least a month, and you couldn't go with her because of exams and money." Jenny's excitement finally seemed to die down as she watched Nicola cautiously. "Are you okay, you look a bit green. You're not gonna puke, are you?"

Nicola felt sick, but it had nothing to do with the hangover. How could Jenny do this to her? How could she make up lies about her life and tell them to her own mum? She didn't trust herself to speak.

"I told my mum you were going to be home alone. She said we'd both be under enough stress with our exams, so she suggested you stay here, instead. She told me to come up and ask you." Jenny now looked worried and embarrassed.

Deep down, *very deep down,* Nicola knew Jenny had done it to help her. But that didn't make it right. There was no way she could pull off what Jenny wanted her to. No way.

"Thank you. But you'll have to tell her, although the offer's very kind, I'm going to have to refuse."

Jenny stared at her. "Why? It's perfect and you're safe here. Don't you like it here, with me?"

The obvious hurt in Jenny's voice made Nicola feel worse. But she couldn't lie to Anne, especially not when she'd been so lovely to her.

"I love it here, Jenny. I wouldn't feel right staying here under false pretences, and I honestly can't lie to your mum. I'll be fine in a hostel."

The silence between them seemed to last an eternity. When Nicola did glance up she saw Jenny was staring back at her. The hurt expression had now been replaced by anger.

"The reason I've done all of this is so you'll be safe. So I can help you. If he's looking for you, don't you think a hostel would be the first place he'd go?"

Nicola didn't answer.

"I do." Jenny folded her arms. "I've seen those films, Nic. I know they're supposedly fiction, but who knows what weirdo they've given sick ideas to. And I don't like lying to my mum, either, but would you rather I'd told her the truth?" She paused, for effect. "No, you wouldn't."

"It doesn't justify—"

Jenny uttered a frustrated sound and shook her head. "I thought you wanted my help."

Irritating as it was, Nicola found Jenny's arguments did make sense. It suddenly dawned on her Jenny genuinely cared about her. She no longer had to deal with everything by herself. Tears brimmed, but she held them back. The time for crying was over.

"I'm a bad liar," she said. "I mean really bad, Jenny."

Jenny flashed a mischievous grin and stood up. "Well, you're about to make up for it now. Uncle, heart attack, and Australia. How difficult can it be?"

Very! Nicola thought to herself as she reluctantly followed Jenny out of the bedroom.

CHAPTER TWELVE

I'm so sorry to hear about your uncle, Nicola. Has Jennifer invited you to stay here? It would be a pleasure to have you."

Jenny watched Nicola carefully and noted her panic-stricken expression before looking down at her plate. Her flushed cheeks and tense body made Jenny squirm with discomfort. *Come on Nic, lying is easy.* Jenny concentrated on eating another small forkful of her breakfast, waiting to see what would happen.

"Thank you, Anne. If you're sure it's not too much trouble, I'd love to stay," Nicola said, as she unenthusiastically prodded the food on her plate.

"Were you close to your uncle, dear?"

That question even took Jenny by surprise. Jenny watched as Nicola paled, looking as if she might pass out or throw up. She jabbed at a sausage with her fork and said, "When I was young, I was close to him. But once he moved to Australia, we rarely saw him. He used to write and e-mail every few weeks and phone on birthdays or at Christmas. I can't believe I'm never going to see or speak to him again."

Jenny tried her hardest to mask her shock. *What the hell was that? Not good at lying? Bullshit!* Either Nicola had been lying all along, or else Jenny had inadvertently created a pathological liar.

"Bless you, you poor thing. Are you religious, Nicola?"

Jenny snapped her head towards her mum and glared. This was the problem with her parents! It was embarrassing, yet understandable, they insisted on saying grace in their own home. But trying to convert other people to Catholicism, especially her friends, was totally unacceptable. Why did they think she didn't invite her friends over?

"My dad was brought up in the Church of England as a child, but that's as far as it went. The last time I set foot in a church was at my dad's funeral."

Jenny watched as her mum nodded solemnly. "Well, as you can't go to your uncle's funeral, you could always come to Mass tomorrow with Michael and me. It would give you the opportunity to say a quiet goodbye and light a few candles. Think about it, Nicola."

Jenny mustered the evilest look she could physically manage and directed it at her mum, but Mum was so satisfied with herself, she didn't see the look or chose to ignore it.

"Thanks, Anne. I'll think about it and let you know," Nicola said politely.

Jenny was speechless. Nicola couldn't seriously be contemplating going to Mass to pray for a dead uncle who didn't exist. *Could she?*

After a few minutes of silence, the phone thankfully rang and Jenny's mum disappeared into the hall to answer it. Jenny seized the brief opportunity and whispered, "Bad at lying? You could've fooled me, Nic. Why don't you go have a shower before she comes back and persuades you to become a nun?"

Nicola placed her cutlery down and headed towards the door.

"Nic?" Jenny said, watching as Nicola turned around. "You did all right. Just like I said you would."

Nicola smiled weakly and left.

Jenny got to her feet. She'd also had enough of breakfast. She'd begun to empty their plates when her mum returned.

"Where's Nicola gone?"

"For a shower. She wasn't too hungry. I think she's still upset."

Her mum nodded and resumed eating her own breakfast. "She didn't look well. She was pale, the poor thing."

"We're going to fetch Nicola's things and then go shopping. Thanks for everything, Mum," Jenny said quickly before leaving. She went to her room and found Nicola sitting on the bed, still dressed in pyjamas.

"I've no towel, toothbrush, shampoo..." Nicola said, clearly embarrassed.

"Sorry, I didn't think about that." Jenny opened a drawer, took out a towel, and handed it to Nicola. "There should be a spare toothbrush in the bathroom cabinet, and feel free to use anything else you need. How are you feeling now?"

Nicola headed out the door and said over her shoulder, "I'm still adamant I'm never drinking again."

Jenny lay on her bed and smiled to herself. Today was going exactly how she'd envisioned it.

As soon as Nicola returned, Jenny took her turn in the bathroom. She'd decided to dress in the bathroom too, so she didn't make Nicola feel uncomfortable. Once back in her room, she dried and then straightened her hair, until it met with her impeccably high standards. Then she started the rigorous routine of applying her make-up.

"Do you do this every day?"

Jenny glanced into the mirror and saw Nicola was watching her reflection. "Yeah. Why?"

Nicola placed her book down on the bed beside her. "I wondered. It seems like a bit of a waste of time. I don't do the whole make-up and hair thing."

Feeling uncomfortably scrutinized, Jenny said, "I like making an effort."

"For other people," Nicola asked, "or yourself?"

Jenny shrugged. "Both, I suppose. I like looking good, and I like other people noticing I look good."

Nicola frowned. "Would you bother doing all this if you weren't going out and people weren't going to see you?"

Jenny was starting to feel irritated. *Someone's obviously feeling better.* "I always do it, whether I'm going out or not. Some people aren't like you."

Nicola looked away, clearly hurt by the comment.

"Nic, I didn't mean that, how it came out." Jenny placed her make-up brush down and turned in her seat. "It's just, you're naturally gorgeous. You don't need make-up, but I do." Nicola had turned bright red and had wrapped her arms protectively around her knees. She still looked upset. Jenny asked, "You don't believe me, do you?"

Nicola looked up and searched Jenny's face. After a few seconds, she finally answered. "I'm not beautiful. You don't need to say it, to make me feel better. You've been nice enough to me, but please don't pity or lie to me. I'm sorry if I bothered you with my questions, I was curious."

"Nic, I'm not saying it to be nice. I'm saying it because it's true. You're beautiful and it's all natural. Do you know how envious I am? I spend a fortune on make-up." She motioned to the dresser which was filled with various tubs and tubes. "Mascara, blusher, lipstick, but you already have it all there." Jenny held up a hand to silence Nicola's retort. "Don't bother arguing with me. I'm entitled to my opinion and I think you're beautiful. That's the end of it."

Nicola remained silent, so Jenny turned back to the mirror and continued applying her make-up. She added the last bit of eyeliner and was finally finished. "Are you ready to go shopping?"

"Not really," Nicola said honestly. "I'm still feeling ill."

"It'll be fun, and if you're a good girl who buys lots of things, I may treat you to a McDonald's for lunch. It's the best cure for a hangover. It's better than an O'Connor fry-up because it comes without the additional sides of interrogation and being forced to lie."

Nicola laughed and got to her feet.

Jenny realized the sound of Nicola's laugh made her feel good. She hoped she'd get to hear lots more of it, before the day was out. "Come on, then. Let's go."

CHAPTER THIRTEEN

The shopping trip turned out to be more fun than either of them had expected. Despite their obvious differences, they'd gotten on surprisingly well. Nicola ended up purchasing more clothes in that single trip than she had in the entire previous year. Although initially she hadn't been keen on using her savings, there wasn't any other choice—she desperately needed clothes and other essentials. Luckily, Jenny knew which shops had the best sales and reductions, so she didn't spend too much in the end, and she even secretly enjoyed it.

The only thing that dampened their day was the ridiculous amount of calls and texts Jenny received from her friends. It'd gotten so relentless, Jenny eventually switched off her phone.

After their McDonald's lunch, they returned to the O'Connor house with plenty of bags in tow. It was once they'd gotten past Anne and were safely in the privacy of Jenny's room that their conversation became heated.

"You can go, Jenny. That's fine. But there's no way in hell I'm going with you. I'm staying here with your parents," Nicola said firmly.

"Mum and dad are going out again—"

"Then I'll stay in by myself."

Jenny crossed her arms and glared. "Nic, please consider it at least. It's just a house party. And I have to go. You saw the number of texts and missed calls I got today."

"I'm not stopping you from going," Nicola said, with a shrug. "In fact, I'm insisting you go."

Jenny began to pace the floor. "We're friends now. Well, *I* consider *you* a friend." She glanced at Nicola and waited.

"I consider us friends too."

"Good. But I've got other friends, and at some point you're going to have to meet them. I want to show them how great you are." Jenny stopped pacing and looked pointedly at her. "You're seventeen, Nic, and you haven't experienced what fun it can be. These are supposed to be the best days of our lives. You're going to look back in twenty years and have regrets."

Nicola sighed. She knew Jenny was probably right, but that made it all the more irritating. She was seventeen and hadn't experienced anything. Not one party, not one date, not even her first kiss. But the thought of actually going to a house party filled her with sheer panic.

"Jenny, I appreciate what you're saying, I do. But I don't think I can do it. Everyone, including all your friends, thinks I'm a complete freak—"

"I don't," Jenny said. "And I don't give a shit what they think." She placed her hands on her hips, which made her look formidable. "I'd never let anyone hurt you, Nic. Never."

The sincerity in Jenny's voice was unmistakable, and a lump lodged in Nicola's throat.

"Come with me tonight. I promise you'll be fine. Who knows, you might enjoy yourself. We'll give it half an hour and then come home if you hate it. If someone says or does something that makes you feel uncomfortable, we'll come home. All you have to do is say, and we'll—"

"Come home. I get the message," Nicola said wryly. "Fine. I'll go with you to the party tonight. But I'm not drinking."

"Excellent," Jenny said with a smile. "It'll be the first of many new experiences for you."

Jenny left the store and scurried over to where Nicola was waiting.

"Did you get everything you wanted?" Nicola asked, concerned because Jenny looked flustered.

"Yeah." Jenny lifted the blue plastic bag, and Nicola saw it was filled with a large bottle of sweet cider and a bottle of cheap vodka. "That guy always serves me, but he's a total creep. The way he looks at me makes my skin crawl. Let's get out of here."

Nicola followed Jenny—she had no idea where the house party was. She wasn't surprised Jenny had received leering looks. She was dressed in ridiculously high heels, a pair of incredibly short denim shorts, and a cropped pink Lycra tank top, all of which left little to the imagination.

Nicola knew she could never wear anything as provocative or revealing, as she didn't have the curves, confidence, or the unblemished skin. But even she was struggling to stop her own eyes from roaming over Jenny's scantily clad body. Her cheeks warmed and her stomach churned, so she decided to focus on looking ahead.

"I got you some cider. I know you said you're never going to drink again, but it'll help your nerves and it's sweet," Jenny said. "So you should like it."

When they entered the house, Jenny led Nicola through the crowded hallway, past the thick mass of bodies, and into the busy kitchen. Jenny searched and found two clean pint glasses. She poured Nicola a pint of cider and then poured herself a large amount of vodka, with a splash of Coke. The smell of the vodka invoked memories from the night before, and Nicola had to take a step away.

"So, what do you think about the cider?" Jenny asked.

Nicola took a tentative sip and was pleasantly surprised. "It's actually nice."

"I thought you'd like it. We've got to hide our bottles to stop skanky tramps from drinking them or pervs spiking them." Jenny made a point of showing Nicola that she'd chosen to hide their bottles in the washing machine. "Right. Ready to meet my friends?"

Nicola took three large gulps of cider before nodding. With a reassuring smile, Jenny took hold of her hand and led her to what looked like a dining room. Just before they reached a small group of girls, Jenny gave a final squeeze and then let go of her hand. Nicola immediately missed the touch and comfort.

She looked up briefly and quickly scanned the faces of the four girls who stood before them. She recognized Laura immediately but had never seen the girl standing next to her. The other two girls she knew by reputation, same as she'd previously known Jenny.

Sarah Wade and Corrina Jinks. Both girls stared at her with obvious surprise. Sarah was slender, tanned, and blond, although Nicola didn't believe the last two features were natural. Corrina was the larger of the two. She had dark hair with red highlights and wore a constant sneer as if perpetually annoyed.

"This is my friend, Nic," Jenny said, giving her a wink before turning to introduce the other four girls. "This is Sarah, Laura, Corrina, and Saz."

Nicola swallowed hard and tried to force a smile but feared it looked more like a grimace.

"Hi, Nic. It's great you've come tonight," Laura said cheerily. She seemed genuinely happy Nicola was there.

"Hey, Nic."

Nicola nodded appreciatively at the other smiling girl, Saz. She had dark hair tied up with two bits hanging down at either side of her face. She was slightly plump compared to Laura and Sarah, but it suited her.

"Hi," Nicola said. She raised her drink and took a hasty mouthful. She wasn't particularly thirsty; it was just something to do.

"So, where were you yesterday?" Sarah asked Jenny, blatantly ignoring Nicola in the process.

"We chilled out."

Nicola felt both Corrina and Sarah's eyes boring into her, their initial surprise now changed to suspicion.

"I wish I'd have been there—" Laura said.

"Shut up!" Corrina said. "So, when exactly did you two become such good friends?" She shot a glare at Nicola.

"We've been friends for a while," Jenny replied curtly. "Have you got a problem with that?"

"Yeah, actually, I've got a big problem with it. You've never mentioned her or the fact you're friends before. So it's a bit fucking weird that all of a sudden she's here," Corrina said. Sarah nodded in agreement.

"I didn't mention it because it's none of your business. What the hell's your problem tonight?" Jenny asked.

Nicola recognized the warning in Jenny's tone and shifted nervously. She glanced at Laura and Saz—they looked as uncomfortable as she felt.

"My fucking *problem* is you're acting weird. Like you decided to miss school and the party yesterday and didn't bother to reply to the texts and voicemails we left you. Then you turn up tonight acting like nothing's happened, with *her*, claiming to suddenly be best friends."

Nicola watched, fascinated, as Corrina and Jenny aggressively eyeballed each other.

"Nic, do you want to come and get a refill with us?" Laura asked quietly.

Nicola gave an appreciative nod. "That sounds like a good idea."

Laura and Saz led her back to the kitchen. She was glad to be out of the room because they'd left in a wake of raised voices.

"I'm sorry about Corrina and Sarah. Don't let them bother you. They take a while to get used to change," Laura said, seeming genuinely embarrassed by her friends.

"Change? Laura, you seriously need to wake up," Saz said, then turned to Nicola. "They're total bitches and they aren't going to change. They still don't acknowledge me because I'm Laura's friend, and I don't go to the same sixth form." Saz poured some neon-green liquid into her glass, from a bottle she'd retrieved from inside the cooker. "We've been going to the same parties for over a year now, and they still ignore me. They're not worth worrying about."

Nicola took her opportunity to refill her glass with the cider. Curious, she asked Laura, "Why do you hang around with them if they're so horrible?" She'd spent less than three minutes in their company, but it had been enough to put her off them for life.

Laura blushed and chose to drink rather than answer.

"I'm lucky enough to only come across them at parties," Saz said and then turned her attention back to Laura. "I honestly don't know how you can stand being around them all the time. Especially when they speak to you and treat you like utter shit. I'd have killed one if not both of them by now if I were you."

Laura shrugged. "They can be okay, sometimes. It's always easier when Jenny's around."

Nicola decided she liked Laura and Saz. They were friendly and honest.

"I think it's nice Jenny and you are friends," Laura said, blatantly trying to change the subject. "Does it mean we're going to be seeing more of you at school?"

"Maybe," Nicola said. "I suppose it depends on if they all survive tonight." All three laughed.

"Well, I hope you do spend more time with us, it'll be a nice change," Laura said.

Nicola was surprised she was actually enjoying herself. The cider was going down well, and she was feeling quite merry. She liked it.

"I'm going to go see what Tom's up to and have a smoke. I'll catch you both later. It was nice meeting you, Nic." Saz stood up and disappeared into the busy hallway.

Nicola felt a little uncomfortable being alone with Laura. Although Laura was lovely, she wasn't used to having to have such close personal interaction.

Laura seemed totally at ease. "Tom's her boyfriend," she explained. "They've been together for about six months. It's depressing how happy they are. Sickening, even."

"Do you have a boyfriend?" Nicola asked.

"No. Unfortunately, not," Laura said with a wistful sigh. "How about you?"

Nicola shook her head. "No, me neither."

"I'd give anything to be as confident as Jenny is with guys," Laura said. "Even if it was for an hour."

Nicola struggled to swallow. "Jenny has a boyfriend?"

"No. Well, maybe. To be honest it's difficult to know." Laura sipped her drink. "She's always going on dates and things, but then the next day she starts seeing someone new. There's this one guy I think she does like, though. His name is Matt." Her brow furrowed as she peered curiously at Nicola. "Hasn't she mentioned him?"

Shit! Nicola tried not to panic. "She mentioned something, but like you said, there always seems to be someone new."

Laura smiled and nodded. "I know what you mean. Matt's here tonight, so we'll see what happens." She sighed dramatically. "I suppose we'd better go back to them. Hopefully, they'll have sorted things out by now."

They reluctantly made their way to the doorway but stopped when they heard shouting.

"Like you'd know!" Saz said.

"I'm not blind. Look at you. It's pathetic!" Jenny said angrily. "You need to…"

Laura turned to Nicola and whispered, "How about we go and see what's happening in another room?" Nicola didn't get a chance to reply before Laura grabbed her hand and jumped up and down on the spot excitedly. "I frigging love this song. Come on."

Nicola was dragged into a darkened room full of people. The music was so loud, she could feel the bass pumping through her body.

Laura headed straight for the group of people dancing in the middle of the room, and Nicola managed to pull her hand away to avoid joining them. She stepped back, uncertain what to do next. She knew she should probably go back to Jenny, but she didn't like confrontation at the best of times. And the fact they were arguing about her made it even less appealing.

She moved against a wall and decided to people-watch for a bit. Laura waved at her from the dance floor, beckoning for her to join her. Nicola waved back and then quickly averted her eyes to look at some non-existent interesting thing on the other side of the room.

She saw a group of six guys play-fighting near the makeshift dance floor. Only girls were dancing, and they all seemed to be trying to catch the attention of the fighting guys with their dance moves. It was like an amusing animal-mating ritual.

"Hi."

She became aware of the close proximity of the guy who'd spoken. He was tall and looked down at her with a lopsided grin. There was something uncomfortable about him.

"I'm Matt. I haven't seen you around here before, have I?"

"Probably not," Nicola said. "This isn't normally my kind of thing."

He flashed a toothy grin, and although she knew some girls would probably find him attractive, she definitely wasn't one of them.

"How about a dance?"

Her initial surprise at the request quickly turned to panic. "Thanks, but I'm okay watching."

Disappointment flickered across his face, but then his grin returned. "How about a drink, then?"

Unease overtook Nicola. *Why is he asking about getting a drink? I've got nearly a full pint in my hand!* She realized suddenly what was making her so uncomfortable. He was drunk. His eyes were bloodshot, he leaned against the wall for support, and he stank of both weed and alcohol.

A flashback bombarded her. Her abuser's eyes, the smell of beer and cigarettes on his breath. His body pressed against hers.

"So, what do you say?"

"No," she whispered.

"Come on. It's a dance, you'll enjoy it," he said, moving closer. "I promise."

Panic rose in her throat. He was blocking her exit and her back was against the wall. Totally trapped. Even if she shouted for help, the music was far too loud for anyone to hear. Tears welled and she barely had the strength to hang on to her glass.

"Get the fuck away from her, now!"

I know that voice!

Jenny.

Matt turned to face her. "Jenny, we're kind of busy here, so why don't you come back in ten minutes?"

Jenny finally came into view and she looked furious.

"Fuck you, Matt. She's not interested in a drunken prick like you. Move." Jenny took a step closer. Matt swayed slightly, but Nicola noted his free hand had clenched into a fist. He wasn't going to move away that easily.

"I think it's cool you're jealous or whatever, but like I told you the other night, I'm not interested in anything more than fun. You're hot, but I've been there and done that. *That* meaning *you*." He laughed loudly and added, "So why don't you back off a bit? Give me and… her a chance to have some fun. If you're desperate, you can join us later."

Nicola shot a desperate glance at Jenny, who met her gaze before turning back to Matt once more, her expression murderous. "I swear to God, Matt, move the fuck out of the way or so help me. Her name's *Nicola* and she's not interested in you. Neither am I. Who would be? Look at the state of you." Jenny lifted her chin and forced her face close to his.

The music continued to blare, but people were noticing something was happening. A crowd started to form. The music was cut in time for Matt's response.

"You didn't think that the other night, did you? I always knew you were a slag, but I didn't know you were a fucking psycho as well." The crowd went silent and then hushed whispers carried through the darkened room.

This time it was Nicola who got angry. It wasn't an emotion she was used to, and it took her by surprise. She opened her mouth to speak, but as always, Jenny got there first.

"I'm a psycho? It's you who's trying to force yourself on a girl who quite blatantly doesn't want anything to do with you. There's a name for guys like you, guys who won't take no for an answer. And since you mentioned it, maybe you're right about me. Maybe I'm a slag. But if that's the case, then trust me when I say that in my experience you were officially the *worst* shag I've ever had. And the fact you still have Spider-Man bed sheets at your age, well, that's fucking creepy."

The crowd gasped, and a few jeers rose through the laughter. Nicola watched Matt shaking. He looked like he wanted to hit Jenny, but after a long moment of hesitation, he stormed out of the room, shouting, "Fucking bitch!"

Jenny rushed over to Nicola. "Are you okay?"

"I am now. I didn't think he was going to leave."

Jenny led her out of the room and away from the murmuring crowd.

Nicola could tell Matt's words had upset Jenny. She wanted to make her feel better but didn't know what to say.

Some of the dispersed crowd hovered around them, whispering and laughing. Jenny glared. "Why don't you take a photo." She turned to Nicola. "Let's get out of here."

"Okay."

They collected their alcohol and left the house. For nearly fifteen minutes, they marched in silence, with Nicola trying to keep up with Jenny's pace. She sensed something deeper troubling Jenny. She'd always been extra sensitive to other people's reactions, moods, and thoughts. She'd developed it as a defence mechanism to save herself from her abuser.

She studied Jenny and sensed the anger, but also something more intense, something darker. Jenny's jaw was locked, her hands balled into fists, and she seemed driven. But what she saw in Jenny's eyes worried her the most. *Desperation.*

Jenny unlocked the front door and let them into the house. She held the plastic bag out to Nicola. "Make us some drinks, I'm going to the bathroom. I'll meet you in my room."

Nicola frowned but took hold of the bag. She reached for one of Jenny's hands. "Jenny, are you okay?"

Jenny pulled her hand away and walked towards the stairs. In a flat emotionless tone she replied, "I'll be fine."

A chill crawled over Nicola's flesh. The calculated coolness of Jenny's tone suggested something really wasn't right. Nicola didn't know what it was or how she could get Jenny to open up to her, but she sensed her time was running out...whatever that meant.

CHAPTER FOURTEEN

Jenny locked the bathroom door and rested her back against it. She tried to put off doing the inevitable, as the seconds sped by. A mixture of raw, agonizing emotions consumed her. Physical pain didn't compare to it. Nothing ever came close to it. It was as though every dark emotion and terrible thought or feeling she'd ever had had somehow turned into a living entity that consumed her. It clawed and bit at her from inside.

She blinked with surprise when she found herself standing by the sink with no recollection of getting there. She avoided her reflection in the cabinet mirror because she knew nothing would look out of place. That was something she'd never understood. How could she feel so shitty on the inside and have nothing show on the outside? At least a broken leg could be treated. When people saw it, they knew it must hurt. But nobody ever saw this pain. It was hidden deep inside of her like a cancer.

She opened the bathroom cabinet and took out one of the four disposable razors. "Shit!" She closed the cabinet door.

Anguish filled her to the brink. The self-loathing, hatred, anger, guilt, fear, and humiliation continued to feed the pain inside—it had grown so horrific, she couldn't stand it. She placed the razor on the sink, undid her shorts, and let them fall around her ankles. What bothered her more than anything was that Nicola knew the truth about her: she was a slag.

She'd never meant to be. It just kind of happened. She'd been looking for something…attention, love? Whatever it had been, she hadn't found it, but in the process she'd succeeded in becoming a joke.

A joke.

The guys she'd been with hadn't loved, cared for, or respected her. But then, why would they, when she didn't even respect herself?

Pain.

Anguish.

Her thoughts hammered her, tortured her until her mind, body, and soul all seemed to crave the same thing.

Release.

A few simple cuts.

A few trickles of blood and it'd all be over until the next time she got this bad. Her body trembled as she acknowledged her darkest secret. There would always be a next time. She was addicted to hurting herself. It was the only way to stop the pain.

She'd tried to stop so many times before, and this time she'd lasted months. She'd actively sought professional help. She'd gone to her doctor and confessed, and although it had been so hard to say the words out loud, she'd done it. The counselling was helping and she'd been trying so hard…but it had become too unbearable this time.

Cutting, slicing, burning, and bleeding gave her short-term release from the ongoing pain inside.

"So fucking sick," she said, under her breath.

She knew after hurting herself, the excruciating pain inside would become bearable, but she'd be left having to cope with the guilt, shame, and regret at her actions. She always felt disgusted with herself afterwards for being so pathetically weak.

For days afterwards, even when the physical pain had faded, she'd look at what she'd done to herself. There was also the anxiety that perhaps this time, she might have gone too far, done some serious damage and have to seek medical help. Deep down, she wasn't convinced she'd have the guts to seek help if she did seriously hurt herself. And that fear was always there, in the back of her mind, tormenting her.

Every day, she'd carefully clean and dress the wounds, checking for signs of infection and making sure no one discovered the truth. Eventually she'd be left with another scar to add to her growing collection, a permanent reminder of how fucked up she was.

But afterwards and right now were two very different times.

She lowered her knickers and looked down at the savagely scarred skin below her hip bone. A sense of calm ruled over her, momentarily making everything numb, even the pain inside. In a matter of minutes it'd be over, and although she would feel shitty, the excruciating hurt inside would be bearable.

With trembling hands, she took the safety lid off the blade and chose where she would press it firmly against her skin. Her intention was to add pressure to the blade and slowly drag it along, feeling as it sliced her.

She heard a sudden gentle knocking on the door.

"Jenny," Nicola's voice called softly. "Can I come in, please?"

The last thing Jenny had expected to hear.

The plastic lid fell from her fingertips. "I'll be a few minutes, Nic."

Shit! Shit! Shit! Could she actually go through with it, knowing Nicola stood outside? The pain remained, eating away and withering inside her, but she knew she wouldn't be able to face Nicola after doing it.

"Jenny, I'm desperate. I think I drank too much cider. Seriously, it's going to get messy if you don't let me in."

"Shit," Jenny whispered to herself. *It's now or never.* "Argh."

She couldn't do it. Not with Nicola standing outside the door. She'd have to bear it for a little longer, and then when Nicola went to sleep, she'd come back in and do it.

The pain inside gave one last excruciating shove, but the opportunity had passed.

"Jenny?"

"Christ, Nic! I said I'll be out in a minute." She heard the mixture of anger and frustration in her voice and winced. She pulled up her knickers and then the shorts before reluctantly returning the razor to the cabinet.

When she unlocked the door, Nicola was waiting, but she couldn't look at her. "I'll be in my room."

"I won't be long," Nicola said quietly.

Jenny stormed past her and went straight into her room, determined to get drunk, in the vague hope it would lessen her need. As soon as she heard the bathroom door shut, she changed her mind about drinking. There would be time for that later. Instead, she tugged harshly at the bracelets on her wrist, snapping two of them as she pulled them off. She stretched the elastic band between her thumb and forefinger, taking it to the verge of snapping, before letting it go. The plastic flew backwards and struck the already bruised flesh hard.

Without hesitating, she quickly repeated the process another five times. Her eyes began to water and her wrist throbbed, to the point she couldn't bring herself to do it again. Wincing, she quickly rolled her bracelets and bangles back over her hand, so they covered the bright redness of her wrist. She walked over to the bottle of vodka, unscrewed the cap, and downed two large mouthfuls. Hot salty tears escaped her eyes as she gagged from swallowing the neat alcohol. She brushed them away and tried to compose herself before Nicola came in.

The urge to cut had died down, but as a result her wrist was sore. She was angry at herself for misusing the band and knew she was going to end up with a corker of a bruise because of it. Was there a difference between cutting and using the band? Didn't they both result in the same thing, only one causing less severe damage than the other? She decided to bring it up when she next spoke to Kathy.

Will I ever be free of it?

She didn't bother thinking of a reply, or of one more lie.

CHAPTER FIFTEEN

Nicola used the facilities, then washed and dried her hands. Worry about Jenny niggled at her. As she turned to leave, her foot brushed something small across the tiled floor. She bent down and picked up what turned out to be a plastic safety lid.

She looked around but couldn't see anything else out of place. She shoved the lid inside her pocket and returned to the cabinet, to open its door. She immediately spotted four disposable razors, one of which no longer had a plastic lid.

She closed the door, baffled. Although she didn't have proof Jenny had been messing with the razor, she somehow simply…knew. Anne was too tidy and would have picked the lid up as soon as she'd dropped it. It was unlikely the pink razor belonged to Michael. That left Jenny and herself, and she hadn't used one.

Jenny hadn't looked like she was intending to shave, which only added to Nicola's worry. With no further clues, she left the bathroom and headed into Jenny's bedroom.

"I wanted to say thank you for tonight," she said, as she picked up her glass of cider and sat down on the bed.

"Yeah, right." Jenny scowled. "Which bit in particular are you thanking me for?" Her tone sounded bitter. "For taking you to a party full of fucking idiots? For letting Matt corner you? Perhaps you're thankful to me for allowing Sarah and Corrina to be complete bitches towards you?"

Nicola had glimpsed this side of Jenny only twice before—the previous morning—first when they'd argued in the kitchen, and then when they were climbing the stairs. Both times, Jenny had been angry at herself, but Nicola had managed to lighten her morose mood. But tonight Jenny's dark mood was in full swing, and the alcohol probably wasn't helping the situation.

"Jenny, I'm grateful. I've never been to a house party before. Laura and Saz are both nice. They made me feel welcome. We both knew Corrina and Sarah weren't going to like me. It's not a big deal." Nicola continued to speak while Jenny shook her head vehemently. "As for the thing with Matt, it was a misunderstanding. He was drunk and I freaked out after...well, you know. But you sorted it. I actually enjoyed myself. So when I say thank you, I genuinely mean it."

The party had been an interesting experience and she was glad she'd agreed to go. She could tell Jenny wasn't convinced by her gratitude, and so they sat in silence for a few minutes. In that time, Jenny had downed her drink and was pouring another.

"I'm so sorry, Nic. You're the most...amazing person I know. You're so selfless and funny. I love that you're happy to be yourself. Never change, I mean it," Jenny slurred.

Nicola looked at her and instinctively knew three things. Jenny meant every word, she was drunk, and she was also hurting.

"Jenny..." She wasn't sure what she wanted to say. "I didn't have anywhere to go, or anyone to care about me, or anyone I could trust. But you've changed that. If anyone should be apologizing, it should be me. You're a great person and I..." *think I love you.* Totally shocked, Nicola tried to ignore the words that had struck her from nowhere. "I'm so grateful I have you as a friend."

Love you? Nicola took a drink from her glass and swallowed hard. *Where the hell had that come from?*

"I'm not a good person, Nic," Jenny whispered into her glass. She slumped down on the bed next to her.

"You're upset by what Matt said, but everyone knows it isn't true. You were protecting me and he was drunk." She hated seeing Jenny so distant. She reached out to hold her hand, but Jenny flinched away from her touch.

Wow, that hurt.

"Matt was right. I'm a slag and everyone knows it."

Nicola tried to argue, but the look Jenny shot her shut her up immediately.

"I am, and I hate myself for it."

Nicola wanted to say and do something but couldn't think of anything that would help, so she remained silent.

"I'm sorry, Nic. I just…I don't like myself sometimes. I'm a horrible, weak, pathetic person. You'd be better off without me."

Pain etched Jenny's expression, but Nicola didn't think it was physical. She knew from personal experience about how painful self-hatred and disgust could be—she'd spent the last few years living with them. It had never occurred to her someone as popular and as perfect as Jenny could feel the same way.

"You're hurting…inside, aren't you?" It came out as a whisper.

Jenny's eyes widened and her body tensed. "I'm weak, Nic. After everything you've been though, you're not bitter or twisted. You've not let it poison you, and that's why you're so special. I'm pathetic. If you knew the truth, you'd hate me."

"You're the bravest person I know," Nicola said. "I could never hate you."

Jenny blanched. "I try so hard to fight it, but it eats away inside me until eventually it gets too much and I have to…let it out."

"Let it out?" Nicola struggled to make sense of Jenny's words.

Jenny turned away. "You wouldn't understand. No one does."

Nicola's stomach lurched and revulsion shuddered through her body. The plastic lid from the razor weighed like a tonne against her leg, heavy with the unsettling realization of what Jenny was confessing. It upset her to think about it, and she'd probably never understand why Jenny hurt herself, but she refused to judge.

"I think I understand more than you realize. You're not weak. People cope in different ways." Nicola reached inside her pocket, grasped the plastic lid, and placed it on the duvet between them.

Jenny's mouth opened in a silent gasp as she stared at the lid.

"I don't understand the reasons why, but that's okay," Nicola said, noting the anguish on Jenny's face. She imagined her own expression when her dark secret was revealed probably looked similar.

"How could you know?" Jenny asked. "And why don't you hate me, after everything you've been through?"

Nicola didn't understand how what she'd been through could possibly make her hate Jenny. She shrugged and said, "I worked it out. But I don't hate you, Jenny. I wish I could do something to help you."

Jenny drank a few mouthfuls from her glass, and Nicola noted her trembling hands. "I don't know what to say."

Nicola smiled. "I know exactly how that feels. Do you want to talk about it?"

"No," Jenny said and then quickly added, "but I think maybe I *need* to talk about it. My counsellor keeps badgering me about finding someone to talk to, but I don't have anyone."

Nicola reached out and gave Jenny's hand a gentle squeeze. "You have me. I won't judge you, Jenny. And I'm amazing at keeping secrets, mainly because I don't have anyone to tell."

Jenny gave a weak smile. "I'm not worried you'll judge me or tell anyone. I trust you completely."

"Then what are you worried about?"

Jenny dropped her gaze. "That when you realize how fucked up I am, it'll put you off me." She picked at some invisible fluff on the duvet and added in barely a whisper. "I'm scared when you start to know the real me, you'll hate me. And I don't want to lose you."

"That won't happen. I promise." Nicola glanced down and nibbled her bottom lip. Jenny's insecurities surprised her. But she understood the difficult risk, trusting someone with a personal secret. If anything, she admired Jenny more now.

"I'm not sure how to start," Jenny said. "I've never told anyone except my counsellor, because I'm ashamed." She caressed the bracelets on her left wrist. "I wouldn't know how to go about talking about it."

"How about I ask some questions? Like you did for me last night."

Jenny expelled a defeated sigh. "We can try, but don't get your hopes up."

Nicola racked her brain, trying to think of an easy question that would allow Jenny to open up gradually. Easier said than done. In the end, she asked the first question that came to her. "When did you start?"

Jenny paled and swallowed hard. "I was twelve, I think. Elizabeth was being a royal bitch to me in front of all her friends, and I was upset. I ended up hiding in the bathroom, but I knew I couldn't cry because Elizabeth would humiliate me more." Jenny's eyes glazed over and she slowly exhaled. "I don't know why, but I started to scratch my hand, over and over again in the same place."

Nicola kept quiet and watched as Jenny absent-mindedly touched her left hand, as if feeling the phantom wound.

"It hurt, a lot, but I kept doing it. Soon I ended up with a nasty friction burn, but the need to cry had disappeared, replaced by calmness. I went back out, proved I wasn't a crybaby, and got on with it. When Mum asked me later what I'd done to my hand, I lied. I didn't do it again for another two years."

Nicola wasn't sure how she should respond. "Did something happen to make you do it again?"

"Yeah," Jenny said, rubbing her eyes, which only succeeded in smearing her mascara a million times worse. "My gran died."

Nicola grimaced. "I'm sorry, Jenny."

Jenny shook her head dismissively. "I've never told anyone this bit. Not even my counsellor. Are you sure you want to hear it? I mean, I don't know if I'll be able to get the words out, but once I say it, you can never go back to not knowing—know what I mean?"

Nicola thought she understood and nodded. Trepidation sat uncomfortably on her shoulders.

"I was close to my gran. Really close." Jenny coughed and reached for her glass. She took a long drink before continuing. "I went to her house every day after school. Elizabeth was in sixth form and I loved it, because it was just the two of us. We had long chats, drank copious amounts of tea, ate biscuits, and watched TV together until my mum picked me up on her way back from work."

Nicola's heart ached.

"It was a Wednesday, and I was given my first ever detention, for talking in class. I was told to stay behind for an hour after school, and I was so caught up in my own fear of being in trouble, I didn't think about phoning my gran and telling her. I did the detention and then started walking towards her house, when it dawned on me. I felt so guilty, I decided to walk to the nearest store and buy her something to show I was sorry."

Nicola nibbled on her thumbnail. She braced herself for the bad she sensed had happened.

"I spent fifteen minutes in the store and eventually decided on a pack of fig rolls because they were her favourites. When I finally got to her house, the door was locked. I knocked loudly and figured she was angry with me. I ended up using the spare key she kept hidden. I let myself in, and when I called out, I got no response."

Nicola watched helplessly as Jenny seemed to relive the whole experience. She had turned an unhealthy pale colour, and with the added smears of black mascara beneath her eyes, she looked a sorry state.

"I found her in the kitchen. She was sprawled out on the floor. I rushed and knelt beside her, not noticing the shattered teacup or the spilled liquid. She wasn't moving or breathing and her eyes...they were open, but they didn't look like hers—they were...cloudy." Pain contorted Jenny's face. "They never show that on TV or films—people's eyes being open."

Nicola shuddered; words failed her.

"I ran to the phone and called for an ambulance. Then I called my mum and told her. She cried hysterically and I panicked about her being fit to drive, but then the ambulance arrived and I ended the call. They gave up trying to bring Gran back near enough straight away. One of them sat me down in the living room and messed with my hand. I realized then I'd cut my hand. It must've been on the broken cup. Blood covered my shirt, the carpet, the bastard packet of fig rolls, and the phone, but I didn't feel anything. I felt nothing at all. While the rest of the family were crying, even at her funeral, I felt nothing. No matter how much I wanted to, I couldn't cry."

Nicola wiped her own tears away and tried to mask her sniffling. "Jenny, I'm so sorry."

Jenny swallowed hard and winced. "Since then, I've never cried. Sometimes my eyes water, but it's not the same because I don't get any release. Everything builds up inside until I'm about to explode from the agony and the only way to release it is by hurting myself. And that's how I've coped ever since the funeral."

"Oh, Jenny—"

"Don't feel sorry for me, Nic." Jenny pounded the duvet between them with her fists. "I deserve this. If I'd not got that detention, if I hadn't wasted time going to that fucking store, she might still be here. I know my parents have forgiven me, but that's not enough. It's my fault. The only person who could actually forgive me is Gran and she's dead. And I have to live with that. That's the real me."

Nicola grabbed hold of Jenny's fists and held them firmly. "I know you won't want to hear this, but you have to. You're not to blame." Jenny tried to pull her hands free, but Nicola held on. "Sometimes people we love die. It's unfair and it hurts so much, but it happens. You can't keep punishing yourself with guilt."

Jenny pulled away.

Nicola softened her tone. "Getting a detention was bad luck, and going to the store was a nice thing to do. You were fourteen, Jenny. From what you described, there was nothing you could do. Punishing yourself for her death is wrong. You need to forgive yourself."

"I could have saved her—"

"Deep down, you know that's not true. You were a child who walked in and found a horrendous situation. Would you blame me for the same thing, if I told you at the age of fourteen, I'd gotten a detention and then gone to the shop, before walking in and finding one of my loved ones had passed away? Would you, Jenny?"

Jenny shook her head.

"And do you honestly think your gran would want you to keep punishing yourself like this? Because I don't, not from the things you've said about her. She loved you, and seeing you blame yourself would be the last thing she would want."

Jenny buried her face in her hands, and Nicola wrapped an arm around her shoulders.

"I miss her so much."

Nicola sighed. "And that's a good thing. It means you loved and cared for her. I believe the more I think about my dad and remember the amazing times we had together, the more he's still with me. He's not forgotten because I make sure his memory lives on."

Jenny sat up and faced Nicola. "I know I haven't talked about hurting myself, but could we leave it for another time, please? I will at some point, I promise. Just not tonight."

Nicola felt a surge of relief. "That's fine. Whenever you're ready."

"What if I'm never ready to talk about it?" Jenny asked.

"Then you never talk about it."

Jenny looked at her for a few seconds, then shook her head softly. "You're incredible."

Nicola's cheeks warmed, and she chose to drink rather than reply.

Jenny drained her glass, placed it on the floor, and lay down on the bed, stretching out. "How are you doing, anyway?"

"Honestly, my head feels fuzzy," Nicola said.

Jenny laughed as she wriggled around, trying to make herself comfortable. After a few more seconds of shuffling, she looked up at Nicola. "Lie down with me?"

Nicola felt a little nervous, but she climbed onto the duvet and lay beside her.

"That's better," Jenny said, reaching out and softly taking hold of Nicola's hand. "Tomorrow, we're going to start planning how to sort your problems out. Have you spoken to your mum yet?" Jenny's thumb absent-mindedly stroked against the back of Nicola's hand.

Nicola struggled to breathe. A mixture of excitement and nervousness coursed through her body from Jenny's touch. She didn't trust herself to speak and so shook her head.

"Well, you need to tomorrow. She must be worried about you."

Nicola knew she should be listening to Jenny and helping to contribute towards a plan, but lying with Jenny and feeling the touch of her caress made everything else seem significantly less important.

The sound of a car pulling up outside disrupted the moment.

"Shit! They're back early," Jenny said, jumping up and grabbing the bottles of alcohol.

"I'm tired anyway," Nicola said, as she fled to the door. "See you tomorrow."

She tiptoed across the landing as the front door opened. Inside the room she allowed a few seconds for her eyes adjust to the darkness, before quickly changing into pyjamas. A timid knocking sounded on the door, and she rushed to get into bed.

Closing her eyes and lying still, she heard the door creak open. After a few seconds it closed, and she sighed with relief. Speaking to Anne whilst tipsy wouldn't have been a pleasant experience.

Gradually her eyelids grew heavy and she willingly succumbed to sleep.

Chapter Sixteen

"Nic, are you asleep?"

Groggily she sat up in bed and rubbed her eyes. "Jenny?" She squinted at the silhouette in the doorway.

"I can't sleep. Is it okay if I come in here and we chat for a bit?"

Nicola wanted nothing more than to lie back down, close her eyes, and go back to sleep. With a sigh, she whispered, "Yeah, it's okay."

Jenny quietly closed the door, tiptoed to the bed, and crept beneath the covers. They lay facing one another as their eyes adjusted to the darkness. Nicola fought against the tiredness and noted Jenny seemed restless.

"Did you see any guys at the party you liked?" Jenny asked, a little too casually.

"I wasn't really looking," Nicola answered, a little suspicious.

"Can I ask you something personal?"

Nicola's heartbeat quickened. As uncomfortable as she felt, she couldn't deny Jenny anything. She nodded reluctantly.

"You don't have to answer, I'm just curious." A pause. "How many boyfriends have you had?"

"I haven't had any," Nicola said as her face warmed with embarrassment.

"What?" Jenny looked surprised. "Ever?"

"I've been a little too preoccupied with trying to stay alive," Nicola said angrily and then immediately regretted it. "I've never had—never will have—a boyfriend, Jenny. You've seen the state of my back. I'm always going to be alone."

Jenny gently took hold of both her hands. "Don't say that. Your back isn't as bad as you think. You're beautiful and there's someone out there for everyone. And that person will see how beautiful, caring, smart, and funny you are…like I see it."

"Thanks," Nicola whispered, her voice hoarse with emotion.

"And to be honest, guys our age are seriously overrated."

Nicola felt her own curiosity stir. "How many guys have you…?"

Jenny grimaced. "I've had far too many boyfriends and kissed way too many guys to count. But in answer to what you really want to know, I've slept with five guys. That's the magic number to get you the title of *slag*."

The low number surprised Nicola. "Well, that proves Matt was wrong. Five doesn't make you a slag, Jenny. If you'd have said fifty-five, it might be a different story."

Jenny smiled. "Maybe."

A few minutes passed, and they lay in a comfortable silence with their fingers interlocked.

"I still can't believe you've never had a boyfriend. My first boyfriend was named Scott. He was seven and I was six. We lasted for about forty minutes. Everything was going so well until he tried to kiss me. I punched him and then we both cried hysterically. My mum was forced to take me home from the park and I never saw him again."

Nicola chuckled. "Well, I've never had a boyfriend, not even for forty minutes. And I've never kissed anyone, so that's—"

"Are you being serious?" Jenny asked, sitting bolt upright.

Humiliation coursed through Nicola, trailed by a shot of anger. "Please don't make me go through the reasons why again. And yes, I'm being totally serious."

"But you're seventeen."

Nicola pulled her hands away and hugged her knees protectively. "I know how old I am. It's not a big deal, Jenny," she said, perplexed. "I wouldn't know what to do, anyway. I'd embarrass myself and—I don't want to talk about this. Can we please leave it?"

"No, Nic. We can't just leave it. Kissing is the easiest thing in the world, but if you keep stressing yourself out like this, you'll end up never kissing anyone."

"I'm never going to kiss anyone anyway." Nicola turned away from Jenny. Earlier, she'd respected Jenny wasn't ready to talk about the cutting and so she'd left the subject alone. Why couldn't Jenny do the same for her now?

"I didn't mean to upset you. I'm sorry," Jenny said, crawling closer to her. "Please look at me?"

Nicola reluctantly turned but refused to look up at her.

"I don't like the thought of you missing out on things. You're young, and kissing can sometimes be nice. It upsets me to think of you growing into an old spinster who has never been kissed. It's tragic."

"It might be tragic to you, but it's not to me. I know I'm going to be the old spinster, Jenny. I'm okay with it. Now, can we stop? I'm tired." Nicola simply couldn't bear to continue with the topic of conversation. Her good mood and giddiness from the cider had worn off, and now she was feeling upset.

"There's nothing to be scared of," Jenny said, before swallowing hard and seeming to hesitate. "I could show you…"

Nicola's breath caught in her throat. "What?"

"I'll show you. Jeez, don't look so horrified. I've kissed Corrina and Sarah lots of times. It's a great way of getting guys interested. Katy Perry made a fortune singing about it. It's just kissing. It means nothing."

Nicola was terrified by the proposal but also shocked by how much she secretly wanted to say yes. A deep ache settled in the pit of her stomach. She'd never wanted anything as much as she wanted Jenny to kiss her at that moment.

"Nic?" Jenny asked, as she moved so close they were practically touching. "What do you say?"

Nicola looked up and saw Jenny's eyes looked intensely dark. Unable to hold the gaze, she lowered her eyes and found herself mesmerized by Jenny's swollen lips. She watched as Jenny moistened her bottom lip with her tongue, making it gleam.

Nicola desperately wanted to feel Jenny's lips against her own. Her voice was barely audible as she said, "Yes." The whispered answer hung in the deafening silence between them.

Jenny slowly leaned forward, closing the last remaining bit of distance between them.

Nicola couldn't breathe. Her eyes automatically closed, which made her hypersensitive to her body and its surroundings.

The gentle brush of Jenny's hair against her left shoulder and neck shot tingles skittering over her skin. The faint scent of mint from toothpaste lingered on the warm breath that caressed her face. The pounding of her heart and the rushing of blood sounded like a thundering helicopter in her ears.

She sensed Jenny's lips a split second before their softness brushed against her own. Her heart skipped a beat and her head swam dizzily. The deep ache spread through her body like a fire, leaving no part untouched.

Jenny's lips pressed firmly before opening. Nicola nearly cried out when the softness of Jenny's tongue met her own. Jenny tasted unlike anything Nicola had ever had before.

Jenny's mouth grew forceful, almost frustrated. She cupped Nicola's face and pulled her in closer, deepening their kiss. As both tongues caressed and teased, shockwaves of pleasure rolled through Nicola's body. She wanted to immerse herself until she disappeared into the exquisite heat they'd created.

A loud moan escaped from Jenny, and a second later she pulled harshly away, breaking their intimacy. Jenny's expression looked like utter panic.

"I've got to go. I…" Unable to finish her sentence, Jenny scrambled out of bed and ran to the door.

"Jenny? Wait…please don't g—"

Jenny didn't look back or even slow down. She tore open the door and ran out, leaving Nicola alone to flinch as her door slammed shut.

Alone in the darkness, the rapid beating of Nicola's heart gradually slowed, and her breathing returned to normal. She'd never felt so alone or rejected, not even during her darkest days of abuse.

She might have somehow destroyed their relationship. She wasn't sure how it'd happened.

But she'd experienced her first kiss. It'd been phenomenal, and she doubted anything would ever come close in comparison. But she'd probably also lost her only friend. Even more unsettling was the possibility she might actually fall in love with Jenny. That prospect freaked her out more than she dared to admit. Exhausted, her final thought before sleep was *How could something that felt so incredibly good supposedly be so wrong?*

Chapter Seventeen

Jenny hadn't slept, again. She was exhausted, confused, angry, and seriously freaked out. After long, lonely hours filled with scrutinizing, contemplating, and convincing, she knew two things: she definitely was not gay and she should never have kissed Nicola.

Even if it was the most electrifying, intense, and glorious experience she'd ever...

"Shit," she muttered. A mixture of frustration and tiredness set in. Just thinking about the kiss made her crazy. As sick and wrong as it supposedly was, it didn't stop the perverse excitement and longing she got every time she remembered it.

But she couldn't be gay! She was Catholic, popular, and even had the reputation of being promiscuous with guys. Plus, she'd never been attracted to women before and remained adamant she wasn't actually attracted to Nicola in any way. She acknowledged Nicola's beauty, but there was a clear difference between acknowledging something and being gay.

It was impossible to deny how strange she'd been acting and feeling since they'd met. In just two days, she'd changed into a practically different person. She'd never openly encouraged physical contact with any of her friends, and yet she seemed totally incapable of keeping her roaming hands and eyes off Nicola.

"Shit, shit, shit!" She buried her face into a pillow to muffle her shouts.

Adamant she wasn't gay, or at least, that she actually couldn't be gay...Was there a difference? Her family, friends, lifestyle, and religion all dictated homosexuality was wrong. Deep down, she knew it was wrong…didn't she?

And what the hell was going through Nicola's head now? As if she didn't have enough shit to deal with already. Jenny listened as the front door slammed, followed by a car engine starting up in the driveway. Her parents were off to Mass, which only added to her guilt.

"It never even happened," she said firmly.

And what if Nicola wanted to talk about it? Surely she owed her an explanation? She shook her head violently, answering her own thoughts. "There's nothing to discuss." The only vaguely positive thing to come out of the experience was the pain inside no longer loomed at the forefront of her mind. It had spun to the background, and the need for release wasn't anywhere near as desperate as it had been. She wasn't sure if the hot lesbian kiss caused the distraction, or if finally opening up about her gran and dealing with the guilt had done it.

She climbed out of bed and considered what to do next. She'd take a shower, make a cup of coffee, and then busy herself with her artwork. In theory that should be enough to keep her occupied and cut dead any inappropriate thoughts. When it came time to face Nicola, she'd be pleasant towards her, but more importantly, she'd keep a safe distance. It would all be fine…

Nicola had been awake for hours but had chosen to hide in bed where it was safe. She knew Anne was in the kitchen because she could hear the faint strains of music, the clatter of pans, and cupboard doors squeaking and closing. In the cold sober light of day, thinking about the kiss caused confusion and hurt. The fear in Jenny's eyes and her horrified look still smarted every time Nicola remembered it. The whole experience had been bittersweet. The kiss had been amazing and intimate, but when Jenny ran away, the whole thing seemed tainted and perverse.

Never one to dwell in self-pity, Nicola wasn't about to start now. She felt more for Jenny than friendship. She loved her. At first she hadn't been sure of her feelings or what was developing between them, but now she knew she was attracted to Jenny. Denying it was useless. The cowardly option would be to pretend the kiss hadn't happened and ignore the consequences. But she knew that option would ultimately make their situation a million times worse. She decided to get up, shower, dress, and then have it out with Jenny. As far she was concerned, the sooner they discussed the kiss, the sooner they could sort things out.

❖

Nicola took a deep breath, knocked on the door, and waited until she heard Jenny's invitation to enter. She released her breath, opened the door, and went inside. Jenny sat at her desk, looking incredibly uncomfortable.

"Hi," Nicola said.

Jenny flinched at her greeting and said coolly, "Have you had breakfast? Lunch will be ready in about an hour."

Nicola shoved her hands into her jean pockets. "I didn't realize it was so late. I'll wait."

Jenny shrugged and turned her attention back to the easel and canvas. Nicola felt like she was intruding so quickly moved over to the bed. Once seated, she started the pretence of reading.

An unpleasant tension hung in the room. Nicola glanced up at Jenny often and noted that, every single time, Jenny's gaze seemed unnaturally focused on her canvas. She also noted Jenny hadn't made much progress—*any* progress, in fact.

After half an hour, Jenny couldn't have actually made it any clearer to Nicola—she had no intention of discussing the kiss with her. She obviously regretted it, and although it hurt, Nicola decided regret was easier to deal with than Jenny not feeling anything at all.

After reading the same paragraph for the ninth time, Nicola couldn't keep up the pretence anymore. "Well, I'll go read in the other room. Please call me when it's time to eat." Without waiting for a response, she fled from the room. As soon as she was back in her bedroom, lying on top of the bed, she breathed a sigh of relief. A little while later, a firm knock sounded on the door before it opened slightly.

"Lunch is ready."

The door slammed shut before Nicola had a chance to reply.

The prospect of sharing a meal with Jenny and her parents filled her with dread, but with no other choice, she made her way downstairs.

❖

The meal ended up being far worse than Nicola had anticipated.

Jenny totally ignored her when she took her place at the table. To make the situation worse, Jenny's parents obviously noticed the frosty atmosphere. Thankfully, they were gracious enough to not make a scene or ask too many prying questions.

During grace, Jenny limply held Nicola's hand, making it clear she'd rather be holding a spitting cobra. Michael insisted on saying grace, and his prayer weighed heavily on Nicola's conscience. He prayed firstly for her fictitious dead uncle and then concluded with how precious the gift of friendship is and how it should be treasured.

The big scene however, came halfway through the meal.

"So girls, what are you doing for the rest of the day?" Anne asked, trying yet again to fill the awkward silence.

Nicola knew if she wasn't quick, Jenny would dictate the answer for both of them. "I've got work at half past four," she said quickly. "Then I'm going to have an early night, I think."

Jenny stared at her in disbelief, and for the first time during the meal, actually spoke to her. "You can't be serious."

"I need the money and I can't let them down," she said quietly. "It's only until half-eight. I'll be fine."

"Well, I think it's commendable, Nicola. We've suggested to Jennifer she get herself a nice little part-time job, but she doesn't seem overly interested," Anne said with a smile. "Elizabeth's always had part-time jobs to support herself—"

Jenny slammed her knife and fork down onto her plate. She jumped to her feet and said, "I'm done!" then stormed out of the room.

The remaining three sat in a stunned silence.

Anne and Michael flicked a glance toward each other before Anne spoke gently to her. "I know it's not any of our business, but we wondered if everything's okay between you girls? You both seem a little bit…quiet today."

Yes, Anne, everything's fine, apart from the fact your daughter and I kissed and now I'm slightly obsessed with her. And she hates me for it. Nicola chose to ignore her guilty conscience. "I think we're both a bit stressed about exams starting tomorrow." She was surprised at how easily Michael and Anne seemed to believe the feeble excuse.

"They do put too much pressure on you young people today," Anne said sympathetically.

Nicola thanked them graciously for the meal and then excused herself. She had two and a half hours until she had to leave for work. She knew Jenny was angry with her but was surprised to find Jenny waiting in ambush when she went into her room.

"What exactly do you think you're doing?"

Nicola had never seen Jenny so angry with someone other than herself. She found it a little unnerving. "I'm going to read for a bit and then I'm going to get ready for work." She found Jenny's blazing eyes, her flushed cheeks, and the tense jaw muscles incredibly sexy.

"You're *not* going to work. Do you think I've been helping you so you can go and get attacked by him?"

Nicola saw the faint pulse throbbing in Jenny's throat and had to force her gaze away. "I'm going to work, Jenny."

"You fucking are not!"

"I *am*. I need to get away for a while and sort my head out. You should probably do the same."

Jenny's nostrils flared and her lips pressed tightly together.

"I'll be fine. He doesn't know where I work and I won't be alone," Nicola said softly, trying her best to reassure Jenny. Seeing it wasn't working, she left the room, choosing to hide in the bathroom for a bit. Jenny needed to calm down, and the idea of a locked door between them—for Jenny's sake as much as hers—also appealed.

Moments ticked by. Nicola focused on smoothing out her shaky breaths, on listening, on waiting. She heard the rustles of Jenny leaving her room and jumped when her bedroom door slammed.

She sighed, wondering if they'd ever sort things out.

CHAPTER EIGHTEEN

Nicola stood outside Jenny's door hesitating, unsure about what to do. Was confronting Jenny about their kiss a good idea? They couldn't carry on like they'd been doing. But what if she made the situation a million times worse?

"Like that's even possible," she whispered to herself while knocking on the door. This time she didn't bother waiting for a reply and burst straight inside. Jenny sat at her desk. Nicola closed the door. "Jenny, we need to talk. No"—she held up her hand when Jenny opened her mouth to interrupt—"let me speak."

Jenny remained silent but glared.

"I know you don't want to talk about last night, but I do. I feel like I'm going insane."

Jenny's expression was unreadable as she said, "Other stuff takes priority. We need to talk about what we're going to do about your mum and your abuser. As for last night, there's nothing to talk about."

"Yes, there's the issue of my mum, and me going back—"

"Good. Let's talk about that then."

"*After* we've talked about last night." Nicola folded her arms defiantly.

"There's *nothing* to discuss."

"Why won't you even hear me out?"

Jenny shook her head as her face drained of colour. "As far as I'm concerned, last night, the kiss," she rasped, "didn't happen. The whole thing was silly. I'm sorry if I confused you or made you uncomfortable. But it meant nothing to me. If we talk about it, you'll end up embarrassed and—"

"Fine!" Nicola turned to face the door.

"It's for the best, Nic. For both of us," Jenny said quietly.

Nicola spun around, seething. "No. It's best for *you*, Jenny. So don't speak for both of us. You're trying to protect your own skin because that's all that matters to you. Isn't it? You don't care about anyone other than yourself." She felt satisfaction as hurt flashed across Jenny's face.

"Please, Nic?"

Nicola turned back to the door, gripped the handle and refused to look back. "I'll leave tomorrow morning. I'd go tonight, but I don't want to upset your parents. You can tell them…actually, you can tell them whatever the hell you want. As you're so excellent at lying, it shouldn't be a problem for you." She twisted the doorknob, but Jenny was out of her seat and between her and the door in a flash. Surprised, Nicola stepped back, and Jenny took the opportunity to shut the door and block it with her body.

"Move," Nicola said, her own voice strangely cold to her ears.

"Nic, you can't…"

Nicola took half a step closer. "I can and I will. I'm not staying here when you won't even talk to me about it. It's killing me, Jenny. I can't stand to be around you."

Jenny looked crestfallen. "Please stay."

"Will you talk about it?"

Jenny closed her eyes and shook her head. "I can't."

Despite Nicola's discomfort seeing Jenny hurt, she knew if she wanted the truth, there was no backing down.

"If you won't talk about it, at least give me your permission to do one last thing."

"Permission?" Jenny whispered.

Nicola tried to appear calm and confident, but inside, chaotic emotions swirled and bucked. "You don't want to talk about it. But I can't even be sure if my memories of last night are real. So you can either talk to me honestly, or let me kiss you, one last time."

Jenny stared at her, speechless.

Nicola closed the remaining distance. She reached past Jenny and gripped the door handle firmly. She suddenly realized how close they were and the tension between them surged with electricity. "Choose, Jenny."

Jenny shook her head tightly, but Nicola noticed the physiological responses. Jenny's breathing grew shallow, and every muscle in her body stiffened and trembled.

"Are you going to talk to me?"

Jenny shook her head again. They both knew the next question.

Nicola's heartbeat kicked into a gallop and she struggled to swallow.

What if she says no?

What if she doesn't feel the same?

A wisp of Jenny's hair was out of place. With a trembling hand, Nicola swept it back behind her ear. Jenny's cheek sought after her open palm and skimmed against it.

"Jenny…" Nicola nervously bit down on her lip.

This was it.

Real love or total rejection.

"The kiss, then?"

Jenny's eyes screwed shut and her jaws clenched in agony.

"Please?" Nicola asked, knowing she would kiss Jenny, but needing to know one way or the other how she felt about it.

Just when the waiting became unbearable, when Nicola knew her body would get its own way regardless, Jenny whispered, "Yes."

Her voice was so quiet, Nicola blinked, wondering if perhaps she'd imagined it. Although her mind struggled to accept the answer, her body had no problem. She found her lips pressing fiercely against Jenny's.

Jenny's lips were soft and smooth, but they resisted her. Nicola began to panic.

Had she perceived the situation wrong?

Had she ruined everything?

Just as Nicola thought to pull away, Jenny's resolve crumbled and she kissed back passionately.

This kiss was different from the previous night's. That first kiss had been soft, slow, clumsy. This kiss was fast, powerful, urgent.

As the kiss deepened, Nicola felt Jenny's fingertips gently stroking her left cheek and travelling down past her throat, to linger lightly on her collarbone. Her skin prickled and pleasure tingled through her body from the delicate caress.

Footsteps creaking on the floorboards of the landing outside alerted them both to imminent danger. They pulled apart, and Nicola ran to the bed and grabbed her book, while Jenny ran to her desk and picked up a paintbrush.

A loud, brief knock sounded before Anne burst into the room. "Well, look at you two, still working hard. Bless you both." She beamed a smile. "We've decided to head out for a walk, as the weather's so glorious. We'll see you when you get back from work, Nicola."

Jenny and Nicola nodded in unison.

Anne turned and left the room as abruptly as she'd entered it.

Nicola dropped her book and saw she'd been holding it upside down. With a sigh, she turned towards Jenny but didn't know what to say. Her idea had only been to kiss Jenny again to see if she also felt something, which apparently she did. But that didn't help either of them now.

"Please come and sit down. It's okay," Nicola said quietly.

"It's not okay, Nic," Jenny said, as she sat down next to her. "I can't be gay."

"Did you ever think you might be before?" Nicola asked, suddenly curious.

"No," Jenny said, a little too quickly.

Nicola watched her in silence.

"What's going on with us?"

Nicola shrugged. "I can only tell you how I feel, but I don't think it'll help you."

Jenny buried her face in her hands. In a muffled voice she said, "Tell me."

Nicola fidgeted, uncomfortable and vulnerable. "Before last night I didn't even know what to expect. But when we kissed, last night and just now, it felt good." She chewed on her lower lip, hesitating. "I never felt I could love a woman in any other way than friendship. Until now," she sighed. "Until you."

Jenny remained silent.

Nicola focused her attention on the floor and continued. "I think I'm attracted to you because of who you are. The fact you're a woman, well…that makes things a hell of a lot more complicated. But it doesn't change or stop the way I feel about you."

"This can't be happening," Jenny whispered, from inside her hands.

Nicola felt hurt and rejected but put on a brave face. "Listen, I never expected you to feel the same, but I had to be honest with you. I'm still moving out tomorrow. It's not fair for me to stay here in your parents' house with you while I feel like this."

Jenny lifted her face and shook her head. "Nic, I can't help the way I feel—"

"I know—"

"Let me finish. Jeez," Jenny said, clearly frustrated.

A little taken aback, Nicola stilled.

"I'm attracted to you too. In the same way." Jenny raised her eyes to the ceiling, as if looking for some divine intervention. "I don't understand it. But you can send my body wild with the simplest of looks or the gentlest of touches. I guess that says it all."

Nicola's elation was short-lived because Jenny wasn't finished.

"I need to sort my head out. My parents, my friends, the church all think it's a sin. That it's unnatural and wrong. Whatever this is, it's serious. It could cause a lot of damage and hurt a lot of people."

Nicola felt the need to defend herself. "I know it's serious and I don't want to hurt anyone. We need to work this out, together. You said your parents and the church would see us…this…as wrong. Is that how you see it?"

Jenny shrugged evasively. "The Catholic part of me does, but the rest of me doesn't. Kissing you feels like the most natural thing in the world."

"Which part's stronger?" Nicola asked, already dreading the answer.

Jenny didn't speak for a few seconds. "The part that thinks it feels okay," she finally said.

Nicola hugged herself. "If we stay as friends, there wouldn't be anything to sort out."

Jenny nodded grimly. She'd obviously been considering the same thing. "Staying friends would make life easier."

"In some ways it'd be easier." Nicola tried to mask her desperation. *Please don't let this end before it's even begun.* "It could also be unbearable."

"I've been fighting with myself all day, not to touch or kiss you," Jenny said, her brow creasing. "I don't think I could go back to being just friends. But I also can't hurt my parents. After what happened with my gran, I swore to myself I'd never, ever hurt them again, and since then, I've tried to become the best daughter I can be. I've never scored top marks in my exams, and I've never come close to making them as proud as Elizabeth has. But I've protected them from the messed-up things I've done and I'm trying to sort myself out. I think if they found out about this—us, they'd never forgive me. I can't do that to them."

"I could never intentionally hurt your parents. They've been so wonderful to me," Nicola said, feeling guilty for already betraying their trust. "I'm only just getting used to having friends and fitting in. I don't want to ruin it all."

Jenny looked perplexed. "What do we do, then?"

"Why can't we keep it to ourselves. We're both good at keeping secrets. And in the end we may end up deciding to be just friends, after all."

Jenny smiled and reached for Nicola's hand. "I suppose that could work. Although I honestly don't think I'll ever want us to go back to being just friends."

Nicola had never felt happier. "Me, neither."

Jenny stood up. "It's time to go." She helped Nicola to her feet. "We don't want you being late for work."

"I can walk by myself."

Jenny shook her head. "I'm not letting you out of my sight. I'll walk you there and then walk you home."

"My hero." Nicola swooned playfully, before kissing Jenny again. A moment later she pulled away, not wanting to start something she wouldn't want or be able to finish. "No more of that right now, or you'll make me late."

Jenny grinned mischievously and wiggled her thin eyebrows. "I get the feeling you're going to be a bad influence on me."

Smiling, Nicola walked over to the door and said, "I hope so."

CHAPTER NINETEEN

Nicola waved to Jenny one last time, before walking through the familiar doors of the convenience store. The loud bell signalled her arrival, as it always did. It'd been a week since she'd last worked a shift, but in that short time her life had completely changed.

"Hi, Nicola."

She smiled and walked over to the serving counter. Jack sat behind it. His blue eyes sparkled and his short blond hair looked suspiciously solid, due to the copious amount of gel he'd used. He was dressed as he usually was, in his green work polo shirt and a faded pair of jeans. He remained seated while they talked, but when he stood he was six foot one. Usually by the end of their shift, Nicola's neck ached from having to look up at him.

Other than Jenny, Jack was the only person Nicola considered to be a friend. They'd only been working together for a few months, but during that time he'd always been kind. The job had enabled her to earn money and, even more importantly, get out of the house for three evenings a week. It had also ensured someone would actually miss her and ask questions if one day she didn't turn up. Thanks to Jack and the job, she wouldn't simply disappear.

"Hey, Jack. How's things?" she asked, leaning on the counter.

He shrugged. "Not too bad." He looked her up and down. "There's something different about you today."

Nicola blushed and said, "New clothes."

Jack tilted his head to one side and seemed to consider something. "The clothes are great, but it's something different. You're kind of glowing."

"Thanks, I think," Nicola said, squirming with discomfort. She decided to change the subject. "I've got a favour to ask."

He raised one of his bushy eyebrows. "Go on."

"I had a huge bust up with my mum on Friday. She basically kicked me out, so I'm staying with a friend. All of my work shirts are at my mum's. I don't suppose you've got a spare I can borrow?"

Jack's smile disappeared. "Are you okay?"

"I'm fine. Honestly. My friend's parents are great and they're letting me stay with them for a while."

"That's good," Jack said quietly. "But if things don't work out with your friend or you need somewhere else to stay, you can always stay with me." His face turned beet. "It has its perks…it's close to work and there's a spare room."

Nicola was surprised by the unexpected offer. "Thanks." Unable to resist, she teased, "You actually couldn't get any closer to work, Jack. You live above the store. How do you even manage to be late?"

"My time management skills are impeccable." Jack shot her a mock glare. "But I do mean it, Nicola. The offer's always there."

"Thanks, I appreciate it."

"There should be a spare shirt in my locker, so go for it."

Nicola was about to leave when she thought of something else. "That's another thing I don't understand. Why do you have a locker in back, when you only live upstairs?"

Jack grinned. "Mostly, because I can."

Nicola laughed and made her way into the back of the store. The storeroom, office, toilet, and small kitchen area were all in the back of the building. She opened Jack's locker and had to dig through a mound of clothing before finding a rumpled work shirt. She lifted it warily to her nose and sniffed. It smelt a little musty but appeared to be clean, and for that she was grateful. Once dressed, the shirt was huge and hung past her thighs. She rolled it up as best as she could, before heading back out front.

"You look like a Borrower," Jack said loudly, before bursting out in laughter.

"That's height-ism. I could take you to court and sue your ass," Nicola said with a playful scowl.

"No, it's an observation," Jack said. "Just because you're short in height, doesn't mean you have to be short in temper."

"Very funny. How about I tell your mum, and we can see how amusing she finds it?" Nicola suggested.

Jack held his hands up in surrender. "Okay, you win. I've actually remembered what I was going to tell you. Dad confronted a thief the other day. He spotted the guy on the security footage, so he locked them both inside and waited for the police."

Nicola gasped. "What happened?"

"The police arrested the guy. Dad gave a statement and handed over the security tape. He's going to prosecute. Apparently the tape has more than enough evidence to prove the guy's guilty."

"That's good but also pretty scary."

Jack nodded grimly. "I know. You can imagine how my mum reacted. She went proper mental, shouting that the guy could've had a knife on him. She has a point though, especially after dad's heart scare last year."

Nicola walked around the counter. "Well, let's hope it never happens again."

Jack dragged the spare stool next to his and patted it. "So, what's new with you, short stuff? Don't your exams start this week?"

Nicola took a seat. Her good mood faltered, as she suddenly felt stressed by the reminder. "Yeah, but I couldn't be more unprepared if I tried. With everything that's happened recently, I've not had the time to revise. I'm going to fail everything."

Their conversation paused as Jack served an elderly woman. When she left, he turned back to Nicola. "Why don't you go into the office and do some now?"

Nicola frowned. "Jack, I can't. I'm at work."

"It's Sunday afternoon, Nic. We're never busy on Sunday, and as much as I love your company, your exams are more important. I'll be fine serving out here, but if hordes of people suddenly come in, I'll ring the bell twice and you can come out and save me."

The offer was appealing, but she hesitated, too guilty to accept outright.

"I can manage." Jack persisted.

"Okay, but only if you're sure."

Jack smiled. "I'm totally sure. Can you remember the password for the computer?"

"Yeah, I think so. You're a lifesaver, Jack." She surprised them both by pulling him into a quick hug before rushing out back and into the office.

She set up the computer and felt another twinge of guilt when she chose to put off doing revision for a little while. She used the Internet search engine and researched homosexuality, the Catholic Church, and other general information on lesbians. Within minutes, she quickly became engrossed in various articles and websites. She discovered a world of lesbian fiction and entertainment and even purchased a few books and DVDs, thankful for her bank card. She wanted to know everything she could, and although Jenny would probably be pissed at her for ordering stuff to the house, she decided she'd cross that bridge when she came to it.

After no time at all, she vaguely heard two buzzes but paid them no attention. A few minutes later, she heard them again. Her attention snapped away from the article she was reading, and she suddenly remembered Jack.

"Damn it!" She quickly exited all the websites and logged off the computer. She rushed into the store and immediately spotted there were no customers. Jack gave a sheepish smile, which only added to her irritation. *Why offer someone the opportunity to do something if you had no intention of letting her actually do it?*

"I'm sorry for disturbing you, but if I left you any longer we'd never be done on time."

Frowning, she glanced at the clock on the till. There was only twenty minutes of their shift left. She gaped at Jack and asked, "Why didn't you call me sooner? I've been in there for the whole shift."

Jack shifted uncomfortably on the stool. "It seemed silly when I could manage by myself. Did you get much done?"

Nicola swallowed down the guilt. "Yeah. I got quite a bit done. How about I go make you a drink?"

"That'd be great, thank you."

She made his usual cup of tea, which consisted of lots of milk and plenty of sugar in it. On the way back to him, she picked up a packet of his favourite chocolate biscuits and placed them and his drink on the counter. She dug in her jean pockets, produced some change, and handed it over. Jack raised a quizzical eyebrow.

"The biscuits are a thank you, but don't get used to them. They're strictly a one-off."

Jack ran the cost through the till. "Bribing me for my silence, eh? What would my mother say?"

"I'd deny it," Nicola said. "Plus, you're too much of a coward to tell her anyway." She playfully swiped at him. "I'll get started on the floors."

While Jack cashed up the takings, drank his tea, and devoured half of the pack of biscuits, Nicola swept and mopped up.

Finished for the day, they both went to collect their things. Nicola asked if she could borrow his shirt for a little longer and Jack happily agreed. She then hung the shirt neatly inside her locker and sprayed a few squirts of body spray on it, trying to be inconspicuous so as not to offend him.

As they walked towards the front door, Jack hesitated and finally blurted out, "I can walk you back if you want."

"Thanks, but my friend's meeting me." Nicola's stomach flipped at the thought of seeing Jenny again, of kissing her. "I'll see you tomorrow."

Jack nodded, his cheeks pink. "See you tomorrow." As Nicola reached for the door, he called after her, "You do seem different today. Happier."

"I am happier," she said with a smile. In less than a minute, she'd be back with Jenny, and the thought filled her with excitement.

"It suits you." Jack opened his arms and grinned mischievously. "How about a quick hug? Or does that go against the new happier you?"

Nicola walked into his open arms and gave him a quick hug. After a few seconds, she pulled away and opened the front door, barely registering the disappointment that flickered across his face.

He looked at the floor and said, "I think I've forgotten something out back. You head off. I'll lock up."

Nicola hesitated out of politeness, still trying to mask her eagerness to leave. "Are you sure?"

Jack nodded. "Yeah. You don't want to keep your friend waiting."

She didn't need any more persuasion and so rushed out of the store and across the road and found herself facing a sullen-looking Jenny.

"Hi," she said in a breathless tone. "Ready to go?" Nicola hoped to assess Jenny's mood by her answer.

"Yeah."

"Okay." Nicola sighed. Definitely not happy.

After five minutes of walking in silence, Jenny finally spoke. "Who's the guy you work with?"

Surprised by the random question and the obvious hostility in Jenny's tone, Nicola said, "His name is Jack. His parents own the store and we work our shifts together."

Jenny focused ahead and said, "You do know he fancies you, don't you? And he's got it bad if those lovesick puppy dog eyes are anything to go by."

Nicola stopped walking. She wasn't sure whether to laugh, be annoyed, or feel flattered by Jenny's obvious jealousy. After a second of deliberation, she chose the latter. "He doesn't fancy me. We're just friends."

Jenny crossed her arms and pursed her lips. "Friends who just *hug* a lot?"

"I can't believe you spied on me, and are now jealous—"

"I didn't spy on you and—" Jenny's mouth opened and then closed. Squirming for a few seconds, she finally admitted, "Maybe I'm a little bit jealous. But he does have a serious crush on you, Nic. You're too innocent to see it."

Nicola drew Jenny into a tight hug and whispered in her ear, "I'm not that innocent anymore." She pulled back, pleased by the look in Jenny's eyes. "Although you being jealous is sweet, there's no need to be. Come on. The sooner we get back, the sooner I can kiss you."

Swallowing hard and speaking in a slightly higher pitch than usual, Jenny answered, "Okay."

After eleven o'clock, Nicola finally managed to pry herself away from Jenny and sneak back to her own room. They'd spent the entire evening kissing and lightly caressing each other. Her lips felt swollen and sore. A deep ache had settled in her lower stomach, and with each kiss, it had grown more intense. It worried her, although now she was in bed alone and away from Jenny, it seemed to have eased off some.

She switched her mobile phone on for the first time that day. The battery was almost gone and she'd forgotten to buy a charger in town. As she set her alarm for the morning, the phone vibrated in her hand, announcing she had received a new text message. The message was from her mum's phone. With a mixture of nervousness and dread, she opened the message and read it.

Bring smokes back after work. Ran out. Mum x

She read the message four more times before switching the phone off and placing it on the nightstand. Anger and betrayal consumed her. It'd been three days since she'd left home, and the only communication she'd received from her mum was that pathetic text. No worried phone calls, no concerned voicemails. Nothing.

Had her mum even noticed she'd not been home?

Did she care?

Nicola refused to cry. She'd done enough crying and now it was time to act. She'd allowed herself to become complacent in the O'Connor home and in doing so had ignored her problems. She now had less than a month until her time here was over and she'd be facing the same mess all over again.

After an hour of thinking, she'd come up with a basic plan. In order for her to return home, *he* needed to leave. She absolutely did *not* want the police involved—she couldn't face the ordeal of having to explain everything. Also, if the abuse came out publicly, it would destroy her mum. So she'd have to force him to leave because he wouldn't go willingly. That thought logically led her to blackmail. If she could get proof, undeniable proof, of everything he'd done to her, then he'd have to go. The frustrating problem was she had no idea how to go about getting the proof. She had her old journals but felt certain they weren't enough. To have the best chance, she'd have to somehow get him to admit it.

Inspiration struck in the form of Jack's dad and his run-in with the thief. If she could somehow secretly record herself confronting him and have him admit what he'd done, then she'd have all the proof she needed. Like a snowball effect, everything quickly fell into place.

There was a webcam on the computer in the living room at her mum's house. Hypothetically, if she could set it up without him knowing and have someone record the live feed, she'd have all the proof she needed. There were a few details she'd have to check out, but Jack could probably answer her questions concerning technology.

Only once she was completely sure her plan could work would she even consider telling Jenny about it. She would, however, ask Jenny to take photos of her back tomorrow after her art exam had finished. She'd confront him with the photos, and once he saw them, he'd realize someone else knew the truth. That knowledge would hopefully be enough to persuade him to leave, but if he still refused, then she'd threaten to go to the police.

The most important aspect of her plan was going to be timing. She'd have to confront him while her mum was at work in the evening, otherwise he wouldn't confess to anything. She calculated that with her mum's shift pattern, her next real opportunity would start a week from Thursday.

She had over a week to perfect her plan and an additional four days in which to convince Jenny to help her.

CHAPTER TWENTY

Nicola loitered outside the door of the art classroom, waiting with both anticipation and trepidation for the bell to ring. It'd practically been a miracle Jenny had even made the exam, considering how difficult it'd been to get her to leave the house this morning. Their kissing and touching had started as soon as they were awake, and it had taken every ounce of self-control for Nicola to demand they rush to school. With less than two minutes to spare, Jenny had made it through the door and into the classroom. The art exam lasted for the whole school day and those hours felt torturously long. Nicola filled the hours by going over and over her plan until her brain hurt. The thought of asking Jenny to take the photos made her even more apprehensive.

What if Jenny wouldn't agree to take them?

What if she did?

How could Jenny ever find her physically attractive again once she saw up close how horribly disfigured her back was?

Their newfound relationship was precious, and Nicola desperately didn't want it to end. But time was running out, and the photos had to be taken today.

The bell sounded. A moment later, the art room doors burst open. Jenny was the first out, flying down the steps until she was standing before Nicola, grinning like a maniac.

"How did it go?" Nicola asked.

"Okay, I think. Let's get out of here," Jenny said with a mischievous wink.

As they walked home, Nicola tried to build up the confidence to ask Jenny about the photos, and her silence apparently didn't go unnoticed.

"What's up, Nic?" Jenny asked with a frown.

"I want to ask you something. You can say no, and that's fine. In fact, I'd totally understand if you did say no—"

"Are you actually going to ask me something?"

Nicola was glad for the interruption. "Do you have a digital camera? One you can upload pictures straight onto your laptop and then print photos off?" It wasn't exactly what she'd intended to ask, but she suddenly realized she wasn't even sure if Jenny had a camera.

"Yeah, I've got a camera. I've also got a laptop, printer, and even some posh photo paper I use for art, but please tell me that wasn't your big question," Jenny said, taking a cigarette out of her bag.

"No, that wasn't it. I needed to check that first. What I wanted to ask you is…" Nicola swallowed hard. She'd known asking would be difficult, but this was ridiculous. "Tonight, after your parents have gone to bed, will you…take some photos of my back? Please?"

Jenny stopped walking and gaped at Nicola, dropping her cigarette in the process.

"Jenny?"

She shook off her surprise. "Of course I will. I wasn't expecting… that." Her weak smile looked more like a grimace. "Can I ask why?"

Nicola shrugged. "I want proof of what he's done to me while it's fresh. That way, whatever I decide to do, I'll have evidence." She'd already decided not to bombard Jenny with her entire plan straight away. She intended to drip-feed it to her, in the most sugar-coated way possible.

"Are you sure you want to do it tonight?" Jenny asked, flicking her hair back.

"I want to get it over and done with. Otherwise, I'll probably chicken out."

"Okay," Jenny said, nodding. "Tonight it is." She rummaged in her bag again and took out a new cigarette.

They started walking, and although neither of them mentioned it again, it hung over them all the same.

❖

Jenny positioned herself on top of the duvet and seductively patted the space next to her. "I've been thinking about kissing you all day. Please, don't make me wait any longer."

Nicola climbed onto the bed and crawled over to her. "I've been thinking about the exact same thing."

Their mouths met and their soft kiss turned intense within seconds. A shudder tore through Jenny's body when Nicola's light fingertips caressed through the material covering her right breast. In a matter of minutes, they were both breathing hard and gasping for intermittent breaths. Nicola suddenly pulled away.

Jenny sat up, startled. "Nic, what's wrong?"

Nicola looked away and began chewing on one of her fingernails.

Jenny tenderly stroked her face and whispered, "Nic?"

"I think there's something…wrong with me."

"Something wrong with the kiss?" Jenny asked.

Nicola's gaze shot to hers. "God, no. The kissing is amazing. It's me. I think there's something wrong with me…inside." Nicola blushed and lowered her gaze again.

Jenny grew worried. "I don't understand. Are you feeling ill? You haven't eaten much today, maybe if you ate—"

Nicola shook her head. "It's not that. It's just, whenever we kiss, well, pretty much whenever I'm with you, I feel strange inside. I've never felt anything like it before."

"Strange in what way?" Jenny asked softly, taking hold of the hand Nicola wasn't nervously gnawing on.

Nicola swallowed hard and her frown deepened. "It's like stomach ache, but lower down. It keeps getting worse and now it's even a little bit painful."

Jenny gave Nicola's hand a reassuring squeeze. "Does it get worse when we kiss?" Nicola considered the question and then nodded. "Can I try something?"

"Yes."

"Are you feeling the ache now?" Jenny asked and Nicola nodded. "I want you to tell me if it gets worse, okay?"

"Okay."

Jenny lay back down and gently moved Nicola's hand away from her mouth and then kissed her deeply. She allowed her fingertips to linger lightly on the base of Nicola's throat, stroking her soft skin, before travelling south and brushing across her right breast. As their kissing intensified, Jenny cupped Nicola's breast and teased the firm nipple beneath the material with her thumb.

A gasped cry escaped from Nicola, and Jenny felt her own body ache in response. She reluctantly pulled herself away, breathing hard. "What's it like now?"

Nicola eyes remained clenched. "It's so much worse. What's wrong with me?" Her face was etched with genuine worry.

"There's nothing wrong with you, Nic. You're just..." Jenny struggled to think of how to explain it.

"What?" Nicola asked. Her eyes opened wide, piercing Jenny with her innocence.

"You're...turned on," Jenny said. This time, she felt her own face flame with embarrassment.

"Are you sure?" Nicola asked, uncertainly. "It feels so..."

"Strong?"

Nicola's face turned scarlet. "Yeah, strong."

"I've never felt anything like it before, either," Jenny said. "When I said you've been driving me crazy, I wasn't exaggerating."

Nicola gave a weak smile. "You must think I'm ridiculous. Is it going to keep getting worse?"

Jenny felt her face grow hotter. "From what I understand, it's going to keep getting worse, until we..." Once again, she couldn't find the right words.

Nicola's expression turned to sheer panic. "Jenny, I don't think— I'm not ready for—I know my body obviously has its own ideas, but I'm—"

"Hey." Jenny took hold of Nicola's hand and tried to ignore the stab of hurt, as Nicola flinched at her touch.

"Nic, relax. It's a good thing we feel this way. It means we're suited to each other. But there's no rush to do anything. So far everything that's happened between us has happened naturally, because it's felt right. If anything else ever happens, it'll be when you and I are both ready and not before."

Nicola's expression looked solemn. "What if I'm never ready? What if it never feels right for me?" Her bottom lip wobbled and her big blue eyes became watery.

"Then nothing happens. We'll take things slowly and ignore our raging hormones, okay? No pressure." Jenny watched Nicola's reaction carefully.

"He always said I'd be alone and I believed him. I've just gotten so caught up in this—in us—I haven't thought about the physical side. Jenny, my back—how could you ever..." Nicola choked with emotion and couldn't finish her sentence.

Jenny pulled her into a tight hug, not knowing what to say. She couldn't deny she felt attracted towards Nicola. She also couldn't deny the memory of Nicola's back had initially been an issue for her, but it wasn't anymore. Deep down, she knew Nicola wouldn't believe her even if she said it. She'd most likely view it as misplaced pity.

Ultimately, the decision for their intimacy to go any further was Nicola's, and Jenny was prepared to wait for as long as it would take.

Her own self-inflicted scars were hard enough to contend with. They were constant reminders that sometimes, she was seriously fucked up. The thought of Nicola seeing them filled her with shame.

Nicola was right.

Their bodies might be craving something more, but for the time being neither of them was ready to fulfil those needs.

She hoped, in time, they would be.

CHAPTER TWENTY-ONE

Nicola pulled the large green polo shirt over her head and began rolling up the bottom of it. So far, her plan was working out okay: Jenny had reluctantly agreed to take the pictures of her back tonight once her parents were asleep. She walked into the store and sat down next to Jack, behind the counter. Her objective for their Monday-night shift was to subtly quiz him about webcams.

"So, how are things going with your girlfriend? I mean your friend. Who's a girl," Jack said, blushing.

Nicola wondered if he somehow suspected the truth but then decided it must be her imagination. There's no way he could know the truth. Especially as Jenny and she weren't even sure what was going on between them.

"Everything's fine, thanks. Do you know much about how webcams work?"

His eyebrows arched in surprise at the abrupt change in subject. "I suppose I know a bit. What do you want to know?"

Nicola tried to remember what questions she'd planned to ask. "Do they record sound?"

He rubbed his stubbly chin. "If your webcam has a microphone, it should record audio alongside the video."

She couldn't be certain if the webcam at her mum's had a microphone, so she decided to move on and ask the next question. "What kind of distance and sound quality would it record?"

Jack wore his *I'm thinking hard* expression. After a few seconds he said, "It'd depend on the webcam. The only way to be sure would be to test it out. What are you thinking of doing?"

Nicola forced herself to remain calm. "It's for my drama coursework. I've got to record a performance and I don't have a video camera, so I figured the webcam would do. I know it'll record the video, it's the audio I'm worried about. I don't want to fail because it ends up being a silent movie."

With bated breath, she waited to see if he believed her. She seemed to be getting better at lying all the time and was even feeling less guilty about doing it. Worrisome.

"The only way to make sure would be to record it on something like a digital voice recorder as well. That way, you could always mix the audio with the visuals afterwards."

A digital voice recorder! *Shit.*

"Where can I get a voice recorder thingy from?" she asked and added quickly, "And how much do they cost?"

Jack beamed a toothy smile. "Well, it just so happens I own a digital voice recorder. I had to use one for school last year. But I have one condition." He presented his hand to her, so they could shake a deal. "You let me see the finished product."

Nicola felt her stomach lurch. *Trust me, Jack. You aren't going to want to see this video.*

"You drive a hard bargain, but it's a deal," she said, forcing a cheerful smile, as she shook his hand.

Jack stood up and stretched his arms over his head, which lifted his shirt and revealed part of his toned stomach. "I'll go fetch it now, but only if you're okay minding the store for a few minutes."

Nicola glared at him. "I'm more than capable of minding the store by myself, Jack." She crossed her arms. "But the sooner you go, the sooner you can come back and protect poor defenseless me."

"Glad you understand your rightful place, woman," Jack said and then laughed. "And don't forget—it's poor defenseless *little* you." He scampered away before she could find something to throw at his head.

A few minutes later he returned, holding a small white device. He handed it over and she inspected it. It kind of resembled a mini iPod but was significantly smaller and lighter. Simple buttons to record, stop, rewind, fast forward, and alter the volume were clearly labeled on the front and side.

Her initial fear that the device would be too complex for her to work quickly faded. As she gripped the discreet recorder, she became confident her plan would work. "Thanks, Jack."

"Not a problem, but you'll probably need some new batteries. It can record up to six hours, and once you've finished recording, upload it onto your computer with a USB cable."

Nicola slipped the recorder inside a pocket and was surprised at how comfortably it fit. "You're officially a lifesaver."

The remainder of their shift was spent rotating stock and stacking shelves. She attempted to stay busy and keep her mind occupied. It worked because the time flew by, and before Jack cashed up for the day, she purchased a pack of batteries.

Before she left, she braved giving Jack a final hug, hoping Jenny wouldn't see. As his arms wrapped around her and he asked if she was okay, she struggled to keep up the pretence of being fine. In the end, she reluctantly pulled away and forced herself to believe that the next time she saw him, she'd be even closer to sorting out her problems.

She walked out into the humid evening air, and her anxiety increased as she realized that in a few hours, she'd have to show her back to Jenny.

As she crossed the road, she met a subdued-looking Jenny. "Are you ready to head home?"

"Yeah." As they started walking, Jenny added, "I've cleared all the crap off my camera. It's all ready. Unless you've changed your mind?"

Nicola didn't miss the weak but unmistakable sound of hope in Jenny's voice. "I haven't changed my mind. I want to do it tonight."

CHAPTER TWENTY-TWO

Jenny sat on the edge of her bed, dressed in shorts and a strap top. She fiddled nervously with her camera. Her parents had gone to bed an hour ago, and now she was waiting for Nicola to return from the bathroom.

This feels so wrong!

The pressure of how to react to the sight of Nicola's back stressed her out. That Nicola seemed to be able to read her like a book at the best of times wasn't helping the situation. The last thing she wanted to do was unintentionally hurt her.

A tiny knock sounded on her door, and as she looked up, Nicola crept inside. She was wearing her pyjama pants and had a towel draped over her shoulders, covering her torso.

"I want it over with," Nicola whispered. She looked pale and her eyes mirrored Jenny's own nerves. "I can't put it off any longer."

"Okay," Jenny said, "let's do it." She stood on weak legs.

Nicola quickly closed the distance between them and kissed her tenderly on her mouth. Even as Jenny closed her eyes and kissed her back, she couldn't ignore the niggling thought that this felt like a kiss goodbye.

Nicola pulled away, turned from her, and walked into the centre of the room. "Whatever happens, I do care for you, Jenny."

Jenny opened her mouth to reply, but before she could speak, Nicola unwrapped the towel and let it fall around her feet.

Jenny took in the sight of Nicola's back, and this time she wasn't shocked or repulsed by what she saw. She raised the camera with trembling hands and took the first picture. On inspection, the image clearly picked up the bruises, scars, and cigarette burns against the backdrop of Nicola's white skin.

Jenny stepped closer, zoomed in, and quickly snapped another four pictures. This close, she noted the old scars and marks on Nicola's skin for the first time. They varied in shape, size, and colour. Some of the old scar tissue had a faint purple tint, like her own did when she grew cold.

She resisted the temptation to reach out and touch Nicola's skin and occupied her hands by taking another few pictures instead.

Nicola was shivering, and quiet sniffles escaped from her. Jenny placed the camera on top of the drawers and moved behind her. She reached out but hesitated at the last moment. *Is this right?*

This time, Nicola shivered more violently, as if answering her question. She allowed her fingertips to softly skim the warm gooseflesh of Nicola's skin. "It's okay, Nic," she whispered and felt Nicola lean back into her.

She delicately explored Nicola's back with light fingertips. She avoided the tender and sore areas but allowed her fingers to trace some of the outlines and feel the raised smoothness of some of the old scars.

She swept Nicola's damp ponytail aside, revealing her slender neck. The faint fragrance of shampoo lingered pleasantly, as she pressed her lips against Nicola's skin. Unable to resist, she tentatively licked Nicola's skin. It tasted both sweet and salty.

Nicola groaned and Jenny took it as a sign to continue. She slowly kissed and licked a trail from Nicola's neck down between her shoulder blades. When Nicola moaned again, Jenny felt a throbbing ache pulse between her legs.

She caressed the flat of Nicola's stomach with her hands, travelling up past her ribs until they skimmed the warm weight of her breasts.

"Jesus!" Jenny said, as the throbbing became painfully more intense. She cupped both breasts, enjoying the feel of their softness and weight. She circled Nicola's nipples with both thumbs, feeling as they grew hard against her touch.

Part of Jenny's mind cried out for her to stop. *I'm touching a woman. It should feel wrong, it should feel so wrong—but it doesn't. It feels fucking amazing!* But were things moving too fast? She didn't want this to feel wrong for Nicola.

"Nicola?" she asked, her voice husky with desire. Nicola slowly turned to face her. Jenny took in the beautiful pale body before her. "God, Nic, you're so beautiful…"

Nicola closed her eyes and winced at the words as if they caused her pain.

Cradling Nicola's face with her hands, Jenny whispered, "Look at me, Nic." Nicola's eyes fluttered open. "You're beautiful. You're the most beautiful woman I've ever seen. I wish you could see yourself how I see you."

A tear rolled down Nicola's cheek.

Jenny wiped it away with a thumb. "Don't cry, Nic."

Nicola wrapped herself around her and whispered, "I thought when you saw my back you'd realize you couldn't…" Her voice broke with emotion.

"I've never wanted anything as much in my entire life," Jenny said, before pulling her even closer and planting a soft kiss. Nicola shivered again. "You're cold. Climb under the covers."

Nicola did while Jenny switched on the bedside lamp and then switched off the main light. The room fell dark, with only the small lamp offering an intimate glow. She walked over to the bed and her heart skipped a beat. *Are we making a mistake?*

"Are you okay with this, Nic? If it's going too fast, we can—"

"The only thing I'm not okay with," Nicola interrupted, "is that you're still standing there."

Jenny pulled back her side of the duvet, but before she could climb beneath it, Nicola spoke again. Her tone was low and seductive. "You need to take your top off first."

"Uh…okay," Jenny said, avoiding Nicola's direct gaze.

Jenny suddenly felt incredibly self-conscious and shy. She pulled off her top in one swift motion and dropped it to the floor, while simultaneously diving into the bed.

"If this feels weird for you we can talk or go to sleep," Nicola said.

It did feel weird. Jenny's body was reacting with a will of its own, but she didn't want them to stop. "Let's see what happens. If either of us gets freaked out, we stop."

Nicola moved in closer, the heat from her body radiating as she whispered into Jenny's ear, "Freaked out yet?"

Every hair on Jenny's body stood on end. She was nervous, but also longing for intimacy. She moved in close and kissed Nicola. As their tongues battled, she caressed Nicola's breasts.

Her own nipples hardened with a tingling sensation as Nicola's hands began exploring her body. "Shit, Nic…"

She'd never felt so aroused before and the longing had now settled permanently as a pulsing ache between her thighs.

She moved into a kneeling position, lowered her mouth to Nicola's right breast, and, sensing no sign of apprehension, drew the taut rosy nipple into her mouth. As she kissed and sucked, she was rewarded with deep groans from Nicola.

She moved her hand to the material that covered the inside of Nicola's thighs and felt a surprising but welcoming heat. She suddenly hesitated.

She'd slept with guys and knew what to expect and, more importantly, what they expected from her. But she didn't know anything about girl-on-girl sex. *What if I do something wrong? What if I hurt her? Shit!*

Nicola must have sensed her distress because she spoke softly. "I trust you. This feels right."

Jenny swallowed hard. "Nic, I don't know what I'm doing. I'm scared I'm going to hurt you."

"You won't hurt me," Nicola said, lifting her head and kissing Jenny softly. "We'll work out what to do together, take our time and explore. It feels good so far, doesn't it?"

"It's amazing."

"Exactly," Nicola said. "I think we should do this next." With a mischievous smile, she stripped out of her pyjama pants and kicked them to the floor. She turned her attention back to a stunned Jenny and said, "Now it's your turn."

As Jenny removed her shorts, excitement coursed through her veins, making her heart pound hard and fast.

Nervously, they came back together, embracing the newly discovered freedom of their nakedness. As their kissing deepened, their wandering hands once again explored and caressed.

Jenny skimmed a hand down over Nicola's stomach and travelled further south, until her fingers met with the tuft of coarse hair. She hesitated, raised her gaze, and looked into Nicola's eyes. She saw only loving trust.

Nicola's hand gently grasped her own and guided her fingers lower. The tips of her fingers met with folds of velvet.

"Christ!" Jenny cried out.

Nicola released her grip, allowing Jenny to explore.

Jenny timidly stroked and caressed, watching Nicola's face. Her eyes were closed, her face was flushed, and her mouth was slightly open, as ragged breaths and incoherent moans escaped.

Exerting a little more pressure, Jenny's fingers quickly became enveloped in a hot wetness. As her fingers slipped and slid, she could stroke faster, without the worry of hurting Nicola.

Nicola cried out and instinctively grabbed for the nearest pillow. She held it over her face as her entire body tensed and her thighs clasped against Jenny's hand, holding it in place. As one final incredibly intense shudder tore through Nicola's body, Jenny heard Nicola's cry, even though muffled by the pillow.

For a few moments, Nicola lay perfectly still. Her breathing gradually calmed and she slowly relaxed her thighs, releasing Jenny's hand.

Jenny never wanted to lose the intimacy, so she kept her hand where it was. The silky wetness was already drying on her fingers, while her own need continued to scream out for attention.

She looked down at Nicola's naked body, and thinking about what they'd done only added to her arousal. She had no regrets because what had happened between them had felt both natural and perfect. She'd never believed sex could be so delicate, tender, sensuous, or loving. *I suppose that's why it's called making love.*

When Nicola finally removed the pillow, Jenny couldn't help but chuckle. Nicola's hair was sticking up, her face remained flushed, and her eyes sparkled brightly. It was her expression, however, that amused Jenny the most. Nicola was beaming a huge satisfied grin.

There was so much Jenny wanted and needed to say, but she couldn't manage a single word. So instead of speaking, she leaned down and kissed Nicola softly. As their kiss deepened, her growing ache of arousal made her gasp into Nicola's mouth.

Nicola sat up and looked sympathetically down at her. "Now, it's your turn."

As if sensing Jenny's desperation, Nicola touched her where she needed it most. Unable to hold back, Jenny pressed herself against

Nicola's hand and began grinding back and forth against her fingers, starting a rhythm.

With each stroke, the fine line between pleasure and pain seemed to merge. The pleasure was so intense, it was bordering on sublime torture.

As another powerful wave crashed through her body, she squeezed her eyes shut and choked back the deep cry that was trying to escape. Blindly, she grasped for a pillow and pressed the dense material against her face.

As her pleasure and pain reached an intolerable high, she tried to speak, to tell Nicola they had to stop, she couldn't take any more—but a sudden almighty explosion tore through her body. She buried her face deep into the pillow, crying out desperately. Fireworks and colours filled the darkness of her closed eyes and were so bright they almost blinded her.

Relief and ecstasy were simultaneous. A gradual sense of contentment followed, leaving her feeling fuzzy. As little waves continued to sweep through her body, she became aware of the part of her that had been aching so badly. It was now hypersensitive and seemed to be humming pleasantly. The insides of her thighs were coated with wetness.

Nicola cuddled in against her, adding both comfort and warmth with her body. Soon, a lulling sleepiness crept over them both.

"Are you surprised this doesn't feel weird?" Nicola asked, midway through stifling a yawn.

"Yeah, but also glad," Jenny said. Her cheeks ached from smiling, but she couldn't stop.

"Did it feel…was it okay for you?"

Jenny rolled her head to the side and looked at Nicola. Her eyes looked uncertain as she chewed on her bottom lip. "What are you talking about?"

"I didn't know if I'd done it right—"

"Did you not see, hear, or feel what happened to me? I've never even had an…orgasm before tonight," Jenny said, knowing she was blushing.

Nicola snuggled in closer and let out a contented sigh. "I wanted to check."

Jenny reached across to the bedside lamp and switched it off, trying her hardest not to disturb Nicola, who was already softly snoring.

CHAPTER TWENTY-THREE

They woke on Tuesday morning, both sprawled out naked on Jenny's bed to the sound of Jenny's mum's voice shouting up the stairs. Jenny rushed to the door in the buff and shouted down she was awake.

Anne left for work a few minutes later. They were both freaked out, but Jenny significantly more so. They could've easily been caught inexplicably naked and sharing a bed. As they dressed in pyjamas, they made a pact—from now on, they'd be extra careful, and Nicola would return to her room every night, dressed.

While Nicola went for a shower, Jenny went down to the kitchen to make them coffee. As she was pouring, the doorbell rang. A delivery man presented Jenny with a large box addressed to Nicola. She signed for it, carried it upstairs, and placed it on Nicola's bed. She was curious and suspicious.

When Nicola came into the room, she looked genuinely surprised. Her eyes darted from the box to Jenny.

"What's in the box?" Jenny asked cautiously.

Nicola was now dressed in her uniform and busied herself with rummaging through the contents of the box. "Just some books and DVDs."

Jenny sat on the bottom of the bed. "I've got loads of DVDs you haven't seen."

Nicola cringed. "You don't have any of these books or DVDs, trust me." She turned to Jenny and said, "I don't want you to freak out. These are important to me."

Jenny shrugged, "Okay, as long as they make you happy."

"Jenny…" Nicola hesitated before sheepishly putting the books she was holding back into the box. "These are lesbian-themed books and DVDs."

Jenny stood gaping, momentarily speechless. How could Nicola do this? After everything they'd talked about—her parents!

"Aren't you a little curious about—"

"What the hell!" Jenny demanded, her temper surfacing quickly. "We said we were going to keep this between us." She glared furiously from Nicola to the box and back again.

Nicola sat down on the bed. "It *is* our secret."

Jenny began pacing up and down, her arms flailing by her sides. "Then why the fuck have you brought a huge box filled with gay DVDs and books into my parents' house? What exactly do you think is going to happen when my mum comes across them? Christ, Nic. What if she'd answered the door? How would you have explained these? You're fucking stupid!"

As soon as the words left her mouth, Jenny stopped pacing. The realization of what she'd said to Nicola hit her like a tonne of bricks. Her hands flew to her mouth. "Nic, I'm so sorry. I didn't mean to say that. I just…" She moved towards her, but Nicola turned away.

"Why did you say it, then?" Nicola asked, her voice full of reproach.

"It just came out. I'm sorry. Please believe me?"

"It was a shitty thing to say," Nicola said, looking undeniably hurt.

Jenny nodded. "I know, it was totally out of order." Without thinking, she plucked the plastic band on her wrist.

Nicola frowned. "I'm not trying to out you to your parents. I'm curious about how women like us live. These books and DVDs show women who love each other and manage to live together in the real world. For them, *this* is normal. I wanted to see what it could be like for us."

Nicola seemed to wait, but Jenny refused to respond. She was too eaten up by her emotions. She plucked the band again, feeling as it struck her already bruised flesh.

"I'll only read the books when I'm alone. I thought maybe we could watch the DVDs together, when your parents are out."

Jenny tried her best to take deep breaths and act rational. But in reality, she was biting at the bit. *How could Nicola be so naive?* This was exactly what she feared happening. If Nicola kept this stuff, it was only a matter of time until their secret was discovered. She flicked the band again and this time winced a little from the smarting pain.

Nicola continued, seemingly oblivious to Jenny's anger. "Even if your mum did find them, she'd only suspect *me* of being gay. She'd never put the two of us together. No one would. I promise you, right here and now, if anyone ever discovers what's going on between us, I'll take the blame. Okay? I really wanted these books and DVDs, but if it's upsetting you that much, I'll send them back."

Jenny rubbed her temples trying to massage away a headache. She didn't want to continue being angry with Nicola. She begrudgingly had to admit Nicola's arguments made a little sense. After another long stint of silence, she finally said, "Keep them, but we've got to be so careful."

Nicola threw herself at Jenny, planting kisses on her lips and cheeks. "Thank you. I'll be careful, I promise." She then kissed Jenny deeply on the lips before turning her attention back to the box.

Jenny watched as Nicola transferred all the DVDs and books into the large rucksack she'd purchased on Saturday. Nicola then loaded her clothes on top and hid the bag inside the wardrobe. They tore the box into pieces, together.

"You go get rid of all this while I take a shower," Jenny said. "We're going to be late if we're not quick."

Nicola was still smiling like a lunatic. "It's okay, we can miss assembly today and then we've only got revision periods." She gathered up the pieces of cardboard in her arms. "Anyway, I thought I was meant to be the good influence in our relationship?"

Jenny shook her head. "Nope, I was right all along." She held the door open, letting Nicola leave first. "You're bad to the core and leading me astray with your wicked charms."

Nicola gave a flirtatious wink. "And you're enjoying every second of it."

❖

The school day dragged. They both had separate revision periods for their lessons, in which the teachers tried to get them to cram as much information into their heads as humanly possible.

Nicola struggled to concentrate. Thoughts and images of Jenny flashed in her mind, making her body react wildly every time. She knew she should be doing her best to listen and pay attention, as she'd hardly done any revision at all. But her mind and body had other ideas and seemed hell-bent on distracting her.

She finally managed to stop thinking about Jenny by going over all the aspects of her plan instead, which ended up being as distracting. She was running out of time and decided she would have to tell Jenny everything that evening. That gave her over a week to sort everything out and ensure Jenny was on board.

They got to spend lunch together and chose to deliberately keep away from Corrina, Sarah, and Laura by hiding in the art room. It was cool and deserted, which allowed them to sneak some furtive kisses and caresses in private.

After lunch, they both had a psychology revision period in the same classroom. They sat together and ended up doing no revision work whatsoever. Their time was spent sneakily touching and caressing in any way they could. When the bell sounded, it was a relief.

"I can't take it anymore. I need to kiss you properly. Can we go home?" Jenny asked quietly, hitching her school bag on her shoulder.

A surge of excitement shot through Nicola. "I was going to suggest the same thing."

CHAPTER TWENTY-FOUR

They spent the afternoon in Jenny's bed, their need to touch and kiss insatiable. They eventually managed to tear themselves apart to shower and dress before Anne returned home. Michael returned a little later, and they all sat down for their evening meal. Once again, the food was delicious and they both ate with gusto before retiring to Jenny's room.

Nicola's nerves kicked into gear. She knew she couldn't put it off any longer…it was time to tell Jenny her plan. She hoped Jenny might not react as badly as she feared, what with her parents downstairs.

She was wrong.

"That's the dumbest fucking thing I've ever heard! He threatened to kill you. He tried to rape you!" Jenny said, her eyes blazing. "It's not happening!"

Nicola chose to remain seated on the bed. She'd expected a bad reaction, but not one as hostile as this. "I'm doing it next Thursday whether you help me or not."

Jenny's fury came off her in waves as she took a menacing step forward. "No, you're not."

Although Nicola hated upsetting Jenny, she refused to back down. "I'm doing it, Jenny. I have to. If you won't help me, I'll find someone who will." Her calmness only fed Jenny's anger.

"Who?" Jenny demanded. "Who'd help you, Nic? You have no one else. So you can forget about this shit, right now."

Nicola knew Jenny's fury was because she cared, but it didn't stop the savage words from hurting her. Which, she supposed, was exactly what Jenny had intended.

She tried to remain calm as she got to her feet and said quietly, "I'll ask Jack." She watched as Jenny's expression changed from surprise to blinding rage. "It'll take a lot of explaining, but I managed to tell you, so I know I can do it. And if he doesn't agree, I'll do it by myself." She folded her arms and raised her chin. "I'm doing it, with or without your help. Don't underestimate me, Jenny."

She registered the impact her words had on Jenny. Her anger had visibly intensified.

Body rigid.

Jaws clenched.

Hands balled into tight fists.

Jenny stalked towards her. "If you think I've helped and cared for you so you can go and get yourself raped and murdered, you're seriously fucking crazy. You're not doing it!"

Their eyes locked, but Nicola refused to look away. "Jenny, I need you." She hesitated and then whispered, "I love you."

Jenny flinched backwards at the admission, as if she'd been struck. Nicola took another step towards her, but Jenny held up a hand to ward her off.

"Don't," Jenny choked out hoarsely. "Don't do that, Nic. That's not fair…" She turned her face away.

Nicola reached out, refusing to give up. She took a firm grip of Jenny's arm and said, "I do love you." She moved in front of Jenny. "I love you and I need you, now, more than ever. Please, Jenny? Please, help me to do this? I'm terrified."

She watched helplessly as Jenny stormed to the other side of the room and stood, facing away. A moment later she heard the pinging sound of rubber striking flesh. What was she doing? Before she could take a step towards Jenny, she heard the same sound repeated.

A flashback of their argument over her book and DVD order earlier that morning struck her, and she remembered Jenny snapping the thick rubber band sharply against her wrist. It had made her feel uncomfortable, and she'd intended to say something, to ask Jenny what she was doing. But then they'd made up and she'd been so happy about keeping the books she'd forgotten all about it.

When she heard the sound again, she rushed forward and stood directly in front of Jenny. She placed a hand beneath Jenny's fingers, preventing her from flicking the band again. "Jenny, stop."

Jenny held her gaze, her jaw set, an unreadable expression on her face. "Leave me alone, Nic."

Nicola refused to remove her hand, and after another minute of silent standoff, Jenny finally let go of the band. She went to pull her wrist away, but Nicola held on and felt a small jolt, followed by a flash of pain across Jenny's face.

"What are you doing with this band?" she asked, dreading the answer.

Jenny looked away and shook her head. "I don't know what you mea—"

"My God!" Nicola ignored Jenny's protest, as she carefully moved the bracelets to one side and looked at her wrist. What she saw made her feel sick. The skin on Jenny's inner wrist had bright red strap marks and was severely bruised. "You did this." It was a statement of almost disbelief, not a question.

Jenny tried again to pull her arm away again, but her attempt was so pathetically lame, it did no good.

Nicola blinked at the boiling salty tears welling in her eyes. "You did this because of me." Her voice was barely audible.

"No, I—"

Nicola shook her head. "I saw you, Jenny. This morning with the box of books, you did it then. And you've done it now because I've upset you. You did this to yourself because of me." Guilt weighed so heavily on her heart, she struggled to draw breath.

"It's not because of you, Nic. I swear. It's meant to help *me*, to stop me from hurting myself—"

"Well, it's obviously not working, is it?" Nicola released Jenny's arm.

Jenny wet her lips before speaking. "It's kinda working. Honestly, I know it looks bad, but it's nowhere near as bad as what I used to do. My counsellor says—"

"She knows about this?" Nicola asked in disbelief, taking a step backwards.

"She suggested it. Whenever the urges are overwhelming, I have to flick the band. It gives a quick shock of pain and then gradually the urges lessen."

"But you're still hurting yourself." Nicola didn't know what else to say. The whole thing seemed ludicrous to her.

"Nowhere near as bad. I still feel a bit crappy afterwards, sure, but it's a million percent better than it was. I used to *hate* myself afterwards. Now, I feel frustrated."

"Why do you do it?" She knew the question was about as personal, as intrusive, as she could get. "I need to know why."

Jenny grimaced. "It's a compulsion, almost like I'm addicted to it. I know it sounds ridiculous, but it's the truth. I've never been able to deal well with my emotions, especially anger and guilt. Hurting myself has always given me a release. The unreachable pain inside is finally reflected on the outside, which I can treat. And afterwards, I feel better."

"It feels *good*?" Nicola blurted, unable to hide her disgust.

"No." Jenny shook her head. "The urge becomes bearable, but I always feel guilty and ashamed afterwards. The biggest fear is someone will find out." Jenny slumped her shoulders, and the words came out in a tumble. "I'm trying to stop. I went to the doctors, and they set me up with my counsellor, and we're working on it. I'm lucky because I have a great doctor. I first went to see her when I was fifteen, about going on the pill. She was nice and supportive. Just over six months ago I made an appointment with her. When I got in there, I couldn't get the words out, so she asked me to write it on a bit of paper. I did, and then we started talking about it. She arranged the counselling, and the next day I had my first session."

"Weren't you scared your parents or someone you know would see you in there and start asking questions?"

"Not really. As far as Mum and Dad know, I've been going to the doctor's by myself since I was sixteen. And the medical centre is massive with loads of different doctors and nurses, so unless you specifically make an appointment with a certain doctor, you end up seeing a different one nearly every time. Plus, from that first appointment about going on the pill and the fact I was only fifteen, I knew she wouldn't—and couldn't—tell anyone."

"There are only three doctors at the centre I'm registered with. I always had the same one ever since being a child, but I haven't dared go back there in years."

"You don't have to go back there, Nic. There are drop-in clinics, walk-in centres, and even family planning clinics that give confidential help for loads of different problems, including abuse, addictions, and ill health. I read about them when I was looking online for help, but in the end, I felt more comfortable going back to that doctor."

"I'll bear them in mind." Nicola was genuinely proud Jenny had been brave enough to go to the doctor to seek help. She tried to remind herself she'd promised to never judge Jenny about the self-harm, and if Jenny was trying to stop, surely that was a positive step. If she could do anything to support her progress, she would. "And the counselling's working?"

Jenny nodded. "I've been going for over six months, and in that time, I've only cut myself once, during the second month. All the talking and thinking about it made it even more difficult to resist. Since then, I've only used the band. And being with you helps too, even though it's only been a short time."

"Yeah, I can see I'm really helping," Nicola said harshly and regretted the sarcasm straight away. "I'm sorry."

"I feel like myself when I'm with you, Nic. That includes the good, the bad, and the ugly parts of me. I know I'm not the easiest person to love—Christ, I'm only just starting to like myself again. My counsellor says it's going to take a while. No quick fix." Jenny lifted her wrist and said, "This is progress, and as sick as it sounds, I'm proud of it. But if you can't deal with it," she implored, "or with me, I understand."

"Come and sit down," Nicola said softly. "You're amazing and that includes the good, the bad, and the ugly."

Jenny sat down on the edge of her bed, and Nicola knelt between her legs, cradling her hands.

"Look, about your plan—"

"We can talk about it later."

"This isn't a game, Nic," Jenny said quietly. "He could hurt you and I don't think I can sit by and watch it happen." She let out an exasperated sigh and then added, "I will, though."

Nicola was confused, then surprised. "You'll—?"

"I'll watch and record it, but only because I don't trust anyone else to do it. First sign of trouble, and I won't hesitate to call the police. That's the deal. Take it or leave it."

"I'll take it." Nicola squeezed Jenny's hands. "Thank you."

Jenny shrugged. "I still think it's a fucking stupid idea."

"I know you do," Nicola said wryly.

"He abused you for years. He told you if you ever went back there, he'd kill you. Nothing's stopped him before. What's going to stop him this time?"

Nicola stood and placed her hands on her hips in an attempt to look confident, even though she didn't feel it. "I'm going to stop him this time. I've got something to fight for, something I'm not prepared to give up on." A flutter of determination swelled in her chest. "I have you."

Colour bloomed in Jenny's cheeks. "Well, you'd better take me through this step by step then."

For the rest of their evening, Nicola explained every aspect of her plan. In return, she listened to the various criticisms and the many swear words Jenny unhelpfully contributed. When Anne and Michael came in to say goodnight, Nicola decided it was time to go to her own room. Exhaustion from the emotional turmoil of the evening pulled at her. She would never feel comfortable with the idea of Jenny hurting herself, but she would do her best to support her efforts to change. Hopefully in the not-so-distant future, Jenny would stop for good, and that was enough for now.

It had to be.

Her English Literature exam was in the morning, and she hoped, against all odds, getting a decent night's sleep might make up for her lack of revision.

As she headed to the door, Jenny called quietly, "Hey."

Nicola turned back, a quizzical lift to her eyebrows.

"Did you mean what you said before? About…love?"

The vulnerability in Jenny's voice was clear, and a lump formed in Nicola's throat. "Yes. I love you, Jenny O'Connor."

Relief blew through Jenny like a cool breeze. She walked over to Nicola and kissed her gently on the lips. "Good, because I love you too." She opened the door and whispered, "So I hope this dumb-ass plan of yours works."

Nicola forced a smile and lied as convincingly as she could. "Everything's going to be okay. I promise."

Chapter Twenty-five

Nicola woke up at stupid o'clock on Wednesday morning. She went downstairs and had breakfast with Michael and Anne before they left for work. She promised Anne she'd wake Jenny up, and then she took a long hot shower and brushed her teeth.

Wrapping her towel around her damp body, she quietly snuck inside Jenny's bedroom. The curtains were drawn, but sunlight shone through a small gap. She hovered by the bed, watching Jenny sleep. She looked seriously cute.

Jenny stirred and her eyelids fluttered open. Nicola quickly planted a soft kiss on her forehead. "Morning."

Jenny rubbed the sleep from her eyes and sat up. "Nic? Are you okay?"

"I'm fine," Nicola said. "In fact, I feel good today."

Jenny combed her fingers through her messy hair, trying unsuccessfully to tame it. "That's great." Her gaze moved from Nicola's face to her bare shoulders and then lingered on her partially covered breasts.

"Are you actually ogling my boobs that blatantly?" Nicola asked, amused.

Jenny snapped her eyes upward, her cheeks blushing. "No. Even though you've come in here wearing only a towel." She wet her bottom lip. "I'm innocently sitting here, on my bed, in my room, and it just so happens my eye level coincides with your boob height."

Nicola raised an eyebrow and fought back a grin. "So, to clarify," she said, while tracing a fingertip across her chest and watching as Jenny's gaze obediently followed, "you *weren't* checking out my boobs, then?"

Jenny swallowed hard and then remembered to shake her head. "No. It's the eye-and-boob height thingy, I explained."

"The eye-and-boob height thingy?" Nicola repeated, as she closed the distance between them.

"Uh…yeah."

"I like your eye-and-boob height theory. I really do. But it has one major flaw…" Nicola said, sweeping her damp hair aside and revealing her throat.

Jenny looked as though she might explode. "Uh…flaw?"

Nicola nodded. "Yes. An important flaw, in that you were *blatantly* ogling my boobs." She moved her mouth within inches of Jenny's and whispered, "Weren't you?"

Jenny flushed. "Yeah," she said huskily. "I was definitely checking out your boobs. Sorry."

"Don't apologize," Nicola said, as she lightly kissed the corner of Jenny's mouth. "It was a good theory."

Jenny wrapped her arms around Nicola and pulled her onto the bed. Their mouths met and their tongues battled.

Jenny broke for air. "What time's your exam?"

Nicola stood up straight. Her lips were gleaming from the wetness of their kiss. She unfastened the towel without saying a word and let it fall to the floor.

Jenny let out an involuntary cry. Her eyes feasted on Nicola's naked body, as if starved.

"We've got plenty of time," Nicola said, climbing back onto the bed. Jenny pounced at her. She pulled her down and began kissing and nibbling her skin. "Jenny?"

"Mmm?" Jenny said as she kissed Nicola's throat.

"You need to take off your pyjamas. Now."

In a flash Jenny stripped, and although they had no reason to hurry, their insatiable desire created a growing sense of urgency.

Nicola lay alongside Jenny, marvelling as a beam of sunlight caught her hair, revealing a kaleidoscope of autumn colours. Her gaze roamed over the curvaceous body lying against her. Jenny's breasts, which were larger than her own, swelled with each breath she drew. The delicately pink nipples hardened beneath her gaze and darkened in colour.

Nicola allowed her gaze to travel lower down, passing over the muscular stomach and stopping at the neat triangle of coarse hair between Jenny's thighs. She remembered their last time together and the burning ache of arousal inside her stoked.

Her gaze fell onto the scared skin below Jenny's hip. She hadn't noticed the scars the previous times they'd made love because it had been dark and they'd been beneath the covers. But in the clear light of day, they were unmistakable.

The memory of the razor lid made her shudder. Seeing the scars and knowing Jenny had inflicted the injuries on herself troubled her deeply. Her only consolation was, true to Jenny's word, none of the scars appeared to be recent.

Jenny moved away from her and covered the scars with her hand. She was clearly uncomfortable.

Nicola noted the hurt projected on Jenny's face. She removed Jenny's hand and silently traced the scars with delicate fingertips. "You're beautiful, Jenny," she said softly. "I love every part of you."

Jenny rolled them over in one fluid motion, positioning herself on top. She kissed Nicola's lips fiercely before lowering her mouth to her right breast and devouring her nipple.

Nicola sucked in a breath. Jenny playfully teased her nipple with her tongue and raked it with her teeth. Her excitement intensified as Jenny's fingers stroked the inside of her thigh. The simultaneous sensations of Jenny's mouth sucking and her fingers caressing made the fiery ache between her thighs unbearable. She moaned loudly and opened her legs wider, craving more of Jenny.

"You feel so amazing," Jenny whispered as she straddled one of Nicola's thighs.

Nicola gasped. She could feel Jenny's centre pressing against her bare thigh.

"Oh God!" Jenny whimpered. Her eyes were closed. Her breasts swayed with the motion of her body as it rocked against Nicola's thigh, keeping in rhythm with each stroke of her hand.

Wetness coated Nicola's thigh as Jenny's fingers exerted enough pressure to induce an almighty orgasm. Nicola cried out, and the sound reverberated through the otherwise quiet house.

Contentment flooded through her body while Jenny climbed off her and lay by her side.

"That was…" She couldn't think of a word to describe it.

"Yeah, it was," Jenny said with a chuckle. "I swear I've never been so…wet."

Nicola rolled onto her side and reached out. Her fingertips followed an invisible trail that descended over the mound of Jenny's left breast, entitling her to give the hardened nipple a playful tweak before continuing southwards. She held Jenny's gaze as she lowered her fingers, feeling the warm, silky wetness coat her fingertips. Apparently Jenny wasn't exaggerating.

Nicola was happily sated and so took her time to explore Jenny.

Jenny's eyes clenched shut again. "Nic…God that feels so good… would you…" She whispered huskily, "I want to feel you inside me."

Nicola asserted more pressure and Jenny moaned as she pressed herself against Nicola's hand, guiding and inviting her to where she needed her caress most.

As Nicola penetrated, she immediately became both aroused and overwhelmed by the delicate tightness that enveloped her finger. She withdrew slowly. Jenny whimpered loudly at the loss and so Nicola thrust back inside. With each thrust, strong muscles tensed around her finger.

Nicola needed to feel more. She desperately wanted more intimacy and so she inserted another finger.

"Don't…stop!" Jenny said between labored breaths.

Nicola continued with firmer and faster strokes. Jenny's back suddenly arched, every muscle in her body seeming to tense, as her cry filled the room.

Nicola waited until Jenny had recovered before slowly withdrawing both fingers.

"Nic. That was was…" Jenny's eyelids looked heavy and her hair was actually now defying the laws of gravity.

Nicola snuggled up against her with a smile. She'd officially had a great start to the day.

CHAPTER TWENTY-SIX

Approximately halfway through her shift, Nicola couldn't pretend to ignore the awkward atmosphere any longer. Jack had been acting weird ever since she'd walked into the store. He'd barely spoken to her. She'd tried joking and initiating their usual banter, but he was having none of it. She decided to wait to see if it would pass naturally, but after sitting for the last half an hour in complete silence, she couldn't take any more. They still had another two hours to go.

"Jack, is something the matter?" she asked, in an attempt to sound causal.

He looked at the floor. "No."

"Have I said or done something to annoy you?" she persisted, watching for any signs she was close to the truth.

"No."

She sighed and nibbled on her bottom lip. There was definitely something strange going on, but Jack seemed to have no intention of discussing it. She thought about what his issue could be, but nothing came to mind. She decided to be more assertive, like Jenny would be. She'd ask him outright.

"Please tell me what's bothering you," she said, "because I'm getting paranoid."

Jack continued to look away from her. "I'm worried about a mate of mine."

It isn't to do with me. She relaxed. "Okay. Well, tell me about it. Maybe I can help."

Jack picked up a pen from beside the cash register and fiddled with it. "My mate accidentally found out something about one of his other friends. A secret. He didn't mean to. He was trying to stop them getting in trouble. But now he's feeling shitty, like he's betrayed her. He's basically scared that if he tells her the truth, she'll hate him."

Nicola considered the situation for a few minutes. "I don't think she'd hate him. It's not like he did it on purpose. Does he have to tell her he knows?"

Jack shrugged. "I don't know. From what he said, it sounded like it was a big secret and I think he's worried about her. She's having a crappy time at the moment and he wants her to know he's there for her if she ever needs him." He glanced beseechingly at her. "What would you do, if you were him?"

Nicola considered her reply as two customers came up to the counter and Jack served them. Once they'd left, she said, "It's difficult, because I don't know what she's like."

Jack shook his head, as if the answer she'd given wasn't what he wanted to hear. "She's like you," he said. The pen dropped to the floor. He sighed and turned to fully face her. "Nicola, it's you. I'm sorry."

She was seriously confused. "Me?"

"Yeah. I'm the guy. You're the girl with the secret," he said, hanging his head in shame.

Nicola was stuck for words. Secret?

He knew about the abuse?

How?

When?

"What secret do you think you know?" she asked, warily.

"I know about you and Jenny." He buried his head even deeper into his hands. "I know you're lesbians."

Wow! She hadn't been expecting that bombshell. All she could manage was, "How?"

"I went back to delete the Internet search history you did on the computer. My mum busted me a month ago for using work time for my own recreational purposes and docked my wages. It was totally by accident, but I happened to see the names of some of the sites you'd been on."

Nicola wasn't sure what to say or do. She'd promised Jenny their relationship would remain a secret and she wouldn't tell anyone. *Do I deny it?*

"I haven't told anyone and I never will." He shifted on the stool but still wouldn't look at her. "It explains why you've changed so much in the last few shifts. You're happier—and you deserve to be. I wanted you to know I'm here if you ever want to chat."

Nicola surprised him by putting her arms around his neck and hugging him. "You're a softie, but I wouldn't change you for anything. Thanks, Jack. I mean it."

He hugged her back and finally seemed to relax. "Just think about the chats we can have about hot women," he said with a grin. "Maybe you can also help me find a girlfriend?"

"Deal," she said, with a laugh.

"I also have a few questions."

"Questions?"

"Yeah. You're the first real-life lesbian I've ever had as a friend."

"Fire away," she said, amused but already blushing at the potential topics he might broach.

Nicola lay beside Jenny on her bed with music quietly playing to give them background noise. Anne and Michael were downstairs, so only kissing and fondling over their clothes was permitted.

"So, no more work until Sunday?" Jenny asked.

Nicola nodded in response.

"That means we get to spend every evening together until then. How will we pass the time?"

Nicola smiled. "I'm sure we'll find something to entertain us."

Jenny laughed. "This new you is rather naughty."

"Would you prefer the old me back?" Nicola asked, planting a quick kiss on Jenny's mouth.

"No way."

"Good, because this new me is here to stay." She rested her head on Jenny's shoulder and added, "The new you is pretty amazing too."

Jenny sighed contentedly. "I actually do feel like a different person. I'm happy. In fact, I honestly can't remember ever being this happy before. You've changed me, for the better. The old fucked-up me is practically gone. Good riddance."

Nicola chewed her bottom lip. She'd had a burning question that she'd not dared ask. *Now or never.* "Jenny, can I ask you something about your scars? If you don't want to answer, that's fine."

Jenny tensed. "Go on."

"The scars are just below your hip—why did you choose to do them there?"

"So no one could see them. During the first few years, I experimented with different things, in different places. But I was always terrified someone would see what I'd done and ask questions. I quickly decided doing it there was the safest place." Jenny agitatedly began tapping her foot.

"Did you always use a razor?" Nicola asked, feeling awkward.

Jenny shook her head. "I'd use whatever was handy." She lifted her head and rubbed the back of her neck. "Razors used to give me a quick fix, though. They're easy to get hold of and are pretty sterile. It'd be over in a matter of seconds."

Nicola couldn't help but feel uneasy at the matter-of-fact tone Jenny used. It was a little eerie. But then, she had asked the questions, so she couldn't complain that she wasn't keen on the answers.

She crawled forward and planted a kiss on Jenny's lips. When she pulled away, she said, "Thank you for being so honest and brave. When the feelings and thoughts get bad again, I want you to talk to me about them. I'll do my best to help you, and maybe you won't even have to use the band. Okay?"

"Okay," Jenny said, wrapping her arms around her and hugging her tightly. "Thank you."

CHAPTER TWENTY-SEVEN

Thursday and Friday both flew by, and so did their exams, including their joint psychology exam. They managed to successfully avoid Corrina and Sarah for the rest of the week.

Laura, however, went in search of them and eventually found them in the art room. Although they were a little annoyed at the prospect of having to find a new hiding place, they both enjoyed catching up with her. She made them promise they'd go bowling on Saturday evening for her birthday.

On Thursday afternoon Jenny went to her counselling session while Nicola sat in the waiting room. For the first time in the whole six months of going, Jenny finally told Kathy about her gran. Although they didn't have enough time left to discuss it in detail, Jenny left the session feeling proud and liberated. Being with Nicola was helping her deal with her problems head-on, more and more every day. Even Kathy had commented on how upbeat she'd seemed, but Jenny had decided to hold off telling her about her newfound sexuality. That would be another bombshell, for another day.

When they returned home, they'd both hoped Anne and Michael would go out, leaving them to their own devices, but it didn't happen. Instead of spending the evening naked, they ended up talking and marvelling about how quickly the week had passed, how things had changed for them both, and how neither of them could wait to be alone together again.

On Friday night their wish was granted.

Anne and Michael went out for a meal with friends.

They made love over and over again until they were both beyond sated. Afterwards, Jenny convinced Nicola to be a nude model for her. They agreed on the pose together, which used Nicola's hair to cover her face and therefore her identity. The finished drawing was excellent and Nicola made Jenny promise they'd hang it in their first home.

Jenny hid the drawing safely in her art folder, along with the very first sketch she'd done of Nicola.

They showered, changed into pyjamas, and cuddled up on top of Jenny's bed to watch the BBC's adaptation of *Tipping the Velvet*. Caught up in that moment, they felt invincible, as if nothing could ruin their happiness.

They were wrong.

On Saturday morning, Nicola heard her bedroom door creak open. She kept her eyes closed and listened to the soft tread of Jenny's footsteps on the carpet. Cool air touched her body as her duvet lifted briefly off her. She floated with the dip and bounce of the mattress as Jenny climbed in beside her.

Jenny moved closer. The heat radiating from her naked body sizzled as she snuggled up against her. Nicola felt a hand slip expertly beneath her pyjama top and glide lightly over her stomach and climb, until it cupped one of her breasts.

"Morning," Jenny whispered. She began to nibble Nicola's earlobe.

"Good morning," Nicola said, rolling over. "What about your parents?"

"They've gone shopping. So we've got about an hour," Jenny said, with a mischievous grin. "It's time for you to get naked."

Nicola quickly undressed. They both took their time to touch and be touched with curious fingertips. Even after making love so many times already, their curiosity remained new and exciting. There were still so many different textures, sensations, and reactions to discover and experience.

Jenny's hand moved to stroke inside Nicola's thigh, but Nicola reached down, stopping her from going further. "I'm sorry, not today."

"Are you okay? Have I done something wrong?" Jenny asked, hurt and rejection flashing in her eyes as she moved her hand away.

Nicola shook her head. "It's not you. It's me and it's... embarrassing."

"Embarrassing?"

Nicola lifted a shoulder in a half-hearted shrug. "I'm just a bit sore, down there."

"Did I hurt you?" Jenny asked, immediately looking guilt ridden. "God, Nic, I'm so sorry—"

"You didn't hurt me," Nicola said softly. "We've been doing *this* a lot recently. My body isn't used to it, which is frustrating, because I'm incredibly turned on right now."

A ghost of a smile touched Jenny's lips. "I've been feeling a little bit tender myself."

Nicola rolled her eyes. "We're as bad as each other."

They lay cuddling, and Nicola's body hummed with arousal. She resigned herself to the prospect of having a very cold shower.

"Are you still turned on?" Jenny whispered seductively.

Nicola sighed. "Yes, and you're not helping."

Jenny sat up, her expression serious. "I think I'd like to try something new, but only if you're okay with it. If it makes you feel uncomfortable or hurts, just say and I'll stop."

Nicola was curious, but she trusted Jenny completely. "Okay."

Jenny's eyebrows narrowed. "Promise you'll say if it hurts. I'm not sure if I'll feel comfortable with it, but I want to try."

Nicola began to feel apprehensive. "I'll say if I want you to stop."

Jenny nodded and threw back the duvet, exposing them both. She kissed Nicola on her mouth, then her throat, breasts, nipples, and stomach.

It suddenly dawned on Nicola exactly what Jenny planned to do. Her mind raced, but so did her body. Jenny's hot mouth and ticklish breath made her body shudder with each wet lingering kiss. Her heart began pounding nervously, but she was also undeniably excited by the prospect.

Jenny continued to tease her way down her body. She spread Nicola's thighs and positioned herself inside them.

Nicola gasped as Jenny's mouth lightly kissed the inside of her thigh. She felt vulnerable, but in a good way.

Jenny's warm breath tickled her sensitive skin, making the anticipation almost intolerable. Her body actually jumped when Jenny's tongue flickered out and teasingly gave the slightest of caresses.

"Jenny. It's torture…" Nicola said, as her body shuddered again.

After what felt like a lifetime, Jenny's exquisitely soft mouth descended and kissed her deeply.

"Oh…Jenny!" Nicola cried out. No pain, no discomfort, only the intimate tenderness a mouth and tongue could give. Her hands ruffled through Jenny's hair, guiding her and drawing her in closer.

The next few minutes were the most intense Nicola had ever experienced. As the second wave of orgasm ripped through her body, she almost began to cry.

Jenny moved back up the bed, wrapped her arms around Nicola, and cuddled her. "That was incredibly sexy," she whispered.

Nicola mustered all her strength and managed to say, "You're so…doing that again."

They were running late to get to the bowling alley on time for Laura's birthday. Nicola made no attempt to hide the fact she thought it was entirely Jenny's fault. Jenny, meanwhile, made no attempt to hide the fact she was sulking.

They were about to reach the front door when Anne appeared from nowhere and blocked their escape route. She made sure she had their attention, then said, "There's something I need to tell you before you go out."

Nicola glanced at Jenny and saw her sulky expression remained.

Jenny said, "We're going to be late, Mum. What is it?"

Anne directed an annoyed look at Jenny. "Elizabeth phoned this morning. She's coming home for a few days."

Jenny's expression darkened. "Why? She hasn't come back during summer for the last two years."

Anne folded her arms across her ample bust, a sign Nicola now knew meant she was preparing for an argument she intended to win.

"Your sister has as much right to come home as any of us do, Jennifer. I don't know why she's decided to come back, but it's happening. So you'd better get used to it."

Jenny folded her arms and glared back fiercely.

Here we go, Nicola thought to herself.

"Where's Nic meant to sleep? You can't expect her to sleep on the sofa."

Anne glared back at Jenny, her irritation unmistakable. "Of course I don't expect Nicola to sleep on the sofa. If you had anything about you, you'd offer to sleep on the sofa and give up your bed. No? I didn't think so."

Nicola watched them both with fascination. They shared the same stubbornness, yet neither of them seemed to realize it.

"So what's going to happen, then?" Jenny asked.

"Nicola will move into your room until Elizabeth goes back to university. I know it'll be cramped, but it's only for a few days." Anne held up a hand. "And I know you're not going to be happy at the prospect of sharing your bed, Jennifer, but there's no other option." Anne's eyes sparkled with a hard determination. She was clearly expecting Jenny to put up a fight.

Jenny, however, had been rendered speechless. Her mouth gaped as she glanced back and forth between Nicola and her mum.

"Jennifer?" Anne asked, uncertainly.

Jenny snapped out of her surprise and regarded her mum coolly. "No, I'm not happy about sharing my bed. I think it's totally unfair to both of us. But, as per usual, Elizabeth gets everything all her own way. She's so bloody selfish!"

Anne unfolded her arms, which Nicola took to be a good sign. "Elizabeth doesn't always get her own way. Sometimes you do act like a spoilt child, Jennifer. Most girls would be thrilled to have their older sister coming back to visit. I'll never understand why the two of you don't get on."

Jenny pouted. "We can't stand each other, that's why. She's a total bit—"

"It won't be a problem, Anne," Nicola interrupted quickly.

Anne smiled appreciatively at Nicola. "She's coming back one day next week, which gives plenty of time for you to move your things into Jennifer's room."

"Are we done here?" Jenny demanded. "Nicola and I are going to be really late, but I'd hate for you to think I'm acting like a spoilt child."

Anne chose to ignore Jenny's comment. "You both look lovely. Now, remember what I said earlier?"

Nicola and Jenny spoke in unison. "We don't need alcohol or drugs to have a good time."

Anne smiled and clasped her hands together. "Exactly."

"Mum, we're going bowling," Jenny said. "I bet you haven't ever heard of any alcohol or drug-fuelled orgies at a bowling alley."

Anne glared at her.

Nicola couldn't resist adding, "Just because it hasn't happened yet doesn't mean it never will, Jenny." Her tone remained serious, but she struggled not to smile.

Anne glanced at her suspiciously and then returned her gaze to Jenny. "My point exactly, Nicola."

Jenny shot Nicola a warning look, and with a sigh of defeat, Nicola said, "Anne, I promise if in the unlikely event anything drug- or alcohol-related happens, I'll make sure we come straight home."

Anne nodded, seemingly satisfied. "Well, have a good night and don't come back too late." She gave them both bone-crushing hugs before allowing them to finally escape.

Chapter Twenty-eight

They left the bowling alley and headed home, but only after Laura had repeatedly begged them to consider going to a house party on Wednesday night.

As they walked up the driveway, Jenny took out her house keys and whispered, "Great, they've stayed up. Probably to make sure you've kept your promise of saving me from the dangers of drink, drugs, and bowling."

Nicola rolled her eyes. "It's nice they care."

Once inside, they hovered in the open doorway of the living room. As expected, Anne and Michael were both awake, dressed in pyjamas and seated on the sofa. They both looked a little surprised by their return.

"Hello, girls. We weren't expecting you back so soon," Michael said cheerily.

"We ate there, so we finished earlier. I managed to beat Jenny twice," Nicola said, ignoring the playful shoulder bump from Jenny.

"Only because I let you."

They all heard the sound of the fridge door opening and closing from inside the kitchen. "Jennifer, don't overreact—" Anne said quickly, but Jenny and Nicola had already turned.

"Hello, Jennifer," Elizabeth greeted coldly, her voice loud enough for only Jenny and Nicola to hear. "Aren't you going to introduce me to your friend?"

Jenny's complexion paled. She stood gaping at the tall blond girl who stood before them in the hallway.

"No?" The icy blue eyes turned their attention onto Nicola. "You must be Nicola. I'm Elizabeth, Jennifer's older sister."

Nicola regarded Elizabeth curiously. She looked so very different from Jenny that under different circumstances she would've struggled to relate them as cousins, let alone sisters. Elizabeth was taller and thinner. Her blond hair was naturally wavy, without a hint of frizz, and fell past her shoulders. The blue eyes were the same colour as Anne's, but that was where the similarity ended. Nicola could sense cold calculation behind Elizabeth's eyes and it made her uneasy.

The clothes Elizabeth wore also made her wary. The blue jeans and sneakers were fine, but the tight-fitted hooded jumper proclaiming *Jesus is number 1* and the obscenely large silver crucifix hanging around her neck made Nicola's skin crawl.

"Yes, I'm Nicola—"

"What the hell are you doing here?" Jenny asked.

Nicola flinched with surprise, but the outburst had little effect on Elizabeth.

"I've come home especially to catch up with you, Jennifer."

"You told Mum you were coming back next week," Jenny said, her face turning red.

"I wanted to surprise you all."

"Why would you do that?" Jenny asked.

"I thought you'd all be pleased to see me. And when Mum told me you had a new lodger staying, I had to come and meet her for myself." Elizabeth's gaze flickered to Nicola and she smiled.

Nicola instinctively didn't trust the smile—it came across as overly fake.

Anne and Michael came into the hallway, which only made the strained atmosphere even more intense.

"You're so selfish. Why lie about when you were coming back? Nic's things are in the bedroom because we weren't expecting you back. Are you actually capable of thinking about anyone other than yourself?"

"That's enough, Jennifer," Michael said firmly.

Jenny clearly remained furious but stopped speaking. Nicola wanted to do something to calm Jenny down, but this wasn't her argument or her family. For the first time, she actually felt like an unwelcome guest in the house.

"It's okay, Dad. Jennifer's probably right—my timing was a little off. I thought it'd be nice to surprise you all. I didn't realize I'd make things difficult. I'll drive back to halls tonight and come—"

"You'll do no such thing, Elizabeth," Anne said, folding her arms. "It was a lovely surprise and you haven't made anything difficult. Nicola and Jennifer can go up now and quickly move the essentials into Jennifer's room. The rest can be moved tomorrow."

Nicola glanced at Jenny, who looked like she might explode. Elizabeth beamed her overly sweet smile at both her parents before turning her attention back to Jenny. "I'm happy to give you both a hand. It's the least I can do."

The muscles in Jenny's jaw bunched, her gaze murderous.

"Shall we go do it now?" Elizabeth asked, her tone sweet. "It's getting late and I'm quite tired after my drive."

Nicola could see Elizabeth was enjoying every second of baiting Jenny and so spoke. "Thanks for the offer, Elizabeth. But we can manage by ourselves. If you give us ten minutes, we'll be done." She felt an intense satisfaction as Elizabeth's smile faltered slightly. A flash of annoyance flickered across her face. *I'm sorry, Elizabeth, did I just ruin your game?*

"I'll be up in ten minutes," Elizabeth said, her smile perfectly placed once more.

"Night everyone," Nicola said, forcing her own fake smile, as she gently touched Jenny's arm. "Come on, Jenny."

They started to climb the stairs when Elizabeth called up to them. "I'm looking forward to the prospect of *really* getting to know you, Nicola." She'd moved to the foot of the stairs.

Nicola saw Elizabeth's smile was gone. A shiver crawled down her spine. "I'm afraid you're going to be disappointed, Elizabeth, there isn't much to know." Nicola forced herself to keep eye contact.

"Don't be so modest, Nicola. From what little I've heard, you're quite the mystery girl. I'll make sure we've plenty of time to get to know each other. It'll be…fun," Elizabeth said, adding an annoyingly fake laugh.

"I'm looking forward to it," Nicola lied.

Anne asked Elizabeth a question and she reluctantly looked away first, much to Nicola's relief. Jenny and she started climbing the stairs again. The belief she'd won the first battle gave her little comfort. Elizabeth seemed intent on something, and Nicola got the distinct impression she could be a very dangerous opposition.

❖

It took them less than the allocated ten minutes to move all of Nicola's belongings into Jenny's room. They moved the bag that held the DVDs and books first, safely stowing it beneath Jenny's bed.

They changed into their pyjamas in silence, and Nicola switched off the light before joining Jenny beneath the duvet. They held hands in silence while listening as Jenny's parents and Elizabeth came upstairs, used the bathroom, and went into their bedrooms.

After a further ten minutes of silence, Jenny whispered, "I'm sorry, Nic. There's something about her that sends me over the edge."

Nicola gave Jenny's hand a reassuring squeeze. "She was deliberately winding you up, but doing it in a sneaky way so your parents couldn't see it."

Jenny turned to face her, but Nicola couldn't make out her features in the darkness.

"No one ever sees what she's really like. So much so, I used to think maybe I was imagining it all. Everyone thinks she's perfect. She's always been amazing at everything."

Nicola remained silent but cuddled into Jenny.

"I used to try so hard at everything because I wanted Mum and Dad to look at me with the same amount of pride she gets. It never happened and eventually I gave up. I know I sound bitter, twisted, and jealous." Jenny sighed. "When we were kids she was always bossing me around and telling Mum if I did the slightest thing wrong, and as annoying as it was, I accepted that's what older sisters do. But after Gran died, she became a complete nightmare. She deliberately interfered with as much of my life as she possibly could, so when she actually went away to university, it was the happiest day of my life."

"Why is she so mean to you?"

"She is hell-bent on making my life as miserable as possible because she blames me for Gran's death."

"That's ridiculous, Jenny. You aren't to blame." Anger crackled beneath Nicola's skin on Jenny's behalf. "Please promise me you're going to stop letting her wind you up. She gets off on your reactions. Once you stop responding, she'll probably get bored and go back to university."

Jenny perked up. "Do you really think if I ignore her, she'll leave?"

"Hopefully," Nicola said. Jenny sounded so wistful, she hoped her plan would work. "And in the meantime, she's given us exactly what we want. We get to spend every night together."

Jenny shook her head. "We've got to be so careful, Nic. Seriously. We can't let her suspect about us."

"I know," Nicola said. "But being able to cuddle and sleep in the same bed as you is more than enough."

They lay in a comfortable silence.

"I love you," Jenny said, stifling a yawn.

"I love you too. Let's get some sleep," Nicola said, snuggling down further. "Tomorrow will be better."

"Nic, are you awake?" Jenny asked groggily.

Nicola refused to answer and lay perfectly still, feigning sleep. She'd been awake for ages, but she didn't want to get up, and she especially didn't want to see Elizabeth.

"Nic, I can see your eyelids fluttering," Jenny said, creeping closer. "I know you're awake."

Nicola remained still and fought the urge to move or laugh.

"Right, you've asked for it," Jenny said, attacking her with tickling fingers. Nicola squealed, opened her eyes, and playfully fought her off.

"I knew you were faking," Jenny said, smiling.

A single abrupt knock sounded on the door as it swung open. Elizabeth stood in the doorway glaring down at them. "What exactly do you think you're doing?"

"Get out!" Jenny said, jumping to her feet.

Elizabeth tilted her head to the side and smiled but showed no signs of leaving.

"Are you deaf? I said get out, Elizabeth!"

Nicola watched the tiny smile flicker across Elizabeth's lips.

"No, Jennifer, I'm not deaf. Which is surprising, after the ridiculous amount of noise you were both making."

Annoyance prickled at Nicola. Elizabeth was once again getting the reactions she wanted from Jenny.

"We were laughing, but I apologize if we woke you up," Nicola said curtly.

Elizabeth's eyebrows narrowed. "You didn't wake me up. I've already been for a run and had a shower—"

"If we didn't wake you up, then I'm a little confused as to what the problem is. Especially as you felt the need to barge in here and yell at Jenny," Nicola said, keeping her tone pleasant.

Elizabeth gave her a venomous glare. "I knocked, actually. But you obviously didn't hear me over the loud childish screaming. I came to inform you breakfast's ready."

"Thanks. The thing is," Nicola said, getting to her feet, "we heard the knock, but we didn't get a chance to reply because you barged straight in."

Elizabeth had regained her ice queen persona. "And your point is?"

Nicola smiled. "Well, to stop future misunderstandings, we'll keep our childishness to a reasonable volume and you can knock, then wait for a response before barging into someone else's room. That way, everyone knows where they stand."

Elizabeth's cheeks flushed. "I think we know exactly where we stand." Her lips curved into an unpleasant smile before she turned away and stormed dramatically out of the room.

Jenny put on her slippers. "She doesn't like you, Nic."

"Thanks, but I gathered that myself," Nicola said, pulling her dressing gown on.

"I've never seen her so openly hostile to someone before. Not even to me," Jenny said, worry etched on her face. "You need to be careful standing up to her like that because she can be really vindictive."

Nicola's frustration quickly turned to anger. "I don't want to speak to her, let alone win arguments and piss her off. But I can't just stand back and watch you make an idiot out of yourself. It's ridiculous, Jenny." It was harsh, but it needed to be said. The last thing she wanted to do was create more of an enemy out of Elizabeth, but Jenny was forcing the situation.

"I'm sorry. I'll try not to let her get at me," Jenny said, hugging Nicola. "We'll keep out of her way."

Chapter Twenty-nine

Breakfast was an unpleasant ordeal, especially for Nicola, who ended up sitting uncomfortably on one of the plastic garden chairs. Jenny had offered to sit in it instead, but Nicola had refused because she didn't want to sit directly opposite Elizabeth.

Throughout the meal, Elizabeth commandeered most of the conversation. She cheerily enforced her opinions and her hard core religious beliefs on everyone. She directed countless digs and snide comments at Jenny, but true to her promise, Jenny didn't respond.

Nicola chose not to comment on anything either and nibbled unenthusiastically on a single slice of cold toast instead. She felt marginally better when Elizabeth excused herself from the table to go and prepare for Mass.

"Look at the time, Michael," Anne said, jumping to her feet. "I refuse to be late for Mass. I say it every week, and every week you cut it too fine." She cleared the table while Michael left the room, muttering something under his breath about always being ready.

The phone rang and Anne disappeared in the hallway to answer it, giving Nicola the opportunity to give up the pretence of eating toast.

Jenny drained the juice from her glass. "I'm going to go shower. You coming up?"

"I'll be up in a minute," she said and remained seated at the table, enjoying the peace and quiet. The rhythmic ticking of the kitchen clock became a comforting background noise in this brief moment of solitude.

"Why are you here?"

Nicola turned her head, startled.

Elizabeth casually walked over to the table and sat down. "I asked you why you're here."

Nicola was surprised by the question but said honestly. "Your parents offered to let me stay here for a while."

Elizabeth shook her head and sneered. "I wasn't referring to your Australian uncle's death. What I want to know is how have you come to be *here*? How've you seemingly appeared from nowhere and managed to worm your way into my family's home?"

The cruelty of Elizabeth's words rendered Nicola momentarily speechless. Swallowing hard, she said, "Jenny and I became friends—"

"Even that's a mystery. Up to just two weeks ago, you and Jennifer didn't know each other." Elizabeth sat back in her chair, her chin raised high. "Explain it to me."

"We've been going to the same school and sixth form for—"

"You go to the same sixth form, but you and I both know up to two weeks ago, you were a pathetic loner with no friends. How did a social reject like yourself and the most popular girl in school suddenly become inseparable best friends?"

Nicola felt sick. *So this is the real Elizabeth.* She'd suspected Elizabeth could be unpleasant, but she'd totally underestimated her cruelty and spitefulness.

"Come on, Nicola. Why the sudden silent treatment? You had plenty to say last night and this morning." Elizabeth's expression looked almost predatory. "Do I scare you?"

Nicola chastised herself for allowing Elizabeth to bully her into feeling so inadequate. She'd promised to never let herself be subjected to any form of abuse from anyone, ever again.

"I've no problem with talking to you alone, Elizabeth. And I'm disappointed to say I find the real you neither scary nor surprising." Nicola interlocked her fingers and rested her hands on the table. "Jenny and I did become friends quickly. It surprised us both, especially considering our obvious differences, but that's the beauty of friendship. I can imagine it's difficult for you to understand the concept of a best friend."

Elizabeth's smile disappeared. "Don't dare to presume you know anything about me."

Nicola smiled, but remained silent.

"Jennifer's changed and not for the good. She's avoiding her friends and missing school. I know it's got something to do with you and I'm going to find out what it is."

Elizabeth's determination filled Nicola with dread. She masked her emotions and said, "You're wrong. Jenny and I went bowling with her friends last night."

The sound of footsteps descending the stairs signalled an end to their exchange, but not before Elizabeth leaned across the table and whispered, "I won't stop until I know the truth, and you leave my sister and our family alone."

Anne rushed into the kitchen, followed by Jenny, who immediately looked panic-stricken at the sight of them both at the table.

"Look at the time. It's the same as always. I warn him, but we still end up being late. It's embarrassing," Anne said, searching for something.

"Should I go and get him?" Elizabeth asked, doubling the intensity of her sickly-sweet smile.

"Yes, please. Tell him if he's not down here within thirty seconds, we're going without him."

Elizabeth left the room, closely followed by Anne.

Jenny rushed over to the table. "What the hell was that about?"

"She hates me and I don't think she's just going to leave," Nicola said. "She suspects me of changing you in some way."

Jenny's eyes bulged and the colour drained from her face. "What do you mean suspects you of changing me? She doesn't know…"

Nicola shook her head. "No. She doesn't know anything, but she's convinced something's going on. She wants me to leave."

"Yeah?" Jenny slammed a fist down on the table. "Well, she can fuck right off. You're not going anywhere."

Jenny sat in her room, waiting for the minutes to hurry up and pass. She hated her own company and missed Nicola terribly when she was at work, especially now that Elizabeth was back in the house.

She'd been downstairs for less than half an hour before she could stomach no more. Once again, everything had turned into the Elizabeth

Show. Her parents were downstairs now, showering Elizabeth with attention and adoration. They were no doubt cooing over her latest achievements and successes, both of them oozing with unprecedented parental pride.

Jenny knew she was jealous. It was an emotion she'd always felt when Elizabeth was around, and it settled over her now like it always had.

Try as she might, which she had done for many years, she'd never been able to compare to her older sister in any way. Her exam results were always adequate, but never spectacular. She didn't have anywhere near the same natural skill and ability Elizabeth demonstrated in sports and crafts. She'd never captained a team, been a president of a club or the main spokesperson and organiser of a group—even if that group *was* the university Christian group, and Jenny had no interest in religion, anyway. Everything Elizabeth attempted, she succeeded at, and in doing so, made Jenny despair at her inadequacies.

"At least I'm better looking," she whispered and then chastised herself for being so shallow.

A knock on the door interrupted her thoughts.

"Who is it?" she asked, knowing it had to be either her dad or Elizabeth.

"It's me," Elizabeth said from the other side of the door. "I want to talk to you."

"I'm busy. We can talk another time."

"Jennifer, this is important and I'm not going away."

Jenny glanced at the clock and saw she only had forty minutes left until she had to leave to go meet Nicola. With a heavy sigh and a shake of her head, she said, "Fine. Come in."

Elizabeth came into the room and sat on Jenny's bed without waiting for an invitation.

"What do you want?" Jenny asked, trying not to get wound up by her sister's audacity in making herself comfortable in somebody else's room.

"I want to know how you're doing. How's school? How are your friends?"

Suspicion immediately made Jenny wary. "I'm fine."

Elizabeth gave a dramatic sigh. "That's not what I've heard, Jennifer—"

"Well, you've heard wrong, then."

Elizabeth shifted on the bed. "Look, I know we've never been particularly close, but that doesn't mean I don't love or care about you. I've come home because I'm worried about you."

Jenny heard what she could only assume was genuine concern in Elizabeth's voice. It surprised her a little. She and Elizabeth had never been close, but she couldn't deny in the past, on rare occasions, Elizabeth had tried to look after her. But when she'd needed her support, Elizabeth had only succeeded in making her feel a million times worse.

"There's no reason for you to be worried. I'm totally fine. Honestly, Elizabeth, I'm happier than I've been in a long time."

"What's the cause of this sudden happiness?"

Nicola. Jenny looked down at her desk, regretting that she'd allowed herself to speak without thinking things through first.

"There has to be something, Jennifer. What's making you happy all of a sudden?"

"Lots of things," Jenny said. "Can't you just be pleased for me?"

Elizabeth shook her head. "I'd love to be pleased for you, but first I need you to explain some things to me. Who is this girl you've invited to live in our house?"

"Her name's Nicola. She's a friend from school."

Elizabeth shook her head. "I know all your friends. I made a point of getting to know them. You've never mentioned her before. How long have you known her?"

Jenny shrugged. "A while."

"When exactly did you become such good friends?"

"What does it matter?"

"It matters to me, Jennifer. She's living in our house. When I asked Mum and Dad about her, they didn't know anything except you invited her home over a week ago. You never bring friends home, so why suddenly bring her?"

Jenny could feel her temper rising. "What I do and who I hang around with are none of your business."

Elizabeth casually flicked her hair and cupped her knee with her joined hands. "You know it's my business. I told you I'd keep checking up on you, and it's a good job I've been doing. You've started missing school again, haven't you?"

Jenny folded her arms. "It was one day. I felt ill, so I came home."

"Was she with you on this day? Did she come back here with you?" Jenny refused to answer, but Elizabeth continued regardless. "You've been ignoring your friends, the people who care about you. You've been sneaking and lying to people, even more than you normally would."

"That's not fair."

"All of a sudden, you're friends with this random girl. A girl who nobody knows anything about. And even more worryingly, since being with her I've been told you've been acting strange. Uncharacteristically strange, Jennifer. Does this behaviour sound peculiar to you? Because it does to me. Does it sound familiar to you too? It does to me."

"Elizabeth—"

"You're on drugs, aren't you?"

Jenny opened her mouth to reply but was too stunned to think of a response. Elizabeth got to her feet and walked over to the desk.

"What are you on? Did she get you started on something—is it coke? Is she your dealer?"

"What's wrong with you?" Jenny looked up at her sister in disbelief. "No, I'm not on drugs, Elizabeth. Okay?"

"No, it's not okay. Every question I ask, you're either evasive or refuse to answer. Why?"

"Because you're wrong."

"You've just done it again. I know something's going on with you and I know it's got something to do with that girl. Tell me what it is and I can help you."

"You know her name, Elizabeth. Stop calling her *that girl*," Jenny said angrily. "Nothing's going on. She's staying here because her uncle in Australia has died, and her mum's gone over there for the—"

Elizabeth slammed her hand down on the table. "Don't lie to me, Jennifer. I know she's hiding something and you're trying to cover for her. If it's drugs, which I think it is, you need to tell me now, so I can help you. I won't let you ruin your life or hurt our parents like this."

"I'm not on drugs—"

"You said that last year, Jennifer. Remember? You missed school, avoided friends, lied to everyone, and stole money from Mum, which I had to replace. You were acting in exactly the same weird way then too."

"That was different—"

"Thank God, Corrina called me that night. Because if she hadn't, we both know you'd be dead right now. I drove you to the hospital, Jennifer. I stayed with you the entire night. *And* I kept my promise about not telling our parents."

"My drink was spiked, Elizabeth," Jenny whispered, as a shudder passed through her body at the memory.

She'd been in self-destruct mode for weeks. The two-year anniversary of her gran's death had been coming up. She'd wanted to feel nothing and decided to try and drink and smoke away the memories that had haunted her. She'd attempted to get stupidly drunk, and then they'd ended up going to a house party. To the surprise of her friends, she'd headed straight for the local bad boy, who she knew was a drug dealer. She'd flirted shamelessly with him in the hopes he'd give her exactly what she needed to forget. The spliff they'd shared had had little impact, and when she'd asked for something stronger, he'd told her it would come at a price.

She'd followed him upstairs and did what he asked and in payment for services rendered, she was given a pill. When she'd asked what it was, he'd laughed and walked away. She'd taken it anyway, and her wish for not remembering everything was granted...but at the expense of her collapsing. Elizabeth had rushed her to hospital, where apparently she'd stopped breathing. Elizabeth had stayed with her through the entire night. When Jenny had eventually come around, she'd told the staff she couldn't remember anything of the entire night, and they'd said Rohypnol was in her system and it was likely someone had spiked her drink.

In truth, she hazily remembered the parts leading up to taking the drug but genuinely had no recollection of anything afterwards. She'd refused any further tests and demanded Elizabeth take her home.

Try as she might, she hadn't been able to get Elizabeth to believe her drink had been spiked. She'd spoken to Jenny's so-called friends and had been told about her dodgy behaviour and the fact she'd actively sought out the drug dealer. Since then, Elizabeth had made no excuses for checking up on her and interfering in her life. She'd blackmailed Jenny into promising she would never take illegal drugs again. With the exception of the occasional spliff, Jenny had kept her promise. She was genuinely too terrified to take another suspicious tablet ever again.

"This is your last chance," Elizabeth said, her tone serious. "Tell me what's going on with you and that girl, or I'll find out myself."

Jenny didn't know what to say. Elizabeth clearly didn't believe the story about the uncle dying, and she had nothing else she could offer up. Nicola's abuse wasn't something she was at liberty to discuss, and she refused to betray Nicola's trust.

"Fine. You only have yourself to blame." Elizabeth turned and stormed out of the room.

Jenny covered her mouth with a trembling hand and considered what had just happened. The sense of foreboding she suddenly felt was overwhelming.

They were screwed.

Nicola was glad to have the excuse of going to work, as it meant she got to get away from Elizabeth for a few hours. She ended up spending the entire shift moaning at Jack about everything, which made her feel marginally better afterwards. When the end of their shift came, she was dreading returning to the O'Connor home.

She met Jenny and they walked back together. Once inside the house, Anne greeted them and informed Nicola her dinner was in the oven. Nicola secretly gave thanks she wouldn't have to go through the motions of being pleasant to Elizabeth during a family meal.

Anne took the dish out of the oven and presented it to her. The mound of mash was covered in a delicious-looking thick stew. The tantalizing smell made her mouth water and her stomach grumble appreciatively.

After a few seconds of watching her eat, Nicola could tell Jenny was bored. She lowered her cutlery and said, "Why don't you go up, and as soon as I'm finished, I'll join you?"

Jenny didn't need any further persuasion and quickly left the room. Nicola continued to eat, savouring each delicious mouthful. She was only a quarter of the way through the plate and was already starting to feel full. Even after a week, she was still struggling with the size of Anne's portions.

A quiet sound from behind alerted her. She glanced over her shoulder and found Elizabeth standing in the doorway watching her. *Here we go again!*

"Evening, Elizabeth," Nicola said, turning her attention back to her food and calmly lifting another forkful to her mouth. Her appetite had suddenly disappeared, but she continued eating, regardless.

Elizabeth marched over to the table, pulled out a chair, and sat down. In a quiet tone she asked, "When exactly did Jennifer and you become friends?"

Nicola remained adamant she wouldn't allow Elizabeth to rile her. She forced down another forkful of food before replying. "A while ago."

"Jenny said two weeks ago," Elizabeth said, with a humourless laugh. "I'd hardly call that a while."

Nicola didn't respond.

Elizabeth smiled triumphantly and leaned forward. "How did you come to be such good friends in just two weeks? What hold have you got over her?"

Nicola placed her cutlery down and pushed her plate away from her. She'd had her fill of both the food and Elizabeth.

Elizabeth continued undeterred. "She may appear strong and feisty, but the truth is she's vulnerable. She can easily be influenced, especially by the wrong sort of person, which is exactly what I think you are."

"You don't know me."

"Exactly my point. And neither does my sister. I'm not going to let you walk in and take advantage of her or my parents."

Nicola's cheeks warmed with humiliation. She couldn't bear listening to any more of Elizabeth's malicious ranting, so she stood up and headed towards the door.

Elizabeth jumped up and marched in front of her, blocking her path. Her hands were pressed to hips, her body language hostile. "I

AMY DUNNE

don't think so. This conversation is over when I say so, and not a second before."

"It's not a conversation, Elizabeth. It's you ranting, and I'm not prepared to listen to any more of it. Please move out of the way."

Elizabeth took a domineering step forward. "How did you end up here, in my family's house? What are you hiding? Why does no one know anything about you?"

Nicola threw her hands up in frustration. Arguing with Elizabeth was exhausting. She was like a starved dog that had found a juicy bone. "Because there's nothing to know, Elizabeth. Jenny and I became friends. It happened naturally, like most friendships do. Your parents invited me to stay for a month, and I accepted. That's it. There's nothing untoward—"

"Do you deny she missed school because of you?" Elizabeth interrupted angrily. "That she's dropped her friends because of you? That she's been lying to my parents and to me in order to protect whatever it is you're hiding?"

Nicola sighed. "It's more complicated than you could possibly imagine—"

"I knew you were hiding something," Elizabeth said with a savage grin. "You're no good for her. All that's going to happen if you continue to stay here is she and my parents are going to get hurt. Do the right thing. Leave us alone."

"I know you want me to leave, but I'm not going anywhere just yet, Elizabeth. Deal with it." She took a step towards Elizabeth, her gaze unwavering. "I may not be a member of this family, but I'm part of their lives, whether you accept it or not."

Nicola walked to the doorway, then hesitated. She looked back and said, "I care very much for your family. I would never intentionally hurt them. Jenny's my best friend, and I only want what's best for her. Can we please agree to remain civil, for their sakes?"

Elizabeth gave no indication she heard her, let alone considered agreeing to the proposal.

Nicola, realizing she was only prolonging the inevitable, gave up and left the room with a frustrated sigh.

❖

"I wouldn't get your hopes up, Nic. She's never backed down from an argument or given up on anything, in the whole time I've had the misfortune of knowing her," Jenny said, after listening to Nicola's version of the argument.

"Surely if there's no way she's going to win, a truce would be more acceptable to her than an outright loss?"

Jenny sat back in her desk chair and considered the possibility but quickly shook her head. "I don't see it. In Elizabeth's warped mind, a truce would be the same thing as losing. The way she sees it, she's right and therefore should automatically win. If anything, I think you need to be more wary of her now."

Nicola gave an exasperated sigh and lay on the bed. "I still don't understand how she knows we've only been friends for such a short time."

Jenny walked over to the bed and sat on the edge. "She'd have found out from Corrina."

Nicola frowned. "She's friends with Corrina?"

Jenny shook her head. "No. Elizabeth's good friends with Claire, who is Corrina's older sister. She gets all of her gossip from Claire. For the last year she's been keeping tabs on me. When it comes to being controlling, Big Brother could learn a hell of a lot from her."

Nicola nodded. "She is controlling, but I think, deep down, her reason for doing it is because she cares about you."

"Well, it feels like she's doing it to punish me, Nic," Jenny said, in a matter-of-fact tone. "And she's got it in that demented head of hers that you're my personal drug dealer."

"What?" Nicola asked, unsure of whether to laugh at the ridiculousness of it or just be downright offended. "Why?"

Jenny puffed out her cheeks and seemed to shrink back in her chair. "Last year, I went a bit mental on the anniversary of my gran's death. I missed school, avoided Sarah, Corrina, and Laura. I stole money from my mum's purse so I could buy alcohol and weed. I went to a house party and got totally wasted. Elizabeth ended up rushing me to hospital because I had Rohypnol in my system. The doctors said my drink had probably been spiked. Elizabeth didn't—and still doesn't—believe that's what happened. She thinks I chose to take it."

Nicola could tell Jenny was holding something back. "Did you?"

Jenny dropped her gaze to the floor. She shifted uncomfortably on her chair and hesitated for a few seconds before replying. "Yes, but I honestly didn't know what it was."

Nicola chewed her bottom lip while she tried to think of what to say.

"I'm sorry, Nic."

"No. I'm sorry you felt you had to do those things. It does make it a bit clearer as to why Elizabeth's acting the way she is. Maybe we should tell her the truth about why I'm here."

Jenny looked up. "We can't, Nic. There's no way she wouldn't tell my parents, and then they'd know we've been lying to them this whole time. Everything would turn to shit. And they'd insist you went to the police to—"

"Okay, we don't tell her." Exhaustion from all the drama dragged at Nicola, and yet she knew the biggest part was yet to come. "Only three more days, and then I can confront Chris and hopefully go home, anyway."

"You haven't mentioned it for a while," Jenny said quietly, crossing her arms. "I was hoping maybe you'd changed your mind."

"If anything, Elizabeth's made me all the more determined to do it. I'm done being the victim."

CHAPTER THIRTY

Monday morning and afternoon passed without incident, and it looked as though Elizabeth might actually have given up her vendetta.

Nicola sat her last exam and felt it had gone okay. When they returned home, the house was empty. Anne had taken the afternoon off work so she and Elizabeth could go out shopping, but much to both Nicola's and Jenny's disappointment, they returned home only a short time later.

The evening meal was still a little awkward, but on a positive note, Elizabeth didn't acknowledge Nicola, which suited her perfectly.

After the meal, she and Jenny hid themselves away in their room. They were both feeling increasingly frustrated by the lack of intimacy they could share. Ever since Elizabeth's arrival, they had remained fully clothed and unable to do anything other than hold hands and share an occasional quick kiss. Sharing the same bed fuelled their raging desires, which made their situation all the more unbearable.

Nicola was actually relieved when she headed into work. The break from Jenny and Elizabeth was exactly what she needed. Jack was a perfect distraction with his stories and banter, and for the first time in what felt like forever, Nicola allowed herself to relax.

Halfway through their shift, the store's door opened and the bell sounded the next customer's arrival. Both she and Jack turned in unison to greet the customer, and Nicola felt her stomach drop.

Elizabeth strolled over to the counter, her gaze focused entirely on Nicola. "I want a word with you, in private."

Before Nicola could muster up a reply, Jack asked testily, "And you are?"

"Elizabeth," Nicola said and watched as Jack's eyebrows shot up in surprise. "Jenny's sister."

"Now that you've finished gawping at me"—Elizabeth shot a dirty look at Jack—"can we actually go somewhere? I haven't got all evening to spare."

Nicola could sense Jack was getting wound up. His grin was long gone and his cheeks were flushed. She quietly asked, "Are we okay to go into the office?"

"You don't have to go anywhere if you don't want to," he said, puffing out his chest and flexing his hands. "I'm more than happy to escort her off the premises."

"Thanks, Jack." Nicola gave a weak smile. "But I'm okay, honestly." She turned to Elizabeth, who was scowling at them both. "Follow me."

She led them into the back office and watched with dismay as Elizabeth closed the door. "What do you want, Elizabeth?"

Elizabeth dusted off a chair before sitting down and crossing her legs. She appeared calm and collected as she regarded Nicola coolly. "You'll want to sit down for this."

"I'm happy to stand." Nicola placed her hands on her hips. *How dare Elizabeth come into my workplace and tell me what to do!* She reminded herself to resist rising to Elizabeth's bait. "You've got two minutes, and then I'm going back out front to do my job."

"This won't take long." Elizabeth plucked at some invisible fluff on her sleeve. "While you and Jennifer were at school today, I went through your things. I'm not proud of it, but you both gave me no choice."

Nicola gaped at Elizabeth's brazen admission. She tried to mask her feelings, knowing Elizabeth would use any weaknesses she saw to her own advantage. Panic quickly replaced Nicola's initial crack of anger. Had she found the books and DVDs?

She must have, mustn't she?

"I knew you were hiding something, and though I thought it was most likely drugs, I now know differently." Elizabeth flicked her hair twice and cleared her throat, seemingly uncomfortable with what she was about to say. "I know you're a lesbian."

Nicola decided it was pointless trying to deny it, and so her main concern now was to protect Jenny at all costs. She would keep her promise and take full responsibility for the books and DVDs. "Yes, I am."

Elizabeth started to fiddle with the silver crucifix that rested on her chest. "I'm aware my parents don't know about this and that's for the best. But does Jennifer know?"

Nicola shook her head. *Time to put my newly acquired lying skills into practice.* "No, Jenny doesn't suspect a thing. She just offered me a place to stay."

Relief flickered across Elizabeth's face. "I also found your home phone number. I called it during lunch, and a woman answered. I asked if you were in and your mum said you were at school."

Nicola's hand flew to her mouth as she fought the urge to be sick. "I can't go home, Elizabeth."

"Because of your sexuality?"

Nicola forced a nod. *If Elizabeth wanted to blame everything on her being a lesbian, that was fine. Rather that, than the truth.*

"Why does Jennifer think you can't go home?"

Nicola had to think fast. "She knows my mum kicked me out of the house, but I told her it was because we had a massive argument."

"Although the Bible makes it clear homosexuality is a sin, I accept we all have free will. What we do with it is entirely up to each person. So I'm not condemning your chosen lifestyle," Elizabeth said diplomatically, "but I'm not condoning it, either."

"Thanks," Nicola said. *I think.*

Elizabeth held up a hand to silence her. "Your sexuality isn't the problem, Nicola. The problem is you've lied and manipulated your way into my family's home. My family trust and care about you, but you've deceived them and betrayed their trust, in order to have a place to stay."

Nicola struggled to swallow. "I never meant—"

"Do you know how much it would hurt my parents if they discovered the truth?" Elizabeth leaned forward, and the chair groaned quietly. "That you and Jennifer lied and manipulated them? That you encouraged Jennifer to miss school? They'd be devastated."

"I'm sorry—"

"It's too late for sorry." Elizabeth sat back and raised her chin. "You have to leave, Nicola. You have to find somewhere else to stay. I can't let you keep sleeping in a bed with Jennifer now that I know the truth." Elizabeth almost sounded sorry. "It's too late to leave tonight, but first thing tomorrow, I want you to pack your things and go. You need to tell my family tonight—you've decided to leave. Do it in a way that will cause the least amount of distress. And you're to sleep on the floor tonight. Okay?"

"What if I won't go—what happens then?" Nicola asked, already knowing the decision was out of her hands.

"Then you leave me no choice. I'll have to tell my parents everything, including all of Jennifer's involvement."

Nicola's legs buckled and she had no choice but to sit down. Tears began to well, as her mind raced with thoughts. Where would she go? There wasn't anywhere she could think of. How could she explain all of this to Jenny, especially after she'd warned her not to keep the books? How could she have been so stupid? And what about Anne and Michael? They'd been so amazingly generous to her, the last thing she wanted to do was upset them.

"There's one more thing," Elizabeth said quietly, looking down at herself as she adjusted her top, to cover the crucifix. "I don't want you hanging around with Jennifer anymore. I know you like each other, but you've shown yourself to be a bad influence on her. You can't be trusted, and for her sake, you're not to have anything more to do with her. As harsh as it sounds, you'll soon be forgotten."

Hot tears cascaded down Nicola's cheeks and she wiped them away. "I'll leave tomorrow morning, but you can't stop me being friends with Jenny."

Elizabeth got to her feet and said calmly, "I can, and I will." She walked towards the door.

"Whatever you're thinking of doing, it won't work," Nicola said, through a barrage of tears and snot. "Jenny won't stop being my friend because you tell her to."

Elizabeth glanced back, her expression pitiful. "I know my sister, Nicola. And as much as she claims to care for you, she cares for herself an awful lot more. When given the opportunity to save her own skin, I have no doubt she'll take it." She opened the door and walked away.

❖

"So, you have my number and I'll wait for your call in the morning. Okay?" Jack asked, as they waited by the door.

Nicola nodded. She knew she should feel some sort of relief that she had somewhere to stay, but the prospect of telling Jenny and then talking to Anne and Michael only filled her with dread. "Thank you so much, Jack." She shifted the bouquet of flowers she held and gave him a one-armed hug.

"She's arrived," he said, as they pulled away from each other. "It's going to be all right."

Nicola wasn't listening. She looked out the glass as pain stabbed through her heart. Jenny stood waiting at their usual rendezvous spot, oblivious to the fact that in a few minutes her world was going to crumble to pieces.

"I'll see you bright and early tomorrow, Jack."

"Good luck. And remember, if anything goes wrong, I'm in all night. You can come over whenever." He gave her a gentle pat on the shoulder.

Unable to take any reassurance from his kind support, she drew a deep breath and braced herself. She couldn't put it off any longer. She left the store and walked over to Jenny.

"Jeez, that is one massive bunch of flowers," Jenny said with a smile. "Are they for me? How romantic."

Nicola couldn't breathe, let alone reply. She practically ran away but Jenny quickly followed at her heels.

"Nic, what's up?" Jenny asked, her voice worried and airy as she tried to catch up. "Did I say something wrong? I was only joking about the flowers."

Nicola continued to flee, her emotions choking her into silence.

How could she do this to Jenny?

How could she say what happened?

Worse still, what would happen as a result?

"Christ, Nic, you're scaring me." Jenny rushed in front of her, blocking her path. "What the hell's happened?"

Nicola had no choice but to stop in her tracks. She looked into Jenny's eyes and knew what she was about to say could end their relationship. "Elizabeth came into the store tonight to confront me." She watched as Jenny's eyes bulged. "While we were at school today, she went through my things and found the books and DVDs. She knows I'm gay, so it was pointless trying to deny it. She asked if you knew."

"Nic—"

"I told her no—"

"What?"

"—and she believed me—at least, I think she believed me." She blew out a breath. "She also knows we lied about my mum being in Australia because she phoned my house."

Jenny paled before Nicola's eyes. Her mouth gaped. She looked faint.

"She gave me an ultimatum, Jenny. I leave for good first thing tomorrow and tell you and your parents a fake reason why tonight, or she tells them I'm a lesbian and you lied and manipulated them to get them to let me stay."

Jenny's legs buckled. Nicola reached out for her, but the stupid flowers got in the way. She quickly shifted the flowers so she could hold a hand out to Jenny.

"Don't touch me," Jenny said, turning her head away from Nicola's hand.

The stark rejection punched her in the gut. Nicola pulled her hand away and fought off yet more tears. "Tomorrow morning, I'm going to move my stuff over to Jack's flat. You should know, she also said we can't be friends anymore, and we have to stop seeing each—"

"Stop!" Jenny scrambled to her feet but looked wobbly. Her fists were clenched, and she was actually biting down on one. "I told you not to keep those fucking stupid books and DVDs. I told you, Nic."

Nicola felt stabs of guilt pierce her. "I know you did—"

"But you had to have it your way. And now she knows you're a lesbian, so in the space of a few days, *everyone's* going to know. And

it won't take long for people to put two and two together and think—"
Jenny closed her eyes and took some deep breaths, as if trying to stop
herself from being sick.

"I honestly don't think she suspects you of—"

"You don't think she suspects me? You don't know how her mind
works! She's never just going to let it go. When she suspects me of
anything, she never, ever lets go, so this—*this is fucking huge!* Don't
you get it? Everything is ruined now!" Jenny spun and stormed off.

Nicola raced after her. "Jenny, please stop." Jenny ignored her,
but she refused to give up, even if it meant talking to Jenny's back.
"We need to talk about this. We need to talk about us and what's going
to—"

"Us?" Jenny spun around so quickly, Nicola actually bumped
into her. The look Jenny gave was one of such vehemence, it made
Nicola stumble backwards. "There is no us, Nic. You've seen to that.
Whatever *this* was"—Jenny gestured between them—"we agreed to
keep it a secret. But within two weeks you've been outed, and now I've
got to try and stop the same happening to me. Well done," Jenny said,
slowly clapping her hands. "Great job, Nic. Very fucking discreet."

Nicola wiped away angry tears with her sleeve. "She said you'd
be like this, but I didn't believe her. I guess she does know you better
than I do." Jenny wouldn't move, so Nicola walked around her and
called back over her shoulder, "I've had my fill of O'Connor shit
today. So screw you too, Jenny."

Gutted didn't even begin to describe how she was feeling as
she walked away. Her heart hurt—actual physical pain—as if it was
tearing in her chest. Each breath she took burned as she struggled to
draw it over the molten lump of emotion wedged in her throat. Every
time she tried to swallow or breathe, more boiling tears poured from
her eyes.

Jenny's voice replayed, over and over again. *There is no us, Nic.
You've seen to that.*

Was it true?

Had their relationship already ended, before it had really begun?

A hand grabbed her arm and pulled her harshly backwards. Nicola
cried out in surprise and watched as the flowers fell to the ground.
As she turned to face the person behind her, she glanced down at the

hand painfully clasping her arm. She felt glad the grip was strong and unrelenting, but…"You're hurting me, Jenny."

Jenny lightened her grip slightly but didn't let go. Her eyes burned fiercely in her flushed face. Her nostrils flared with each quickened breath, her jaws clenched tight.

Nicola had never seen Jenny look so furious or so incredible sexy. Her vision faltered, and the familiar ache of arousal settled between her legs. "It's getting late. I have to speak to your parents before they go to bed." She waited for a response from Jenny, but after a long moment passed, it was clear she wasn't going to get one. "I don't know what else you want me to do or say."

Jenny swallowed hard and winced. "I love you. I don't want you to go."

"I know," Nicola said softly. "But this isn't going away. I have to leave tomorrow."

"But—"

"There's no way around it. If I don't, Elizabeth will tell your parents. I won't have them hurt or you blamed because of me."

Jenny closed her eyes. "Maybe I should tell Elizabeth the truth."

"That would only make things a million times worse. She'd tell everyone, Jenny. Everyone at school would know—"

"Screw everyone at school."

"You say that now, but they could make your life miserable. And it would only be a matter of time until your parents found out. We both agreed we wouldn't hurt them with this."

"Shit," Jenny said, rubbing a temple with her free hand. "What do we do, then?"

"I tell your parents tonight and I go to Jack's in the morning." Nicola gently stroked Jenny's cheek. "And then we don't see each other for a while—" Jenny started to speak, but Nicola placed a finger softly over her lips. "It'll give us both time to think things through and see how we feel, without us hurting anyone. Eventually, Elizabeth will have to go back to university, and then we can talk."

Jenny moved her face away from Nicola's finger. "You're putting us on a break?"

"I suppose I am," Nicola said with a humourless laugh. "But isn't that better than splitting us up?" Jenny refused to answer, so Nicola continued. "It might only be a few weeks. And at the end of it, you'll be able to decide whether our relationship is worth the sacrifices or not."

Jenny let go of her arm and stepped back. "I'll decide?" she asked, her tone accusing. "How can you put this on me?"

"You're the one who has the most to lose." Nicola bent down and picked up the flowers. "I don't have any friends or family who can get hurt by this." *But it is killing me, and I'm terrified you'll decide you don't love me anymore.* Nicola tried to ignore her thoughts and glanced down at her watch. "Look, it's getting late. Please, let's not waste any more time fighting about this. Let's do what we have to, okay?"

Jenny's shoulders slumped, and Nicola knew that meant she'd accepted the inevitable. Unable to stop herself, she pulled Jenny into one final tight embrace. She tried to record everything to memory… the smell of her and the feel of being held in her arms. Try as she might, she couldn't shake the feeling this might be their final private embrace.

Telling Anne she was leaving was one thing, but trying to get her to accept it? A different thing altogether. It was clear Anne was hurt, and the flowers did little to help. While she tried to convince Anne and Michael that leaving was for the best, and that she would be perfectly safe, Jenny stood silently in the doorway brooding. In the end, there was actually nothing Anne and Michael could do to prevent her from leaving. It took a while, but Anne begrudgingly accepted it. There were hugs, fairly emotional goodbyes, and an open invitation for her to come back and stay at any time.

That was it.

Her time with the O'Connor family was almost up.

In the morning, she would leave for good.

Nicola masked her feelings well, but Jenny ended up leaving the room, seemingly unable to deal with the situation. Elizabeth was there too, and although she hadn't spoken, her smug smirk made her feelings perfectly clear.

Nicola packed up her belongings, while Jenny printed the photos of her back so she could take them with her. They hadn't really spoken since arriving at the house…but then, there wasn't anything to say.

Jenny offered the photos to her. "I want you to promise me you won't go through with your plan to confront him."

Nicola carefully slipped the photos into one of her books to protect them from damage, then packed the book away too.

"Nic, promise me," Jenny said, her face etched with worry.

Nicola looked into Jenny's eyes and told a barefaced lie: "I promise." Even with the two crossed fingers behind her back, she felt guilty. "Jack's fine with it and his mum said I'm fine to stay as long as I need to. The only reason I planned to confront Chris was because my time here was running out. Now, I have someplace else to stay, so I don't need to confront him or go home." She forced a smile before glancing down to zip up her bag.

She'd damn well still confront him. It was her home and her mum. His time of freeloading and taking what belonged to her was almost over. But her decision to do it Thursday had changed. Without Jenny's help, she was too vulnerable. Her plan was to leave it until her mum's next shift pattern. That would give her enough time to talk to Jack and see if she could persuade him to help.

"Right. That's everything. I'm packed and ready to go tomorrow," she said, looking up at Jenny. "Will you help me make up a bed on the floor?"

Jenny folded her arms. "You're not sleeping on the floor."

"Jenny, I have to. She made it perfectly clear. If she barges in here and sees I'm not, things are only going to get worse."

"You're not spending our last night together sleeping on the floor. We'll set everything up on the floor, but you're sleeping next to me tonight."

Nicola shook her head. "And when she takes us by surprise and sees that—"

"There's no way I'll be able to sleep, Nic. So let me hold you tonight—I need to be with you, and I'll keep watch. If I hear anyone get up to go to the bathroom, I'll wake you up. Okay?"

"All right."

They made up a bed on the floor—a sleeping bag, a pillow, and a couple of blankets. Just as they'd finished, they heard the creak on the landing. Nicola dropped to the floor and Jenny dived onto her bed. A moment later, an abrupt knock sounded on the door before Elizabeth burst in. She looked down at Nicola and then across at Jenny. After a few more seconds, she turned and left without saying anything.

"I fucking hate her," Jenny said angrily once the door was shut.

Nicola got up and walked over to the bed. "Maybe I should sleep on—"

"No." Jenny shuffled over and patted the duvet. "Come on."

Nicola lay down but made sure she was facing the door, just in case. Jenny snuggled closer, wrapped her arms around her, and gently spooned her.

"Relax, Nic," Jenny whispered in her ear. "I'll look after you."

The stress of the day had clearly taken its toll because exhaustion smothered her. She resigned herself to a sleepless night but dozed off a few minutes later.

When she awoke, daylight was shining into the room. She turned her head and saw Jenny, already awake and watching her. She looked dishevelled, and the dark bags under her eyes suggested she hadn't really slept.

The tension between them was unmistakable and impossible to ignore. Nicola quickly decided she couldn't bear to drag out the pain of leaving. She skipped a shower and dressed quickly, all while Jenny watched her in silence. She called a taxi and picked up her bags. Time to leave.

As she headed to the door, Jenny rushed over to her and begged her not to leave. It took all of Nicola's strength to deny her. She promised it would only be a few weeks, and then they could talk things through. Jenny looked so vulnerable that Nicola worried about leaving her but knew she had no choice. With a final kiss, she pulled away and left, refusing to look back and knowing Jenny wouldn't follow.

Downstairs, Anne told her off for booking a taxi and not accepting a lift. She gave Anne and Michael one last hug before heading outside into the humid morning. As she walked down the driveway and waited on the pavement, she could feel Jenny's gaze burning into her back, willing her to look back up one last time. She couldn't do it. She clung to the tiny amount of resolve she had left, feeling it corrode beneath the assault of jumbled emotions inside her.

When the taxi pulled up, she practically threw her bags at the driver and scrambled into the back of the car. A few seconds later, they pulled away, and she sent Jack a text telling him she was on her way.

Only then did she finally allow herself to break down.

CHAPTER THIRTY-ONE

Jenny watched helplessly as Nicola climbed into the taxi. She pressed a trembling hand against the bedroom window. She wanted to hammer on the cool glass, to scream and shout to get Nicola's attention. She needed to see her face one more time.

But Nicola never looked up, and before Jenny could open her mouth or raise her hand in one last feeble attempt, the car had sped off.

Time passed, but she remained at the window, unable to move. What was the point? She watched as her dad left for work first, and then her mum followed shortly afterwards.

The silence was deafening, and so she easily picked up on the soft creak of footsteps on the landing. She waited for the knock on her door, which came, but she didn't respond. A few seconds later, Elizabeth knocked again, this time louder. Jenny kept her gaze focused on the view outside her window, looking at nothing in particular.

The door eventually opened, but Jenny didn't turn around. The tread of soft footsteps crossed over the threshold, then abruptly stopped.

Elizabeth cleared her throat. "Jennifer, you need to get ready. You'll be late for school." Her voice was surprisingly meek. "I'll give you a lift."

Jenny didn't move, speak, or even blink. Her anger, which had been raging away to such an extent it had almost reached full-blown fury, had been replaced by a stark numbness. She literally felt nothing. Bad sign. The only other time she'd experienced something similar was when she'd found her gran and in the months that had followed. When and if she did start to feel again, it was going to hurt like a bitch.

"I thought I'd pick you up after school—if you'd like? We could go out and do something. Maybe get something to eat and have a chat. It's my treat, so you can choose…" After a few more minutes of silence, Elizabeth changed tack. "Jennifer, I know you're upset about her leaving, but that's not an excuse to ignore me. Don't be rude."

Jenny heard the steps that came towards her and sensed the hand before it touched her shoulder, but she didn't tense or move at Elizabeth's touch.

"Jennifer, stop this," Elizabeth said, worry, rather than annoyance, in her voice.

No reply.

She moved to Jenny's side. "Look at me." When she refused, Elizabeth gently cupped Jenny's chin and turned her face towards her.

Jenny finally looked at her sister. From all appearances, Elizabeth was distressed. Instead of brimming with her usual overzealous energy, she seemed deflated. And under Jenny's unrelenting gaze, she hugged her arms protectively and shrank back.

"Uh…go shower and then get dressed. I'll wait for you downstairs."

Jenny watched as Elizabeth hurried out of the room. Under normal circumstances, she would have found it amusing to see Elizabeth back down. Not today.

As she surveyed the room, the severity of the situation began to dawn on her, which in turn made her begin to feel again. Loneliness unlike anything she'd ever experienced hit her square in the chest.

Nicola and her belongings were gone, leaving only the faint lingering scent of her perfume behind. Resounding echoes of vivid and vibrant memories they'd shared crushed her already sore heart until it all became unbearable.

"What have I done?" she whispered to herself, grieving Nicola's loss so acutely she couldn't bear to stay in the room.

Blinded by her need to escape, she stripped and pulled on the nearest clothes she could find, which ended up being a pair of baggy jeans and a black T-shirt. Without checking her reflection or brushing her hair, she picked up her bag and practically ran from the room. She rushed down the stairs, tore open the front door, and hurried down the drive, all the while ignoring Elizabeth's shouts of protest. When she was certain she'd gotten far enough away and Elizabeth wasn't following, she slowed down and caught her breath. She had no idea what to do next. Her mind seemed hell-bent on tormenting her with loud, blunt questions she couldn't tune out, no matter how hard she tried. Lost in thought, she walked aimlessly, letting her feet take her where they wanted to go. Where she ended up shocked her system.

Gran's house.

She stared in disbelief at the house she hadn't seen in over three years—she'd refused to return after the funeral. The house looked pretty much the same as she remembered it, with the exception of having a new lick of paint and the absence of Gran's hanging basket of flowers out front. She fought an irrational urge to cross over and knock on the door as if, by sheer will, she could conjure up a miracle and Gran would answer.

"Shit, that hurts." She gripped a handful of skin on her chest and squeezed to relieve the pain that stabbed her heart. It failed. Two harsh flicks of the band on her wrist helped to force herself to walk away, even though part of her still wanted to go knock—the same part that refused to delete Gran's old phone number. With every new phone, she transferred the contact name and number over. She knew it was beyond ridiculous because she knew the number by heart. More ludicrous still, because neither the number nor the person she wanted to speak to existed any longer.

"I'm fucking mental," she whispered angrily, under her breath.

The more she walked, the more her mind raced, and the more she hurt. She tried to convince herself she should deal with her thoughts and emotions like a civilized person, but old habits died hard, and the desire for a quick fix ended up being too hard to resist.

After being refused service from four different stores because she had no ID and looked like an underage tramp, she finally managed to bribe a weird old guy to go buy what she wanted. It cost her ten quid for the privilege, but she was rewarded with a bottle of vodka, which she safely stowed in her bag. She ignored her mobile phone, which rang six times. The caller ID listed the home phone and Elizabeth's mobile. On the seventh time, she switched it off.

She came across a deserted bench next to a canal and decided to sit. The need for release was already consuming her, eating away at her like maggots at a rotten core. Loneliness filled her to the brim. She flicked the band three times in quick succession, flinching at each painful sting. It didn't help. The compulsion to hurt herself continued to fester away inside.

She took out the bottle, unscrewed the cap, and raised it to her lips, drinking deeply. The neat alcohol burned as it went down. She heaved but persevered, needing the sensational void into which she'd eventually fall.

She desperately wanted to phone Nicola, to hear her voice, but she couldn't bring herself to do it. What could she say? Nothing had changed and she had no answers.

She took another long pull from the bottle.

She wanted a future with Nicola, but in choosing that life, people would get hurt. In the end, she decided her parents' pain once they found out trumped her own. The answer was elusive.

Thoughts of Nicola hurt so much, even the anaesthetic numbness from the alcohol couldn't block it out. A gaping, raw hole occupied the place where her heart had once been.

She drank more, her thoughts sluggish. Something else had been bothering her, and she used the alcohol to shove it to the forefront of her mind.

Why had she ended up at her gran's house?

Maybe her subconscious wanted a trip down memory lane, but it felt like something more than pining for the past. For the first time in years, she wanted to actually talk to her gran, instead of begging her for forgiveness. She wanted to talk to her about Nicola and hear her advice on everything. This transformation in the way she now thought about Gran and her role in her death was huge, and the change had started when she'd confessed to Nicola.

Perhaps I've actually started to forgive myself?

Or maybe I no longer believe I need to be forgiven.

The thought offered a tiny shred of light in an otherwise pitch-black scenario.

She missed both Gran and Nicola desperately—the two people she loved most in the world. She wondered what they would have made of each other and couldn't help but smile. They'd have gotten on like a house on fire. No doubt about it.

"I wonder what you'd make of this whole gay thing…" she said, squinting as she looked up into the sky. Her gut feeling said Gran would've been fine with it, as long as it meant Jenny was happy.

Jenny recalled their frequent heart-to-hearts. Gran always reminisced about Grandad, about how much she loved and missed him. He'd died six years before Jenny was born, but she always felt like she kinda knew him, thanks to Gran's countless stories.

Gran had been widowed for nearly twenty years, but she'd flat out refused to consider finding someone new, even for company's sake. It used to frustrate Jenny because she knew Gran was lonely, deep down. But now she had personal insight.

Although it had only been a few hours, she still wanted to be with Nicola more than anything in the world. She couldn't imagine this need lessening with time. It hadn't for Gran. It was the sign of real love. The memories engulfed her mind, body, and soul. She found herself grieving for their house, their children, and the dog they'd dreamt up together—a future she feared would never happen.

She had a few weeks in which to reach her decision, and hurting herself or getting stoned or off her tits on alcohol was not the way forward. She needed to focus, strategize, weigh every single option so she could make informed decisions. This new outlook empowered her and gave her a purpose, a mission. She was ready for the challenge, totally psyched. And then, she was spectacularly sick. Twice.

She wiped her mouth on the back of her hand and looked around. Fortunately, the canal path remained deserted. She grabbed her bag but chose to leave the half-empty bottle of vodka where it was and stood up straight, which only made the vertigo worse. She ended up being violently sick again.

In the back of her mind, panic stirred.

Did she know the way home?

Could she make it by herself in this state?

God, she needed Nicola.

She took her time staggering along, avoiding people and cursing the unrelenting heat as the sun beat down on her and made her feel a hundred percent worse. Eventually, she recognized familiar streets and made her way home.

She stumbled into Elizabeth's car, which was parked in the driveway.

"Shit," she slurred. She rummaged inside her bag for her door keys and then spent the next few minutes trying to get the wrong key into the lock. She must have made a racket because the door swung open and Elizabeth stood, glaring down at her.

"Where have you been? Why haven't you been answering your phone? Have you been drinking? You have, haven't—"

Jenny didn't have time to respond because the urge to be sick became her most pressing concern. She shoved Elizabeth aside, scrambled up the stairs, and barricaded herself in the bathroom.

Later, she crawled away from the toilet bowl, picked up her bag, and staggered to her room. With blurred vision, she gazed around the deserted room. Her heart ached again. She pulled the duvet from the bed and onto the floor. She couldn't sleep in the bed. Not without Nicola.

It was only a matter of time until she had to rush back to the bathroom to continue being ill. When she eventually went back to her door, she found a pint of water and a plastic basin waiting for her. Her initial thought was to ignore them—she didn't want to accept anything from Elizabeth. But after a few seconds of drunken deliberation, she picked up the glass and took a well-needed gulp of water. Begrudgingly, she also picked up the basin and returned to her makeshift bed.

CHAPTER THIRTY-TWO

The taxi pulled up outside the store, and Nicola paid the driver and told him to keep the change. He thanked her, opened the trunk, and started lifting her bags out.

"I'll take them off you, mate."

Nicola watched as Jack took all the bags from the driver. She'd never felt so grateful to see him.

He smiled sombrely. "Come on. Let's go in and have a chat."

Nicola didn't trust herself to speak for fear of bursting into tears again. Jack led the way up the stairs and into his flat. Nicola was relieved to see it was relatively clean. The last time she'd been inside, it had been rather filthy.

Subtly, she covered her nose, fighting the burning sensation in her nostrils that was caused by the pungent smell of apple air freshener that hung in the air like a thin mist.

Jack led them to the spare bedroom door and struggled to turn the handle with his elbow. Unable to watch him suffer, she reached past him and opened the door.

"Thanks," he said. He managed to make it through the doorway and carefully shrugged off the bags.

Nicola followed closely behind and was pleasantly surprised by the room. A comfy looking double bed made a welcoming focal point, complemented by a wardrobe, a chest of drawers, and a full-length mirror. A small flat-screen TV rested atop the drawers. A relatively basic room, yes, but clean and spacious. She liked it. "It's lovely, Jack."

He blushed and shoved his hands inside his pockets. "It's not how I would've decorated, obviously, but you know what my mum's like." He pointed to the drawers. "There are some clean towels in there, but they don't match. Sorry."

She wrapped her arms around him, needing some physical comfort. With her head buried against his chest, she said, "Thank you so much, Jack. I'd nowhere else to go."

He tightened the hug and said, "You know you're welcome here, anytime."

She burst into tears and made to pull away, but Jack kept her close.

"It's okay," he said in a soothing tone. "Let it all out."

A few seconds later she pulled away and wiped her face with both hands. Embarrassment and self-consciousness battled for space in her chest. "Sorry. I'm a bit upset."

Jack smiled. "Let's go have a cup of tea, and you can fill me in on everything."

She followed him into the living room and sat on the sofa while he made the drinks. Although emotionally drained and reluctant to go through it all again, Jack deserved to be updated.

"Here you go." He handed her a cup and then took a seat. "So?"

She avoided looking directly at him as she described the events of last night and the morning. He listened silently. Once she'd finished, he asked questions.

"If you don't mind me saying, it sounds like Jenny was happy for you to take all the blame," Jack said, putting his cup down. "That's shitty."

Nicola shook her head, even though secretly…she kinda thought the same thing. "I don't know what to say…I love her so much. I'm so scared I'm going to lose her." Tears welled up in her eyes once again, but she didn't have the energy to cry.

Jack's expression softened. "She'll come to her senses. She'd have to be crazy to let you get away." A pause. "You look awful."

Nicola snorted, a mixture of a laugh and a sob at the same time. "Thanks."

Jack smiled. "Go get a few hours' sleep. I'll wake you for our shift."

"Okay." She stood, checked her phone for the millionth time, to no avail, and then headed to the bedroom.

"After some rest, it'll all seem better. If you need anything, give me a shout."

Nicola glanced back, forced a weak smile, and lied. "I'm starting to feel better already."

Once inside the room, she closed the door and lay on top of the bedcovers, not having the strength to change out of her clothes.

She looked at her phone again. Nothing. She needed one text or call, just to know Jenny was okay. To reassure her Jenny actually cared enough to check if *she* was okay. After fifteen minutes of staring at the blank screen, her eyelids grew heavy. She checked the volume was on the loudest setting and placed the phone within hand's reach.

I love her so much.

I can't bear the thought of losing her.

Just one text or a phone call, that's all I need...

She drifted to sleep.

She chose to ignore all of Jack's three attempts to wake her by feigning sleep until he eventually gave up and left her alone. She felt guilty but couldn't face going through the motions of pretending to be okay. She heard him leave for their shift and responded by wrapping the duvet even more tightly around her.

The night had been exhausting and insomnia ruled. Once the darkened sky started to lighten, Nicola drew back the curtains and returned to bed to watch the sunrise. Her head hurt from churning things over until her emotions were frayed and unstable. One minute, hot bitter anger sluiced through her veins as she remembered how Elizabeth had treated her and the less-than-satisfactory response from Jenny. The next minute, terrible guilt slammed her for having put Jenny in such an awkward situation. But mostly, she felt afraid and lonely.

The sound of movement from the living room broke her depressive thought cycle. She decided to get out of bed and face Jack.

"Did I wake you? I'm sorry, I tried to be quiet," Jack said, as he tied his laces.

Nicola sat down with a sigh. "You didn't wake me. I've been up since five."

He winced. "I guess that answers my next question about how well you slept. I'm heading out for a run if you fancy joining me."

Nicola couldn't think of anything more unappealing, except for the thought of facing Elizabeth again. "I'll pass," she said. "Thanks for the offer though. How long will you be? I'll make us some breakfast."

"I should be back in half an hour and then I'll grab a quick shower." He hesitated and blushed. "Uh—I need to nip downstairs to get us some food in."

She waved a hand dismissively and said, "I'll find us something." Jack looked unconvinced, but she insisted. "Go on. Go for your run."

"Okay." He plugged headphones into his ears and, with one final cheesy grin, left.

Nicola headed into the kitchen where her faith in producing a decent breakfast waned. Dust and clutter filled every cupboard, although some were worse than others. The sell-by dates on the flour and spices had passed a good few months ago.

She salvaged a large onion from a dark corner and deemed it edible. Hope greeted her when she opened the fridge, in the form of a huge box of eggs, milk, three rashers of bacon, and half a bag of grated cheese—all still in date. Bacon, onion, and cheese omelette would do.

She prepared the ingredients but ended up having to dismiss the milk, as it smelled unhealthily sour. She began cooking, and a few minutes later Jack returned, sweating and out of breath. He crowded into the kitchen and perused the counter. "What are we having?"

"Nothing, until you've showered. Don't you dare sweat near this food," Nicola said, feigning a spatula swat.

He jumped out the way and laughed. "Okay. Here. Consider these a peace offering." He placed a carton of orange juice and a bottle of fresh milk on the counter.

"Thanks. Go shower and it'll be ready when you get out," she said, turning her attention back to the frying pan.

"Yes, boss."

She turned to swipe at him again, but he was too fast. The omelette smelled delicious, and Nicola was surprised to feel her stomach rumble in response.

Must only be my heart that feels like it's dying.

"That really does smell amazing," Jack said, as he reappeared minutes later dressed in white board shorts and a blue polo shirt. He took a seat and marvelled at the plate in front of him.

"Bacon, cheese, and onion omelette," Nicola said. "Go ahead. Tuck in." Her intention was to warn him to be careful because it was hot, but he had already shovelled a forkful into his mouth.

"Delicious," he mumbled, shovelling in another steaming forkful.

Nicola smiled. It was nice to cook for someone and have him appreciate it. She carried her plate to the table and sat. "Why do you have so many eggs?"

Jack poured himself a glass of orange juice. "I like eggs. Would you like some?" He lifted the carton.

"Thanks." She watched him fill her glass. "I gathered you liked them, from the sheer amount of them in your fridge. Would you eat them all?"

He nodded enthusiastically. "Not all at once, obviously, but yeah, they'd probably last me three or four days. They're easy to cook."

Nicola resisted the urge to tease him further. She suspected he didn't have much cause to cook for anyone other than himself, and that she could relate to.

❖

Jack went to work his day shift, leaving her to contemplate what to do with her day and possibly the rest of her life. She had no intention of going to school—of that she was certain. After ten minutes of torturing herself with thoughts of Jenny, she could stand no more. She jumped up and glanced around the room helplessly, and then her gaze settled on the kitchen. She suddenly knew exactly how to spend the next few hours, and none of it involved thinking.

She searched through all the cupboards but didn't find anything of use. She decided to repay Jack's kindness by cleaning his kitchen like it had—obviously—never been cleaned before. She went down to the store, filled a basket with cleaning products, and after having a heated debate about who would pay, she suggested they go halves and Jack reluctantly agreed. She returned to the flat, donned protective gear—a dust mask, gloves—and set to work. She could obsess about Jenny just as easily with her hands occupied.

CHAPTER THIRTY-THREE

Daylight penetrated the curtains and forced Jenny to bury her head deeper beneath her pillow. She felt like shit, and the fact that it was self-inflicted only added to her misery. A rapid hammering shook the door before Elizabeth burst in.

She peered down at the makeshift bed on the floor with disgust. "You kept us all awake last night with your vomiting. I had to convince Mum and Dad you'd come home from school with a bug. And I had to phone school and lie, saying you were sick and wouldn't be in yesterday or today."

Jenny hoped if she pacified Elizabeth, maybe she'd go away. "Thanks for covering for me. I'm sorry," she said weakly.

Elizabeth folded her arms. "Sorry? The closest you get to sorry is what you're feeling for yourself right now. I phoned, and you deliberately ignored me. Where did you go? Who were you with?"

Jenny closed her eyes and took a deep breath to stop the room from spinning. Using a quiet tone and hoping Elizabeth might follow suit, she said, "I went by the canal alone and drank."

"Why should I believe you, Jennifer?"

"Why would I lie?"

"All you seem to do is lie. Do you actually expect me to believe you got into this state by yourself?"

"I'm telling the truth. You think I'm so stupid and pathetic, I can't manage to drink alone?" Jenny said, squinting up.

Elizabeth didn't look convinced. "You really were on self-destruct yesterday, weren't you?" The question must've been rhetorical, because she didn't wait for a response. "You dropped these on the stairs." She held out a packet of cigarettes. "Do you know what would happen if Mum and Dad came across these?"

Jenny remained silent, resisting the urge to laugh bitterly. She hadn't smoked for nearly a week. Her parents discovering that she *used to* smoke was the least of her worries.

Elizabeth tossed the packet onto Jenny's bed. "Get up and sort yourself out. We need to talk."

Jenny massaged her temples. "Not today—"

"Yes, today," Elizabeth said. "I'll be downstairs, waiting." She stalked towards the door and glanced back. "Why are you sleeping on the floor like an animal?"

"I always sleep on the floor when I'm ill. It grounds me," Jenny lied. "Stops the room from spinning as much."

Elizabeth frowned. "I don't understand why you feel it necessary to poison your body with alcohol and tobacco. The way you treat God's precious and loving gift of life is disgusting. You need to sort yourself out, Jennifer. For good. It's getting ridiculous."

Jenny nodded, then fought the fresh stab of vertigo.

"I'll be waiting."

"Where the fuck is my phone?" Jenny demanded furiously as she burst into the living room.

Elizabeth's eyebrows narrowed. "What are you talking about?"

"You thieving bitch. Give it back now!" Jenny fought to hold back the tears born of both anger and frustration. "I need it back, Elizabeth." She'd searched everywhere. Twice. She'd tried phoning it from the house phone, but it remained switched off. She'd thought herself clever yesterday for not writing Nicola's number down anywhere else, but now she realized she'd been plain stupid. Her phone was gone and so was Nicola's number. She had no way of getting in touch with her unless she went by her work.

"Stop swearing, Jennifer. Why on earth would I take your phone?" Elizabeth asked nonchalantly.

Elizabeth's response made Jenny question her accusation, but if Elizabeth hadn't taken it, then she was screwed. She slumped down on the sofa and covered her face with her hands.

"You were in a dreadful state yesterday. Perhaps you dropped it, like you did your cigarettes," Elizabeth said, sipping from her cup. "Have you tried calling it?"

"I switched it off."

"Have you got an old phone you can use?" Elizabeth asked in a sickeningly helpful tone.

Jenny gritted her teeth and nodded.

"Well, that's good, Jennifer. Look, I know you're feeling delicate, but we do need to talk."

Jenny folded her arms. Her anger with and dislike of Elizabeth were back, full force. If Elizabeth wanted a chat, Jenny wasn't going to hold back.

"I know you've been acting out because Nicola left—"

"She didn't leave. You forced her to go." Satisfaction coursed through Jenny at the flicker of surprise on Elizabeth's face. "You should be ashamed of yourself."

"Did she tell you...?"

"That she's gay? Yeah, she did."

Elizabeth looked flummoxed. "Well, then you know why I asked her to leave."

Jenny clenched her fists. "We both know you didn't ask her, you blackmailed her, so cut the crap. Secondly, the only reason she needed to go is because you're a bigoted, bitchy bully. Ever since you came back, you've wanted her gone. You refused to get to know her and see how amazing she is."

Elizabeth placed her cup down and turned to fully face her, clearly riled. "She lied to everyone. She was a bad influence, Jennifer. You can't honestly tell me you're okay with her being a lesbian."

Jenny gave a humourless smile. "I'm more than okay with it."

"But she's—"

"An amazing person!" Jenny snapped, her temper bubbling ever nearer the surface. "She's selfless, caring, brave, intelligent, and being with her made me feel happier than I've ever been. You took one aspect of her life, her sexuality, and you purposely chose to ignore the rest. How very fucking Christian of you."

Elizabeth jumped to her feet. "Don't make me out to be the bad guy—"

"You are the bad guy!" Jenny stood and held Elizabeth's stare. "You always are!" She scoffed, shook her head. "Why do you hate me so much?"

Elizabeth looked stupefied by the accusation and it took her a few seconds to speak. "You don't honestly believe I hate you?" When Jenny refused to reply, Elizabeth took a step forward and reached out to her.

"Don't." Jenny evaded her touch. "You have to stop blaming me. Can't you see I've punished myself enough for both of us? I've lived with the guilt every second of every fucking day," Jenny said hoarsely, her raw emotions forced to the forefront. "Stop *punishing* me, Elizabeth, because it's killing me."

"Punishing you?" Elizabeth whispered, softly shaking her head. She actually started to cry.

Jenny swallowed hard. "You've made my life a living hell because you blame me for Gran's death, but you have to stop—"

"Jennifer, no!" Elizabeth said, her voice pleading. She closed the distance between them and took hold of Jenny's arms. "I swear to you, I've never, ever blamed you for what happened."

Jenny folded her arms, shrugged out of her sister's grip. "Then why have you been so evil to me all these years?"

"Evil, how?" Elizabeth asked, her despair palpable.

"The constant interference in my life, forcing me to be friends with Sarah and Corrina, even though I can't stand them. Telling me what I can and can't do."

"I've been looking after you, protecting you," Elizabeth said, through sobs and tears. "After what happened with Gran, I needed to make amends to you. I knew how it affected you, how broken you felt."

"Affected me? How could you possibly know how I felt, Elizabeth?" Jenny asked with frustration. "You don't even know me."

"Of course I know you—"

"No. You never have and you never will," Jenny said, clenching her fists tightly so her nails cut into her palms. "I've spent the past three years punishing myself every single day for Gran's death. You won't ever know what that was like. During the first year, whenever I closed my eyes I'd see her lying there dead on the kitchen floor. Did you know that?" Jenny demanded.

Elizabeth looked horrified at the revelation. Her lips were moving but only sobs came out.

"I was convinced everyone blamed me. Hell, I blamed myself," Jenny said, as pent-up bitterness seeped to the surface. "I had no one to talk to and nowhere to go. Drinking didn't even help drown the pain. So do you know how I ended up coping, Elizabeth? What I ended up doing—to myself—just to deal with it all?" As soon as the questions left her mouth she regretted them.

"Tell me," Elizabeth begged through a shower of snot and tears. "Please."

Jenny opened her mouth to tell her to forget it but hesitated. Elizabeth had never listened or tried to get to know her before. In fact, other than the screaming matches, mild threats, and blackmail, they'd never really had a personal conversation. Jenny sensed that what was happening between them right now was different. Perhaps in this instance they had an opportunity to forge some kind of sisterly bond—something that had always been missing and that she'd secretly longed for.

It was worth a shot.

"I cut myself," Jenny said quietly. She pulled down one side of her trousers to display the ugly reminders. "And I kept on doing it, until six months ago."

"Jennifer..." Elizabeth's expression was unreadable, her eyes fixated on the scars. "I never...I'm so sorry."

Jenny shrugged. "I'm having weekly counselling sessions and cognitive behaviour therapy to deal with it. But Mum and Dad obviously don't know—"

"I won't tell them, I promise," Elizabeth said. She wiped her face, smearing tears. "You shouldn't have gone through that all by yourself."

"What choice did I have?"

"I should have been there with you—"

"But you weren't."

"I should've been," Elizabeth insisted. "I should have talked to you about everything, made you understand it wasn't your fault. But I swear to you, everything I did, I honestly thought was helping you."

Jenny had never seen this side of Elizabeth before and it made her question everything.

Had she been wrong all this time?

Had Elizabeth really only been trying to help her, even though she'd actually done the exact opposite?

Her pain seemed genuine.

Jenny spread her arms wide. "How was always putting me down and making me look stupid, while you went and easily achieved every award and qualification, helping me?" Jenny asked, forcing herself not to look away. Elizabeth looked ugly when she cried.

"I was trying to encourage you." Elizabeth blew her nose unattractively on a gross-looking wad of tissue. "I thought if you saw what I could achieve, it would make you want the same." Her tone went stuffily nasal. "And it isn't easy, Jennifer. I have to work so hard, and now it's just expected that I'll get the best scores and come out on top. I get no free time—every waking moment, I'm studying, praying, or trying to keep fit. You don't know how envious I am of you."

Envious? What the hell? Shit had officially got weird.

"How can you be envious of me?" Jenny asked. "My life sucks."

Elizabeth shook her head fervently. "Everyone likes you for being you. Mum and Dad don't expect you to do well in exams—no offence."

Jenny waved a dismissive hand.

"You're popular. You always have loads of fun and you're so confident with guys..." Elizabeth blushed.

That's one way of putting it. Jenny sighed. "Then why interfere?"

"Because your judgement is impaired. You do stupid and dangerous things all the time without thinking through the consequences." Elizabeth sniffed loudly. "Like the time you took drugs—"

"Why won't you let that go? Jeez, it was one lousy mistake—"

"That nearly killed you, Jennifer." Elizabeth had finally stopped crying. Her face was blotchy, her nose bright red, and her eyes were puffy. "Everything I've done was to protect you, Mum, and Dad from getting hurt. All I've ever wanted is for you to be safe and happy. I'm sorry."

Jenny slumped back down onto one of the sofas. "I can forgive you for that," she said grudgingly, "but I can't forgive you for how you treated Nicola. That was shitty, Elizabeth. Really shitty."

"I guess…I'm not proud of myself." Elizabeth sat down opposite her. "But I still think she's a bad influence on you."

"Because she's gay?"

"No." Elizabeth chewed on her bottom lip. "Maybe."

"And there's the truth."

"You've always been easily swayed by other people, and she has some weird kind of hold on you. Don't look at me like that."

Jenny reduced the death glare and rolled her hand impatiently for Elizabeth to continue.

"Mum and Dad would freak out if they knew, especially because you shared a bed. And they'd be totally hurt by the lies you told them."

"Then don't tell them."

"I won't, providing you stop being friends with her."

Anger flared in Jenny's chest. "You're doing it again!"

"This is the final thing I'm going to insist on. Please. Agree to this and I'll make a conscious effort to back off from your life." Elizabeth held up her hands in defence. "I really will."

"I can't agree, Elizabeth, because it's complete bullshit."

Elizabeth sat back in the chair, lacing her fingers in front of her. "What is it about her? I've never known you to be this involved with someone before. Can't you see it's unhealthy? She's changed you. I can tell by your sulky expression you know what I'm saying is right."

Jenny sighed. Elizabeth would never understand, not unless she revealed everything, including Nicola's abuse, their relationship, and her own sexuality. And that wasn't going to happen. She gave one last attempt to show Elizabeth how much Nicola meant to her. "She did change me, but in a good way. For the first time ever, I cared about someone more than myself. I lied to Mum and Dad so she could stay here. I'm the bad influence, not her. I did it because I wanted to protect her—"

"From what?" When Jenny refused to answer, Elizabeth puffed out her cheeks in frustration. "Even now, after everything we've just said, you still won't tell me the truth about her. All I know is, she's shrouded in mystery and lies. You say you want to protect her? Then tell me what you're protecting her from. Can't you understand why your evasiveness worries me?"

Jenny looked at the floor and shrugged. To be fair, it all sounded dodgy, even to her own ears.

"There's a house party tonight, isn't there?"

Jenny blinked, surprised by the question and sudden change of subject. "Yeah, but I'm not going. I can't face drinking after yesterday."

"You should go, Jennifer. This evening will be the perfect opportunity for you to make up with your friends and for everything to go back to normal."

The idea of going to the party filled her with dread.

"I won't force you to go tonight, but I think it'll do you some good." Elizabeth picked up her cup, took a sip, and then grimaced. "Perhaps it will take your mind off things."

Jenny knew she had to go to the party for two reasons: to appease Elizabeth, yes, but more importantly, to see if she was prepared to give up her old life permanently for the sake of a new one with Nicola. Now or never. "Okay. I'll go."

❖

Elizabeth shouted up the stairs that Laura had arrived.

Jenny sat in her room, guilt ridden about Nicola. She should've phoned her yesterday when she'd had the chance. Instead, she'd put it off, and now she couldn't call. She gathered her things to leave and glanced at her reflection in passing. The old Jenny, wearing too much make-up and slutty clothes, stared back at her. It was like looking at someone she used to know but had never liked. She shouldered her bag and left her room.

Elizabeth stood in the hallway, preaching something at Laura, who shot Jenny a beseeching look.

"We're off, Elizabeth," Jenny said, interrupting politely. "I sent you a text with my number, and I've got the old brick—sorry, *phone*—with me. See you tonight."

"Have fun and be safe," Elizabeth warned, before heading back into the living room.

Once outside and walking down the driveway, Laura whispered, "Is Nicola okay? What's going on?"

Jenny's temper spiked from the lie she had to tell. "We've had an argument, which I don't want to discuss. She's moved out and we aren't speaking at the moment."

They walked in silence for a while.

"I understand you don't want to talk about her, but can you please give me Nicola's number? I need to talk to her."

Jenny halted abruptly. "What do you need to talk to her about?"

Laura's cheeks burned. "You don't want to know."

"We've fallen out, but I still care for her," Jenny said. "If there's something going on, you should tell me."

Laura squirmed, clearly uncomfortable.

"I might be able to help," Jenny persisted, trying to rein herself in, to appear coolly detached. "And if you don't tell me, I won't give you her number."

Laura gave a defeated sigh and Jenny knew she'd won. Laura never could cope under pressure.

"It's cruel and I wanted to warn her—"

"Warn her about what?" Jenny asked, trying to mask her growing sense of panic.

"There's a rumour going around about her. Even if it's true, which is fine with me if it is, I just think she has a right to know. So she can prepare herself—"

"What rumour?"

Laura cleared her throat. "It's that she's…a lesbian."

"Who told you that?"

"Corrina and Sarah. They didn't say where they'd heard it, but then, they never do. It's gone around the whole school. I honestly don't get what the big deal is. I thought she should know."

How the fuck could they know? Elizabeth! She'd promised Nicola she'd see to it their friendship was over. *Two-faced, manipulative bitch!*

"Jenny, are you okay?" Laura asked.

"Have they said anything else?"

Laura winced, making Jenny dread the answer.

"They said she tried to…you know, turn you. So you kicked her out. But I don't believe that. Nicola's lovely. It isn't true, is it?"

Jenny had never hated anyone as much as she hated Elizabeth right then.

"Jenny?"

"No. It isn't true."

Laura nodded, clearly relieved. "So what happened?"

Jenny started walking again and Laura struggled to match her pace. "I don't want to talk about it. But Nicola never tried anything with me. How dare they go around spouting shit when they haven't got a fucking clue."

"Will you tell Nicola?" Laura asked timidly, as if wary of receiving the brunt of Jenny's anger.

"Yeah. I've lost her number, but I'm going to try and sort it tomorrow."

"When you speak to her, please give her my number, and tell her I'm free if she ever wants a chat."

Jenny felt a stir of gratitude towards Laura and said, "I will. I'm sure she'll be grateful."

Jenny and Laura loitered outside the house.

"They're waiting for us in the kitchen. You sure you want to do this? We can go back to mine, if you want," Laura said quietly.

Jenny didn't reply, leading Laura into the house instead.

When they found the kitchen, she immediately spotted Sarah and Corrina. Anger clenched her stomach like an iron fist. Her heart hammered and her palms were sweaty.

Sarah spotted them first. "Look who it is."

Corrina turned and immediately glared. "So, where's the dyke?"

"Nicola isn't coming tonight," Laura said. "She's visiting a friend."

Jenny felt indebted to Laura and tried to convey her thanks with a nod.

"She's probably off trying to gay-rape someone else," Corrina said.

"Even I didn't guess she was a lesbo rapist," Sarah added.

Jenny's hands automatically clenched into fists. She fought to remain calm, but her temper reached an all-time high. "Nicola never tried to rape me. That's ridiculous."

"If it wasn't rape, then you must have wanted it," Sarah said bitterly. "Decided you've had enough men? First the school bike and now a dyke."

Corrina, Sarah, and a few other people in the kitchen erupted into laughter.

"Did she manage to turn you, then?" Corrina asked.

"She must have. Look, she keeps checking out your boobs," Sarah said, getting more laughter from the growing crowd.

Jenny staggered beneath her anger and humiliation. Her conscience screamed at her to defend Nicola, but in doing so, she knew she'd only succeed in making things more difficult for herself. She chose to remain quiet, hoping they'd stop, and hated herself for it.

"It's so disgusting to think I ever got changed in front of you. Or that we actually shared a bed. God knows what you were thinking and doing while I was asleep," Corrina said, dramatically shuddering for her audience.

"People like you and her should be locked up to protect the rest of us," Sarah said with equal disgust.

"I'm not gay," Jenny said, hearing the desperation in her own tone.

"I don't believe you," Corrina said.

A growing mass of bodies continued to surge into the small kitchen, making it hot and claustrophobic. The whispers and sideways looks amplified.

"Well, that's your fucking problem!" Jenny said, angrily.

"Prove it," Sarah said.

"Yeah," Corrina goaded, "Prove it."

"Fuck you." Jenny turned to leave but found herself facing a group of fifteen people or more.

"Oh, come on, Jenny. You never had a problem fucking guys before, so what's the problem now?" Corrina asked snidely from behind her.

The group whispered, laughed, pointed. She wanted to run and hide but there was no escape. The situation had quickly spiralled out of her control.

"Let's get out of here," Laura said quietly, clearly distressed by the turn of events.

Jenny shot glances—first one way, then the other—at people she'd seen before but didn't know. Strangers. Why was she trying to deny who she was to these people? The truth was, she loved Nicola. She wanted to spend her life with her. She wanted a future, with the house, children, and dog. But those dreams would never become reality if she didn't give their relationship a fighting chance.

In a little over a year, they'd both head off to university. She wouldn't see or keep in touch with any of the people surrounding her.

Did their scornful opinions really matter?

No…

No!

The answer was a sudden epiphany.

She spun back to face Corrina and Sarah. "You know what? I don't care what you think about me. And I don't have anything to prove to you."

Fury flared Corrina's nostrils. "Then you're a dyke."

Jenny smiled, which seemed to only infuriate them more. "Nicola never turned me. I'll let you in on a secret. It doesn't actually work that way in real life, only in your messed-up heads."

"She's a filthy dyke," Corrina said. "You betrayed us for some weirdo you didn't even know."

"A freak who tried to rape you, Jenny. That you kicked out of your house," Sarah said in frustration.

"She never tried to rape me and I didn't kick her out. She's gone to stay with a friend because Elizabeth's being a total bitch. You've been spreading malicious lies that my psychotic sister has fed you, and you lapped it up like brainless sheep."

Some of the crowd cheered, while others shouted comments at Corrina and Sarah, who looked stupefied.

"I love Nicola. And she loves me," Jenny declared. The whole room fell silent, but she lifted her chin and carried on, regardless. "I don't care what any of you think about us. And I'm not going to hide away because it makes you uncomfortable."

She turned to address no one in particular. "I'm not here to offend anyone. I want to be able to live my life with the person I love." She scanned the faces in the crowd, noting they all had similar expressions of surprise. "If you don't like it, that's your opinion, which you're entitled to. All I ask is you leave us alone, and we'll happily give you the same courtesy."

Silence.

She turned to Laura. "Ready to go?"

Laura nodded.

The crowd seemed to sense the drama was over and was already starting to disperse. Rumours and gossip were only exciting as long as there was an edge of secrecy and scandal to them.

"Laura, if you leave with her, that's the end of our friendship!" Corrina said.

The whole room stilled again and turned in unison.

"You need to decide, Laura. Them or us," Sarah said.

The room hung in a suspenseful silence. Laura shifted uncomfortably and gave an apologetic glance to Jenny before taking a step towards Corrina and Sarah.

Betrayal knifed Jenny, but she shouldn't have presumed Laura would just take her side.

"With friends like you," Laura said in a loud voice, smiling sweetly. "Who needs enemies?"

"Laura, don't be so—" Corrina started.

"Shut up and let me finish for once!" Laura yelled.

Corrina's mouth gaped in shock.

"You're not even friends with each other. Best friends don't give their best friend's younger brother a blowjob."

Gasps. Laughter.

"Or get off with their best friend's boyfriend while she's on holiday in Spain."

Whoops. Shoving.

Jenny watched with fascination as Laura's words struck blows. Corrina and Sarah simultaneously made the connections and lunged at each other, screaming insults and clawing away. The crowd surged forward to get a better view of the drama as it unfolded, and the chant of *Fight! Fight! Fight!* grew louder.

Laura grinned mischievously. "*Now* we can go."

They walked out into the cool evening air. Jenny turned to Laura and said, "There's loads I need to tell you, but I've got a favor to ask first."

"Sure."

"Can I please stay at yours tonight?"

Laura rolled her eyes. "Of course you're staying at mine." They walked a few more steps and Laura added, "I actually thought you might go through with letting them force you into sleeping with a guy."

Jenny laughed bitterly. "For a split second, I thought I'd go through with it too. But I love Nic too much. I need to ring Elizabeth—" As she took her phone out, she realized the huge mistake she'd made. "Shit!"

"What?" Laura asked, her brow creased with worry.

"I've been so stupid. Corrina's going to tell Claire and she'll immediately tell Elizabeth. Once she knows I've outed myself—I want to tell my mum and dad before she can twist it."

"Ring her now and tell her you're staying at mine. Don't worry about Corrina, I'll deal with her." Laura took out her own phone and walked a few feet away from Jenny

Jenny phoned Elizabeth, told her she was having an amazing time and was grateful she'd insisted on making her come. She asked if it was okay to stay at Laura's, and Elizabeth begrudgingly gave her permission.

With a triumphant grin, Laura explained she'd blackmailed Corrina into not saying anything to Claire. The two examples she'd mentioned earlier were only the tip of the iceberg of scandals she knew about.

Jenny hugged Laura. "You're amazing."

"I know I am. But right now, I want the full story," Laura said, stepping away from the embrace. "We've got a slow walk home. So start spilling."

Jenny started from the beginning and Laura listened in silence. They ended up getting back to Laura's house, changing into pyjamas, and lying on her bed, before Jenny actually finished talking.

"What are you going to do?" Laura asked, smiling.

Jenny shrugged. "The first thing I want to do is speak to Nic. I don't know where Jack lives, but tomorrow morning I'll go straight to the store. I'll wait all day if I have to, but I'll make sure he takes me back to her. And if he refuses, I'll follow him."

"Whoa there, stalker," Laura said, chuckling. "What happens after you've spoken to her?"

Jenny's good mood faltered. "I tell my parents."

"How do you think they'll take it?"

Jenny shrugged. "I honestly don't know. I suppose they'll either accept me or disown me."

"They'll probably freak out, but you can stay here for a while if things get bad," Laura said, climbing beneath her duvet. "You need to sleep, mate, because tomorrow's a big day."

Jenny grimaced. "The biggest day of my life."

"No," Laura said, shaking her head softly. She snapped off the light. "Tomorrow's the *first* day of the rest of your life."

Hope soared inside Jenny. She climbed beneath the duvet and started thinking through her plan. So many variables. She hoped Nicola would listen to her. She hoped her parents would accept her. She hoped the nightmare was ending, not beginning. Could she handle it?

As if reading her thoughts, Laura whispered, "You did a brave thing tonight. Just keep on being brave."

CHAPTER THIRTY-FOUR

After five hours of cleaning, Nicola poured with sweat. Muscles she hadn't known she had ached.

The kitchen sparkled clean, including the oven, grill, every cupboard, all the dishes, the floor, the worktops, and even the inside of the fridge. She surveyed the room, imbued with a buoyant sense of achievement.

She'd had no messages or phone calls from Jenny. In the end, temptation got the better of her. She dialled, held her breath, but her heart twisted when the call went straight to voicemail. She listened to the familiarity of Jenny's voice asking her to record a message and decided to not leave one. Instead, she sent a text: *r u ok?*

No reply.

She decided to put Jenny and the whole situation out of her mind.

Jack returned from work, marvelled over the kitchen, and, after changing, said he'd treat them to takeaway pizza. Nicola suspected the pizza offer came because they had nothing but eggs in the flat, and also because eggs were all Jack could cook. She happily agreed to the pizza, as it meant the kitchen would remain spotless at least for the rest of the night. They watched a DVD and gorged on pizza, and although Nicola enjoyed herself, she couldn't get Jenny out of her thoughts.

Towards the end of the film, her phone vibrated.

A text.

She snatched the phone up with a trembling hand as a whoosh of nerves assaulted her tummy. She swiped it on.

From Jenny.

Her heart thudded. With bated breath she opened it:

Don't call or text me again, as I won't reply. This is best for both of us. If you care about me and my family, please respect my decision. Jenny

Her blood ran cold. The words swam before her eyes.

"Is everything okay?" Jack asked.

"No."

"What's happened?"

Nicola reread the message a few more times before clearing a tight throat. "Jenny's split up with me by text."

"No way!" He held out his hand for the phone.

"Yes way." She passed it to him. "She never wants me to contact her again," she said, in a watery tone.

Jack read the text, then glanced up. "Nicola, I'm so sorry." He swallowed hard, clearly unsure of what to do next. "I...don't know what to say..." He handed the phone back.

Nicola took her phone and switched it off, placing it beside her. Numbness. She wasn't entirely sure how she should react.

It's over.

We're over.

I'll never kiss, hold, sleep, talk, or laugh with her again.

"Can I get you anything?" Jack asked softly. "I can make you a hot chocolate, with all the trimmings."

"No, thanks." She picked up her phone and stood. "I think I'll go to sleep. Thanks for the pizza and film." She didn't wait for a response before escaping to the bedroom. Once inside, she lay on top of the duvet and cried.

Why had she allowed herself to open up to love and friendship? She'd willingly made herself vulnerable and now she had nothing except hurt and regret. When she was finally too exhausted to shed another tear, she lay in silence contemplating her future. It didn't take long to decide what she had to do next. Tomorrow, she would confront Chris and get both her mum and her home back. It wasn't going to be easy without Jenny, but she'd manage.

"As of tomorrow," she said under her breath, "I refuse to be a victim anymore."

❖

Nicola woke to the gentle shaking of her shoulder.

"Nicola?" Jack said quietly.

"Yeah?" she mumbled, stretching out. She felt worse today than the day she'd been ill after drinking the vodka. That memory brought her current situation crashing down on her, all over again.

"I'm sorry for waking you, but there's something you need to see." He walked to the window and threw open the curtains. "Urgently."

Nicola sat up, squinting into the glare and trying to make sense of this. "What is it?"

Jack took hold of her hand and ushered her out of bed. "Come on, quickly."

She reluctantly followed, her annoyance spiking with each hurried step. He led her to the window in the living room, then stood aside, hands resting on his hips. "Well? Look out, then."

Nicola shot him a dirty look and moved closer to the filthy net curtains. She glanced outside and saw it was raining. The heatwave was over. Great.

"Look across the street at the bus stop," he said impatiently.

At first she didn't notice anything out of the ordinary. Then a hooded figure turned around and glanced up at the flat window.

Nicola gasped. "Jenny," she said in disbelief.

Jack nodded. "Yeah. She's been out there for over an hour. She refuses to leave until she gets to speak to you."

Nicola took a step back from the window but kept her gaze on Jenny. "How does she know you live up here?" Her heart raced and her stomach flipped.

"As soon as Dad opened up the store, she was in there. She asked about you and he told her you were staying with me up here. She woke me by repeatedly banging on the door and pressing the buzzer. I went down and she demanded to see you. I told her you weren't here, but she won't take no for an answer."

Nicola didn't know if she should be happy or angry about Jenny's sudden appearance, didn't know if she could face speaking to her or if she should ignore her. Even her body seemed confused, at one moment excited, with a racing pulse and butterflies, and in the next moment, sick and faint.

"What are you going to do?" Jack asked.

Nicola shook her head. "I'm not sure."

He drew her away from the window and looked her in the eyes. "You don't have to decide yet. She'll wait." He smiled and said, "You do need to have a shower and get dressed though."

Nicola nodded. "Okay."

Jack let go of her and she rushed to the bathroom.

Twenty minutes later she was clean and dressed. She walked into the living room and Jack raised a curious eyebrow.

"So, you want me to bring her up, then?" he asked as a smile twitched across his lips.

Nicola nodded. "Yes. Please." She sat on the sofa and tried her hardest to look casual.

"Nicola?" She turned and he winked at her. "You look good. Make her squirm." He then left the room.

She tried to prepare herself. She and Jenny were over—that was clear. So she'd deal with whatever Jenny came to say and then send her away. She already had big plans for today, and she wasn't going to let Jenny ruin them.

In no time at all, Jack returned with Jenny, then quickly headed for his room to give them privacy. Nicola's heart skipped a beat and her stomach flipped at her first glimpse of Jenny.

I've missed you so much!

She was surprised at how dishevelled Jenny looked…wet, frizzy hair tied up in a ponytail. Stranger still, she wore no make-up, not even to mask the dark circles beneath her eyes. She wore ill-fitting clothes, not her usual style. The blue hooded jumper was soaked through, as were the jeans, which were a little too short. Even her sneakers— sneakers Nicola had never seen her wear—looked old and battered.

What was going on?

"Nic, I've missed you so much. You look great," Jenny said, rushing to her.

Nicola turned away from Jenny's open arms, but not before seeing the hurt flash across her face. In a cold voice, she asked, "I have no time for manipulations. What do you want, Jenny?"

Jenny remained standing, but her shoulders slumped and she fiddled with her fingers nervously. "So much has happened that I want to tell you…and I needed to see you, to check you're okay."

"It's a bit late, don't you think?"

"What do you mean?"

"How'd you think I'd be feeling after how you've treated me? I'm far from okay," Nicola said, refusing to look up at Jenny.

"Nic, I'm sorry," Jenny said, kneeling next to the sofa. "I wanted to contact you sooner, but—"

"You're a coward," Nicola said abruptly, finally looking into Jenny's eyes. "Don't you think I deserved to be treated better?"

Jenny swallowed hard, her expression both confused and guilt ridden. "I should've handled this better, I know. Fear, and some of it I couldn't control, but that doesn't matter. I want to make it up to you, to tell you what's happened. Please?"

"You have a nerve!" Nicola said hotly. "After what you said last night, you expect to come here today and for things to just be okay?"

Jenny pulled back, her expression confused. "Last night?"

"The text, Jenny! Don't play stupid."

Jenny went very still. "I haven't sent a text to you."

"Liar."

"Nic, please listen." She held up her hands in a placating gesture. "I lost my phone on Tuesday."

"That's convenient." Nicola picked up her phone, retrieved the message, and thrust the screen in front of Jenny's nose. "Explain this, then." She watched as a range of emotions flickered across Jenny's face.

"The conniving bitch!" Jenny said, her cheeks flushing. She handed the phone back to Nicola. "I knew Elizabeth stole my phone. She must've sent you that message."

Nicola folded her arms. "Why should I believe you?"

"Why wouldn't you?"

She let the question hang in the air.

Nicola wavered, hated herself for it.

Jenny got to her feet and approached slowly. "I came today because I had no other way of contacting you. Your number is in my phone, nowhere else. So I stood out in the rain, getting soaked, wearing Laura's old clothes, hoping you'd speak to me. Why would I have done that if I could've sent you a message or called?" She spread her arms wide and glanced down at herself, then back at Nicola. "Look at me."

Nicola couldn't help but snicker. "Okay, I believe you."

"What's so funny?" Jenny demanded.

"You look…different." As quickly as her amusement had cropped up, it dissipated. Sober, scared, Nicola got to her feet and stood in front of Jenny. "So you don't want to split up with me?"

Jenny shook her head. "No. God, no. Especially since I managed to tell the entire school about us."

"You what?" Nic shrieked.

"It's a long story," Jenny said, shivering.

Nicola hugged Jenny and planted a big sloppy kiss on her mouth before pulling away. "Take that jumper off before you catch your death. Then you can fill me in on everything."

It had taken some serious convincing, but in the end Jenny agreed to help Nicola confront Chris that day. They'd been waiting at the bus stop opposite Nicola's mum's house for nearly an hour. They'd barely spoken and their growing fear was almost tangible. It felt like torture. Jenny wasn't sure she could take much more.

After midday, Nicola's mum and the monster appeared. They headed off in the direction of the betting store, just as Nicola had predicted. As soon as they'd disappeared from view, Nicola rushed across the road and into the house. Her plan was to set up the computer and the webcam, while Jenny waited at the bus stop keeping a lookout.

Nicola made it back to the bus stop just in time to see her mum and the monster appear from around the corner.

Jenny switched Jack's laptop on and checked the live feed. It worked, and for nearly fifteen minutes, they both silently watched the screen. The sound was incredibly poor quality and disjointed, making them grateful for the voice recorder as a backup.

"Right, we've a few hours until your mum leaves for work. What do you wanna do?" Jenny asked, taking the initiative to switch the laptop off. In her opinion, Nicola had grown worryingly pale.

"I don't know."

Jenny wrapped an arm around her shoulders and asked, "How about we go to the cinema, take our minds off things? It can be our first official date."

Nicola didn't look overly enthusiastic. "Okay."

❖

Jenny hadn't been able to pay attention to the film, and after four handfuls of popcorn, she'd given up on that too. It'd tasted stale and kept getting stuck in her throat. Three hours later, she sat alone in the coffee shop in Brassley town centre. All of her attempts to convince Nicola that it was safer for her to go along had been futile. So now she sat watching the laptop screen, waiting for Nicola to arrive in the shot.

Jenny's eyes bored into Nicola's abuser. Molten anger burned inside the pit of her stomach, forcing itself upward and scorching the back of her throat. She clenched her jaws and ground her teeth painfully, fighting to swallow it down.

She glanced away from the screen and looked instead at the neatly folded piece of paper beside her hand. Nicola had written her mum's address and her school locker combination on it. All her journals from the last five years were stored in the locker. In them, Nicola'd told her, she had described everything about the abuse.

As Jenny had taken hold of the paper, Nicola had whispered she loved her and left. The rain had come down heavier a few minutes later. Dark clouds continued to gather menacingly in the sky, and each occasional growl of thunder rumbled closer. It would be an almighty storm.

Jenny's premonition of foreboding sat like a boulder on her conscience. Her phone lay next to her on the table, within easy reach if she needed to call the police. Merely a precaution, sure, but it actually felt like an omen. Her gaze snapped back to sudden movement on the screen. Nicola entered the living room.

Jenny struggled to choke back the acidic nausea caused by sheer panic and pressed record. With nothing else to do, she helplessly watched the silent video footage.

She had never felt so desperate or helpless in her entire life, and she found herself doing something she hadn't done in years: she prayed.

CHAPTER THIRTY-FIVE

Shortly after Nicola had left the coffee shop, the heavens opened up and drenched her. As she walked towards the house, fear gripped her with sharp talons. She'd never felt so scared in her entire life. Her heart hammered against her ribcage and her teeth rattled in her skull.

She was grateful for two things: firstly, Jenny wasn't there to witness her cowardice, and secondly, that she remained a safe distance away. She'd insisted Jenny stay inside the coffee shop, in case things went wrong. Jenny had argued and pleaded, but in the end, Nicola got her wish. She reached inside her coat pocket with a trembling hand and pressed the record button. She'd already tucked the photos safely inside one of the pockets in her jeans. She took a final deep breath of fresh air, pressed down the door handle, and walked inside the house.

Her mum brushed past her without so much as a glance. In a distracted but cheery tone, she said, "Hey, honey."

Nicola watched, seething, as her mum picked up a white waterproof jacket and then returned to the living room. Fear quickly replaced anger as she carefully shrugged off her soaking coat. She walked into the living room and shot a glance at the webcam. She quickly averted her eyes, walked to the far sofa, and placed her coat down, making sure the pocket with the recorder was positioned on top.

The TV was on and some trashy afternoon game show blared out. She made a mental note to mute it before the confrontation began. Unable to put if off any longer, she turned to face him.

His eyes burned with hatred.

How could her mum not see or feel it?

He sat on the sofa. One of his hands clenched the neck of a bottle of beer so tightly it turned his knuckles white. Three empty bottles lay discarded beside the sofa and they all screamed the same conclusion: she was in deep shit.

His unwavering gaze bored into her. From jaw to fists to feet, his entire body sat rigid, fury radiating off him like a stink.

Just as she was considering grabbing her coat and escaping, her mum rushed back into the room, now wearing the white waterproof jacket. She bent down to kiss the bastard goodbye but pulled away suddenly, confusion and hurt in her eyes. "You okay, babe?"

He tore his gaze away from Nicola and looked briefly into her mum's eyes. His jaws unclenched and he forced a smile. "Never been better, darling." He pulled her mum in close and kissed her, but his hard gaze returned to Nicola.

Nicola felt sickened, so she glanced towards the computer and then quickly to the floor. After what felt like an age, the sickening embrace finally ended, her mum giggling like a lovesick teenager and playfully pushing him away.

With an embarrassed smile she turned to Nicola. "Have a nice night. I'll see you both tomorrow," she said as she left the room.

Nicola knew Mum would only see one of them tomorrow.

She watched as Mum fished out her car keys, pulled her hood up, and opened the front door. She sensed his gaze penetrating her, but she refused to acknowledge him. Instead, she watched as her mum walked out into the rain, closing the door behind her. The faint jingling of keys, then the distinct clicking sound as the lock engaged.

Shit!

She hadn't considered her mum might lock the front door!

Out of the corner of her eye, she saw a flash of movement as he stood. Fear seized hold of her body, rendering her helpless. Her window of opportunity was rapidly closing and her mind reminded her of Jenny.

She had to try for Jenny.

He took a step forward, and she ran to the TV and switched it off. She spun to face him, making sure the coffee table stood as a firm barricade between them. An oppressive silence filled the room. Her only consolation was the recorder would be able to pick everything up now.

She reached inside her pocket and withdrew the photos. Alert to his potential movements and keeping as safe a distance as possible, she lowered the photos onto the coffee table.

His eyes remained firmly fixed on her. He didn't glance down at the photos. As she pulled her hand back, he exploded into motion. She managed to duck in time but felt a rush of air go over her head, as the bottle he'd thrown smashed against the wall behind her.

That was close!

"What did I tell you about coming back here?" he demanded, clenching his fists.

"You said you'd kill me."

"Do you have a fucking death wish? Or did you think I was messing with you?"

She remained silent.

He stepped towards her, but she resisted the urge to step backwards. She refused to let herself be cornered by him again. She needed to stay in sight of the webcam.

"You made it perfectly clear you meant it."

He flexed his fists and asked, "Then why come back? You want to die? Or do you want me to finish what we started the other morning?"

She flinched at the reminder and immediately regretted doing so as he grinned cruelly.

"Is that it? You came back because you want me to fuck you into your proper place?" The gleam in his eyes and the snarled grin on his face showed his excitement at the prospect of controlling her by whatever means necessary. He took another menacing step towards her.

"No. I don't want you near me. I don't want you to touch me ever again!"

"Why are you here?" he bellowed.

"I came back because I want to know why. The beatings, the burns, the cuts, the bruises—all of it. I want to know why you've hurt me." She clung on the verge of hysteria. Her emotions surfaced in quick explosions that left her struggling to remain in control.

He took two quick steps around the table towards her, and she immediately took two quick steps to the side. Now she stood directly in sight of the webcam, but it did little to comfort her.

"'Cause every time I look at you, I want to smash your face in. It's just something about you. Even your own mum can't stand you, but you still won't go."

"Mum loves me."

"She doesn't! No matter how many times I've tried to beat it into you, I ain't never been able to get the message through your thick skull."

Tears threatened. Her breaths came in fast, short, ineffective bursts.

"But you've wasted all your chances, bitch. Tonight, you're going away and you ain't never coming back. They'll never find you," he said, spittle gleaming on his lips. "Well, every bit of you, anyway."

"If I repulse you so much, why did you try to rape me?" As soon as the words left her mouth, she knew she'd made a terrible mistake.

His mouth opened in a vicious snarl as he kicked the coffee table out of the way. She managed to jump back in time, to avoid it hitting her. The ashtray smashed and the photos fluttered down onto the soiled carpet.

"You asked for it! Teasing bitches like you always ask for it."

"I didn't—"

"Shut up!" he growled. "Thought you were pretty fucking clever that morning, didn't you? Trying to make an idiot outta me. *No fucking prick-teaser does that to me.*" He looked manic—red-faced, eyes dilated.

"I didn't do anything!" she said, terrorized to her core. "I just wanted to leave for school without you hurting me again. But then you tried to…to rape me." She heard the fear and desperation in her voice and hated sounding so weak.

He took another step towards her, and one of the photos crumpled beneath his boot, but he didn't seem to notice. His gravelly laugh was cold and humourless. "Hurt you? Up to now, I've been holding back. You ain't got a clue how much it would hurt if I didn't. But you're going to find out."

Nicola froze, silent, unblinking. Had this been the biggest mistake of her life, coming here? He was going to hurt her badly, maybe permanently, and she couldn't stop him. There was madness in him tonight unlike anything she'd seen before. Her only hope was Jenny.

"You see, bitch, I have the power. I can hurt you. I can fuck you. I can kill you if I have to because no one gives a shit about you. You don't exist."

"That's not true," she said, in a wobbly, uncertain voice. "I'm here now."

He took another step towards her. "Has she noticed you've been gone?"

Tears filled Nicola's eyes. She blinked them away with urgency, didn't want to lose sight of him.

"When I get around to killing you, there's nothing you can do to stop me. She can't help you now, not that she would." He laughed again. "I've hours until she gets back and finds you've gone away again, typical slut teenager. Only this time, you ain't coming back."

Nicola stumbled backwards.

"She didn't even realize you were gone—doesn't that show how little you mean to her?" He cracked his knuckles. "No one's gonna report you missing. I tell her you left, she's not going to doubt me. And when I'm done, they won't be able to identify you."

All her thoughts of the webcam and recorder disappeared. He meant every word, and she desperately needed to escape. Her only option was the back door, but she wasn't sure if it was unlocked.

Her eyes flickered in the direction of the kitchen, but he saw and stepped to the side, blocking her escape route. Her final chance was to run upstairs into the bathroom, lock the door, and hope Jenny called the police. But as there was no audio, Jenny probably wouldn't know what was happening. Help might arrive too late.

"I'd have gone easy on you the other morning. But tonight when I'm done with you? You'll beg me to kill you." He lunged forward.

She started to run but hesitated a split second too long. He grabbed her arm and dragged her backwards. Her body slammed against him and he forced her onto the sofa, pinning her under the full weight of his body.

She fought him, kicking and bucking, but nothing seemed to make contact. She heard her own voice screaming, *"No! No!"* over and over again, until his grip tightened around her throat, choking her screams into silence.

His other hand tore at her jeans. Her feeble fighting was useless against his brute strength, but she refused to give in.

He tore open her jeans and viciously ripped them down. In desperation, she dug her nails down hard, clawing at his face, and felt satisfaction as he cried out in pain. His grip on her throat momentarily loosened, and she managed to draw a breath—but a second later, his fist struck the left side of her head. The blow was hard and left her reeling.

One hand returned to her jeans, trying to tear them down, while his other grabbed a fistful of her hair. Her scalp erupted in fiery agony at the same moment that she felt his hand jam inside her jeans and tear painfully at her underwear.

She freaked out and instinctively kicked out, managing to catch him off guard. One of her knees struck him hard between his legs. His grip slackened, as he rolled off her and fell backwards onto the floor, cradling himself.

She flailed to get up, but her head spun from the blow. She needed to get out now, but her vision swam, unfocused. She sucked in a breath and nearly managed to get to her feet, but her knees buckled.

"What the fuck is this?" he said from below her.

She looked down and saw, with horror, he was holding one of the photos.

His eyes shot from the photo in his hand back to her. "Who took this? Who took it, you stupid bitch? Who did you show? *Who?*" With an animalistic roar, he leapt and savagely pulled her down. Her head smacked the floor as he stood over her, screaming the same questions over and over.

"Who did you show? Who?"

Punches and kicks rained savagely down over her body. She tried to cover her head and curl up into a protective ball, but his lashings were relentless and randomly placed. Her body felt each blow as his cries of rage deafened her.

Crack!

She screamed, knowing a bone had snapped, but couldn't identify which part of her body it had come from. A scalding, coppery liquid filled her mouth and she realized it was blood. Struggling to breathe, she gagged and spit, the hot stickiness cooling instantly and congealing on her chin and throat.

Another hard blow struck her face, snapping her head to the side with its force.

Everything went dark.

In the darkness she was aware he stood over her. She could distantly hear his voice shouting at her, but it grew fainter with each passing second. The metallic taste filled her mouth, but it no longer upset her. He continued to strike her body, but she no longer felt pain. To draw each breath remained a burning struggle, but it no longer panicked her. The realization he would most likely rape and kill her seemed to no longer matter. Everything around her grew deeper, calmer, more peaceful by the second. She no longer wanted to stay with his shouting, punches, and kicks. So she stopped fighting.

A fleeting thought of Jenny flashed in her mind's eye as the darkness enveloped her completely.

Chapter Thirty-six

Jenny's lungs were on fire, her feet pounded the slick pavement, and raindrops pelted her. She turned onto Wavery Street, saw blue flashing lights, and picked up speed. When she reached the house, she saw the front door had been forced open. Without hesitating, she rushed inside.

She burst into the living room and abruptly came to a halt. A female police officer was kneeling on the floor next to someone. The officer snapped her head up and regarded Jenny with suspicion while speaking into the radio attached to her vest.

"Eighty-two seventeen to control. Need backup and ambulance at this location. One suspect detained but hostile. Victim: young female Caucasian. Difficulty breathing and head trauma. Over."

A crackling voice calmly replied, "Backup dispatched and on way to location. ETA one minute. Ambulance also on way, ETA three minutes."

"Who are you?" the officer asked, her voice testy.

Jenny struggled to catch her breath, but managed to choke out, "Jenny O'Connor."

"You know her?"

Jenny nodded. "She's my...friend. Nicola." She glanced around at the trashed room. A sudden cry of rage sounded from beyond the doorway that led to the kitchen, and it made her jump.

"He tried to run. My partner's got him handcuffed out back. You're safe."

"That's Chris. Her mother's boyfriend. The monster."

The officer nodded, wrote something down in a notebook
Jenny swallowed hard and looked at the person on the floor. She
could only make out a pair of legs. "Is that Nicola? Is she okay?" She
craned her head for a better look, but the officer blocked her sight line.
The officer looked down and spoke softly. "Nicola, can you hear
me? Nicola, stay with me. That's it, stay with me. Good girl."

Terror seized Jenny's heart and painfully squeezed. She suddenly
didn't want to see any more, she knew she couldn't cope with the
truth—but her legs carried her closer, anyway. Jenny couldn't
recognize the girl lying on the carpet. She didn't resemble Nicola at
all. Blood covered her face, hair, and clothes. A wheezy gurgling sound
was coming from her mouth. Beneath the matted blood, her face was
badly swollen. One eye was swollen completely shut. The other eye
fluttered open, and in that instant, Jenny saw a familiar flash of blue.

A strangled sound escaped her mouth.

"Jenny, are you okay?" the officer asked. "Jenny?"

Jenny was too horror-struck to reply.

The sound of sirens grew closer until they were directly outside
the house. Heavy booted footsteps charged into the room. They
glanced at the officer with Nicola.

"Back there," she said.

Three police officers ran past them into the kitchen.

A stern voice drew Jenny's attention away from Nicola. "I need
your help, Jenny. Come down here and speak to her, let her know
you're here. We need to keep her awake, do you understand me?"

Jenny understood the command but was unable to move or speak.

"Jenny!" the police officer said, finally snapping Jenny's attention
away from Nicola's battered form. "Come here and talk to Nicola.
Backup's arrived and I need to speak to them."

As realization dawned on her, Jenny suddenly freaked out. "You
can't leave me with her, she might…" *Die.*

The officer shook her head, her hard expression softening. "I'll
stay in the room with you, but I have to go talk to the other officers."

Jenny reluctantly knelt down next to the unrecognizable body that
was supposed to be Nicola. With each gurgling breath, a tiny bubble
of blood swelled and burst from the corner of Nicola's mouth. The eye
that wasn't swollen shut watched her, and tears trickled from it.

"Nic..." Jenny started but had no more words. Nicola's eye closed and panic gripped Jenny once more. "Nic! Nic, stay with me!" Nicola's eye fluttered open again. The desperate gasping sound from her chest had a disturbing rattling.

A firm brown hand gripped Jenny's shoulder. "Jenny, the paramedics are here. You can step back now. You did a good job."

Two male paramedics pushed past her to get to Nicola. Jenny got up, staggered, and moved away with the female officer, but her eyes were unable to look away from Nicola. The paramedics busily swarmed over her. They talked to her and then to each other in hushed voices, using words Jenny didn't understand.

She watched numbly as one paramedic opened his green bag and took out a huge syringe. The other paramedic cut through Nicola's bloodied top and revealed her bra as two male police officers entered the room. Jenny felt an overwhelming need to protect Nicola's dignity.

"What the hell are you doing?" She started towards the paramedics.

The female officer intercepted her and pulled her back. "Jenny, you have to let them do their job."

She stared in horror as the first paramedic held the syringe high above Nicola's chest. *What if it goes too far? Too much force might accidentally pierce her heart.*

She flinched as the hand touched her shoulder.

"Jenny, were you the one who called the control room?"

Jenny nodded. A sudden burst of sound erupted from the officer's police radio, making Jenny jump with surprise.

"One-six-one-three to control. We are escorting suspect to the van now. Make custody aware he's a lively one."

The female officer watched Jenny carefully. In a wary tone, she said, "Jenny, I'm going—"

Something snapped inside of Jenny. One minute, she was letting the radio announcement sink in, and the next minute, she was running out the front door and back into the rain.

He was being escorted by two male officers and about to enter the back of a police van. His hands were cuffed behind his back.

Jenny charged forward, but before she got within a few feet of him, strong arms grabbed her around the waist and held her back. She fought viciously against the restraints, but her gaze never left him.

His dark sadistic eyes gazed coldly at her while his lips curled into a smirk.

With a cry of rage, Jenny tried to throw herself forward, but the strong arms remained locked around her waist. "You sick fucking bastard!" she screamed.

Blood was splattered over his arms, top, and jeans.

Nicola's blood.

He had scratches down one cheek.

"Bastard!" Jenny screamed again.

The two officers forcefully took him into the van and out of sight.

"Let go of me!" Jenny cried out, her voice hoarse and sore. "Let go!" Snot and tears started to flow simultaneously. She gave up fighting and her legs buckled, but the strong arms that had infuriated her seconds ago now cradled her and prevented her from falling.

"It's okay, Jenny." The voice and arms belonged to the female officer. She watched through burning tears as the police van engine started up and it pulled away from the house. She watched until it disappeared from view.

"Come on, Jenny. Come back inside. You're getting soaked."

Jenny looked around, suddenly aware of all the people watching her. Humiliation mixed with the anger and made her cry harder. The floodgates had finally opened, and all the tears that had been building up for the past few years surged out of her.

The strong arms released their grip from around her waist and shifted position to help support her weight instead. Jenny allowed the officer to lead her back into the house, away from the prying eyes, whispered voices, and the unforgiving rain.

As they entered the hallway, the paramedics rushed through with Nicola on a trolley. Jenny was grateful when the strong arms caught her once more.

"We're going to take her to St. Mary's," the leading paramedic said to the female officer as they wheeled by.

"I have to go with her," Jenny said desperately.

The second of the paramedics gave the female officer a brief shake of his head, as he rushed the trolley outside.

Jenny no longer had the strength to physically fight, so instead, she turned to the officer and begged. "Please, I need to go with her. I don't want her to be alone. Please?"

The serious brown eyes held her gaze.

Outside, the ambulance doors slammed shut and a few seconds later the engine started, followed immediately by a piercing siren.

"Please?" Jenny begged again.

The police officer hesitated and then finally gave a curt nod. "I'll drive us. We'd have only slowed them down. Wait here while I let people know." She hesitated, watching Jenny warily as if assessing the wisdom of leaving her alone.

Jenny looked at the floor, embarrassed. "I'll stay right here. Thank you."

"Back in a minute, and we'll head straight there. My name's Officer Palfrey. Donna. You can call me Donna."

Jenny silently watched Donna approach three police officers, who stood in the living room. They spoke in hushed voices, shooting odd glances her way.

A few seconds later, Donna returned. "Let's go."

Jenny had expected Donna to use the journey as an opportunity to interrogate her, but they drove in silence. She secretly watched Donna with genuine curiosity, having never met a female police officer before. Her long black hair was tied up in a smart ponytail. Her brown skin was unblemished, and she wore no make-up. Her eyebrows arched perfectly. She clearly took pride in her appearance.

As the car came to a halt, the hospital loomed huge and daunting before them. Jenny had never felt so alone or helpless.

"Are you sure you want to do this, Jenny?" Donna asked softly.

"I need to do this for Nic. She has no one else. I'm just..." She couldn't finish the sentence.

Donna gave a sympathetic nod. "When we get in there, I'll do all the talking and find out where Nicola is. Later on, I'll need to take your statement, but not until you're ready."

Jenny was surprised to feel a soft, warm hand gently squeeze her own. She looked up and met Donna's concerned eyes.

"They're doing everything they can for her, Jenny. We all are."

After speaking to a staff member at the main reception, Donna led them through a maze of seemingly identical corridors until they reached a smaller, quieter reception area. The thick smell of disinfectant filled Jenny's nostrils and made her shudder.

Donna spoke to a woman behind a desk, then led Jenny to a coffee machine.

"There's no news. We'll have to wait in the family waiting room." Donna looked pointedly at her and said, "You should phone your parents."

"I'll call them later. I love my mum, but as soon as she knows, she'll freak out. I'd rather do my statement thingy without her being here."

"You don't have to give your statement tonight. You've been through a lot. Another officer can take it tomorrow."

Jenny shook her head. "I want you to take it tonight. Please?" For no real reason, she trusted and respected Donna. She'd rather explain things to her than to a complete stranger who probably wouldn't care.

"Okay, as long as you phone your parents afterwards." Donna sighed. "Coffee?"

"No, thanks," Jenny said, as she headed into the room.

❖

Jenny sat on one of the green plastic-covered sofas. A few minutes later, the door opened and Donna entered, carrying two plastic cups. She placed one on the table, in front of Jenny.

"I got you a hot chocolate. You don't have to drink it, but the sugar may help you feel better."

"Thanks," Jenny said.

Donna sat on the sofa opposite and took a sip from her cup. She cringed and placed it down on the table. "Ugh—it gets nastier every time I come here."

Jenny felt too nauseous to drink but held the cup anyway. The warmth from the hot chocolate was a comfort from the coldness of the room, which seemed to be seeping into her bones.

"I need you to listen carefully," Donna said, as she took out a notepad and pen. "Your statement is your opportunity to give a true and accurate account of what happened tonight. You must tell the truth, Jenny, because if aspects are found to be conflicting or untrue, it could result in the perpetrator getting off. Earning justice isn't the job of a foolish vigilante. Are we clear?"

Jenny felt inexplicably guilty. "Crystal."

Donna nodded. "Okay. If you need a break, just say." She clicked the top of her pen, releasing the nib, and held it poised. "Let's start with Nicola's last name and date of birth."

"Her last name is Jackson, but I don't know her date of birth. Sorry."

Donna made a note and then glanced up. "Do you know what month her birthday's in?"

Jenny shook her head. "I don't have a clue." She felt ashamed for not knowing when her own girlfriend's birthday was. It had never come up in conversation between them.

"Okay, why don't you start with how long you and Nicola have been friends, then work your way up to what happened tonight?" Donna encouraged.

Jenny nervously began to talk. She stuttered and mixed up her words, but gradually found talking became easier. Donna was a patient listener and showed no judgement about any of the things she told her.

Jenny described how they'd met and how she'd manipulated her parents into letting Nicola stay. She told of how she'd accidentally come across Nicola's scarred back. She relayed everything Nicola had told her about the abuse and finally spoke about the attempted rape, and Nicola's plan to confront him.

Donna sat up straight and moved to the edge of her seat when Jenny mentioned the webcam and photos.

"Shit!" Jenny jumped up and took two running steps towards the door.

In a flash of movement, Donna appeared in front of her. "What?"

Jenny fought tears. "When I ran to the house, I left Jack's laptop in the coffee shop. It's got the recorded web feed on it. I'm so fucking stupid."

Donna held up a calming hand. "I'll get someone to go over and see if they've still got it."

Jenny tried to swallow, but the lump lodged in her throat was painful. "If it's gone, then Nicola went through all that for nothing. That's all I had to do, and I managed to mess it up. I've failed her."

Donna guided her back to the sofa. "Chances are, the staff will have kept it safe, especially because you made such a big scene when you left. Where's the voice recorder?"

"In Nic's coat pocket, on the sofa, in the living room."

Donna's expression looked sorrowful, but she remained silent.

Jenny answered the look with her own question. "She went in there knowing what was going to happen, knowing what he'd do to her, didn't she?"

Donna sighed. "It sounds like it."

A wave of anger rocked Jenny. Anger directed towards Nicola, for lying to her and making her believe exactly what she'd wanted to hear—that everything would be okay. She redirected the anger towards herself, then, for having believed the lies.

Donna closed her pad and placed it with the pen on her lap. A deep line furrowed her brow. "I've got to go and let people know. Are you okay waiting here? I think you should phone your parents." Donna had an urgent energy about her, which made Jenny feel all the more useless and exhausted.

"I'll be fine," she said, rubbing her grainy eyes.

"You've been a good friend," Donna said and hurried to the door. She glanced back before leaving and said, "Ring your parents now." Then she left.

Jenny sat for a few minutes, trying to decide what to say. So far, she'd taken responsibility and acted like an adult, but the facade was fast slipping. She felt scared, lonely, unable to cope with the situation. Her heart ached with the need to hold Nicola, to kiss her soft lips and taste her. The realization that she might never get to do those things again rocked her fragile world.

She retrieved her phone, typed the familiar number, and pressed call. Hot, salty tears started to spill down her cheeks as the first ringing tone engaged. She seemed unable to stop crying. A strange strangling sound escaped from her when she heard the second tone, and by the third, she was sobbing uncontrollably.

Please don't let Elizabeth answer!

A familiar comforting voice answered the line. "Hello?"

Jenny listened to her mum speak again, the worry tangible in her tone, but she was unable to talk through her sobs. After taking a deep breath she managed to speak. "Mum, it's me. I'm at St. Mary's hospital. Nic's...she's hurt and they're operating and I don't know if she's going to be okay. We're on the third floor—"

"What happened, Jennifer? Are you okay?" Mum's voice was filled with sheer maternal panic.

In a voice that sounded nothing like her own, Jenny said, "I'm fine. It's Nicola who's hurt. I wasn't there, but I should've been—"

"We're on our way. Stay safe until we get there. We love you, Jennifer!"

She returned her love through disjointed sobs before her mum hung up with the promise of arriving there soon.

All she could do now was wait.

Her parents arrived within fifteen minutes of her making the call. When the door opened and she saw them, all composure left her and she started to cry all over again.

Her mum's eyes were red and puffy as she rushed over and gripped Jenny in a vice-like hug. They remained locked in the silent embrace for a few minutes, and Jenny felt truly safe for the first time since arriving at the hospital.

Her dad perched on the opposite sofa. He looked both pale and uncharacteristically sombre. "What happened, Jennifer?"

Before she could speak, Mum said, "Please tell me it wasn't drugs. You know how we feel about dr—"

"It wasn't drugs!" Jenny snapped. "Nicola isn't like that."

Her mum was clearly taken aback by her outburst, and Jenny's anger quickly turned to guilt.

"I'm sorry, Jennifer," Mum said. "I just worry so much about your generation. But you're right. Nicola isn't like that."

A quick knock sounded on the door, and Donna entered the room. She looked at Jenny's parents and hesitated. "I'm sorry for interrupting, I can come back later." She turned to leave.

"No." Jenny jumped up. "Please stay? Mum, Dad, this is Officer Donna Palfrey."

Both parents stood up. Her dad walked over and shook Donna's hand. "Thank you for looking after our daughter, Officer."

Donna blushed. "It's not necessary for you to thank me. You must be proud to have such a mature daughter." She shot Jenny an unreadable glance.

Her dad smiled wanly and her mum announced, "We are proud of her."

Jenny sat next to her mum while Donna and her dad sat on the opposite sofa.

"Jennifer, please tell us what's happened to Nicola," Dad asked quietly.

Jenny gave Donna a beseeching look, but Donna's expression made it clear she had no intention of helping her out.

With a sigh, Jenny looked at the floor. "I'll tell you. Just…please don't…overreact." She glanced at her mum, who scowled at the accusation. She told them almost everything, including the fictitious uncle and his equally fictitious death. The only parts she left out involved drinking, kissing, and sex. When she'd finished talking, the room hung in silence. Naturally, it was her mum who chose to break it.

"Jennifer, you should've had more sense than to let her go through with it!"

Jenny knew her mum was right and the regret felt like it was killing her.

"Mrs. O'Connor, I believe Nicola wouldn't have listened to reason. And if she'd attempted to do it without Jenny's help, she would certainly be dead now."

Horror kicked Jenny in the gut.

"Jenny could never have foreseen what was going to happen, but thanks to her bravery and fast thinking, we were able to respond quickly, giving Nicola the best chance."

Jenny's heavy burden of guilt lightened a little with Donna's kind words.

"Be that as it may, it does not excuse the lying, Jennifer. Your father and I have been praying and lighting candles for a dead man who doesn't exist. You should have told us the truth from the beginning. We trusted you both, and you lied to us."

"It wasn't my secret to tell. We lied about the uncle, and it was me that came up with it, but I did it for Nic. In hindsight, it was stupid. I see that. But at the time, I was trying to look after her. I'd promised to keep her secret."

She could feel the stares of everyone in the room, but she refused to meet them. The awkward silence returned, looming over them for a short time.

Dad finally said, "You did what you felt you needed to. But in future, you need to be honest with us. No more lies. We'll leave it at that now." He focused his attention on Donna. "Do we know what's happening with Nicola?"

"Not much, I'm afraid," Donna answered. "The surgeon in charge will come speak to us as soon as they can."

Jenny thought she heard a hint of apprehension in Donna's tone but wasn't sure if she was being paranoid.

"What about Nicola's mother?" Her mum asked, surprising them all.

"My colleagues have gone to her workplace to inform her."

Jenny wanted to change the subject from Nicola's mum. "Any news about the laptop?"

"That's what I came in to tell you. We got it." With a smile, Donna added, "The manager kept it safe. Apparently you made quite a scene when you stormed out."

Before Jenny could reply, the door opened and a man dressed in green scrubs entered. He was tall, had a white beard, and regarded them coolly. "My name is David Smith. I'm the chief surgeon who operated on Nicola Jackson."

Jenny's stomach twisted into a tight knot and her mouth went dry. She felt the urge to bolt out the door but forced herself to remain seated.

"Nicola was in a critical state when she came in. Our main concern was her lung being punctured by two broken ribs. The paramedics inserted a syringe into her chest cavity, but when she got here, we had to go a step further and insert a chest tube. Once that was secure, our main priorities were the linear skull fracture and severe bruising caused by internal bleeding." He met each of their gazes in turn. "There's a strong likelihood of severe concussion, and Nicola will have to be kept in ICU. A number of problems could still occur because of the severity of her injuries. We do, however, remain optimistic."

Throughout his speech everyone had remained silent and still, apart from Donna who scribbled hasty notes in her pad.

Jenny felt stupid. She'd barely understood a word he'd said, but she thought she'd managed to grasp the gist: Nicola was alive.

"How long until I can speak to her?" Donna asked.

The surgeon raised a bushy eyebrow. "She'll not be fit to speak to anyone for some time. She's in critical condition. I understand you're eager to speak to her, Officer, but my priority is Nicola's health alone." He paused, let his words sink in. "At least three or four days, and that's only if there are no further complications."

Donna blushed from the scolding and gave a nod.

The surgeon addressed them all. "Tomorrow morning, I or one of my colleagues will assess if she's stable enough to take visitors. Until then, I've nothing further. Excuse me." He turned and left the room as abruptly as he'd entered.

Everyone remained silently stunned.

"Well, it's a good job he's a surgeon. If his patients were awake they probably wouldn't think much of his bedside manner," Mum said, with a huff.

Donna smiled. "I'm going to get some coffee, does anyone want anything?"

Jenny's dad stood. "I'll go with you."

Mum also stood. "I need to go and ring your sister. She'll be wondering where we all are."

Jenny watched as everyone left. The mention of Elizabeth filled her with dread. She needed to tell her parents about her and Nicola's relationship, but she didn't dare do it today. They'd already been through so much.

Jenny remained seated and felt Laura's ill-fitting clothes begin to dry out. When the door finally did open, Jenny was initially surprised and then furious to see Elizabeth.

"Get out!" Jenny said, jumping to her feet.

Elizabeth continued towards her, unaware she'd left the door slightly ajar, in her haste.

"Mum sent me. She's waiting with that black policewoman for Dad to get back from the long-stay car park. We don't have much time, so you need to listen—"

"Get out, Elizabeth, before I do something we'll both regret. You've no right to be here after everything you've done."

Elizabeth shook her head. "Mum's told me everything. Why didn't you tell me the truth about her abuse? I could have done something."

Jenny tried to keep control of her temper, but fury seethed beneath the surface. "We didn't exactly get a chance, with you being such a goddamn bitch the whole time."

"I'm sorry."

"For what exactly?" Jenny asked through painfully clenched teeth. "Kicking her out of our home even though we told you she had nowhere to go? How about outing her to the whole school? Or maybe you're sorry for stealing my phone and sending her that text, is that it?"

Elizabeth's face reddened. "I'm sorry for it all. I was only trying to protect you—"

"It was Nic who needed protecting, not me." Jenny closed her eyes and exhaled slowly, trying to restrain herself from leaping at Elizabeth and tearing her limb from limb. "Remember how you said all you ever wanted was for me to be happy?"

Elizabeth nodded sheepishly. "Of course. That's honestly all I—"

"I'm gay," Jenny said, feeling a huge weight lift from her shoulders.

The colour drained from Elizabeth's face. "You're not gay, Jennifer. She's confused you."

"I *am* gay," Jenny insisted adamantly. "Nicola took the blame to protect me. But it was me who kissed her first and it was me who initiated our lovemaking." Jenny watched with great satisfaction as Elizabeth stood dumbstruck. Feeling liberated, she continued, "I love Nicola and we've been in a relationship for the last two weeks. You stumbled across the truth but didn't realize it."

"You're not gay. You're just—"

"I'm gay. Really, really gay and ridiculously happy because of it. God made me this way, and I believe he loves me for who I am."

Elizabeth stumbled backwards, gripping her crucifix. She opened her mouth, only to close it again.

"I *love* her, Elizabeth. We're both going to transfer to the sixth form in town and then we'll go to the same university. Once we've graduated, we'll move in together, and eventually we'll get married and have babies. It's all planned. Don't give me an ultimatum because I'll choose to be with her. Always. I want you, Mum, and Dad to be a part of our lives, to accept us."

Elizabeth looked like she might faint. "So this is what's changed you. You're really in love with her?"

"I am and she makes me happy," Jenny said, taking her sister's hands. "I've never asked or begged you for anything before, but right now, I'm begging you with all my heart. Please. I need you to support me, Elizabeth. I need you to stick up for me, especially when I tell Mum and Dad."

Elizabeth swallowed hard, gave a curt nod, and opened her mouth, but before she could speak again, a shrill voice spoke from the doorway.

"You've both got some explaining to do," Mum said as she stormed into the room.

Jenny lowered her head, unable to bear the hurt on her parents' faces and the surprise on Donna's. She knew she should at least try to explain, but before she could gather the courage and open her mouth, Donna spoke.

"If you'll excuse me, I've got to go make some calls and update my sergeant." She hastily left the room, and Jenny wished she could escape too.

The awkward silence returned, and it felt like it was never going to end. In the end, it was Elizabeth who spoke. "Mum, Dad, I don't know how much you heard, but Jenny has something she needs to tell you."

Jenny glared at Elizabeth. *Bitch! As if this isn't difficult enough.*

Elizabeth ignored the look and continued, "It shocked me at first, but I want you to know I love her and I fully support her with this... decision."

"It's not a de—"

"With this announcement," Elizabeth amended. "I think you should too."

Tears rolled down Jenny's cheeks at her sister's words. She mumbled the first thing that entered her head, "Mum, Dad, I'm so sorry…"

Her mum gave her a comforting hug. "What's going on?"

Jenny wiped her tears away with her hands, wishing she had some tissue. "I wanted to tell you both, just not today and not like this." She hesitated for a moment. Her stomach lurched and her throat restricted, making it difficult to speak. "I'm gay and so is Nicola. We're in a relationship."

Silence.

Finally her mum cleared her throat. "Lots of girls have strong feelings towards their best friends. That doesn't make them gay."

Jenny felt a bitter laugh building inside but managed to choke it down. "Mum, please don't try and convince me, or yourself, the feelings I have for Nicola are just friendship. I'm not a child. I know the difference between loving friends and loving a partner."

Elizabeth, Mum, and Dad all grimaced, and Jenny felt a stab of guilt.

"You have to understand, this is hard for your mother and me to understand," Dad said. "You've never shown any indications of being…well, that is…you've always liked boys."

"I was raised to like boys, but honestly, I don't like them much. Not in that way."

"You've never even had a proper boyfriend," Dad said, blushing and darting nervous glances around the room.

The last thing she wanted to do was tell her dad about her reputation for being promiscuous, but at the same time, she had to somehow make them understand this was real. "I've had boyfriends in the past—"

"She's had loads—oops, I didn't mean that how it came out." Elizabeth shot an apologetic look at Jenny. "I just meant—"

"Be quiet, Elizabeth," Mum interrupted testily. "Let your sister speak."

Jenny took a breath and tried to continue with the lost trail of thought. "Basically, being with guys never felt right, and I ended up thinking there was something wrong with me." She clasped her hands together. "I know it's hard for you all to understand, but this isn't a phase. It's not going to go away. It's a part of who I am."

Her mum shook her head. "Why have you never spoken to us about this before?"

Jenny heard the accusation in her mum's tone. "I needed time to come to terms with it myself. And I knew if I told you, you wouldn't let Nicola stay with us. She had nowhere else to go."

Mum folded her arms and pursed her lips, preparing for an argument.

"That isn't fair," Dad said. "Of course Nicola would've stayed with us."

Mum gave a huff and said, "Do not look at me like that, Jennifer. We would've let her stay—but there would have been rules. Lots of rules, and we most certainly wouldn't have insisted you share a bed. You've betrayed our trust again."

Jenny winced. "It was never our intention. We honestly didn't want to hurt you."

"You're both children," Mum said.

Jenny's frustration grew. "Just because you treat us like we're children doesn't mean we are. In a few months we'll both be eighteen. We'll be going away to university in over a year. How old were you when you started courting Dad?"

Her mum's eyes narrowed and her cheeks flushed. "That's not the same thing."

"It's exactly the same thing," Jenny said.

"It kinda is, Mum," Elizabeth said cautiously.

"You were sixteen," Jenny said before turning her head. "Dad, you were eighteen."

"Jennifer, it's—"

"You've always said, even at that young age, you knew you loved him and that you'd marry him. Why can't you accept Nicola and I love each other and want the same thing?"

"Because I don't want that kind of life for you," Mum answered honestly.

The words were a proverbial slap across her face. They rendered Jenny speechless.

"We haven't got a problem with gay people or how they live their lives," Dad said quickly, sliding an arm around Mum's shoulders. "Being gay is more widely accepted these days. But there are still a lot of people who will never accept it. We don't want you to struggle through life."

Jenny saw the unconditional love in her mum's and dad's eyes. She knew their words weren't said in malice but were said out of love. "I know you want to protect us. You think if we live a normal *straight* life, then everything will be okay. But it won't." She leaned forward and gently cupped her mum's warm hands. "I went for two days without being with her. I tried to ignore my feelings, and it was hell. The thought of a lifetime of doing that—it's unbearable."

The anguish she saw on both of her parents' faces showed they were finally beginning to understand.

"All we want is for both of our daughters to be happy," Mum said, squeezing Jenny's hands. "And if that means you're gay and you're with Nicola, then so be it. It'll take us some time to get used to it. That's okay. But please, don't go shave all your hair off and get tattoos and piercings."

Jenny smiled. "I won't."

Elizabeth raised a mischievous eyebrow and said, "That's what university is for."

Jenny watched her mum's expression darken, but the rest of them laughed.

CHAPTER THIRTY-SEVEN

A knock on the door caused them all to look up. Donna entered. "Any news?"

"No," Dad said. "Nothing as of yet."

Donna walked over to them. "Well, I've some news from my sergeant. Nicola's mum is on her way here."

They all sat in silence and waited. Jenny was particularly apprehensive about meeting Nicola's mum.

How could she not have known about the years of abuse?

Nicola wouldn't be in here if her mum hadn't been so selfish.

A short while later, a timid knock on the door announced her arrival. Jenny braced herself, ready to tell Nicola's mum exactly what she thought of her. When the small, thin woman walked in, all of Jenny's anger immediately faded. Nicola's mum had the same colour hair, pale skin, and freckles, as her daughter. Her brown eyes were puffy and red, as was her nose. Her body trembled as she continued to sob uncontrollably into a handkerchief. Jenny had never seen anyone look so guilt ridden, vulnerable, and terrified, all at the same time.

Jenny's mum rushed to her. She introduced herself and explained briefly how she knew Nicola. In response, Nicola's mum introduced herself as Angela. She hugged Jenny's parents, Elizabeth, and finally Jenny herself, thanking them all so much for looking after Nicola.

They sat down, and Angela talked and cried intermittently. She'd never suspected anything but now berated herself for being so ignorant. In hindsight she realized Chris had manipulated her from the beginning. It'd been his suggestion to move in with them, so he could offer a supportive male influence to Nicola. She'd noticed Nicola had withdrawn and had wanted to talk about it, but he'd told her it was probably a mixture of grief and adolescence.

As Jenny listened, she felt sorry for Angela. It was clear she genuinely hadn't suspected anything. Not only did she feel guilty for not suspecting, she also felt guilty for enabling it to happen, and for not being someone Nicola trusted enough to tell. Her whole world had fallen apart, and the thing that ate away at her most was thinking she might lose Nicola and never get the chance to make amends.

"My shift ended hours ago," Donna said once Angela had talked herself out. "I need to go get some sleep. What are you all going to do?" She stifled a yawn.

"I'm staying," Jenny said, then added, "if that's okay?"

Her dad nodded. "We'll stay."

Donna got to her feet and stretched. The bags under her eyes were dark and heavy. "There's nothing more I can do tonight, but I'll come back first thing tomorrow morning." She placed a business card on the coffee table. "Here's my number, in case you need it."

"Thank you so much, Donna, for everything," Jenny called after her.

Donna turned and gave a sad smile. "I'm sorry we've had to meet under such horrible circumstances. If you ask the receptionist, she'll get you all some cots, blankets, and pillows. Night, all."

Exhaustion plagued Jenny, but she was too emotionally wired to sleep. She ended up resting her head on the arm of the sofa.

"Do you want me to go and ask for a cot for you, Jennifer?" Dad asked, getting to his feet.

"No, thanks," Jenny said with a yawn. "I won't be able to sleep anyway."

He nodded and sat back down.

There was nothing they could do other than wait, and so Jenny resigned herself to the prospect of an incredibly long and draining night. Two minutes later, her dad gently placed his jacket over her and planted a soft kiss on the top of her head.

❖

The gentle shake of her shoulder woke Jenny.

"Jennifer, it's time to wake up, sweetheart," Mum whispered.

Reality assaulted her and erased all traces of sleep. She opened her tired eyes and grimaced at a painful twinge in her neck and stiffness throughout her body. She looked around, but only her mum and she were there. "Where's everybody?" she asked, stretching.

"Your dad had to go into work, but he'll be back as soon as he can. Elizabeth drove home early this morning, and Angela's gone in to see Nicola. How are you feeling?"

Jenny sat up. "I can't believe I managed to sleep."

Her mum gave a tired smile. "Almost as soon as your head went down, you were out like a light. There's a canteen nearby if you want to go and get something to eat."

Jenny shook her head, flaring the aching pain in her neck. She winced. "I'm not hungry, but you should go and get something."

Exhaustion and worry carved lines on her mum's face. She looked ill. "Your father got me something earlier."

"Any news about Nic?" Jenny asked.

"She's still stable, which is a good sign. Angela went in about an hour ago and the nurse said we can go in shortly. That's why I woke you."

Mum yawned. Jenny was about to suggest she go home and rest when the door opened and a man wearing a suit and white jacket entered.

"Mrs. O'Conner? Jennifer?"

"Yes?" they said in unison.

"Morning. I'm Dr. Craig Jenkinson. I need to talk to you before I take you to see Nicola."

Jenny stepped forward. "Has something happened?"

"Nothing new, no. She's stable and has come around from the anaesthetic. Doing well, but she's in a significant amount of pain. We've administered a high dosage of pain relief, but the drugs cause her to slip in and out of sleep."

"That's okay. She should sleep," Jenny said.

He nodded. "We've also cleaned her up as best as we can, but there's a lot of severe bruising, especially to her face." He paused, seeming to weigh his words.

"Okay," Mum said, cautiously.

"I'm telling you this to prepare you." He pressed his lips into a grim line. "Her appearance, the injuries, the machines she's attached to…well, it might be shocking to see. Nicola won't be able to speak to you because of her injuries. As I said before, she'll slip in and out of sleep, but that's normal." He looked from one to the other. "Do you have any questions before I take you to her?"

Jenny was struggling to breathe. Her mum gently took hold of her hand and gave it a reassuring squeeze. "Are you sure you want to do this, Jennifer? I can go in alone if you'd rather stay here."

Jenny had to go in, she owed it to Nicola. She wanted to go in. "I'm sure." She turned to the doctor and asked, "Will she know we're there, or will she be too out of it?"

Dr. Jenkinson smiled kindly. "It'll probably be a bit of both, to be honest. She should be able to hear you though, so talk to her."

Jenny stood. "Will you come with me, Mum?" She didn't think she could manage going in alone.

"Of course I will, sweetheart." Mum gave a final, reassuring squeeze of her hand as they followed the doctor.

Jenny was grateful, for the first fifteen minutes, that Nicola was asleep. It allowed her time to get over her initial shock. Although the doctor had done his best to prepare them, the sight of Nicola was far worse than either of them could've envisioned.

Her face was a total mess. The entire left side was covered with dark bruising and disfigured from the swelling and bloating. Nicola's left eye remained swollen shut, and for the first time, Jenny noted the severe gash on her forehead and scalp. Nearly two inches in length, the hair around the wound had been shaved, and the stitches made it look particularly grotesque. Jenny suspected the gash had been the source of most of the blood she'd seen. A sheet lay over Nicola's body, but her arms and hands lay on top of it. Large bruises covered her arms, and Jenny felt certain the rest of Nicola's body would look the same. A nasal cannula brought Nicola a steady stream of oxygen. A thin strip of white tape attached to her right cheek held the tubing in place. Various other wires and tubes were protruding from Nicola, and a constant beeping sound kept a steady rhythm.

Jenny stood rooted to the spot as she stared at Nicola with a mixture of disbelief and horror. Mum walked to the bed and placed her hand atop Nicola's. A lump stuck in Jenny's throat and tears threatened as she watched her mum gently stroke Nicola's hand.

"Hello, Nicola. It's Anne. I'm here with Jennifer. Your mum has nipped outside. We're all going to stay with you for as long as you need us. We're going to help you get better."

With trepidation, Jenny walked over to the bed and stood beside her mum. Nicola's right eye hazily looked up at them and then focused solely on Jenny. It pierced her soul.

Jenny feigned calmness and enthusiasm. "We're here and we're not going anywhere, Nic. You're going to be okay. The doctor said you won't be able to talk for a few days, but Mum and I will do enough talking for you."

The blue eye slowly blinked twice and then remained closed. Jenny verged on panic, but Mum whispered quietly, "She's fallen back asleep, Jennifer."

Nodding, Jenny swallowed, forcing down the panic.

"I'm going to phone your dad and tell him. Will you be all right without me for a few minutes? I'll just be outside."

"I'll be fine," Jenny said, sitting in the chair next to the bed. Once her mum had left, she reached out. Nicola's hand felt cool to the touch and her fingers twitched. Jenny saw the lone eye watching her again.

She moved her head closer and whispered, "You scared me, Nic. I thought I'd lost you. I love you so much. It's all going to be fine, honestly. You need to concentrate on getting better. Your mum knows the truth and is here for you. I also told my mum and dad and Elizabeth about us, and to be fair, they've been really good about it."

The blue eye blinked and the hand twitched again.

"Please don't ever scare me like that again. I need you, Nic."

The blue eye watered, blinked a few more times, and then remained closed—but Jenny felt certain Nicola had heard and understood everything.

Jenny's mum returned with Angela a short while later, both of them carrying plastic chairs. "Elizabeth will be here in five minutes,"

Mum whispered. "She's going to wait for you in the car park. You're going to go home, have some food, sleep, and a shower. I'm going to stay here with Angela. Elizabeth will drop you back later on." There was a steely determination in her voice Jenny knew all too well. It was the *don't even think about arguing with me* tone.

"Mum, I'm fine, honestly. I'd rather stay. I got some sleep, but you didn't. You should go—"

"You're going home. That's the end of it. I'm not prepared to have two sick girls on my conscience. There's leftover lasagna and salad in the fridge, and I know exactly how much is there, Jennifer. After you've eaten you'll have a shower because, quite frankly, you need one. Then you'll get a few hours' sleep." Mum paused for breath, then said, "Nicola needs us to be strong for her, and making ourselves ill will do none of us any good. There'll always be one of us here with her, I promise."

Jenny didn't argue because, frustratingly, her mum's logic made sense. They sat for the remainder of time in silence, listening to the continuous beeping and watching Nicola sleep. After two minutes, Jenny stood, kissed her mum and Angela goodbye. She left the ward with the directions her mum had given her and managed to find her way to the car park. While waiting for Elizabeth to arrive, she sucked in a large breath of fresh air and held it. As she exhaled through her nose, the stench of disinfectant was cleansed from her nostrils.

Nicola happily gazed out the car window. She was glad to be free and no longer cooped up in hospital.

When Michael spoke, his voice so quiet, she had to strain to hear him. "There are many things in this world I don't understand. My faith helps sometimes, but I still struggle to understand how God can let bad things happen to good people. Mostly, I think it's not God's fault. We all have free will. But what happened to you, Nicola, upsets me greatly." His voice croaked with emotion and it took him a few seconds before he was able to continue. "Annie and I want you to know you're a loved member of our family." He reached across and gave her hand an affectionate squeeze before returning his hand to the steering wheel.

Nicola tried to keep her composure. "Thanks, Michael."

He glanced at her, his green eyes sparkling. "I'm a man of few words—mainly because Annie speaks enough for the both of us. But the words I do manage to say, well, I mean every single one of them." He swallowed hard and turned his attention back to the road ahead. They continued the journey in silence, and a short while later, the car pulled outside the familiar house. She could remember the last time she'd ventured inside but had no recollection of leaving it. She looked at her mum's house with a mixture of emotions, but when the living room curtains twitched, she couldn't help but smile.

"I hope you've got your appetite back. Annie and your mum are as thick as thieves, and they're both determined to fatten you up," Michael said, undoing his seatbelt. "When I left the three of them, there was already enough food to feed a small army."

The front door swung open, and her mum, Anne, and Jenny rushed out to greet them. For the first time in a long time, Nicola felt she was home.

CHAPTER THIRTY-EIGHT

Jenny sat fidgeting in the back of the car. The collar of her shirt was aggravating her neck. She glanced at her mum in the front passenger seat. She wore her best dress, but her make-up did little to hide the dark rings beneath her eyes. Jenny flicked her gaze to her dad. He'd donned his best suit, but fatigue was clear on his face too.

None of them had slept because they'd been dreading today.

Panic flickered inside Jenny. *I don't feel ready for this!* All she wanted to do was hide and let the day pass by without her. But she wouldn't let Nicola down, not ever. But especially not today, of all days.

"I'll have to let you out here," Dad said quietly, pulling the car to the side of the road opposite the courthouse.

Jenny and her mum got out and silently watched as the car disappeared into the heavy flowing traffic.

"Should we wait inside the entrance?" Jenny asked, feeling self-conscious about where they were standing. Her mum nodded and they slowly made their way up the steep stone steps. Jenny wished she could see Nicola one last time before it all started, but there was no time.

"Hi, Jenny."

Jenny had to do a double take. She was surprised to see Donna wasn't dressed in her police uniform but was wearing a dark suit instead. A shorter blond woman in a dark blue jacket and skirt stood next to her. She smiled shyly.

"Oh, how rude of me!" Donna exclaimed with embarrassment. "This is my partner, Gemma." She indicated Jenny and her mum. "Gem, this is Jenny and Anne."

Gemma said a quiet hello, to which Jenny and her mum politely replied.

"Where's Michael?" Donna asked, looking around. "It's going to begin in a few minutes."

"He's gone to park," Jenny said, trying to sound calmer than she felt. "He'll be here any minute."

Donna nodded thoughtfully. "Traffic's always mayhem around here. Well, we'll head in, but we'll speak to you both afterwards."

Jenny watched as Donna and Gemma disappeared through a door. Two minutes later, her dad appeared at the top of the stairs, face flushed and out of breath. "I'm sorry. Traffic is terrible and parking was a nightmare."

"You're here now, that's the main thing," Mum said, taking hold of one of his hands. "Come on, we'd better hurry inside."

When they entered the room, Jenny was surprised by the number of people she saw and the eerie silence in which they all sat. They walked up the centre aisle towards their seats. Donna, Jack, his parents, and Laura were all seated, sombre expressions on their faces.

Dad led them to the front and then stood aside, so Jenny and her mum could enter the row first. Jenny shuffled along until she was next to Angela, who looked up with relief.

Angela's hair had been professionally dyed and styled. She was dressed in an elegant long black skirt and a grey blouse. Although she remained painfully thin, her skin was now a healthier colour, especially compared to the first time Jenny had met her.

A short man with a neat grey moustache and balding head walked purposefully up the aisle. He wore a long black-sleeved gown over a white shirt. The stiff collar of the shirt had two rectangular bands hanging beneath it. As he turned to address everyone, Jenny's breath caught in her throat.

No turning back now.

"All rise for the Honourable Judge Johnson."

The whole room stood as one. After the initial sound of creaking benches and the shuffling of feet and clothes, the eerie silence fell over the room once more. A woman emerged from a door at the front of the room. She wore a red-and-black gown and a white horsehair wig.

It was then Jenny recognized Penny Dyson, the prosecuting barrister, standing near the front. Her own wig and black gown had initially camouflaged her.

"Please be seated," the judge said, her voice both regal and authoritative.

Everyone sat.

"Good morning. My name is Judge Annabelle Johnson. Firstly, I wish to address you, the members of the jury."

As the judge spoke to the jury, Jenny scanned their faces. Surely they had to find him guilty. Didn't they?

The judge then turned to address those in the gallery, Jenny included.

"We're here today for the case of the Crown versus Mr. Christopher Weston. Before we begin, let me make myself perfectly clear. I run a strict court. I'll tolerate no nonsense, including outbursts of any kind. If I have to address any individual or members of the gallery, you shall be removed immediately, and I'll hold you in contempt."

Everyone in the gallery remained silent, but a few people shifted uncomfortably under her stern gaze.

The judge turned her gaze to Penny Dyson and the prosecution team, who were seated on the table to the right. Before the judge opened her mouth to speak, the man at the left table stood up. He was tall and also wore a black robe and wig. He nervously cleared his throat and the judge slowly turned her head. She regarded him coolly.

"Your Honour. May I please interject?"

The judge frowned and pursed her lips. Jenny felt grateful she wasn't on the receiving end of the death stare.

"Interject? As far as I'm aware, Mr. Mosley, we haven't begun yet." The judge's voice was sharp, and after a few long seconds of awkward silence, she continued. "Don't make a habit of interrupting proceedings in my court, Mr. Mosley. You may go ahead, but this once."

Mr. Mosley wiped his palms on the sides of his trousers. "Thank you, Your Honour. I've received instructions from my client minutes ago. He's informed me he wishes to change his plea to guilty, with regard to all charges laid against him."

The judge's gaze bored angrily into Mr. Mosley. "Please explain to me exactly why your client has left it until this ridiculously late stage to change his plea?"

Mr. Mosley shifted uncomfortably. "I'm afraid I cannot answer that question, Your Honour."

The judge leaned forward, seemingly unsatisfied with the answer. "You can't answer? Well, in that case, let's hear from Mr. Weston himself and see if he can shed some light on this mystery." She turned to the two uniformed men, who waited in the wings. "Please bring Mr. Weston into court."

They disappeared down some steps, inside the wooden dock.

Jenny watched as Mr. Mosley picked up a glass of water and took a sip. She was close enough to see his hands were trembling.

Angela's body suddenly stiffened. Concerned, Jenny glanced at her and saw terror in her expression. She took hold of one of Angela's hands and gave it a reassuring squeeze. Angela blinked twice, glanced at Jenny, and then returned her eyes to the dock.

One security guard emerged, and following directly behind him was Nicola's abuser, dressed in a grey suit. Jenny watched as hate boiled inside her like molten lava. She remembered clearly the last time she'd seen him. He was being escorted into the police van, covered in Nicola's blood. He'd smiled at her as she'd stood in the middle of the road, screaming at him in the rain.

His hair was longer now, but he was cleanly shaven and his suit looked relatively smart. The jagged scar down his face was still visible, and his eyes remained cold. Rather than face the judge, his eyes immediately found Angela and fixed her with a menacing stare. A flicker of a sneer touched a corner of his mouth. Even handcuffed and surrounded by guards, his presence remained unnerving. Angela held his gaze, though tears welled in her eyes.

"Please state your name for the court," the judge instructed.

He tore his attention away from Angela and faced the front, replying, "Christopher Martin Weston."

The judge asked, "Mr. Mosley is your legal defence representative, is he not?"

He nodded.

"Speak! Do not nod," the judge said, with clear irritation. "I know from your record this is not the first time you've been in court, Mr. Weston. You should know better."

"Sorry," he said. "Yeah, he is."

"Is it correct that you informed Mr. Mosley a few minutes before court began today that you wish to change your plea to guilty?"

"Yeah. I mean yes."

The judge raised her chin. "Were you given the opportunity to plead guilty when you were interviewed by the police?" Her tone sounded almost conversational.

"Yeah, I was," he said warily.

"And was it made clear to you that you could change your plea to guilty at any time during the process leading up to today's court case?"

He hesitated and turned to look at Mr. Mosley.

"Well, Mr. Weston?" the judge asked. "Do not waste my time."

Turning back to the front, he shrugged and answered, "Yeah."

The judge sat back in her chair, her eyes locked on him. "Then why did you choose to change your plea today, minutes before this court began?"

His neck and cheeks flushed as he turned and shot a nervous glance at Mr. Mosley again.

"Well? Mr. Weston, it's a simple enough question. Why today?"

"I was told…I thought it was time to be honest," he said lamely, with no conviction.

The judge's expression was void of emotion as she declared, "I acknowledge and accept your plea of guilty, Mr. Weston. However," she added firmly, "you were given ample opportunity to plead guilty throughout the different stages of the process leading up to today. I believe you chose to change your plea today because your legal counsel warned you, once again, of the severity of the charges laid against you. Throughout the process, you've shown no signs of remorse or guilt for your actions. It's my opinion that you are a sly and calculating man, and the reason for your late admission of guilt is nothing more than an attempt to save your own skin. For that reason, you will not be eligible for a reduced sentence."

He snapped his head up. "You can't do that! You can't fucking do that!" He turned to Mr. Mosley and pointed at him with cuffed hands. "You told me if I pleaded guilty, I'd get a reduced sentence. You fucking lying bastard!"

"Mr. Weston!" The judge stood and rapped her gavel.

He turned back to face the judge as both security guards rushed to take hold of him from either side.

"You'll now be taken back to the cells and your case is remanded until a later date, for sentencing. I must warn you, due to the serious nature of the offences and your vile outburst in my court, you are likely to receive a significant custodial sentence."

"You bitch! You can't—"

"Get him out of my sight. Take him to the cells now," the judge ordered angrily.

The guards struggled to escort him down the steps. Even with his hands cuffed, he fought against them. Another two guards rushed into the room and grabbed hold of him to help. Jenny could still hear him shouting expletives from the bottom of his lungs, long after he'd been dragged from the courtroom.

The judge sat down, composed herself, then turned to the jury. "I apologize for that disgusting display and that your morning has been wasted. Thank you for your service, but I shall waste no more of your precious time." She turned her attention to the rest of the courtroom. "Court adjourned!"

"Please rise," the court usher bellowed.

Excited energy built in the room as everyone got to their feet, but the room remained silent until the door to the chambers closed. Then, cheers erupted.

"I'll be outside!" Jenny shouted to her mum, trying her hardest to be heard over the raucous noise. Her mum and Angela were too busy chattering to Jack's parents to take any notice of her. Energized, Jenny slipped out of the room and looked around. She immediately spotted her, standing by the balcony on the floor above. Before her brain had engaged, she took to the staircase, two steps at a time. Her heels slapped noisily on the floor, announcing her presence and drawing all gazes to her. Donna, Gemma, and Penny had turned to watch her run the final few steps.

Unable to control herself, Jenny lunged forward and gripped Nicola in a tight hug that nearly toppled them both over. "Nic! God, I've missed you," she said into the soft dark hair. She felt the gentle rise and fall of Nicola's shoulders as she laughed.

"You only saw me yesterday afternoon," Nicola teased, but her arms squeezed back just as tightly.

"Jenny, do you think you could let her go for a minute?" Donna asked.

Jenny begrudgingly released Nicola but moved to stand by her side, intending to stay as close to her as humanly possible.

Nicola smiled and said, "I'm sorry, Penny. You were saying?"

Penny laughed. "Well, I genuinely didn't know what to expect from Judge Johnson. She's renowned for being a battleaxe, but honestly, it couldn't have gone better for us."

Nicola nodded. "So what happens now?"

"Nothing," Penny said happily. "She accepted his plea of guilty. He isn't going to get a reduced sentence, and after his tantrum, I should imagine he's feeling very sorry for himself."

"So I don't have to testify today?" Nicola asked, tucking her hair behind her ears uncertainly.

"You don't have to testify at all."

"Ever?"

Penny nodded. "You never have to see him again. He's being carted back off to prison where he'll remain until he's sentenced." Penny smiled. "It's over."

Nicola looked unconvinced and opened her mouth to ask another question, but everyone's attention was suddenly drawn to the stairs. A mass of excited familiar faces approached like a stampede.

"Nicola! It's over," Angela cried, surging forward and showering her daughter in kisses. For the next few minutes, Nicola was hugged, kissed, and patted and had her hands shaken by everyone. She remained modest throughout, clearly embarrassed by all the attention, which made Jenny love her even more.

"Everyone," Jenny's mum called out. "Angela and I would like to invite you all to a party to celebrate this wonderful day. Please. We want all of you there. It's at our house, and you all know where we live. Six o'clock this evening."

The crowd cheered.

Finally, everyone began to disperse. Penny left first, but not before Jenny's mum forced her to agree to come to the party.

"Girls, are you getting a lift back with us?" Jenny's dad asked.

Jenny glanced at Nicola and caught the twinkle in her eye. With matching grins, Jenny answered, "Thanks, but I think we'll walk back and get something to eat on the way."

"Will you be okay, Nicola, if I go and help Anne get ready for the party?" Angela asked.

Nicola nodded, "That's fine, Mum."

Angela hugged Nicola again, planting a few more sloppy kisses on her cheeks. "Okay. I love you."

Jenny felt a surge of excitement and knew Nicola was feeling the same. They'd have Nicola's house to themselves, and the prospect made their grins grow wider—but they weren't going to get away with it easily.

"Where are you going?" Jenny's mum asked, her eyes narrowing with suspicion.

"We're going to have a slow walk back and get something to eat," Jenny said, trying to sound innocent.

"We've got plenty of food at home—"

"Let them go," Dad interjected before Mum could finish. He shot her a warning look. She returned the look with a deathly glare before turning her attention back to them. "Fine. Make sure you're at our house for half five, at the latest. And don't eat too much—"

Jenny's dad coughed loudly. Her mum's shoulders tensed and her mouth thinned. "Just be good!"

"We will," Jenny said, blushing.

Clearly dissatisfied, Jenny's mum finally gave in and all three parents left. Only a few others remained behind.

Jack had his arm protectively around Laura's shoulders and they both seemed ridiculously smitten. "We better get off as well. I'm so happy for you, Nicola. We'll celebrate properly tonight," Laura said, managing to tear herself away from Jack long enough for the three girls to hug.

"I told you it'd all work out," Jack said with a goofy grin, giving Nicola a bear hug. "We'll see you later." As soon as the hugging was done, Jack and Laura became conjoined once again and continued to gush with soppiness.

Jenny watched as they walked away.

Who would've thought? Jack and Laura—a couple?

Ever since they'd met in the hospital while visiting Nicola, they'd been inseparable and sickeningly loved-up. Sometimes, it made Jenny queasy.

A sharp elbow jabbed her ribs.

"Ouch!" She gave an apologetic smile to Nicola, while rubbing her side.

"Right. We're headed off as well," Donna announced. "I'm proud of you both."

"You're coming to the party, aren't you?" Nicola asked, glancing from Donna to Gemma.

Donna flashed a mischievous grin. "Like I'd miss it. I've been getting withdrawal symptoms for Anne's cooking."

"And you'll come as well, won't you, Gemma?" Nicola asked.

Gemma smiled. "It would be a pleasure. Thank you."

Nicola nodded with satisfaction. "Great. It'll be nice to get to know you better."

Donna looked a little embarrassed as she said, "I've got to go get changed—I'm not used to wearing a suit. Give me my uniform any day. See you tonight."

"Lovely to meet you both," Gemma added shyly.

They said goodbye and watched as Donna and Gemma walked away. As they started to descend the stairs, Donna subtly brushed her hand across Gemma's back affectionately.

"Did you see that?" Jenny asked, staring with genuine surprise.

"Yes," Nicola said, amused.

"Do you think…nah…do you? I mean, they can't be…can they? Not if they work together."

"Work together?" Nicola burst out laughing. "Gemma's a primary-school teacher."

Jenny frowned. "Donna said they're partners."

Nicola laughed harder, as Jenny struggled to make the connection.

"Not work partners, but *partner* partners? Wait—Donna's gay?" Jenny gasped.

"How could you not know?"

Jenny stared at Nicola in disbelief. "How long have you known?"

"I knew from the moment I met her."

Jenny shook her head. "I honestly never saw it."

Nicola grinned and ruffled her hair playfully. "It's a good job I love you for more than your observational skills and awful gaydar."

Jenny laughed. "So, what now?"

Nicola's eyes glinted. "I thought we could celebrate."

"How would you like to celebrate?"

They began walking to the stairs and Nicola whispered, "Have I told you, you look pretty sexy in that suit?"

Jenny didn't reply until they got outside. "As it happens, I don't believe you have."

"Well, you do. But as good as it as looks, I'd still like to strip it off you as soon as possible," Nicola said, her voice husky and seductive.

"As long as you wait until we're back at your house, it sounds good to me," Jenny said, not even trying to mask her arousal.

Nicola opened the door and they both walked inside. In a flash of movement, Nicola pressed her body firmly against Jenny's, forcing her back against the door. Their mouths met and melted into a passionate kiss. Nicola began to fumble with the buttons on Jenny's shirt, only managing to undo three before she pulled her mouth away and gasped, "Upstairs, now."

Jenny responded with a throaty moan and obediently followed as Nicola ran up the stairs and into the bedroom.

"How long have we got?" Jenny asked, unbuttoning Nicola's top and pulling it over her head.

"Five hours," Nicola said.

"Only five?" Jenny asked, her tone sulky.

"Yes. So let's get naked and stop wasting precious time," Nicola suggested, removing the rest of her clothes. As soon as she was naked, she leapt onto the bed. "Hurry up."

Jenny crawled across the duvet cover. Nicola's swollen lips gleamed from their last kiss. Jenny was unable to hold back, wrapping her arms around Nicola's warm body.

"I can't describe how much I love you, Nic," she whispered before kissing Nicola's mouth softly. When she pulled away, she said, "But if you'll let me, I'll do my best to show you, every day for the rest of our lives."

Nicola answered by devouring Jenny's mouth with hot passionate kisses.

Five hours would never be enough, Jenny thought, but a lifetime would do just fine.

About the Author

Amy was raised in Derbyshire, England. She attended Keele University and graduated in 2007 with a BSc in philosophy and psychology. After graduating, she worked for a while with vulnerable young people until she moved on to deliver training and educational courses. She is currently in the process of setting up her own speech writing business aptly named, Gift of the Gab. She and her lovely partner Lou celebrated their Civil Partnership at the start of this year. They share a love of Dolly Parton and live with their two gorgeous cats and very naughty puppy.

Soliloquy Titles From Bold Strokes Books

Night Creatures: The Immortal Testimonies Book Two by Jeremy Jordan King. In the early 1980s, a young man transforms into a night creature to save himself and his loved ones from a mysterious illness sweeping New York. (978-1-60282-971-8)

Secret Lies by Amy Dunne. While fleeing from her abuser, Nicola Jackson bumps into Jenny O'Connor, and their unlikely friendship quickly develops into a blossoming romance—but when it comes down to a matter of life or death, are they both willing to face their fears? (978-1-60282-970-1)

Meeting Chance by Jennifer Lavoie. When man's best friend turns on Aaron Cassidy, the teen keeps his distance until fate puts Chance in his hands. (978-1-60282-952-7)

Asher's Fault by Elizabeth Wheeler. Fourteen-year-old Asher Price sees the world in black and white, much like the photos he takes, but when his little brother drowns at the same moment Asher experiences his first same-sex kiss, he can no longer hide behind the lens of his camera and eventually discovers he isn't the only one with a secret. (978-1-60282-982-4)

Lake Thirteen by Greg Herren. A visit to an old cemetery seems like fun to a group of five teenagers, who soon learn that sometimes it's best to leave old ghosts alone. (978-1-60282-894-0)

The Road to Her by KE Payne. Sparks fly when actress Holly Croft, star of UK soap Portobello Road, meets her new on-screen love interest, the enigmatic and sexy Elise Manford. (978-1-60282-887-2)

Kings of Ruin by Sam Cameron. High school student Danny Kelly and loner Kevin Clark must team up to defeat a top-secret alien intelligence that likes to wreak havoc with fiery car, truck, and train accidents. (978-1-60282-864-3)

Swans & Klons by Nora Olsen. In a future world where there are no males, sixteen-year-old Rubric and her girlfriend Salmon Jo must fight to survive when everything they believed in turns out to be a lie. (978-1-60282-874-2)

The You Know Who Girls by Annameekee Hesik. As they begin freshman year, Abbey Brooks and her best friend, Kate, pinky swear they'll keep away from the lesbians in Gila High, but Abbey already suspects she's one of those you-know-who girls herself and slowly learns who her true friends really are. (978-1-60282-754-7)

In Stone by Jeremy Jordan King. A young New Yorker is rescued from a hate crime by a mysterious someone who turns out to be more of a something. (978-1-60282-761-5)

Wonderland by David-Matthew Barnes. After her mother's sudden death, Destiny Moore is sent to live with her two gay uncles on Avalon Cove, a mysterious island on which she uncovers a secret place called Wonderland, where love and magic prove to be real. (978-1-60282-788-2)

Another 365 Days by KE Payne. Clemmie Atkins is back, and her life is more complicated than ever! Still madly in love with her girlfriend, Clemmie suddenly finds her life turned upside down with distractions, confessions, and the return of a familiar face… (978-1-60282-775-2)

The Secret of Othello by Sam Cameron. Florida teen detectives Steven and Denny risk their lives to search for a sunken NASA satellite—but under the waves, no one can hear you scream… (978-1-60282-742-4)

Andy Squared by Jennifer Lavoie. Andrew never thought anyone could come between him and his twin sister, Andrea…until Ryder rode into town. (978-1-60282-743-1)

Sara by Greg Herren. A mysterious and beautiful new student at Southern Heights High School stirs things up when students start dying. (978-1-60282-674-8)

Boys of Summer, edited by Steve Berman. Stories of young love and adventure, when the sky's ceiling is a bright blue marvel, when another boy's laughter at the beach can distract from dull summer jobs. (978-1-60282-663-2)

Street Dreams by Tama Wise. Tyson Rua has more than his fair share of problems growing up in New Zealand—he's gay, he's falling in love, and he's run afoul of the local hip-hop crew leader just as he's trying to make it as a graffiti artist. (978-1-60282-650-2)

me@you.com by KE Payne. Is it possible to fall in love with someone you've never met? Imogen Summers thinks so because it's happened to her. (978-1-60282-592-5)

Swimming to Chicago by David-Matthew Barnes. As the lives of the adults around them unravel, high school students Alex and Robby form an unbreakable bond, vowing to do anything to stay together— even if it means leaving everything behind. (978-1-60282-572-7)

365 Days by KE Payne. Life sucks when you're seventeen years old and confused about your sexuality, and the girl of your dreams doesn't even know you exist. Then in walks sexy new emo girl, Hannah Harrison. Clemmie Atkins has exactly 365 days to discover herself, and she's going to have a blast doing it! (978-1-60282-540-6)

Cursebusters! by Julie Smith. Budding psychic Reeno is the most accomplished teenage burglar in California, but one tiny screw-up and poof!—she's sentenced to Bad Girl School. And that isn't even her worst problem. Her sister Haley's dying of an illness no one can diagnose, and now she can't even help. (978-1-60282-559-8)

Who I Am by M.L. Rice. Devin Kelly's senior year is a disaster. She's in a new school in a new town, and the school bully is making her life miserable—but then she meets his sister Melanie and realizes her feelings for her are more than platonic. (978-1-60282-231-3)

Sleeping Angel by Greg Herren. Eric Matthews survives a terrible car accident only to find out everyone in town thinks he's a murderer—and he has to clear his name even though he has no memories of what happened. (978-1-60282-214-6)

Mesmerized by David-Matthew Barnes. Through her close friendship with Brodie and Lance, Serena Albright learns about the many forms of love and finds comfort for the grief and guilt she feels over the brutal death of her older brother, the victim of a hate crime. (978-1-60282-191-0)